In the thrilling sequel to *Magic, Monsters and Me*, Elijah Delomary steps into a whirlwind of challenges that test his strength, his identity, and the depth of his relationships. Confronting Zid'dra, the diabolical king of the menacing Gloom, Elijah faces a web of deceit spun by the sinister force, luring him toward his demise. However, his escape is orchestrated by the intervention of the Áuqala, who guides him back to Earth with a crucial message—to believe in his innate magic. Meanwhile, Elijah's mother undergoes a profound transformation, shifting her focus to support her son, amend past mistakes, and discover a newfound love for herself along the way.

Elijah's journey isn't just about reclaiming his powers and rekindling his relationship with Austin, his boyfriend; it's a battle against Zid'dra's relentless pursuit. As he struggles with his identity and seeks reconciliation, he becomes entangled in a dangerous game with Zid'dra, all while being shadowed by Devlina, his nemesis. An unfortunate accident sidelines Elijah, forcing him into a period of introspection and healing, where he grapples with self-acceptance and finds his true essence.

Amidst a summer blooming with rekindled love, Elijah is drawn into a chaotic conflict as the battle between Zid'dra and Devlina escalates into a full-blown war, pitting the coven against Devlina. Faced with a terrifying revelation, Elijah is pushed to protect his family, Austin, and the very fabric of existence. The weight of these challenges tests Elijah's strength, forcing him to confront the darkest forces while proving the unwavering strength of his love to Austin.

RESURRECTING MY MAGIC

Magic, Monsters, and Me, Book Two

Timoteo Tong

A NineStar Press Publication
www.ninestarpress.com

Resurrecting My Magic

All poems translated by Colman Watkins, Winchester University Press.

CONTENT WARNING:
This book contains fade to black sexual situations and depictions of homophobia, homophobic slurs, LGBT slurs/discrimination, bullying, fat phobia/shaming, on-page violence, supernatural war, anxiety disorder, mention of underage sex.

For Mom, who encouraged me to write, dream, and believe stuffed animals were alive.

Boxey
Belinda Delomary
Ocho
Austin Kang Jr.
Elijah Delomary
Austin Kang Sr.
&
Cecilia Kang
Devlina
Barn Wong
Orville Conry
ZID'DRA
Blair Winchester

Prologue

LONG, LONG AGO, under a layer of red and brown smog in the sprawl of the San Fernando Valley, northwest of downtown Los Angeles, before Elijah Delomary lived in the purple-and-white Victorian mansion at the top of Magnolia Boulevard in Burbank, a terrible event happened that changed the trajectory of his life. His mother, Belinda Delomary, made a mistake, setting in motion the course of events culminating with him in a field in Homer's Glenn watching Devlina, the Queen of the Gloom, battling monsters named *Henges,* or "Zusqoe" in the Dark Language. His mother was very much the reason why Devlina was at war with the Gloom.

Belinda Delomary stood in the dining room of the tiny ranch house painted olive green—not her choice, but rather her ex-husband's. Ex—that described him. Gone from her life. And yet, here, in the fading light of another terrible day after he walked out on her and their young children, he was present, still able to inflict pain on her.

"Notice of foreclosure," emblazoned on top of the official document, with the seal of the court and signed by some bureaucrat in a courthouse downtown, instructed her the sheriff would evict her and her children from the house in the next week due to nonpayment of mort-gage. Belinda fumed, balled up the paper, and tossed it in the trash can. She went to the kitchen, opened the back door, and walked across the rutted, overgrown backyard to the detached garage, closing the door behind her. She proceeded to scream at the top of her lungs for ten minutes.

When her red-hot anger subsided enough for her to not use her magic to smite the world, she marched out of the garage, back across the knee-high grass. Larry, her ex, had promised to give her a wonderful garden, but instead, she had a weed-strewn mess. Just like Larry, all promises and no action. She stumbled over a worn tire he had left among the weeds.

"Goddamn it!" she cursed out loud. "I hate you and your very birth, Larry Eugene Smith!" She walked carefully up the rutted, concrete steps—another item from the honey-do list Larry had never completed—and back into the house. She went to the den, Larry's preferred room—with the awful paneled walls, stone fireplace, and mini-bar filled with bottles of whiskey, his drink of choice. The room smelled of his cologne, Brash, a foul-smelling holdover from the eighties. She sat down at his little desk and stared at the landline. She hated the thought of making this call. She had ignored her mother's warnings to not marry the man, to be smart, to be a "Delomary."

"Be better. Think twice, girl," her younger sister Lisa, the pragmatic, brainiac one, had warned her.

"I love him," she'd told Lisa and the youngest sister, Christine, the afternoon before they were set to elope and get married in Vegas.

"He looks like a crook," Christine, the no-nonsense sister, said, filing her nails at the kitchen table in their parents' mansion in Holmby Hills. "And he smells like mothballs."

"That's his cologne," Belinda had said.

Christine gagged, "Brash? That's a sign. He buys his cologne at the chain pharmacy. No good. No good."

"Elitist," Belinda had said.

"Brainless."

"Belinda," Lisa had interrupted them, "I think you know we're right. He's not right for you."

"I love him," Belinda had said, then stood and stalked across the large, sunlight-filled kitchen. "You're either with me or against me!"

"Bye, fool," Christine said.

"Bye, haters."

The joke, of course, was on Belinda. She married Larry at a drive-in wedding chapel off the strip in Vegas and then they honeymooned at a motel far off strip, infamous for being a hotspot for homicides

Her sisters and mother warned Belinda and yet she married him and he had ruined her. She had no money and was about to lose her children's home because she believed him when he assured her he'd pay the mortgage in lieu of child support. She gritted her teeth, prepared to hear her mother's words, "I told you so." Still, she had to hear them. Her mother wasn't wrong, and now she needed the family money and the family lawyers to save her—from herself and her bad choices. She was terrible at making decisions. She was terrible at love. She had fallen for a con artist. A man who pretended to be something he wasn't. A prince in shining armor. Instead, she got a magician of sorts. No, he wasn't magical. Instead, he was good with sleight of hand. He paid the mortgage with one credit card, then opened another to pay the first credit card. He never worked; rather, he lived off credit and a game of cat and mouse with the creditors until the game ended, and he lost. She lost. The kids lost. In a few days, the sheriff would come and evict them from their home.

Late at night, as rain thundered off the roof from a late season storm from the Gulf of Alaska, Belinda accepted defeat and called her mother.

"Delomary Estate."

"Hi, Martha, is my mother in?"

"Hello, Miss Delomary."

"Mrs."

"Your mother was clear you are to be referred to as Miss Delomary."

Belinda's face grew red.

"Fine." She fought back her anger. "Can I speak to her?"

"She's having drinks with John Stewart and Oprah."

"It's almost midnight."

"You know your mother doesn't keep track of time when she's networking."

"Fine, Martha, then can you tell her I need to speak to her urgently?"

"More urgent than Oprah?"

"Yes, because I am her daughter."

"But Oprah won't like it," Martha said, "and your mother doesn't like to mess with Oprah."

"Martha."

"As you wish," Martha relented. "Hold the line."

A peppy, jazz version of *Valley of the Dolls* played while Belinda waited and waited. Yes, her family had music playing while the call was on hold. Talk about excess.

Her mother picked up after ten minutes.

"I was having an enlightening talk with Deepak about reincarnation, dear."

"Mother, I'm in trouble."

"Magicals can reincarnate; you know this."

"Mother."

"Belinda, we are our having port. Oprah loves port."

"Mother, I'm losing the house. I need your help."

Her mother paused on the other end of the line; Belinda imagined a smile creeping across her face.

"You need *my* help?"

"Yes."

"Well, well, well," her mother said. Belinda imagined her walking across her elaborate study with the fussy Louis XIV gilt-edged furniture, paneled walls lined with original works by Picasso and Cassatt, to close the double doors and sit behind her large desk where she deftly managed the numerous tentacles of the family business.

"Mother."

"So, you've finally come to your senses," her mother said in the same voice she used to the affiliates of the family's television network when instructing them to air a "must run" op-ed denouncing the moral majority or attacks on abortion healthcare rights.

"We're being evicted."

"Serves you right," her mother said. "Why would you want to live in a ranch house?" her mother said in a disgusted tone. "What is it, fourteen hundred square feet? Yuck."

"Not everyone wants to live in a mansion masquerading as a French chateau."

"And that's the problem with America."

"Mother."

"Fine," her mother said. "I'll help you, not because I think you deserve my help after all you've done to wound me, snub me, embarrass me. You are my *famille*—my family." Her mother paused. "I will sacrifice my pride to help you."

"That's big of you."

"You'll have to work, of course."

"Fine. I can be a vice president? I was good at managing staff before I left the company to take care of the kids."

"Oh, Bel." Her mother chided her, "You can't be an executive."

"Let me guess. I'll be a secretary?" Belinda could see it now, sitting outside her mother's office in the soaring glass and steel skyscraper on Wilshire Boulevard in West LA, fetching coffee, delivering mail, answering the phone. Being punished for daring to live her own life.

"No," her mother said, "you are not fit to be a secretary."

"Please tell me I don't have to work in the mail room."

"No," she said, "actually you'll be my assistant."

"Isn't that a secretary?"

"Executive assistant."

"Executive assistant is code for secretary. I'm terrible at typing, just so you know."

"You'll use a laptop. My goodness, you act like you'll be doing stenography and taking diction on a pad with a pencil. Times have changed."

"You haven't."

"The mouth on you."

Belinda relented. She needed money. She could use her magic to make the eviction notice disappear or spirit away the judge who signed it. But she had taken an oath to use magic for the good of humanity not her own gain. Stupid oath.

"Can I do something else? Maybe something in the creative department. I majored in graphic design."

Catherine Delomary laughed. "Oh, honey, aim higher. I'm not having you create flyers and mailers or spending your day creating, what are they called, viral videos?"

"Mom, you sound outdated."

"Keep being obstinate and I'll hang up."

"Fine, Mother, what do you envision me doing?"

"Well, you learn to be me," Catherine Delomary said. "Teddy, Lisa, and Christine are not fit to take over for me when I retire."

"You're never going to retire."

"I have to," her mother quipped, "per the Delomary Corporation bylaws."

"Surely you don't follow the rules."

"That is the only rule I have to follow. When I turn sixty-five, I must step down."

"Aren't you sixty-five already?"

"No one is the wiser."

"Breaking your oath to change time?"

"Do you want my help or not?" Catherine grumbled. "Anyway, you can start tomorrow."

Belinda gagged.

Her mother complained, "I am not a bad person!"

Yes, yes, she was. Overbearing, opinionated, short tempered, possibly narcissistic, and definitely insane to one degree or another.

"Belinda?"

"Yes, sorry, Mother."

"This will be good for you."

Belinda knew better. She glanced down at her nails, painted bloodred. She'd have to remove the color and apply light-pink nail polish, also known at Delomary corporate as "Delomary Pink."

"Or for you?"

"Don't be ridiculous," Catherine said. "This is good for you. Return to the fold. Ride in limousines, live in penthouses, have money, power, and control."

"Not everyone wants to be like us."

"A million women would kill to be us."

Belinda groaned. "What if you just loaned me some money?"

"Oh, stop," Catherine said. "You've been living like some hobo in the Valley. You will return at once to the estate."

"Mom, I like this house. The kids call it home."

Catherine grumbled, "It's a ranch house!"

"Mother."

"Fine," Catherine said. "You'll learn the ropes. How to be me."

Belinda almost hung up the phone.

"Are you sure Lisa or Christine or Teddy can't be groomed to take over?"

"Teddy is too busy living it up. Lisa is in law school. Christine is working the graveyard shift at a supermarket and singing in a band. She's written off."

"Mother!"

"You're the only one who can do it."

"I don't want to."

"I don't care what you want. If you want money to pay for your house, you will accept my terms. And those are my terms."

Belinda wanted to summon a hurricane to swirl over the estate in Holmby Hills and blast the mansion apart and suck her mother through a portal to Old Earth where she could wander around alone for a few years and leave her be.

The wind howled down the chimney of the fireplace. Rain pattered against the windows. She thought of the kids down the hall, fast asleep in their beds. She couldn't let them down.

"Fine, Mother, fine."

"And, you'll need a makeover. Get a sensible haircut. No more sundresses from the thrift store. No more sandals, for crying out loud. You'll wear heels and an array of pantsuits."

"Mother."

"Powerful women don't have luxurious auburn hair falling to their shoulders."

"I'm not going to have a coif like yours. No helmet hair for me!"

Her mother fell silent. Belinda imagined her touching her silver hair, spun like a bird's nest on top of her head.

"It's not a helmet."

"Well, you do your hair your way, and I'll do mine as I like."

"Fine."

"Fine."

"Good. I'll have the lawyers draw up our contract and pay the bank and maybe threaten them a little for daring to foreclose on a Delomary."

"Mother, don't."

"Why not? It's what we Delomarys do. Show our strength. Threaten, intimidate. It's who we are, dear."

"Mother."

"Actually, I think I'll just buy the bank when the markets open in a few hours, then fire everyone from the CEO to the janitorial staff as revenge. And whoever signed the eviction notice will get their just desserts as well. Surely, the judge is up for reelection sometime soon." Catherine sounded excited. Her mother loved revenge. She chuckled through the phone; ice sloshed in a glass. Her mother must be drinking whiskey.

"I thought you were having port."

"I was until I heard you called, dear. Then I poured myself a stiff one."

"Goodnight, Mother."

"Night, darling."

A while later, she switched on the turntable. She always listened to Dionne Warwick when she was upset. She pulled a bottle of whiskey off the shelf. An hour later, she crawled into the attic and fished out a box labelled: *NEŃUNSO TOCÃ! PÉRÁIGO!* Carrying it back down the hall to the den, she noted the box smelled of cheap cologne sold at the drug store. She realized she was probably not thinking clearly, but she hated Larry so much right now. She read the words written in the Old language in her sister Christine's blocky writing: "NEVER TOUCH! DANGER!"

She stirred the logs in the fireplace, then went back to the box, opened the cardboard top and rummaged around—pushing aside a skull, some femurs, dried shrunken heads, souvenirs from Disneyland, a dried bat, a souvenir from one of Christine's creepy goth boyfriends, until her hands settled on a cold, leather-bound book. She pulled it out and carefully read the old English script stamped in gold on the front of the book:

Livris De Malacins Malactanenans or *Ixotei sie Malac Malactańena* or simply, "The Book of Black Magic."

This book was forbidden by the Alliance, her family, her ancestors, the Áuqala, everything sacred and holy in the universe. And yet, she was very angry at this moment—angry with Larry for fooling her, angry at herself for being played, and angry that, for all her attempts to live her life, she found herself on the verge of living her mother's plan for her.

She shook her head and cried out, "I WILL NEVER BE CATHERINE DELOMARY!"

She opened the book. The lights flickered. The flames in the fireplace leapt and crackled. Groans and moans sounded in the shadows and corners of the room. This book was a gateway to the monsters and covens of the Gloom, the darkness of the underworld.

She paused for a moment. She could close the book and put it back in the box and hide it in the attic. Seal the door and forget about her need for revenge. That was the sensible thing to do, but Belinda, in her current state, was not in a mood for being sensible.

Thunder sounded in the distance. She noticed the foreclosure notice balled up on the floor. She gritted her teeth. She wasn't a victim.

"Nunma in viacadeima," her ancestor Dirk Delomary had whispered on his death bed. She flipped through the book to find the spell she wanted. She knew of a Malevolent, a fallen Immortal, who lay trapped under the *Oceana sie Tranqauilimenta,* between the *Ilxas sie Tubo* and Minerva, confined by magic after a great war between herself and the Magicals. This Malevolent was terrible and lusted for power and destruction. Perfect. Belinda lusted for the destruction of Larry! And this Malevolent would do her bidding and ruin Larry.

She cleared her mind and pricked her finger with a needle, then drew the words of the Malevolent on the surface of the desk. She lit one black candle and said the spell. She remembered one part of the spell, very important for it to work correctly.

"Should I use my blood?" she whispered. "If I use my blood, there's always the chance the Malevolent will turn against me. Maybe I'll use one of the kids' bandages in the trash."

She stood and went to the bathroom where she found a used bandage.

"I'm an asshole," she said before grabbing a used bandage from the trash. The drop of blood would link the spell to Larry. She returned to the table placing the bandage on top of the name she scrawled on the *Livris de Malcins Malactanenans.*

"Compellum Malactans Sujurat!" she said the spell again, dripping black wax on the bandage.

The fire cracked and popped in the fireplace. The groaning and moaning disappeared. The thunder dissipated. She opened her eyes.

"Puxhàredo!" she cursed in the Old Language. "Jesus, I can't even work dark magic right!" She closed the book, returned the box to the attic, wiped the table clean and put out the fire. She crawled into bed, pulling the covers over her head. She was a total failure. She couldn't even cast a spell to punish Larry. And in a few days, she would be a servant to her mother—her worst fear realized—thanks to dear old Larry Smith.

Over the next seven years, Belinda graduated with a Master's Degree in Business Administration and Graphic Design, and finally put her degree to use. She preferred working at the cooperative grocery in Reseda and singing in a piano lounge on occasion. That had been the good life. She worked to live. Now she lived to work. Following her mother from meeting to meeting, traveling in the family jet across the globe, making deals, schmoozing with unsavory foreign regimes to ease "regulatory issues," thwarting the competition, and learning the art of managing a corporation nicknamed the Octopus of Death.

One time, she returned home after a day of meeting with a group of men who were part of a shadowy operation that fixed "problems" for the family. The dark underside of the family business that protected the family and its interests, no matter the cost or legality. She had signed off on doing something highly unethical and possibly bordering on illegal, immoral, and wrong. This was her new life. She hated the *New Belinda*.

Belinda walked in the door, tired after the long commute over the 405 from the West Side, kicked off her heels, and undid her bra.

"Mom!" Elijah called to her from his bedroom.

"Hi, hon," she said, sinking into the oatmeal-colored, overstuffed sofa in the formal living room fronting Kittridge Street. She closed her eyes.

She dreamed of the piano lounge, the flickering candles in red glass holders on tables leaning one way or another. The smell of wax and scotch. The good old days when she crooned at the Lamplighter Lounge on Vanowen Boulevard. Only the smell changed in the living room to...farts?

Her eyes flew open. A woman stood in front of her wearing black stilettos, black fishnet stockings, a black leather miniskirt, and black bodice. She had very pale skin, tinged green, with dark eyes, and hair cut in a severe bob, framing her face. She was smirking.

"I'm here, baby."

Belinda lifted a hand to bind the monster. The woman raised her own hand, holding a riding crop. "My power is stronger than yours, knave!"

"Who—who are you?"

"Your best friend. Come to avenge your husband!"

"Come again?"

The woman rolled her eyes irritably, "You conjured me!"

"That was a long time ago!"

"Time is different on Old Earth."

"You're the Bane of Biscayne? Pàràsafàna! Máu Licuria, the Goddess of Lust!"

"IT IS I!" the woman shouted, the sky outside darkening. Crows sounded. "However, turns out I have no desire to punish a man—I am sympathetic. I have seen this ex of yours. He looks like Neil Diamond run over by a metro bus, dropped in the ocean, left to be eaten by sharks, raised again and reincarnated, then beaten, stabbed and left by the side of the road..."

"He's not that bad."

"He is no Ryan Gosling."

"Fair."

"Anyway, Mrs. Delomary—I applaud you changing yours and the children's last name back to your maiden name after the divorce. This should be standard. Children tend to go with the mother, so why carry the deadbeat's family name?"

"Right?" Belinda reached for her phone to text her sister to come and help her. Paràsàfàna was the Queen of the Gloom, a powerful Malevolent. She had meant to summon an entity named *Péraseana*, a Malevolent more like an Áucúitu—a wraith of sorts to do her bidding. Mainly haunt Larry for six months and then vanish without a trace. She knew Larry was scared of his own shadow. Some chain rattling at night, doorknobs turning on their own, and sounds of moaning while he used the bathroom would be enough to turn him into a nervous wreck.

Paràsàfàna raised her hand, pulling Belinda's phone toward her. "Trying to call someone?"

"To be honest, I meant to summon someone else. Not you."

"Why?"

"Because you're the Queen of the Gloom."

"You got the best, baby!"

"Mom? Are you talking to yourself again?" Elijah called from the back of the house.

"No, honey. I mean yes."

"Look, Belinda, plans have changed. I need to conquer Old Earth, and you, as the former Queen of Minerva are my key."

"I was the Queen only because no one else could do it. And I passed the mantle to someone else right away."

"Bore someone else with the details of your life. You will come with me."

"No, I have my kids. My work. My macramé?"

Paràsàfàna looked at the orange and yellow macramé plant holder hanging from the slanted ceiling and waved a hand, turning it to dust. Belinda watched the sand fall to the white Berber carpet, the pothos plant tumbling to the floor.

"Hey, my macrame took a long time to make!"

"Well, here's the deal. You summoned me, and, well, I need your help, so think of this like *Thelma and Louise*. Two badass women about to shake things up."

"I'm not helping you conquer Old Earth!"

"Are you sure?"

"Yes!"

"Fine, then I will *vovo compùlsa*. Compel you!"

"No, think about the kids!"

"You should have thought of that before opening the Malac Malactańena when you were drunk. Now come with me!" A black portal opened near the fireplace, black jellylike light flickered. "Go!"

"Mommy? Are you okay out there?"

Belinda lamented about what to do. Why had she been so stupid? Devlina grew impatient.

"Fine. I will suck your soul into the other dimension!" Devlina lifted her hands, which produced a black light, tugging on the white aura of Belinda's soul. Belinda screamed as her soul was pulled from her body and into the portal. Devlina laughed maniacally as the portal popped and disappeared.

Belinda's body fell to the floor. Elijah came out from the hallway.

"Mom?"

Elijah stood in the front hallway, holding his stuffed lion, named Tubby, in one hand, squinting his eyes, trying to see what was lying on the floor in the dark formal living room.

"Elijah!" His older sister Victoria "Tory" Delomary pushed past him. "Call 911 right now!" She hurried into the living room. Elijah dropped Tubby and ran to the kitchen to call 911 on the landline.

A week later, heavy rain fell from black storm clouds hanging low over the San Fernando Valley—a late season storm. Elijah stood at the doors of the white chapel perched on the side of Forest Lawn Cemetery, on the eastern side of the famous Hollywood Hills. To the west, stood the aluminum-and-steel sign luring dreamers for over a hundred years to Hollywood, seeking fame and fortune. Elijah stood in the rain watching the rows of grave markers stretching down the hillside. LA was a mirage. In the abundant sunshine, there was life, and in the darkness, death, magic, and monsters. Too many monsters.

Part One

Rain in Southern California

Oreistànsa sie Ráumonna
I dreamt of Ramona,
The old groves of orange trees irrigated with water from somewhere
else,
Snowcapped mountains from another world;
All of Los Angeles is a desert, man,
Filled with chaparral and sand,
Los Angeles is a mirage, man,
Lights! Cameras! Action!
All a sham, don't you see?
When it rains in the desert,
All the paint and makeup covering the mountains,
Valleys and beaches,
Melts away revealing the intricate plan,
From long ago.
They came for one reason,
Fame.
A mirage.
All of life is a stage and we're nothing but sand, man.

Ansolandérr Càstronevès
"Ama Assundra veo Echàngrantzea" 1968.

Chapter One

Cor Oscurimenta

"WATCH OUT ELIJAH!" a voice called, and a moment later, I tumbled head over heels, like Alice down the rabbit hole. My head throbbed, and my stomach threatened to release its contents at any moment. I was surrounded by darkness. Occasionally, monsters circled me, claws out, eyes red, desperate to pull me into the shadows.

I landed on my rump on a springy surface, bounced to my feet, lost my balance, and fell on my stomach. I lifted my head. I was in a ravine surrounded by jagged stone cliffs on three sides. In front of me stretched a long, flat plain punctured by twisted, blackened tree stumps, plumes of smoke circling to the heavy, black clouds overhead. Tongues of flame dotted the horizon. Lightning flashed and thunder rumbled.

"I think I'm in the puxhàredo Gloom!" I grumbled, rolled to my side, and struggled to my feet. My balance faltered. I almost fainted.

"*Bona Venra Adda Oscuriment,*" a voice boomed from the shadow of the caves gaping like angry mouths to my left.

"So, I *am* in the Gloom," I said, clutching my head and breathing in the smell of phosphorus. Crow-like birds circled overhead, screeching, "Oscuriment!"

"*Velsonavets enta ispirina?*"

I squinted into the cave, trying to decipher the body talking to me in hushed tones.

"I could use an aspirin," I said. "Who are you?"

The air, thick with smoke, rippled around me. A figure approached the edge of the cave. I squinted to make out the shape of the figure. Red eyes with yellow pupils shone among the darkness.

I stepped back reflexively.

"Who are you?"

"*Ent Amans Antico, Elijah mala deo Oscurimenta.*"

"Old friend?" I muttered, and my mind raced. "Haddo?"

Puxhàredo. I hoped he wasn't back from the grave me and Barn sent him to. Without my magic and Barn and Austin, I was in terrible danger.

"*Adcunma ent picant plus emportanted, iunio,*" the voice said. The figure shuffled closer to the edge of the cave. Áucúitus flew overhead shrieking and crying out. God, I fricking hoped I was dreaming. I had been hit by a massive rock that knocked me out. I was in a coma probably. I was hallucinating. Yes. That was it. How did I wake myself? I pinched myself.

"Ouch!" I cursed. Burning embers floated down from the clouds streaked with red and orange and black.

"*Nunta sogno Iunio,*" the voice assured me I wasn't dreaming.

"What do you want?"

"*Sulla prove ijustavets.*"

"Only to help me?" I asked skeptically.

"*Morosa adve passare sents et aquent podet ijust.*"

"How do you know what happened to me and how to help? Who are you?"

"*Ent amico.*"

"A friend, huh?" I folded my arms across my chest skeptically.

"Okay, so what happened to me?"

"*Tragica plus horribilibis.*"

"My magic," I whispered.

"*Podavets retroclaummenavets Macicens tuae sic enduravets gralle.*"

"If I push myself very hard, my magic will come back."

The shadow nodded. "*Tu sentavets aquela podavets lom complenet.*"

"Push myself how?"

"*Pro demonstrare aquelve est pro patris rente.*"

"To show I'm...not my father?"

"*Macicants non relaxicare edve mes?*"

"Right, Magicals don't give up. And I'm a Magical!"

"*Bona, iunio.*"

"Puxhàredo!" I complained, "So how do I get out of here?"

"*Tu deccia sicme dere alcuns,*" the voice called out ,and a creature stepped out of the cave. "You can leave once you've given me something." The creature had the lower body of a goat and the upper body of a man—well defined abs and pecs and arms—sorta hot actually—and the head of a stag with long horns curling up to the sky. Its red and yellow eyes glowed among the ash and embers falling around us.

"Zid'dra!" I screamed, and innately something forced my feet into motion. I was running as fast as I could away from the King of the Gloom, the scourge of the Shimmering, the antithesis to the Áuqala.

"No, no, no," I said. "I am not giving you anything. Not my soul or whatever."

"*Sic tu non ralcipricare morta desi tua!*" Zid'dra's voice followed me as I sprinted as far away from the caves as I could.

"I am not reciprocating, so kill me."

"*Ergo podum tua enbellissare!*"

"I don't want you to make me great. I want nothing to do with you."

"*Tu non podere fugired deme, iunio!*" Zid'dra's voice echoed around me as I ran through the ravine as fast as I could.

"I am going to get away from you!" I shouted, turning back and spotting Zid'dra transform into a magnificent black stallion, eyes red and yellow with flames shooting from its nostrils.

"Oh, fuck," I said, turning around and trying to run faster. "I am going to die!" My foot connected with a flaming, fallen tree. My body flew over the flames, and I tumbled several times until I lay on my back, short of breath, ash and embers falling onto my face softly.

The horse appeared among the smoke and cinders.

"*Tu devents sapens aquela matterna conjurunta mäu Licuria cuna sangro deve?*"

I huddled under the stallion staring up at its red eyes and the flames shooting from its nostrils."

"What do you mean my mom summoned Devlina with my blood?"

"*Hexa utilunt matterna deve proa mäu Licuria conjuret cuna sangro deve aquel sorprens comvinet dus.*"

"Mom used my blood in a spell to conjure Devlina?"

The stallion whinnied and blew smoke out its nostrils; its eyes flashed yellow.

"So, what does that mean?"

"*Battarant-no et pro diminuir potencia dega tuxa tu!*"

"Wait, hold on." I squirmed to move away from the stallion. "What do you mean you need a part of me to weaken Devlina?"

"*Est deo mannerad relquicitarunt, placiddo Iunio.*"

"Look, maybe Mom used me in a spell, but surely you and Devlina will patch things up. She calls you pookie, for crying out loud!"

"*Proaccivare sum prove nullificare!*"

"Okay, you want to be proactive," I said, "but there's no need to jump to conclusions. Maybe Mom linked me to Devlina—" My mind spun back in time to Tynenium when I was engaged in hand-to-hand combat with Devlina. Every time my sword sliced a wound into her arm, my own arm burned with pain. We were inextricably linked. Devlina had been coming around me, wanting me to join her. Now I understood. She needed me to help her destroy Zid'dra. But no. My magic was gone—no, diminished. Surely, I was no use to her. I couldn't be. I hoped I wasn't.

The stallion reared back on its back hooves, lifted its front hooves into the air and head up and shot two long tongues of flames into the air.

That doesn't seem like a good thing, I thought to myself.

The stallion returned to face me, *"Bombba adda conversacibo enra-no, tuxa deve desi mim!"*

"Let's be reasonable," I said. "Just because you're tired of talking doesn't mean you need to kill me. Think about it. Devlina loves you. She does. Maybe just apologize to her. Cut a few wives loose. Tell her she's a great cook!"

Suddenly, the stallion was over me, flames licking at its nostrils.

"Zid'dra non relens iamais!"

"There's always a first time to apologize, Zid'dra!"

The stallion dug its hooves into the sand in front of it, reared up on its back legs and unleashed two streams of flames at me. I winced, bracing myself for the heat and the inevitable...and a second later, the temperature plunged suddenly. I shivered as the flames were extinguished by a dazzling white light. I was momentarily blinded.

Something cool and soft fell against my face. The smell of phosphorus and smoke retreated. I opened my eyes. Snow fell around me.

The stallion stood motionless, its eyes dark and its body covered with ice.

Hundreds of pinpoints of light floated above the stallion, at least fifty feet high.

"Elijah," a soft voice called to me from above, "you must hurry now. My magic won't last long down here far away from where I belong among the stars in the heavens."

"You're the Áuqala!" I said as the pinpoints of light came to resemble a tall woman with long flowing hair falling past her shoulders, wearing a long dress, holding a sword in one hand and a shield in the other.

"I am Evangeline, your great-great-grandmother."

"Holy cannoli!" I exclaimed. "Did you come to save me?"

"Of course, my love." The pinpoints of light twinkled each time she spoke. "Now I need you to stand quickly, my love."

I hurried to my feet.

"Place your feet together, hands at your sides, and close your eyes."

I did as instructed.

"Reach deep inside you and touch the magic within, love."

"There is no magic."

"There is. You know it is."

"I can't use it."

"You can."

"Not like before."

"Those bastards at the Còngréhassa..."

"Grandma Evangeline!"

"I can use bad words on occasion."

I laughed.

"Feel the light inside you," she said.

Among the shadows and darkness within me, buried under layers of self-loathing and hatred of brands and plans and especially of Mom's failure to succeed in love and my vile father who despised boys who liked to kiss other boys, there was a slight sensation of.... What was that....hope?

"Yes, Elijah, reach for the hope."

"The hope?" I asked.

"Yes, Elijah, inside you is an *eqaulibreo,* a balance. Between hope and anguish. You've moved too far into anguish."

"The darkness."

"Yes, Elijah."

"What can I do with hope?"

"Hope is the absence of fear. You will release yourself from the Gloom and then you will return to Burbank and find your mom and she will help you. And you will seek out Máurso, the God of War, and you will learn how to use magic in a different way. And you will struggle along the way and suffer, but you will turn to the light. And in the end, you will be stronger than before."

"Do I have to do the suffering and struggling part?" I asked. "Or is that maybe negotiable?"

"Elijah," Evangeline said firmly. Just like Mom when she was ending a conversation simply with the tone of her voice.

"Okay."

"Elijah, you will be great again, I promise."

"Ugh," I said, "I don't feel great. And I really messed things up. My boyfriend—"

"He's still there."

"And Barn, my brother. Well, he hates me."

"He loves you."

"And I love him. And Austin."

"They will help you."

"You think?"

"I know, my cherished one."

"So..." I stammered, "I mean, me and my mom haven't been doing too well."

"Yes," Evangeline said in a regal tone, "but you two will help each other."

"You think so?"

"You are my blood."

"Well, looks like you're made of stars."

"Elijah." Evangeline's voice wavered. "Stop stalling. You are a stubborn boy, aren't you?"

I hung my head. "Okay, yeah. I hear you. Mom and me."

The earth trembled violently underfoot. The snow turned to mist. Áucúitus howled in the distance. The stallion's eyes flickered red.

"You must go now, Elijah! Reach for that sparkle of hope within you. Go to the light, my dearest one!"

I closed my eyes and dwelled on the strange flicker of hope deep within me. Austin's face flashed before my eyes. His hand reached for mine. I grasped for him. Suddenly, my body became light as a feather, my feet lifted off the ground, and in a split second, I was hurtling up and up and up.

Chapter Two

Waking Up, Alive

AIR RUSHED INTO my lungs; my heart beat furiously in my rib cage. My eyes flew open. I looked around me. I was sprawled out on the grass, my shoes dangerously close to a smoldering fissure in the ground. Steam and smoke lifted into the night air. I sat up and crawled toward the fissure. Hot air and the smell of phosphorus buffeted my face. A crack to the Gloom had opened in Homer's Glenn.

"Oi," a familiar voice called to me, "Elijah, is that you, mate?"

My eyes focused on Barn standing across the fissure holding his PlasmX defensively. "I heard a terrible explosion while I was watching a wuxia movie in the second-floor front parlor and came to investigate. Looks like a gate to the Gloom opened up."

"Yeah, I was down there." I pointed toward the fissure.

Barn lifted effortlessly over the smoke and steam and landed softly next to me. He closed up his PlasmX and put it in his pocket.

"Mate," he said, "I've been worried about you."

"I know, Barn."

"You've been acting loco, mate."

"I know."

"You gotta stay away from your dad."

"Shit, tell me about it."

"Austin, he loves you."

I looked away. I loved Austin. But, I was broken inside. There was a spark of hope inside me but too much darkness and anguish as well.

"Mate." Barn kneeled next to me. "You have burns on your face."

"Embers from the Gloom." I explained, "They rain down from the sky."

"Shit," Barn said. "You really were there."

"Yeah, this boulder flew at me..." My voice trailed off as I spotted a large rock embedded in the grass nearby. "Devlina, she was here battling Henges."

"The Elite Guard of Zid'dra."

"Those two are fighting."

"Ouch."

"Yeah, well, I got knocked into the chasm and right into Zid'dra's lair."

"What did that wanker want?"

"He says my blood is linked to Devlina." I didn't tell him about how Zid'dra said to push myself because that's what Magicals do. I wasn't like my father; he gave up long ago. I was going to be nothing like him. I was going to push myself to be better than him.

"Yeah?"

"Yes."

"Bollocks," Barn said. "That would explain why that daft cow has been lurking around you the last few months. She wants something."

"Zi'dra says she needs me."

"Aye," Barn said. "To wreak havoc for him."

"Yup," I said. "And he wanted to kill me because he said that would weaken her."

Barn stood and pulled out his PlasmX.

"Well, that's not happening."

"Barn," I said, "the Áuqala saved me!'

"Wait, what?"

"Yes, she appeared. Evangeline. My great-great grandmother."

"That's brilliant."

"She says I can make things better."

"Of course, you can."

"She wants me to see Máurso."

"Good," Barn said. "He will train you in Xem Sen Ou. And to meditate and you will become a powerful warrior just like me and Austin."

Suddenly, tears welled in my eyes. I stepped forward and pulled Barn in for an embrace.

"I missed you."

"I missed you too."

Two powerful beams of light cut through the smoke and steam drifted out of the fissure. I squinted while Barn covered his eyes with his hand.

"Oi," Austin called to us, "Anti-coven League! Here to check what's going on!"

"We have weapons," Cecilia Kang chimed in, "lots of powerful weapons that can destroy monsters in a blink of the eye!"

"It's us, mates!" Barn shouted.

"Barny?" Austin called back.

"Yes, Lostin," Barn called back, "along with Elijah."

Austin gasped. "I thought...well, I hoped...I mean, I feared for the worst...."

"I'm okay, K-kangy."

Austin leaped over the fissure, landing softly between Barn and me. He peered at me through his thick glasses.

"You have burns on your face," he said, examining my body, "and cuts on your arms and hands, mate."

"I got in the middle of a battle between Devlina and the Zuscoe."

Austin suddenly pulled me into a tight embrace, and tears erupted from his eyes.

"Kangy? Are you crying?"

"I thought you were dead..."

I hugged Austin tighter. "I'm alive, Kangy."

We clung to each other for another moment.

"Do you know where Devlina went?" Barn asked.

I shook my head. "I don't know," I said. "She warned me of a boulder flying at me, and the next thing I knew I was tumbling into the fissure there."

Austin glanced over the side, wrinkling his nose in disgust. "Smells like farts and feet."

"The Gloom."

Austin's eyes widened. "Mate, you fell to the Gloom?"

"Yeah," I said softly, the cuts on my arms and burns on my face becoming painful.

"Okay, let's get you home," Austin said.

"I can stay here—" Barn began but was interrupted by the ground heaving underfoot. Barn swayed, trying to keep his balance, but fell over. Austin wrapped his strong arms around me and sank to the ground. I gazed into his eyes. He smiled softly.

"Austin!" Austin's parents called from the other side of the fissure, "Are you okay?"

Black smoke poured out of the fissure before Austin could answer. The smoke twisted into the shape of a large body with thick arms and neck, a square head with two triangular horns. Red eyes blinked. A jagged mouth smiled wickedly.

"Well, hello, boys." A deep bass boomed over the meadow, shrouded in darkness, the half-moon blotted out by the smoke from the fissure. "Looks like I'll be finishing off a bunch of pests in one fell swoop."

"Sod off, freak!" Barn said lifting his glowing PlasmX protectively with both hands.

Austin winked at me and leaned over to pick up his own PlasmX.

"We aren't push arounds, monster," he shouted.

"I am Tartáuranno, the *Manatäuro Ombralle*, the Shadow Monster, the protector of the realm of the pits of darkness below the foundations of the Gloom."

"What brings you here then, tosser?" Barn shouted up at the monster, fire shining behind its mouth and eyes. Embers fell from its nose as it breathed.

"Why, to fetch Elijah Delomary, Bane of the Gloom, and while I'm at it, you as well."

I gulped. Shit. I certainly did not want to return to the Gloom or the pits below the Gloom.

"We'll see about that!" Austin said, lifting off the ground, throwing his body toward the head of Tartáuranno, Barn hard on his heels. They shouted in the Old Language as they began their offensive by kicking Tartáuranno in his head. He growled and spewed flames at them. Barn yelped, "Wanker, that was my arm!" He spun around, lifted his PlasmX over his head, and brought it down on Tartáuranno's head. The PlasmX sparked and ricocheted off Tartáuranno before falling to the grass. I raced for it as Barn flew toward him, fists out ready to clobber the monster.

I looked across the steaming fissure; Cecilia was on her phone, talking animatedly. Austin Sr. took out his PlasmX and joined the fight. Tartáuranno swatted Austin Jr. with his large square fist, sending him flying over the meadow disappearing into a ring of Coastal Live Oaks. Barn recovered his PlasmX and ran a few paces before lifting off toward Tartáuranno. Austin Sr. shouted some words in the Old Language as he soared over the monster. His body began to glow with a purple light. His PlasmX burned brighter. He held it up and behind his head then swung it toward one of Tartáuranno's eyes. Tartáuranno lifted himself out of the fissure, his enormous, muscular body lit from below by the flames emanating from the chasm. Austin Sr.'s PlasmX plunged into Tartáuranno's head which shuddered and cracked, fine lines glowing with flames from within. He grunted and swiped Austin Sr. to his left, sending him flying back over the fissure, then disappearing behind a cloud of smoke.

I fidgeted with my phone. I had to call Mom. We needed help, desperately.

Mom picked up right away. "Elijah, where have you been? I've been worried."

"Mom, I'm in Homer's Glenn. Devlina was battling Zuscoe who tossed a boulder at me, but she deflected it with her stiletto's—"

"Damn, that had to hurt—" Mom interrupted.

"Mom, I fell to the Gloom, and, well, long story short, there's a monster named Tartáuranno here, and Austin and Barn and his parents are fighting, and they need help. I think Cecilia called the League for help—"

"Stay where you are," Mom said. "I'll be there shortly."

She ended the call. Tartáuranno stomped across the grass, embers shooting out of his nostrils, flames licking behind the cracks on his face. He loomed over me.

"Let's make this easy, shall we?"

"No," I said. "I shan't."

"I think you will, *iunio*."

"I'm not a boy."

"You are," Tartáuranno laughed. "A wee little pest in the greater scheme of things. I shall reach down and squeeze you until all the blood and guts come spewing out of you!"

"Go fuck yourself!" I said standing up, digging my heels into the grass, putting my fists together as Julio taught me when we practiced boxing in the gym. The same moves that had wiped the floor with Orville.

Tartáuranno lifted his head back and chuckled, the sound reverberated across the Glenn.

"Iunio," he said, "you can't possibly fight me!"

I ran as fast as I could toward him, fists up as I shouted with some primeval sound that came from deep within me. I charged him; my fists connected with his ankles. I pummeled him with all my force.

"Hey, you stop that, iunio!" He shouted.

"No, I want you to die!" Tears slithered down my face as I screamed and pounded him with my fists. I kept striking him even as my hands erupted into searing pain.

A bright flash of purple light lit up the meadow and the steep slopes of the mountainsides.

"Elijah!" Mom called to me in a gentle voice. "You can stop pummeling the monster."

I dropped my fists to my side, looking up at Tartáuranno. His eyes focused on something behind me. I turned, glancing at my hands, raw and bleeding. Mom stood in a shimmering purple portal, with her softly lit bedroom behind her. She wore a white jumpsuit and held a tall silver staff topped with a glowing star at its end.

"Mom?" I broke down sobbing. Mom stepped out of the portal.

"Looks like Mama to the rescue," Tartáuranno said, although his voice cracked. He sounded less confident than before.

"Tartáuranno, you know you belong far below the Shimmering," Mom said, walking confidently across the rutted grass, littered with smoldering boulders from Devlina's battle earlier, as well as those hurled from the Gloom when the fissure opened up.

"Well, yes, Belinda—"

"That's Ms. Delomary to you, because I know you are nasty," Mom said assuredly, "and not the good nasty."

Tartáuranno growled and opened his mouth, "I will smite you!"

"Oh, Tarty," Mom said shaking her head, "you forget my power."

Tartáuranno closed his mouth. He glanced at Mom, worry crossing his face.

"I mean...look, can't I take Elijah, and we can just go our separate ways? Master will be very angry if I don't."

Mom wagged a finger at him. "No."

"How about an arm, at least?"

"No."

"His hair, then. Surely, it would be in his best interest to be rid of that bright-red hair."

"Absolutely not."

Tartáuranno mumbled to himself. He drummed his large, square foot against the grass. The earth trembled under me. I looked at Mom and then up at Tartáuranno.

"Look, no offense, but I just have to bring back something—" Tartáuranno leaned down toward me. I scuttled out of his way.

Mom shook her head and drummed her staff against the ground. In an instant, a blinding white light erupted from the star atop her staff. I closed my eyes and hugged my knees with my arms. A shockwave of energy sent me toppling onto my back. Tartáuranno howled. The ground jumped with each of his steps. I opened my eyes and watched the wave of energy crash into his large, blocky body. He screamed and raged, throwing his arms into the air, stumbling backwards. Mom dropped her staff, which flashed and turned into a twisted umbrella she had picked up at the drug store years ago. The most powerful Encantreinus had staffs, including Mom, Aunt Christine, and Grandma Delomary.

Mom hurried to my side. "Elijah come with me quickly!" She pulled me toward the fissure and waved a hand which summoned a strong breeze to carry us to the other side.

Cecilia joined us. "The League are almost here."

"Good," Mom said, brushing my hair off my face. She lifted her index finger, the end glowing with a soft pink light. She traced it across my face and arms and hands. For a moment, the pain subsided. "This will do until we can see Dr. Hu."

"Thanks, Mom."

Mom pulled me in for a hug. Across the fissure, Tartáuranno stumbled, his body split in two. Out of the night sky, Austin and Barn appeared, flying toward him with their PlasmX's aimed right at him.

"Hoooousà!" they shouted in unison as they flew toward him. "No one messes with us!"

They approached Tartáuranno and, unexpectedly, crossed their PlasmX's. Purple sparks shot skyward as they dug their weapons into Tartáuranno. My eyes widened as I watched Tartáuranno's appearance separate from his body. Austin and Barn floated down, sparks circling into the night sky. Tartáuranno's exterior peeled off his body and glided to the ground, like a clown stepping out of a costume and leaving it behind.

"Housà!" Austin and Barn bumped fists, walking toward the fissure. Austin Sr. appeared behind them. "Bollocks I wanted to help out!"

"Too slow, Dad," Austin called over his shoulder. He had cuts on his face and dirt smeared across his arms. His glasses were crooked. He had a huge smile on his face. Barn looked a lot like Austin with bleeding cuts on his face and his arm. He looked very satisfied.

I leaped up and ran to the edge of the fissure waiting for them to cross over. After a moment, we all embraced.

"Kangy," I mumbled.

"My Eli."

"Don't forget me, yeah, mate?" Barn quipped.

"Thank God you guys came to help me."

"What?" Austin said pulling back peering at me. His left lens was smashed. His eye swollen. His nose was bleeding. "I am your Coaugelo. Of course, I would come."

"Yeah and I'm your Coaugelo too. Sheesh." Barn grunted. "Oh, he only wants to hang out with Encantreinas, my ass. You know, Elijah, you are selfish. You know that? And maybe prejudiced. Just cuz I'm straight doesn't mean we can't hang out."

"Barn, I'm sorry."

"Yeah, well, you better be."

Austin Sr. drifted down to the earth. Cecilia rushed to him, talking softly in Cantonese behind us.

"Anyone care about a middle-aged woman who probably won't win the Mom-of-the-year award?"

We all chortled really hard, steam and smoke wafting around us.

*

AGÉCENDRUS, IN THEIR standard issue black-and-white suits, milled around the fissure or stood over the lifeless image of Tartáuranno and scanned the crumpled stone body that he once inhabited.

"We did all the work, yeah?" Austin grumbled, watching the agents from the Macistráuto or XAQ2 survey the scene. Agécendrus from the Anti-coven League and XAQ2 did not get along. The former was scrappier, boots on the ground. XAQ2 was more by the book and following up after the League intervened with monsters.

A senior agent, her black hair pulled off her face and wearing sunglasses, drew Mom aside to talk to her.

"Always the way with those wankers," Barn agreed.

"All right, boys," Cecelia chided them, "you know how the world works. The League comes in first to respond to the situation and deal with it as necessary. Then the Macistráuto comes in to investigate and write up a report to send to the Alliance. We're the police, and they're like the FBI."

"Unsung heroes more like it, yeah?" Austin said, holding a tissue to his nose.

"You're heroes to me," I whispered softly.

Cecilia sighed. Austin Sr. said something in Cantonese. Austin and Barn nodded.

"Our reward is seeing the faces of the people—Encantreinos—we save."

Of course, we all came in for a group hug again. I was feeling emotional and in need of hugs.

After a moment, we separated. The agent with the ponytail said something to Mom. She paused and threw her head back to holler at the agents near Tartáuranno's image.

"*Qauanabo, sega irano porgo torqauãe!*" She ordered them to step aside as Mom moved forward and waved her hands over the crumpled remains of Tartáuranno's image. In an instant, it rolled up like a carpet and floated toward the fissure. With a snap of her wrist, the rolled-up image of Tartáuranno disappeared into the fissure. Mom held her hands aloft. The ground shuddered, rumbled, and the fissure sealed. Tiny wisps of steam and smoke curled into the night air.

Mom walked over to us. "The Macistráuto will clean up so we can go home. Tomorrow, I'll take you to Dr. Hu. And Commander Akuba will come by to interview you."

I nodded.

"You'll submit your report to League headquarters?" Mom asked of Cecilia and Austin Sr.

"Aye," Austin Sr. said. "We'll have a full report."

Mom leaned in to whisper something to them. They nodded again.

"Come on, JuneBug," Cecilia said. "Let's get you cleaned up."

"I'm not named JuneBug, Mum!" Austin complained.

"JuneBug?" I said.

"He hates it, yeah, mate?" Barn laughed.

"It's not my name. I'm Austin or Kangy or His Majesty!"

"You might be concussed," Cecilia teased. "You are definitely not royal, son."

"Yes, I am, Mum," Austin said. "I am a Leo, king of the forest!"

Everyone sniggered as we walked toward Cecilia's black sedan.

"Need a lift?"

"I can open a portal," Mom said, waving a hand. A squirming purple portal appeared.

Aunt Christine appeared inside, hands on her hips. "Why the hell wasn't I included! I heard reports over the League's ham radio of the incident!"

"Oh, get stuffed, Christine!" Mom complained.

Chapter Three

Leap of Faith

MOM SAT ON the yellow satin sofa across from me, sipping tea, wearing pajamas under a yellow robe. I was across from her in a yellow wingchair near the marble mantel at the foot of her bed. Her room, the Yellow Suite, was decorated in shades of yellow from the Persian rug in the center of the room to the sheets and duvet on the four-poster bed to the sateen wallpaper on the walls and the silk drapes pulled across the floor-to-ceiling windows overlooking the front gardens.

"Tell me everything, Elijah."

I squirmed in my seat, picking at the scab on my hand from where I had punched Tartáuranno's ankle.

"I've been talking to Devlina," I said.

"Excuse me? Why would you do that?"

"You're angry."

"Of course, I am."

"I'm sorry."

"Elijah…" Her voice trailed off. *Here it comes*, I thought, *one of her lectures.*

"What does she want?" she said. No lecture, I guessed.

"Well, yeah. She wants me to help her." I glanced at the painting of Evangeline and Dirk astride horses with their young kids wearing matching white outfits roaming Homer's Glenn. Evangeline seemed to be listening to us.

"Help her?"

"Take over the world."

"Typical," Mom said, then paused to sip her tea.

"Mom, did you do something to connect us?"

Mom choked on her tea. "What do you mean?"

"Zid'dra said my blood was used to connect us."

Mom sank into the sofa, pulling her robe close to her. "Well, yes. The spell I cast asked for blood. And, well, you know how squeamish I am. And there was a used bandage in the bathroom. I thought it was mine."

"But it was mine."

"Most likely."

"Shit, Mom." I paused. "Why do I feel like you're not telling me the truth?"

"I am." She stirred her tea. "I'm not. Anyway, I used your blood. I'm sorry."

"Why?"

"I figured it was safer."

"For whom?"

"Me."

"Mom!" I was livid.

"I'll never win any awards at parenting," Mom snapped. "I fucked up. Is that what you want to hear?"

I mouthed the word *language.*

Mom stiffened. We sat across from each in tense silence.

"Mom," I said after a few minutes, "remember when I came to find you three years ago? At the time, Devlina was syphoning off my magic to make herself stronger."

Mom coughed, looked away.

"Zid'dra implied that the same thing is happening."

"Can't be," Mom said. "Your powers were taken away."

"Devlina researched in London. She says I still have them."

"Maybe," she said. "Yes. Probably. Somewhere. The Càsticanta can remove magic, but I guess it's like how a computer erases something. It's always there, but the computer ignores it. Like it doesn't exist."

"Mom, is it possible my magic is helping Devlina?"

"Maybe," Mom said, "but I doubt it. She's powerful on her own. She's a Malevolent."

"Can I get my powers back?"

"Like before?" Mom shook her head." No. I know you and Christine tried every spell imaginable."

"None worked."

"Yes."

"Evangeline said I should seek out Máurso. She said he can help me."

Mom tapped a finger on her teacup. I glanced at Evangeline astride her horse. She had her hand cupped around her ear. Was the picture always that way?

"Yes, Ma'm Sáu Eu," Mom said, "will help you." She stood and crossed the room to stir the logs in the fire." You're a fighter Elijah." Mom said, "That much is clear. My fault really. You should just be a boy, but I made you this way. I think it will be good to work with Máurso. He is a powerful Immortal. I think you can learn the Hygienic Arts."

"Be a Coaugelo like Austin and Barn?"

"Yes," Mom said, "and maybe, in time, your power will grow stronger."

"What will the Còngréhassa do?"

"Nothing, I hope," Mom said. "I'm lodging a formal complaint with the *Eqaulibradêro*. You were almost killed by the Zuscoes battling Devlina, by Zid'dra and then Tartáuranno."

"Yeah," I said. "Who knew I was so popular."

"The actions of the Còngréhassa put you at risk," Mom said, "by what they did to you."

"I'll say."

"You will train with Máurso so you can defend yourself."

"Okay, Mom."

Mom smiled at me." Honey, there's more."

"More?"

"I talked to Sweetie," Mom said. "You know, I think coming out has been hard on you. And your father didn't exactly help you. I'd like for us to go to a support group for queer young Magicals like you."

"What?"

Mom nodded." Yes, there's a weekly group that meets in West Hollywood."

"No way."

"We'll go together."

"Yeah?"

"Yes."

Mom came around and squeezed my shoulder.

"I think we'll drop a lot of your extracurriculars as well."

"No way," I said. "Like choir and basket weaving and tap dancing?"

"Ah, but I like you tap dancing."

"Mom!"

"Okay," Mom said. "And maybe you should drop out of *Oklahoma!*, the All Valley Swim Competition, aca-deca, and the Burbank 5K."

"No way," I said. "No. I want to do those, Mom. I'm not into tile glazing, miming, or learning ancient Greek. But I want to do the other things. I can do them. I want to prove to myself I am a winner."

"But, honey, you're a winner."

"No, Mom," I said leaning over to ruffle L'Ocle's feathers as he sat on the edge of my wingchair." You don't understand, I really fucked a lot of things up—pardon my French—with Austin, and you know I want to prove that I can be better than Dad."

"Elijah, you have nothing to prove."

"To me."

"Honey."

"Mom, please."

"Elijah, I don't want you to do too much." Mom returned to the sofa." You've been pushing yourself so hard for too long. Because of me."

"Yes, but Mom now I get it. Dad is scum. I am different than him. I can prove it. To him."

"You don't need to prove it to him."

"Yeah, when I show him all my awards and accomplishments."

"You are not to see him."

"I'll post them to social media," I said. "I think he follows me."

"Block him!'

"Mom, I'm going to do this."

Mom looked upset. "Elijah, I don't think this will end well."

"Mom, don't you believe in me?"

"It's not that. I just think you need to cool your jets."

"Says the Queen of Brands and Plans?"

Mom hung her head." Fine, yes."

I smiled. "You're going to be proud of me."

Mom sighed. "I am proud of you."

The grandfather clock in the hallway chimed ten times. The fire cracked and popped. L'Ocle closed her eyes and hooted softly.

"What about Austin?"

I grimaced. "I—I dunno."

"You're going to get back with him."

"Mom, no," I said. "I mean look at me. I messed things up terribly."

"Yeah, so?"

"Well, I mean. Look, I'm going to follow my plan and then when I am a winner he'll take me back."

"You're totally senlàpso," Mom said with a laugh. "I mean, you know what, it's good you have me to guide you."

I frowned. "What the hell does that mean?" *She had to be kidding me.*

"Elijah, you don't have to do a million little things to win back Austin."

"So, what do you suggest?"

"Flowers, chocolate, and a big apology."

"No way," I said and folded my arms across my chest, glancing up at the painting over the fireplace. Evangeline held up a sign that read, *Sega coendégallo* or "She's right, y'know?"

"Shit, Mom did you put up Evangeline to do that?"

Mom's eyes darted to the painting. "No." She smiled." But she agrees."

"I don't think I can."

"Yes, you will," Mom said. "I'll help you."

"What?"

"Well, we'll go together. Tomorrow."

"No one wants their mom around when they are with their boyfriend."

"Normal kids, yeah," Mom said, "but you need me there."

"So little trust in me."

"It's my fault, son," Mom said. "But I'm going to fix you, me. Us."

I caught my breath. Was she for real?

"Can we be...helped?'

"Yes, we can."

"Okay, Mom." I was going out on a limb; I was going to trust her.

Mom's phone vibrated. She picked it up off of the coffee table.

"That's the Macistráuto," she said. "Gotta talk to them. You should go to sleep."

I sighed. "I'm not tired."

"You had a long day."

"Yeah," I said, standing and stretching. L'Ocle ruffled her feathers and chirped. "Mom, what exactly happened to Tartáuranno?"

"Oh, well, I used a powerful spell that loosened his soul from his body. I hoped to destroy him, but even my magic isn't that powerful."

"Yeah?"

"Yes, Elijah," Mom admitted." Then Austin and Barn combined their PlasmX's and peeled his soul from his body. Effectively diminishing his power. Then we rolled him up and sent him back where he belongs."

"In the basement of the Gloom."

"Yes, where he'll stay for time immemorial." Mom tapped on her phone. "Hi, yes this is Belinda Delomary..."

I walked to the double doors leading to the hall.

"Mom?"

"Can you hold?" Mom said into the phone. "Yes, honey?"

"I think I mean this—thank you. And I love you."

Tears welled in Mom's eyes. "I love you too, darling."

That was weird, but good. I think.

*

CLOUDS THREATENED TO unleash another torrent of rain over the Valley the next day. Mom and I went to see Dr. Hu. She gave me a clean bill of health.

"You look tired," she said. "Are you getting enough rest at night?"

I didn't want to tell her about the darkness lingering inside me.

How I had trouble falling asleep and staying asleep. "I'm okay."

"A young man as active as you needs plenty of rest."

Mom shot me a look. "You'll be happy to know I've canceled most of his extracurriculars."

Dr. Hu raised an eyebrow. "Am I dreaming? Is this really Belinda Delomary?" she asked flatly. Dr. Hu was no nonsense. She didn't joke.

"Very funny," Mom said. "Elijah still wants to push himself. So, don't blame me."

"I've got things to do," I said. "And we have a plan." I looked at Mom. She nodded.

"I thought plans were done?" Dr. Hu said.

"This is his plan."

Dr. Hu walked to the window." Well I don't see any pigs flying," she said. "Though that could be because you cast a spell on me."

"You've got a million jokes today, Dr. Hu," Mom said. Dr. Hu was a Mùn Tái, a type of Encantreina specializing in healing.

"I suppose I could cast a spell on you," Dr. Hu said pointedly to me. "But, instead, please get some rest, Elijah."

A half hour later, we drove downtown to the offices of the Macistráuto in a mid-century office tower resembling an air conditioner on stilts. I was there to give my account of the *malpàssuncto* or the "disturbance," as they called it. The building loomed over one side of the Spanish-style Marcého Imradomensanaballen, the open-air marketplace and gathering place for Magicals, covered with a gramora that made the place resemble an abandoned factory.

I gave my account of what happened to a sour-faced, heavyset woman with her hair slicked off her face and pulled into a tight ponytail.

"As I explained, I was running away to Old Earth," I said. "It's better there, for gay boys like me."

"Unwise for a minor, to flee to another dimension," she said. "Something could have happened to you."

I ignored her." Then I heard a commotion and crawled back

through this vortex between dimensions—"

"A vortex? Where? That's extremely dangerous, should probably be sealed with runes—" she said, head down jotting notes into her tablet.

"I ended up being caught in a battle between Devlina and Zuscoe,"

"That's not very smart; she was a Malevolent and you have no powers."

"Eventually, I fell into the Gloom."

"Unheard of," she said, wagging an eyebrow at me. "Haven't you read the Pàcifimenta? Magicals are forbidden from being in the Gloom."

"I didn't go willingly." She had to be kidding me, right?

She kept up her barrage of questions. "And you say you confronted Zid'dra?"

"He was waiting for me."

"You're lucky to be alive. Zid'dra hates Magicals."

"Am I a Magical?" As far as I knew, I was no longer magical.

"Technically, yes, but maybe not in practice."

"You suck."

"Elijah," Mom said, "it's not her fault."

The woman looked at me. "Go on."

"The Áuqala appeared and saved me."

The woman stopped typing notes into her tablet. She looked at me skeptically." Son, the Áuqala is busy guiding the Shimmering. She also has a hands-off policy. She doesn't interfere with direct engagements between Magicals and monsters."

"Yeah, well, I'm telling the truth."

The woman glanced at Mom, who nodded.

"Maybe it's because you're related," the woman said. "Nepotism isn't allowed per the Pàcifimenta," she continued, summoning a small, blue book out of the air. "I think you need to read this carefully, son."

"I don't need a copy of the Pàcifimenta."

"My son is alive thanks to the Áuqala," Mom said angrily, "and no thanks to the Pàcifimenta. My son was powerless to protect himself."

The woman paused, looked at her tablet, and said, "I am just here to take a report, ma'am."

"Go on, then, ma'am." Mom said viciously. *Wow, Mama Lioness*, I thought.

"Can we keep this professional?" the woman asked, then looked toward me." Please continue."

"A great monster appeared out of a fissure. He was named Tartáuranno."

"Oh, him," the woman said, shaking her head. "Yes, he is a terrible one. Zid'dra's second in command." She paused and looked at me. "You have formidable enemies, perhaps the Delomary family can hire body-guards?"

Mom grunted, focusing her eyes on the woman's head. A red spot appeared and a wisp of smoke.

"Mom!" I shouted.

The spot disappeared. Mom was close to setting the woman's head on fire. The last thing we needed was Mom being taken away for assault on an XAQ2 agent.

"Eventually, Mom and several agents from the Anti-coven League came to save me."

"Oh, the League," the woman said, shaking her head, "I suppose they do something useful."

"Yeah," I said sharply. "They saved me."

"Good," the woman said, turning over her tablet. "Keep them close." She stood. "I'm done with my report." She extended her hand to Mom who rolled her eyes.

"Well," the woman said, "I'd keep those people who saved you close by. You seem to be on the radar of the man with horns." She used her fingers to imitate horns on her head, chortled, opened the door, and walked outside into the brightly lit hallway.

"I swear to God," Mom said, grinding her teeth, "I was this close to setting her ablaze. She has no compassion."

"Yeah, I noticed," I said and stood. "Let's get out of here before you do something you'll regret, Mom."

"Good idea."

The woman's advice to keep Barn and especially Austin close bounced around my head as we drove back to Burbank. My palms were getting sweaty. Today was the day. I was going to make things right with Austin.

At home, in the living room, Mom appeared from the hallway with two bouquets of flowers, several gold boxes of candy, as well as boxes of cosmetics and cigars.

"Don't get any crazy ideas," Mom said, pointing to the cigars. "These aren't real but, rather, magical. They burn and smoke like true cigars, but they aren't. Cigars and smoking are vulgar. Don't take it up."

"Who are these for?"

"Austin Sr.," Mom said, walking to the wet bar and pouring herself some scotch. She chugged it.

"Mom, it's only two o'clock!"

"I'm nervous."

"Me too." I added, "If smoking is evil, why are we giving Austin's dad fake cigars?"

"Because he loves them. We were at a gala dinner at the Temple of Magic last week. They are his one vice."

"Okay, so?"

"Look. You are going over there to apologize to Austin and his family. Bring gifts. Trust me."

I rummaged among the cosmetics made by Aunt Christine herself. "Is the lipstick for Austin?"

"His mother, Elijah."

"The flowers?"

"Red for Austin, white for his mother," Mom said. "Trust me, you gotta shower them with gratitude. How do you think I get things done at work?"

"Why aren't you at work?" I asked, my fingers tracing the soft petals of the flowers.

"Mental health day," Mom said. She noticed the look on my face. "I told you, I'm a new me."

"Wow, one who skips work," I said, then rubbed my chin and asked, "Do you eat ceviche?"

"What?"

"Mom, ceviche from a stand at the beach. Do you eat it?"

"Absolutely not, unless I want to risk my stomach health. Why?"

"Just checking to make sure you're really you and not some impostor. Remember our questions to test if we are who we say we are?"

"Right," Mom said. "Like if I ask if you like yams, and you say yes, then I know it's clearly not you."

"Exactly."

"Well, I'm not Tartáuranno, here to torment you."

"You do like to torment people," I said sharply, "especially your kids."

"Touché."

Aunt Christine appeared in the door along with Uncle George.

"Are you going to patch things up with Austin?" she asked. "If so, come here so I can cast a spell on you so you don't act stupid."

I rolled my eyes.

"I'm going with him," Mom said, handing me the flowers and cosmetics and cigars in a bag, then putting another bag of the candy around my neck.

"You cannot be serious, B." B was either short for Belinda or bitch. We never knew which meaning Christine was using. "You think Elijah wants you lurking around while he tries to get his man back?"

"I will cast a gramora!"

"Fine," Christine said, "then we're coming too!"

"Aye, moral support mate," George said. Soon I was walking along North Sunset Canyon Drive, looking like a complete weirdo with two bouquets of roses in my right hand, a bag of lipsticks and skin cream in my left, and candy dangling around my neck. With three adults walking quickly behind me cheering me on.

"You got this, honey!"

"You are going to slay, Elijah!"

"Mom," I complained, "you're too old to say 'slay.'"

"Whatever," Mom retorted.

"March on and conquer love, mate!"

A few minutes later, I appeared at Austin's house and stood at the bottom of the hill staring up at the white stone and glass mansion looming above me. Shit, what if Austin refused to see me? What if he hated me? He had every right. I was terrible to him. I was a terrible person when alone in my head. *No, he hugged me last night. Just relax, Elijah.*

I glanced over my shoulder. Mom and Christine and George were all smiles. George gave me two thumbs-up, and Christine blew me kisses. Little red lips floated toward me, dissolving before my face.

"The gramora!" I hissed.

"Yes, sorry, darling," Mom said. The air rippled, and they disappeared. I looked up at the house and then at my hands. I didn't have any way to use my phone to call Austin to ask him to come outside.

"Kangy!" I shouted at the top of my lungs. "Kangy!"

The red door to his house opened. Austin stood on the porch squinting in the afternoon sun.

"Eli," he called, "why are you shouting my name...and...uh...what are you doing?" He swaggered out onto the porch, a smile on his face, and jumped down to the lawn that sloped toward the sidewalk. "Have you decided to become a street hawker?" He strode down to meet me, then examined the flowers in my right hand, the bag in my left, and the candy around my neck. "Maybe you should get a wee cart to push up and down the street, yeah?"

"I'm not hawking these," I muttered, staring down at my shoes. "I umm...well, they're for you."

Austin pushed his thick black glasses up his nose—these were new, replacing the ones broken the night before. "Yeah? For me?"

"Austin..."

"Kang-ee!"

"Okay, I'm sweating here, and it's not really hot out, y'know?"

"Aye," Austin said, hands on his hips, an amused smile on his face. "What would make you sweat though, little Eli?"

"I'm nervous," I whispered.

"Why?"

"Because."

"Tell me more."

Austin was not going to make this easy.

"I...umm...okay, the flowers are for you."

"Hopefully not the white ones. Those are for funerals in China."

"Shit, I didn't know," I said, dropping them to the ground. Austin leaned over to pick them up. He held them in his hands. His left eye was still slightly swollen; his face had scratches and bruises.

"I'm joking," Austin said. "The red ones, would they be for me?"

I nodded. "Yes, Kangy."

"Just because?" Austin was clearly enjoying himself.

"Because I wanted to...say I'm sorry."

"Sorry for what, mate?"

Aunt Christine's voice called out from behind the gramora, "Dammit, why is this taking so long?"

Austin turned left. "Who's with you?"

"I mean, just Mom and Aunt Christine and Uncle George."

Austin glanced at me. "Needed emotional support, yeah?"

"Yes!" I said. "Look, I messed up," I finally spit out. "I have roses for you tind gourmet chocolates—"

"Chinese lads from Hong Kong go wild for chocolate. Smart move." Austin winked.

"And gifts for your Mom and Dad."

"Brilliant," Austin said, standing close to me, peering down at me through his thick glasses. "Bribe the folks, sweet-talk the former boy-friend."

"Yeah," I said, "I feel awkward, Kangy. I don't know what I'm doing. I know I didn't treat you right, and well, I'm working on myself, and I want you in my life."

"Yeah?" Austin said. "How so? Like a bro?" He emphasized the word with a flat, American accent. "BFF? Perhaps someone you look up to because he might be more put together than you?"

My face was red. Clearly Austin was punishing me in his way. I deserved it.

"No. More."

"Saucy minx." He lowered his voice. "Friends with bennys?"

"No!"

He burst out laughing, pulling me into a hug, "I forgive you my wild, feral cat. You love to lash out at poor Kangy. Give him the claw treatment, yeah? Push him away, yeah?"

"Yeah, I'm sorry."

"Sorry, what?"

"Sorry, Kangy."

Austin looked to his left, raising his voice, "I think you all can go home. I have accepted Elijah's groveling." The gramora vanished. Aunt Christine, Mom, and Uncle George came over and hugged both of us. Uncle George and Austin fist bumped after we all separated.

"It was only inevitable," George said. "These Delomarys are crazy."

"Tell me, mate."

"I don't know what we did wrong in a past life to deserve this treatment."

"Aye, Uncle George."

Aunt Christine rolled her eyes." There is nothing wrong with us. We have feelings! We have passion! We are French Creole!"

Uncle George grabbed her by the waist and pulled her close." Relax, pretty lady. I'm just teasing."

Mom cleared her throat. "Let's give them some space," she said. "The last thing they need are middle-aged people showing affection."

"Actually," Austin said, "I love seeing old folks like you acting romantic. My parents are, and it's why I'm a big romantic, right, Eli?" He winked at me.

"Please note, Elijah," Uncle George said, "spend more time around people who love each other and you. Understand me, lad?"

"Yeah, I do," I said. "You're right."

"Of course, I'm right," George said. "I'm very smart. Right, babe?"

"Yes, sure, Georgie," Christine said.

"Enjoy the flowers," Mom said. They turned and walked slowly back to the house.

"I could have made you grovel some more, yeah?"

"Yes, you could have."

"I'm very generous though."

"Is that so?"

"Yes, it is."

"Kangy?"

"Yes, Eli?"

"Can we go inside already? I feel pretty stupid with this bag around my neck."

"Aw, like a little pack mule. A burro, I believe it's called."

"Kangy?"

"Yes, Eli?"

"Stop talking, yeah?"

Austin burst out laughing, reaching around my neck to grab the bag of candy, then putting his arm around me. We walked slowly up the lawn to the house.

Chapter Four

Red Roses and Chocolate

RAIN FELL STEADILY past Austin's picture windows overlooking the front yard and the Verdugo Mountains. "Stay" by Lisa Loeb played from a vinyl record spinning on the phonograph nestled in a warren of floating shelves Austin had recently installed.

"I did it all myself, Eli," Austin said, flexing his biceps. "Does knowing I'm a handyman turn you on?"

I sat up straight on the edge of his bed, nervous and unsure how to act. Austin pointed to the top shelf, lined with gold plastic trophies. "See those? Trophies from my Dáu Xhà in Hong Kong for being a right brilliant Coaugelo. Lucky you."

I kicked my legs nervously against the white duvet. I glanced out the window at the sheets of rain. Another atmospheric river. LA already had received three times the normal amount of rain for the year.

Austin sat next to me. "Eli, you can relax." He placed his hand on my knee. I watched his hand, the faint spread of blue veins resembling a river feeding a delta with nutrient-rich water.

"Kangy, it's hard."

"To what?"

"Be here."

"This is your home, mate."

"I know—it's just—"

Austin fell back on the bed with a whoosh. "Eli," he said, "did I ever tell about the time I broke my Mum's favorite vase? It was very old, imported from Old Earth! Mã-Lo in fact. From a palace or temple or some such place. Anyway, Mum loves porcelain collectibles, hence why her fake job is to be an importer-exporter." Austin laughed. "Anyway, here's the thing. I was mad at my mum. She wouldn't let me eat a dozen Chinese donuts with my morning congee."

I sniggered. Austin's appetite was endless.

"So, I got up from the table and I walked over to the vase and threatened to kick it if she didn't relent. Dad, of course, told me to stop acting like a git, but, Mum, well, she sat eating her congee. I went and kicked over her vase! It made a terrible sound as it broke, and shards of porcelain went everywhere including into my knee. I was bleeding! I felt so stupid, mate."

"What happened then?"

"Mum took me to the bathroom and cleaned my knee, and then she told me that she knew that sometimes my eyes were bigger than my stomach. Sure, I could eat a dozen donuts, but I also had to be realistic. Three was enough for a boy like me."

"Shit, wow. You got off easy."

"No, mate," Austin said. "The thing is I asked Mum if she hated me. And she said she hated that I broke her vase but she loved me, nonetheless, because I was her son."

I choked up.

"Just like I love you, Eli," Austin said. "I hate what you did, but I still love you."

"Oh, Kangy…"

"Aye," Austin said, "you can say it, Eli. You are lucky to know me, Austin Kang Jr."

"I am."

"What was that, love?"

"I AM!" I hollered.

Austin smirked. "Good."

"Anyway, Eli," Austin said, raising off the bed, then walking back to the bookcase." See? I have candles and plants! And a menagerie of stuffed animals, just for you."

I sat up on my knees, tears in my eyes, watching Austin pull out each stuffed animal and present them to me.

"This is Amber. She's a daft cow. Get it? She's a cow!" Austin chuckled. "And this is Jinjuh. She's a ginger cat, like you. Watch her claws!"

"Do I have claws?" I whispered.

Austin choked. "Um, yes, mate, you do."

"Sorry."

Austin paused, setting Jinjuh back on the shelf. "I might be a sadist, Eli," Austin said. "I sorta like the excitement of being with you. You're not meek or boring."

I laughed in spite of myself. Austin did too.

"And you're one of a kind, Kangy."

"This is true," Austin said. "I'm a superstar, yeah?"

We both dissolved into laughter. Austin sat beside me on the bed.

"Not really sure what to do, mate," Austin said. "I want to kiss you, but it's sort of awkward right now, yeah?"

"Yeah."

"I have some feelings too, you know."

"You do?"

"Yeah," Austin explained, "not as intense as you. Maybe I'm a little skittish. Yes. Those claws." He glanced at my hands. And tittered awkwardly.

"Kangy—"

"My Eli."

We sat side by side for a while, the rain drumming against the roof overhead and tapping against the window.

"I'm going to get help, Kangy."

"What kind of help, Eli?"

I coughed. I was embarrassed to admit, "Um, a support group for young Magicals."

"Support group?" Austin looked perplexed.

"Yeah, with a counselor. Talk about what I'm going through."

Austin nodded. "Aye," he said, "that's brilliant, mate. I think it will help you."

"You do?"

"Aye," Austin said, "you've been through a lot, Eli. Much more than Ol' Kangy. Trauma, yeah? You need to process it."

"Process it?"

"Aye," Austin said, "that's what Mum calls it. Once a week we get together, before dinner and sit at the table and share feelings. Well, I'm usually very hungry and perhaps a little standoffish, yeah? So, I'm hesitant at first, but you know Mum studied psychology and counseling when she was at uni in Hong Kong before she studied applied hygenics. She really knows how to tease out things from me and Dad."

"Does it help?"

"I'd never admit it," Austin said. "I mean she's my mum and she can be a little bit of a know it all, yeah?"

"Hmmm...who does that remind me of?"

Austin batted my arm with a pillow." Not funny, Eli. You're still in groveling mode. You need to be buttering me up, remember?

"Eli," Austin said, "this will be good. You'll go and process the trauma of the divorce, battling that slag Devlina—twice, sheesh—coming out, dealing with your dad. Breaking a certain Leo's heart."

My eyes widened. Austin smiled. "Ah, it's okay, Eli. I'm adding, um...levity to the situation. One of Kangy's specialities."

"You're the best, Kangy."

"Say that again," Austin said, standing and walking to the door. He opened it and turned to me." Say it very loudly, young Eli."

"You are the best, Austin Kang Jr.!"

"You're taking the groveling thing to a new level," Cecilia called from down the hall.

"Leave the boy alone, yeah, son?" Austin Sr. chimed in.

"No way," Austin said, turning to face me. He examined my face. "Ah, Eli," he said, his voice cracked. "You're so beautiful. My beautiful cat."

I stood. He walked over to me. We hugged each other tightly. For the first time in a while, the world was right again.

"Mom is coming to counseling too," I said after a while, when we separated. "Turns out she needs a little help too."

Austin sank into his bean bag chair by the window." This can't be happening. Belinda Delomary seeking help? Am I dead? Am I a ghost?"

"No, Kangy, it's true."

"Brilliant," Austin said. "I am glad to hear this. Honestly."

"There's more."

Austin's mouth fell open." More? What more can possibly happen?"

"Mom talked to Máurso. I'm going to train with you and Barn."

Austin bounded out of the bean bag." Eli!" He pulled me off the bed excitedly." That's ace! Wow. You're going to learn to be a fighter!" We spun around the room before he let go, and we fell onto the bed, panting and in stitches.

"I'm excited," I said, "for the first time in a long time."

"I am too," Austin said. "You've always been a fighter. A soddin' good one too. And now you'll learn the Hygenic Arts. And that's going to help you feel confident, mate."

"I hope so."

"I know so," Austin said, "Máurso is a brilliant teacher. You'll grow under him."

"Yeah?"

"Yes."

"Like maybe to be six three?"

Austin looked over at me." Not likely, mate. You don't have tall genes like me."

"I could have a growth spurt."

"You're almost seventeen."

"Kangy!"

"Easy, Eli," Austin cautioned. "Put them claws away, yeah?"

We convulsed with laughter.

Cecilia appeared in the doorway." I hear you boys giggling. Must mean you're hungry. I brought you some oranges."

"I love oranges, Mum!" Austin said.

"I know, son," Cecilia said, tossing an orange to Austin and one to me.

As we peeled the oranges, I said, "I've come up with a plan, Kangy."

Austin choked on his orange.

"Plan?"

"Yeah, for the next few months until school is over, I am going to seize life by the cajones."

"The k-huh-what is?"

"The bollocks you call them."

"Sounds painful, mate."

"Yeah, well, I want to step up and show the world that I, Elijah Delomary, am not some loser. I am more than that. I am a doer!"

"Eli," Austin said slowly, setting down the rind of his orange in a tissue from the box next to his bed, "you don't have to prove anything."

"I do, Kangy."

"What do you mean?"

"I feel like I've been moping around for too long under other people's sway. In their shadow. And now I have a chance to break free, to stand up, and show who I am."

"You're a wonderful boy, Elijah Delomary."

"That's just it. When I was in the Gloom with Zid'dra breathing down my neck, and I didn't know if I was going to live or die, something snapped inside."

Austin's eyes darted over my face. "Yeah, Eli?"

"Yes, Kangy," I said, "it's like I have a second chance. You know. And I want to do stuff. I want to win the All Valley Swim competition, the Gold for BHS in the Academic Decathlon. I want to be in *Oklahoma!* I want to run the Burbank 5K. I know I can do all those things. I know I can."

"I understand, Eli."

"I can show them, Kangy. I can show them all. That I'm a new Elijah."

"I think we know you're new—"

"No, Kangy," I snapped. "I'm sorry, but I have to do this. I want to do this. Do you believe I can do it?"

Austin hesitated. "I worry, Eli. You've already been through so much."

"So, you don't believe in me?"

Austin reached for my hand, lacing our fingers. "No, Eli. I believe in you. I always have."

Tears welled in my eyes and streamed down my face. Austin reached up to wipe the tears off my cheek.

"I know you can do anything, Eli."

"Thanks, Kangy," I said. "Listen...about us... I wanted to ask is it okay if we take it slow? I mean, I put you through a lot. I want us to become stronger. I want to show you that I'm okay. I'm well. I won't hurt you again."

Austin brushed his hand against my cheek. "Aye," he said. "I think that is very wise, Eli. I think we both need to ease back into what will someday be known as the greatest love story ever."

I laughed out loud. "Kangy, you are too funny."

"Aye," Austin said, "one of my many charms. As I said earlier, levity, mate."

"Someday I'll be able to levitate you again. When I get my magic back."

"Is that a promise, boy?" Austin said, swinging his legs over mine, looming over me. "Sounds kinky, yeah?"

"Does it?"

"Yeah, I dunno," Austin said, grinning. "Anyway, I think we should finish these oranges and listen to some Tupac. I bet you have forgotten all about the genius of hip-hop."

"I'm not really into hip-hop. Grunge, remember?"

"Ach," Austin said, scrambling off the bed and pulling a vinyl record off the shelf. "Boy, you can like more than just one genre of music. Tupac is genius."

"If you say so, Kangy."

"Of course, I do, Eli."

Austin removed the black vinyl from the dust cover and slipped it onto his turntable. He lowered the needle. Feedback momentarily seeped out of the speakers before Tupac began rapping.

"Now, while Tupac raps, I suggest you take this pad and write down one hundred things you are grateful for. Most should involve Kangy, mate. Then you take this home and put it up in your room and when the darkness or whatnot makes you loco, you read this and remember how lucky you are to have me."

"Isn't Tupac talking about humility?"

"What? No, Eli. Let me translate for you."

I tossed a pillow at Austin who ducked." Oi, settle down, Cat! Respect the Kang!"

A moment later, we roared with laughter.

*

LATER THAT NIGHT, I was up in the music room on the third floor, tugging on the collar of my tuxedo and standing next to Barn in the back of the room near the gold chintz curtains, which hung over the windows that overlooked the Valley. Yo-Yo Ma was playing the grand piano in the center of the room while a string quartet joined him under the glittering chandeliers. The room was filled with A-list guests Mom was hosting as a fundraiser for the local Democrat running for the House. The air was stuffy. I was bored. Barn appeared to be sleeping with his eyes open, a trick Coaugelus could pull off.

I elbowed him. "Are you asleep?"

Barn jolted awake." Bloomin 'hell, Elijah. I was sleeping."

"This is stultifying."

"Your mum is giving you stink eye." Barn motioned toward my mom in the front, by the double doors leading to the hallway. She wore a sparkling, slinky cocktail dress, her hair piled on her head, covered in jewels.

"We're looking important!" She communicated with her eyes. "It's only for a while longer. We're a team."

Team. This was a new concept. She had told me about the fundraiser earlier and mentioned that donors love to see happy families. And since they're liberal, it's a plus I'm queer. I was wearing a tux with a rainbow pin on the lapel.

I understand, I motioned back. She smiled, relieved.

"Pssst," a voice called to me from nearby. I rotated, my gaze falling over the heavy chestnut and marble lowboy in between the windows, the elaborate anniversary clock with its three-ball pendulum spinning silently to itself and set between two large gilt lamps.

"Elijah," Barn whispered, "pay attention, mate. This is Yo-Yo Ma. He is bleedin 'famous."

"I thought I heard something."

"Yeah," Barn replied, "me telling you to listen!"

The clock chimed nine times. I shifted my weight and clasped my hands behind my back. Servers were circulating with flutes of champagne. I licked my lips, then caught sight of Mom. She had her "absolutely no way" face on. I bit my lip. She was right; champagne tasted awful. Well, Austin told me that.

"Yoo-hoo!" a voice called to me from behind a potted palm. I spun around and spotted a swirling cloud of charcoal gray dust in the gilt mirror hanging on the wall in a corner.

"I got to pee," I told Barn.

"This is Yo-Yo Ma!"

"I'll be right back."

"Maaate!"

I made my way to the mirror, blocked from view from the room by a potted palm and two decorative columns.

The cloud swirled in the mirror.

"Hello?" I whispered.

"Elijah!" the cloud said, shifting and twisting into what appeared to be Devlina's face.

"Devlina! What are you doing?" I said. "I thought you were dead!"

"Oh, I was, honey," she said, "or so Zid'dra thought, but, well, you can't keep me down for long."

"I'm glad you're alive."

"That's shocking," Devlina said. "Elijah Delomary, Bane of the Gloom, is glad I'm alive."

"I misspoke," I corrected. "I had champagne."

"Sure, Elijah, sure."

"Whatever."

"Enough about me I hear you met my hunny bunny in person."

"Oh, yeah," I said, "after you deflected that boulder from killing me, I toppled into a fissure and landed deep in the stinking pit of the Gloom and met him face to face. He's scary!"

"All bark, no bite."

"He was going to kill me."

"I doubt he would."

"He said he would."

"He likes to talk tough, Elijah."

"He seemed to mean it. He was talking only in the Dark Language."

"Oh, well, maybe you're right," Devlina admitted. "He means business when he's speaking in that evil tongue."

"Devlina, he says that when Mom summoned you with her Malac Malactańena spell she used my blood to bind us."

The cloud swirled, as she pondered my words. "I didn't want to tell you so as not to scare you, but he is right."

"If we're bound together, then he wants to kill me."

"Hmmm, that would be a smart way to hurt me."

"Shit, so am I on his hit list?"

"What do you mean?"

"Well, did you two make up?"

"No!" Devlina said sharply. "Sure, he came and apologized, but then he told me he refused to give up his extra wives, and so I lay waste to half his coàcubenas!"

"Devlina!"

"I know, I know," she said. "Watch your temper you'll caution me. But that's like telling the snake not to slither or the spider not to spin its web."

"I'm just saying, you get wound up."

"Look who's talking, Mr. Temper."

I fell silent. Devlina's face swirled in the mirror. After a moment, she said, "Anyway, we're mad at each other again."

"Devlina, Zid'dra told me that he would kill me to diminish you."

"Did he? Based on what?"

"My mom's spell using my blood to link us."

"Fine, but listen...Ziddy will never do that," Devlina said, "and I'm strong enough to stop him."

"If you are so powerful, why are you swirling around in a mirror talking to me? Why aren't you here in person?"

"Zid'dra destroyed my body. I'm regenerating."

"Are you using me to help you regenerate?"

"No. Yes. I mean, I don't know."

"I've been feeling out of sorts lately."

"Not that darkness business."

"Yeah, I'm tired."

"Well, I dunno. I suppose that what he does to me could affect you."

"Can you maybe talk to him? Or cast a spell and remove our bond?

"Elijah." Devlina laughed. "I can't do that."

"Devlina, you can. You said so yourself—you are an omnipotent Malevolent."

"I am!" The cloud in the mirror spun around. "I'll try, Elijah, no guarantees."

"And no siphoning my powers?

"Fine," Devlina said. "Is that all you have to tell your Auntie Devlina?"

"You're not my auntie."

"Lighten up, kid."

"Yeah, well, look, I've decided that I am done being some door-mat. Some loser—"

"Like your dad!"

"No," I said. "Anyway, a new Elijah is coming. I am going to get my magic back. I am going to train to be a Coaugelo, and I am going to show the world I am a badass."

The cloud turned into two hands that began clapping.

"When you become a badass, do let me know, so I can siphon off some of your power to defeat Zid'dy and claim dominion over this planet."

"No, Devlina. You are not siphoning my power. Remember your promise?"

"I had my fingers crossed behind my back when I promised."

"Devlina!"

"Okay, sure, whatever."

"And, look, your plan can't succeed. You can't destroy Zid'dra! Doing so would threaten the balance of the universe. You know this."

"Is this the part where you say you'll stop me?"

I chewed on my lower lip. She knew I couldn't do that anymore.

Devlina relented, "Okay, I will consider your warning."

"Good. Maybe just take some time apart from Zid'dra. Let your emotions run cool. Think clearly."

Devlina laughed, "Says the emotional teenager."

"Shut up!"

"Perhaps you're right," Devlina said, "but maybe you're wrong. Anyway, you know I covet power."

"I do," I said. "That's why you're called the Goddess of Lust. But you also love Zid'dra."

"Fuck," Devlina said. "Yes, things are complicated. I should destroy him and this awful world. Start anew."

I shrugged. "Maybe it's getting better."

Devlina gagged." What did you say?"

"Yeah," I said. "I think things are looking up."

"Screw you, Elijah," Devlina said. "Did you fall and smack your head on the pavement?"

"No!" I said. "I made up with Austin."

The cloud morphed into the word "Hallelujah."

"Praise be," Devlina said. "You finally did something right."

"Yes, I did."

"That's my influence. Did I not teach you to be true to yourself?"

"I am not giving you accolades, Devlina."

"Such a petulant child."

"I would think you'd be happy for me."

"I'm happy when the world is miserable."

"Figures."

"I suppose I should congratulate you on mending things with Austin."

"Thank you," I said. "Maybe I'm happy. Do you think you could be happy?"

Devlina choked, and lightning bolts crashed behind her. The mirror shook on the wall.

"I am not the happy type!" Devlina exclaimed.

"You can try to be happy."

"Barf!" Devlina said. "Bye, Elijah!" In a flash of light, Devlina's image disappeared from the mirror.

I turned around to face Mom.

"Was that Devlina?"

"Yes." I hung my head.

"What did she—" She chugged her champagne. Glass two. She was gonna be tipsy soon. "—want?"

"I don't know. One minute, she loves Zid'dra, the next, she hates him. They're at war. They're not at war. She covets power. He wants to be the alpha. She wants to be the alpha. What's news?"

"Headache," Mom said, rubbing her temples.

"Right," I said. Noticing her sway slightly, I reached for her arm. "Mom, the blood you used to summon her. Does that mean I have to worry?"

Mom shook her head." I doubt it," she said, flagging down the server. "It was like two teeny drops."

"Mom?"

The server brought the tray of champagne. She reached for a glass. I intercepted her hand.

"You have donors!"

"Dammit," she complained. "Look who's the parent now."

"Do I need to worry about Zid'dra possibly coming after me because I may be bound to Devlina, and in order to win his battle with her I may need to be dealt with?"

Mom stared at me intensely, like she was a computer processing a request. Her eyes blinked. She smiled.

"No way."

"Are you sure?"

"Yes."

"Why don't I believe you?"

"Because you like to make me out to be the bad guy," Mom said. "Come on, let's have some canapes and go to the ballroom. Seth MacFarlane is performing, and Austin arrived, and you get the first dance."

"We're taking it slow."

"What does that mean?"

"Mom, I was a mess. I hurt him twice. I need to fix me."

"You think too much."

I guffawed, "Says the Overanalyzer-in-Chief."

"I'm drunk, honey."

"I know, Mom."

"Can you introduce Seth and do my speech?"

"God, Mom," I said reaching for her phone where she had her speech written." We've come one-eighty. Now I'm representing you!"

"You love it."

"I suppose."

"Oh, and Elijah." Mom stopped me before we stepped into the hallway." I am going to talk to your dad tomorrow."

"Wait, what?"

"Yeah," Mom said, "I have some choice words for him."

"You don't need to do this for me."

"Yes, I do," Mom said. "I'm trying to make up for being a shitty parent all these years."

"But, Mom—"

"Elijah, I should have protected you from him. That's my job. I got so caught up in my own head and my own hatred for him that I lost sight of you." She added, "He caused a lot of anguish for you. He needs to be held accountable."

Wow. Mom was being...awesome?

"Thanks, Mom," I said. "When was the last time you talked to him directly, not through the lawyers at the Delomary Family Trust?"

"Ten years," Mom laughed. For once, she looked more at ease, comfortable.

"Please don't tell him that I'm gay," I said. "I want to come out to him on my own time."

"You don't need to do that ever."

"I do, someday. For me."

"Okay, son." Mom and I walked down the long hallway, lined with mirrors and fussy gold velvet settees and sparkling chandeliers floating overhead. We entered the ballroom. I looked around. Floor to ceiling windows on two sides, stained glass ceiling created by Tiffany overhead, stage on one side and huge fireplace in the other. More chandeliers. I swear our house had more chandeliers than the local LightMax Lamp superstore across from Conglomo-Mart.

Mom nodded for me to go to the stage. I looked around nervously at the room, packed shoulder to shoulder with famous actors, luminaries, business people, and rich people.

"You'll do just great, hon," Mom said.

"Nothing like you."

"Better," Mom said. "Plus you're young and handsome. Sex sells."

"What does that mean?"

"Everyone loves listening to beautiful people talk. Go up there and schmooze and make the donors open their pockets!"

I sighed, headed to the stage, and spotted Austin with Barn near the bar. He smiled and shot me the peace sign.

I grinned ear to ear at him. He winked at me.
Okay, I could do this.

Chapter Five

The God of War

HE WAS AT least nine feet tall with dark skin and a body made entirely of muscle. He had high cheek bones, a chiseled jawline, coal-black eyes with a scar that meandered over his left eyebrow. His presence filled the room. He was Mars, the God of War.

Máurso, as he was known in the Old Language, examined me thoughtfully, his enormous hand rubbing his chin.

"Aye," he said skeptically, "you are well-built, if a bit short."

I tried my best to stand at attention in the center of the rambling Dáu Xhà, set in a strip mall between Maxie Mart and La La's Nail Salon across from BHS. Outside, the Dáu Xhà looked like an ordinary store-front with glass windows emblazoned with posters that publicized mar-tial arts for health, longevity and protection. Inside, the Dáu Xhà was large enough to house a football field, a pool, and a separate area filled with weightlifting equipment and what appeared to be a dance studio. The aesthetic was Roman temple chic—marble columns, flaming urns, statues of various immortals; Aveana, Goddess of forests, Pàsadono, God of the oceans, Telémalora, Goddess of land. And the statues, it turned out, talked, a lot.

"Look at this numpty." Telémalora's statue scanned me head to toe.

Aveana shrugged." Máurso is losing his golden touch."

I stuck my tongue out at them. They grunted and fell silent.

"Can you lift weights?"

"Bench press four hundred, Dáumo."

"Small, powerful."

"Almost five eight, Your Majesty."

Máurso glanced at me." Dáumo here, lad."

"Okay, Dáumo." I changed the subject. "How is this space so big?"

"Qu'el of course," Máurso said. "It is just the right size for an Immortal such as myself, laddie." Máurso stroked the black fur of a cat sitting on his shoulder, its tail wrapped around his neck. Another cat lounged in an empty cardboard box nearby, while another slithered among the stone arches soaring overhead. I scanned the room counting at least twenty cats sleeping, stalking invisible enemies, or sitting on top of various equipment or on students resting between sets.

"This is where we learn to battle monsters," Máurso explained. "The physical body is the most important tool for a Coaugelu. Using mind, body, and soul to withstand Malac Malactańena and keep Ordinaries safe. You must be alert, agile, and think quick. There's no time to cast or conjure or summon, lad."

I frowned. Máurso moved on. "That pool is for training to battle water monsters. Cràcoas, you know? Above, is where we train to battle flying monsters such as those blasted Àzmadus."

I fidgeted nervously next to Máurso, taking in the room. Barn and Austin were on the turf behind us practicing *escrimago*, a tactical move to dodge monsters in the field. The room was filled with the sound of shouting and hollering. The ruckus of fifty Coaugelus from as young as five to as old as eighteen learning their craft.

Máurso's cat jumped off his shoulder and circled me, then rubbed against my leg.

"Oi, look at that, appears you have Pumpkin's blessing." He conjured a slushie out of the air, then put the straw to his mouth. He chugged it down in one second flat, the plastic cup deflating in his large hand.

"I love slushies, laddie," Máurso said, flinging the cup into the air, where it transformed into a white dove that flitted over to an overgrown rainforest behind bleachers near the locker rooms.

"Yeah, I heard," I mumbled." Is that a rainforest?"

Thunder rumbled. Rain began falling. Birds and monkeys chittered.

"Aye," Máurso said, "I have a fondness for animals." He led me around the field. "And plants. Bought a few dracaenas from a big retailer, and, well, they somehow turned into that wee forest. Not sure how."

"Maybe because you're a god."

Máurso paused, rubbed his chin, then threw his head back and laughed loudly. The entire room trembled. A cat fell off one of the arches overhead. The lights flickered.

"You're funny, Elijah," Máurso said, "and tense. I can tell. Don't be, laddie."

"You're a god," I said. "You laughed and made the room shake!"

"Aye," Máurso grumbled. "Hate it. One time I went to watch a movie about gods, some Hollywood rubbish, yeah? And, well, I couldn't stop laughing because everything was so wrong. I couldn't stop. The whole theater collapsed around me. I had to intervene to save everyone!"

"Wow."

"Aye," Máurso said. "You see, Elijah, having power is a great gift and a burden. I know you understand."

"Yeah, too well."

"Your family has helped the Immortals for millennia, laddie," Máurso said. He paused to lean down to pat a tabby cat rubbing against his leg." You're good people. And I don't particularly care for the

Còngréhassa or all the rules of the Alliance.

"I believe that Encantreinus and Coaugelus should train and fight together as equals. The Alliance believes Encantreinus should stick to magic while Coaugelus concentrate on fighting, each doing what they are trained for. I think both should train together. And that's why I'm glad you are here."

"I don't understand. Encantreinus and Coaugelus fight together."

"The Alliance wants Magicals to stick to their role. I think roles are shite. You can be a good Encantreinu who knows Xem Sen Ou. You can be a great Coaugelu and conjure and summon."

"I thought Coaugelus can't do that."

Máurso shook his head. "Of course they can, maybe not as much as an Encantreino like you, but they can." Máurso walked me to a set of glass doors leading into the waiting room outside the locker rooms. A small woman with black skin and dark eyes peered at me through horn-rimmed glasses.

"Marva, this is Elijah."

Marva lifted her hand, blowing a white powder into my face. I sneezed. The room glowed momentarily.

"Yeah, Mars, baby," Marva said in a husky voice. "He has it, his magic. Coaugelu level."

Máurso glanced at me. "Sorry, laddie, had to test you again."

I sneezed several more times. Marva handed me a white Qi'Xhè, the traditional robe worn by students at the Dáu Xhà. "You can change in there, hon."

Máurso turned. "I'll meet you on the field, laddie."

Moments later, I jogged across the field where Máurso stood encircled by a dozen Coaugelus. Barn grinned. Austin shot me the peace sign.

"We have a new *êtudiranto* in our Dáu Xhà," Máurso said. "This is Elijah Delomary. He is going to train with us and become a jolly brilliant fighter like some of you lot." He surveyed the students. "*Dàlcqordo?*"

"Okay, Dáumo!" everyone chanted. Gazes fell on me; there was whispering and eyes surveying me.

"You're the one the Còngréhassa punished," a girl chewing gum said. "I hate old people. They were mean to you. That sucked."

"Yeah," I said and shrugged.

"That is neither here nor there, Xiomara," Máurso said. "As you know, I am both the God of War and the God of Peace. What does that mean, Deonte?"

A tall, lanky guy around my age with dark skin responded, "We have a duality, Dáumo! Life is not black or white!"

"Aye, Deonte," Máurso said. "There are shades to life. We are going to do our best to help our mate become a Coaugelo."

"But, Dáumo." A small Asian girl around ten looked up at him. "He was banned from practicing magic."

Máurso stiffened. The lights dimmed. "Topanga, Elijah is a Magical. Period. He is here to train his mind and rekindle the magic in him. He might never be an Encatreino again, which is neither here nor there, but he can be a Coaugelo. Life is colors. We will work within the colors of life."

"But what if they shut you down?" A muscular guy named Roddy, whom I recognized from the football team at school, argued, "What if we get in trouble? Maybe he should learn somewhere else?"

Máurso's eyes darkened—the whites disappearing—a sign I would learn over time meant he was very angry and trying to control it. "Am I not an Immortal? Was I not born on Morra Êímpagońena? Am I not your Dáumo?"

Roddy looked down at the grass below his bare feet.

"If any of you do not trust in me to do what is right for Elijah and all of you, then I suggest you take off your Qi'Xhè and leave now."

Silence followed, save for the growls of some cats fighting somewhere in the back of the Dáu Xhà.

"I trust in you, Dáumo." Austin stepped forward. "And your decisions, and personally, I can vouch for my mate Elijah."

"Here, here!" Barn added, "He's not some monster. He is the Bane of the Gloom! Monsters fear him!"

"That is right, lads and lasses," Máurso agreed." You are lucky to train with him. Probably could learn a thing or two from him."

"Well, I'm Topanga." She put her small hand out toward me. "*Avenelcáumo ãe Dáu Xhà!*"

I shook her hand. Barn and Austin came over to pull me into a hug. Roddy sighed and shook my hand too. "Yeah, well, good luck."

"Thanks."

"Etiendo!" Máurso shouted. The cats in the corner stopped fighting. Everyone stood at attention, hands folded behind their backs. "We're going to start with M'am Sáu Eu." He walked the line, straightening backs and surveying everyone. "Xiomara, why do we practice meditation?"

"M'am Sáu Eu helps us clear our heads, Dáumo!" Xiomara said. "Center our Xei and prepare to battle."

"Xei?"

"Our energy, mate!" Barn teased. "I've told you that word many times."

"Sàlenqo!" Máurso growled. "M'am Sáu Eu allows you to tap into your glimmer of magic and use it to your advantage. We are going to help Elijah do that."

"Will...it...umm... Do you think it will work...?" I asked.

Máurso stiffened. "Am I not a god?"

"Yes, Dáumo!"

"Drop and give me twenty for doubting me," Máurso said.

I blinked at him.

"NOW!"

I dropped to do push-ups. Deep inside, I was nervous but also very excited to be here with the God of War and Austin and Barn. I was certain things were changing in my favor now.

*

I PRACTICED EVERY day after school with Máurso at the Dáu Xhà. At first, it was hard meditating. My mind didn't want to stop spinning. The darkness hovered on the edges of my consciousness. I struggled to concentrate, distracted by the sudden rainstorms in the forest, the sound of fists connecting with legs and arms, the occasional cat fights.

"You'll get better," Máurso told me on Friday evening as I walked with him out of the Dáu Xhà, Barn and Austin waiting for me outside. "Just keep bringing your hunger, laddie."

"I am hungry, Dáumo. I think we're getting burgers, care to join us?"

"No," Máurso laughed. "Hungry to better yourself. Get stronger, connect with your power. Be who you were meant to be."

"Who would that be?"

"A warrior that will save the world someday, laddie."

I chuckled. "I would just like to feel confident again."

"In time," Máurso said, holding the glass door open for me. "Remember, you can tame a great river with a dam but the river will always be powerful."

"Hey, can we eat, Elijah?" Austin said, levitating a few feet off the top of the pavement by his car.

"Yes, Dáumo, we're hungry," Barn added.

Máurso nodded. "Aye, go and have fun boys." He paused, watching a tabby cat zip out the open door heading toward the street. "Blasted cats!" he shouted. "Princess, I will turn you to stone if you don't get back here!" I watched Máurso chase the cat in circles around the parking lot as I put my gym bag in the back of Austin's car.

Máurso eventually caught the cat with his enormous hand. "Lloromo-amã!" The cat clawed his arm. He growled. The sky darkened, and he rubbed his arm.

"Bleedin' cats have claws sharper than the teeth of a Cràcoa!"

We all began laughing as Máurso retreated inside with the squirming cat.

*

I WOKE CLOSE to three AM. Heart pounding, sweat drenching my T-shirt. I groaned, kicked the duvet off my legs. I rubbed my face with my hands. I hated waking like this every night. Moonlight slanted through the windows on the blue and red carpet in the center of the room. The house was filled with a strange absence of noise and commotion. The bustle of daily living in the old mansion. Shadows stretched out from corners of the room. I closed my eyes and tried to concentrate. M'am Sáu Eu. *Concentrate, Elijah.* My heart was beating faster and faster. My eyes flew open. Long tendrils reached for me. Two red dots appeared in the hallway separating the walk-in closet from the bathroom.

"Zid'dra?" I whispered. Silence. The dots glowed deeper. I retreated toward the wall. "What do you want?" I panicked. Zid'dra was in my room. I couldn't stop him... Could I?

I tried to meditate, find the hope...no...magic within me. I could do this. I had to do this.

The clock chimed three times. The witching hour! I closed my eyes. *Boxey, I wish you were here with me.* Thunder growled far off in the Valley. Rain again?

A feeble white light radiated from my hand. *Yes, that's it! Make a ball and shoot it at the red eyes.* The light faded around my hand. The red dots grew bigger and bigger.

"Puxhàredo!"

I gave up and pulled the duvet over my body, trying desperately to distract myself from the dread inside me. The void, the vacuum. The fear and frustration. I was afraid of the darkness. Then, I heard it.

Breathing.

Breathing.

Breathing.

That wasn't me. I was holding my breath. Were the red eyes over me, on the other side of the duvet? Was I going to die?

Boxey, where are you tonight? I miss you. Austin, we're back together. It's not the same. Why can't things go back to the way they were when we first met? Easy, simple. When my life was bathed in golden light?

"The mundane days when we just go about life, when things are easy. Those are what we call the "good old days," Arnulfo, the salt-and-pepper-haired middle-aged Filipino man who lead support group, said. "Cherish those days."

"What if I can't cherish them?"

"Why do you say that, Elijah?"

"I don't want mundane days, Arnulfo. I want something bigger and better. I want to be beyond this place. I want to be....fifty-five and settled, riding a bicycle in the country with my life figured out."

"Elijah," Arnulfo said softly, "you can't skip any part of your life. Why would you want to?"

"Because then I wouldn't have to deal with myself. With this darkness. This uncertainty. I would be able to know who I was."

"Why don't you want to deal with yourself?"

I clung to the duvet cover, breathing softly through my nostrils. The ragged breathing filled the room. Two dots hovered over me. I was sure of it. I wasn't alone in my room. The runes protecting the house must have failed. The mansion wasn't safe from evil anymore.

"Because I'm a monster," I said after a long pause. Arnulfo sighed. Mom sat beside me, rigid in the hard-plastic chair. My eyes scanned the room, a diverse group of queer young Magicals watching me. The great and glorious Elijah Delomary, the Bane of the Gloom. What has he become? *Nada.*

"Oh my God," this girl said when Mom and I stepped out of the elevator an hour earlier. She was short, round, with a shaved head, brown skin and eyes, tattoos on her neck, and a dazzling smile.

"I can't believe you are here, in person."

"Do I know you?"

"No, of course not," the girl said, sticking out her hand. "I'm Stylo Gutierrez, the youth coordinator here. And I'm a huge fan of yours."

"Of me?"

"Yes!" Stylo said. "My Aunt Dora works for the League, administration, you know. And she documents the life and times of Magicals battling to save Ordinaries. For posterity, so future Magicals know what we did and why it's important to persevere."

"I'm sorry, I don't understand."

"Dora, well, she covers your family," Stylo said. "The Delomarys. You fought Devlina twice! You destroyed a Po'auco at your school! You exorcised Haddo the Horrible out of a tween on your way to school."

"Oh," I said softly. "Past tense."

"I don't care," Stylo said. "You are my hero."

"Shut up."

"No way," Stylo said. "You were brave! You stood up to the Còngréhassa! You gave up everything to save your familiar. You understand love, Elijah. You understand sacrifice."

Sacrifice.

Sacrifice.

Sacrifice: an act of giving up something valued for the sake of something else regarded as more important or worthy.

The words pounded in my head. The light faded; I was back in my room again. I held my breath. The ragged respiration was closer. Thunder rumbled across the Valley. Another atmospheric river set to drown Southern California with five inches of rain.

"Anyway," Stylo had said. "I'm gushing. I do that. Why don't you come in. We have donuts, vegan if you're into that. And fair-trade coffee for the lady, your sister?"

Mom chuckled. "You are quite the smooth talker."

"Yeah, my uncle Ozzie says that. I should run for office. Maybe I will. Be the first Pinay dyke congressperson from the Valley. Imagine that."

"I can," Mom said. "Where should we sit?"

"Anywhere," Stylo said. "My uncle Arnulfo is the facilitator. He's a psychiatrist, you know, former marine. He has a husband and two daughters. Beautiful."

"You don't say," Mom said, walking over to a circle of pink plastic chairs in the center of the brightly lit room at the LGBT Center in West Hollywood.

"Yeah, I'm talking too much," Stylo said. "I'm sorry, I do that. I'm nervous! Ha." Stylo sank into a pink, plastic chair. "You know you remind me of someone famous. Jessica Chastain! Yes, wow. You're really his mother?"

"Yes," Mom said, "I am." She looked at me. "Elijah are you okay?"

I was struggling to breathe. My heart raced. Two red dots in the corner glowing. Zid'dra was here. In my bedroom.

Rasping, wheezing, panting.

My heart exploded in my chest. I couldn't catch my breath. I panicked. Zid'dra was here in WeHo.

"Elijah, you look pale. Take a seat, please."

"Does he need water? I'll get him water!" Stylo jumped to her feet, hurrying to the table with the vegan donuts, fresh fruit and a glass pitcher of water with lemon slices floating on top.

I sat down. Stylo handed me a cup of water. I took a sip.

"Yeah, I'm better." I looked over, and the dots were gone. I was breathing normally again.

"Can you define monster, Elijah?" Arnulfo said ten minutes later.

"We fight them," I said flatly. "Soul reapers, life feeders, blood suckers."

"Yes, those kinds of monsters prey on Ordinaries." Arnulfo rubbed his clipped beard. "You said you were a monster?"

"I feel like one."

"You're one of the good guys, Elijah. Whether you fight monsters or not."

"Not really."

"Elijah, you being you is simply enough."

"What?" My brain didn't compute his words.

"You don't have to do things to be a good person, you know that?"

I glanced toward Mom. She was grimacing into her three thousand dollar designer luxury purse.

"Being alive means you're doing what you're supposed to do. That's all that is expected of you. *To be you.* That is all."

I was confused. Mom rummaged in her bag for some chewing gum. We were both disoriented.

"Elijah, what do you do for fun?"

"Skateboard, surf—I'm a SoCal stereotype."

"There is nothing wrong with skating or surfing."

My eyes drifted to Stylo, seated on the edge of her chair, huge smile on her face as she listened to me intently. I relaxed.

"I like to play with my stuffed octopus. His name is Ocho. That sounds deranged, right?"

"I have a stuffed spider named Anthrax I play with!" Stylo shouted, almost toppling from her chair. I chuckled. She grinned.

"And I...want to be an architect someday, you know. Build things. Homes."

I didn't want to look at Mom. Had she really changed?

"That's awesome," Arnulfo said. "What else do you like to do?"

"Academic Decathlon, so I can win gold. All Valley Swim Competition, gold. Burbank 5K, gold."

"Wow that's a lot of gold."

"I love gold!" Stylo said. "See my necklace!"

"Everyone loves a winner," I said.

"I find value in you simply showing up to compete? What does anyone else think?"

"I agree, Unc," Stylo said. "I mean I could never do any of those things."

"Me either," this girl with pink hair agreed. "I think it's amazing you want to do all that."

"Makes me tired," a boy with black dreads said. "I'd rather be in my Qu'elicadêro creating spells!"

"I love naps, Unc!"

"All those things are wonderful. Even taking naps, Stylo."

The room dissolved into laughter. Including Mom and me.

"The thing is..." My mouth was open; words tumbled out to the floor and marched around the carpet. I couldn't stop them. "I'm a fool, you know? I stood on a field and gave away my pride to three hundred kids at my school. And, well, the aftermath sucked and I wonder if I shouldn't have come out."

Silence. I cast my eyes to the pink and blue and gray carpet. *Why had I said that, aloud?*

Mom reached for my hand. I squirmed in my chair. A clock ticked loudly on the wall.

"I think that was brave," Tasha, the girl with pink hair, said. "Very brave."

"One hundred percent," Antoine, or Ant, for short—he of the dreads—muttered.

"Thanks," I said. "Then I came out and fell in love with my best friend. And yeah, I'm stupid and I treated him like crap...not once, but twice. There's something about me, something wrong. A monster inside me, I tell you."

I closed my eyes; I was in my room again. I couldn't breathe. The air was hot under the duvet. The panting and wheezing continued. Two red dots floated over me and bored through the cotton duvet. Rain hit the windows. Another storm sweeping into LA. Look at the mess I had created with my life. Look how far I had fallen. Bane of the Gloom? No more. Monster hunter? No more. I was being hunted by Zid'dra. The runes failed us. Our house was under the attack. I opened my eyes and the lights came up. I was sitting in a large room with a vaulted ceiling surrounded by fellow Magicals, Arnulfo, Stylo, and my mom.

"Mom." I looked at her. "You know you were right about me." My heart was beating wildly in my chest, my face flushed. I couldn't stay here anymore. And then I was on my feet stumbling toward the elevator, desperately pushing the button to go...anywhere.

I ended up outside on the street, trying to catch my breath. Stylo followed me outside onto Santa Monica Boulevard. Palm trees lined the median.

"Hey, you okay, Elijah?"

"Yeah, no," I said. "You know I don't think I should be here."

Stylo leaned against the wall. "Yeah, I hear you."

My heart raced in my chest. Traffic thundered past us. A silver balloon floated high overhead. I watched it zigzag over the palm trees. What tiny hands let it go? Why did they let it go? *No, they shouldn't have let it go.* My heart broke.

Stylo spoke softly, "My first session was hard too, you know?"

"Huh?"

"When I came to session, a year ago."

"You don't seem like the type who struggled to accept yourself."

"Yeah, duh. I struggled to be this other girl because I thought that's what the world wanted of me. Have long hair and love makeup and lipstick! Toss my hair back and laugh for no reason. Skip meals to be thin, thin, and thin, attract the gaze of boys. That wasn't me. It couldn't be me."

"Médedo."

"Shit is right," Stylo said. "I got better because I came here, fool."

"Fool?" I asked. "I thought I was your hero? Look at me. Some hero."

"Coming out isn't easy, Elijah. I always knew. I mean Dora and Ozzie knew better than to buy me dresses. I loved boots! And playing with trucks," Stylo said, reaching in her pocket and pulling out a packet of gum. She offered me a stick. I shook my head.

"Yeah, well maybe it was clear to them. But I wasn't so sure. We went to church, and they said girls don't love girls. And you know I didn't want to disappoint Him. He watches over me ever since my parents left to fight in the *Ozungantu Wars* in the Sixth Dimension. He keeps them safe. I couldn't let Him down."

"I take it you're Catholic."

"Yeah," Stylo said, "but you know what? He can love me and protect my parents too. It's not one or the other."

"Sure, it's not."

"You sound cynical."

"I don't know."

"Maybe come back inside, Elijah?"

"Why? I'm a complete ditmêro. I mean I embarrassed myself."

"No one is embarrassed by what happened," Stylo said. "The girl across from you, Tessa, she has blonde hair? She's an Astroísta. Powerful, she stopped a train carrying radioactive waste from crashing into a neighborhood in Indiana last week. And she's not even thirteen. Anyway, she said she decided that being gay was an illusion. Witchery, she said. Well, we all know better. She does too now, after coming to session. So do you."

"Maybe Máunadas cast a curse on me. Us."

"You know that's not true," Stylo said. "Máunadas want the absolute destruction of light and goodness in the universe. They don't sweat who's in love with who. They just want all humans—ordinary and Magical alike—dead."

We stood a few feet apart for another minute.

"Look, Eli—"

"Eli?" Austin called me that.

"Yeah, your nickname. I decided."

"Did you?"

"Yeah."

"Okay," I relented.

"Look, when you come out you have to reimagine yourself and so do others. It's not easy. It just takes time. You have to go through the feelings. And then, one day you'll be fine."

"Are you fine?"

"Do you think I'm *fine*?" She meant the other fine—as in hot.

I chuckled. "Yes, Stylo. I do."

"Cuz I'm masc?"

"Stylo, you are a *ditmêra*!"

Stylo cracked up. "Wow, got you to lighten up."

"Yeah, okay," I said. "Maybe we should go back in."

"Yeah?"

"I mean, I feel like a *senlàpso,* but maybe you're right."

"It gets better."

"Does someone pay you to say this stuff?"

"No, fool," Stylo said. "I'm just a genius."

Stylo sure talked a lot like Austin.

"Sure, okay."

Upstairs, Mom was waiting for me outside the elevator. "Elijah, darling."

"Hi, Mom."

"You're not a monster."

"I guess."

"Elijah—"

"It's okay, Mom."

Mom fell silent. Arnulfo walked over; he was only slightly taller than me.

"Come and rejoin us, Elijah. First time is the hardest. Okay?"

"Yeah, that's what Stylo says."

"She's right you know."

"See," Stylo said, "I know my stuff."

More garbage fell from my mouth in the next hour, followed by tears and shaking and trembling hands. Tissues and some hugs. Mom was stunned. She was crying herself. She stood up. When the surgeon opens the chest cavity and the heart pumps it's actually kind of disgusting looking—red and white and pink and slick and slimy. Not red and beautiful like they say. Strip away the layers and sometimes what they saw was disturbing.

Mom didn't say much on the ride back home. She was listening to Kenny G on the radio. I watched the low-slung buildings hugging Santa Monica Boulevard, salons, boutiques, Thai restaurants. I hadn't expected to show my heart to anyone, a group of strangers, let alone my mom. I was raw and out of balance. I wasn't used to this.

As the car maneuvered the Cahuenga Pass from Hollywood to the Valley, Mom said, "I'm glad you spoke freely. I was worried you'd hold back."

I didn't respond. I couldn't.

"I don't know what to say, frankly, that won't sound trite or ridiculous. Everything is going to be fine. You're fine. I'm fine. God."

Kenny G played the hell out of his flute or saxophone on the radio. Really belting out a catchy tune.

"I guess, you know, what the hell. I'm just so mad, really. That you are feeling this way. That you are going through this."

I sat silently.

"I blame them. Those people. We know who they are. I'm going to drop a billion to destroy those politicians, you know? We'll launch a coast-to-coast blitz of must-run segments on all our affiliates at the network and streamers about gay rights. We'll show them."

Mom gripped the steering wheel, hard. Her lips pursed. She was mad. Not at me. At the world.

"I'll show those people. Two can play the game of let's use our money and power. I'll use it to *help people*. Those people are sick, you know that..." Mom rambled on.

Austin came to mind. Him and me. Us. In his room a few days ago. Reconnected but still feeling the distance and hurt and pain. From the world around us. From me. I wanted to be in love with him again, like before.

"I just don't get why you can't cast a spell and make me fifty-five!" I begged Aunt Christine last week. "Me and Austin, we'll be together somewhere happy. Settled."

"Magic doesn't work that way, babe."

"Please, Auntie?"

"Elijah, time goes by so quickly. Before you know it, you'll be my age and wishing you were sixteen again. The time slips away. You have to be the grains falling away..."

"God, what is that supposed to mean?" I snapped.

"Elijah, you need to relax."

"I can't. I can't."

At the end of session, before we drove back to Burbank, Arnulfo took me aside.

"I know this is hard, Elijah. But give us a chance."

Chance. Austin had given me so many chances. I couldn't fuck up again. I had to prove myself to him. I had to keep coming to group therapy and showing my slimy, disgusting heart to a roomful of strangers, and worse—my mother—to get better.

Keep pushing yourself Elijah, the voice whispered. Keep it up. Don't give in. You don't want to be a loser like you know who. He who would drink the spit of a server because he has no pride.

"No, no, no!"

I was back under the duvet, the red dots infesting my bedroom. Snickering filled the room. Cold and cruel.

"I think you'll fail, Elijah," the voice said. "You're not strong enough. Just like she isn't strong enough. And when you fail, Devlina fails. And you know what? The universe will keep on spinning because I matter. You? Not so much!"

I pushed the duvet back, staring at the two red dots dancing on the wall, growing larger and larger. Until the red light filled my head.

Fail.

Fail.

Fail.

Iunio desi faltur destinens deve est.

Boy, you will fail. It's your destiny.

"Elijah, mate?" I heard Barn's voice. The door opened. The red light faded. Barn was in the doorway wearing his pajamas decorated with lions. "You were screaming. Are you okay?"

My heart was racing. I couldn't catch my breath.

"Elijah!" Barn hurried over to the bed. "Take a breath, mate. It's okay, just a nightmare you know."

He leaned over to switch on the lamp by the bed. Warm, yellow light filled the room, chasing away the shadows. Pinky slithered in the room, her fur glowing orange.

"Want me to sleep in here, mate?"

"You wouldn't mind?"

"Nah," Barn said, "of course not." Barn sank onto the bed, hands behind his head, sticking his bare feet out. "I think your bed is more comfortable than mine."

"Your bed is new!"

"Yeah, exactly, not broken in yet, mate."
We laughed.

I scooted against the wall. Pinky circled me three times before sinking into the space between me and Barn.

He switched off the light. In a moment, he was breathing softly. Pinky was snoring. I lay awake listening to the rain on the windows and the wheezing, rasping. Zid'dra was still in my room.

Do not fail, Elijah. Or maybe then you'll really lose Austin for good.

Chapter Six

What A Boy Wants

"BREAKING THE GIRL" by Red Hot Chili Peppers played from the speakers poolside as I pulled myself out of the water.

"You think I have what it takes to bring home the gold, Amanda?" I said grabbing a towel, water sliding off my body.

"Yes," Amanda said, tapping into her tablet. "Your times are excellent." She stood up from the bench poolside and surveyed my face. "But something is off. Are you getting rest?"

"Yeah, sure."

"Why don't I believe you?"

"Because you're an adult. It's what you do."

"Elijah, you're an athlete. Athletes need sleep."

"I sleep," I lied. "In my next life maybe," I teased.

"Get more sleep," she said. "That's an order."

"Fine."

"Okay," Amanda said, "you're doing very well. But I know you're also training for the 5k and doing *Oklahoma!* and Aca-Deca. That's a lot. I thought you were doing less these days?"

"That is less," I said. "No more tap dancing, band, tile-glazing, underwater basket weaving!"

"You know," Amanda said, handing me a bottle of water, "doing one event, winning one event, is more than enough. You know that right?"

"Sure, Amanda," I said, "but why win one when I can win three competitions and star in a musical?"

"Elijah, you're either an overachiever or have supernatural powers."

Amanda didn't know the half of it. She was ordinary. Not clued into my real abilities. Former abilities. No, I was progressing at the Dáu Xhà. I channeled my magic just last night. What a rush to feel it again, the burning heat in my chest as I summoned a mini-candy bar in the air. Before I could eat it, it dissolved.

"Wow!" Barn said. "You did it!"

"Brilliant, mate!" Austin said, leaning over to hug me. I breathed in his smell, citrus and eucalyptus. He smelled like heaven: love and acceptance. I couldn't fail him. I couldn't let him down.

I stayed late at the Dáu Xhà learning how to *escrimàgo* and to *aveàtra,* or fly into the air to evade monsters.

"You are a quick study," Máurso boomed, two white cats perched on his shoulders. "I knew you could do it, Delomary. There is Immortal blood in ya!"

I was doing it. I was getting better.

"Are you listening to me?" Amanda said. I snapped to. "You can win, but you need some rest."

"I'm going to nail the competition, Amanda." I ignored her order or advice or whatever. I could sleep later. I swaggered to the locker room to take off this ridiculously small bathing suit.

*

CLOUDS FLOATED OVERHEAD, blotting out the moon from time to time. The grass was wet from a deluge earlier. The rain subsided, and the storm trekked east over the Verdugo mountains, leaving in its wake a flotilla of fluffy clouds over the Valley.

"You know this is sacred," Austin said as we stood at the edge of the bamboo forest growing past the barn and livestock buildings. "*Aveàtrimenta*, we call it. Flying, yeah?"

"I mean, I flew too, once, Kangy."

"That's different, mate. You used spells to fly," Austin explained. "What we do is innate. We dissolve gravity to move effortlessly up and into the sky."

Austin pointed to the tops of the bamboo, rustling with the soft breeze. "Aveàtrimenta is what we do to fight monsters."

"You and Barn are excellent at it."

"Yeah," Austin said stretching out his hand. "Come on, let's do it together"

I stared up at the twenty-foot tall bamboo trees.

"I think I can do ten feet max," I said. "I mean, I'm a *Coaugeláido*. That's what Máurso calls me. The baby Coaugelo."

"No, love," Austin said. "You can do it. I know you can."

I gazed at the bamboo. Daunting. If only I could snap my fingers and fly again. I concentrated. My feet lifted off the ground. I opened my eyes. I sank back onto the grass.

"Kangy," I said, "maybe we just skip it for now."

"Eli," Austin said, "you can do it!"

"I can't."

"I believe in you!"

Austin always believed in me. *Always.*

"Okay."

I concentrated. My sneakers lifted off the grass. And a second later, I sank back.

"This is hard."

"Try again!"

I attempted to fly for another twenty minutes. To no avail.

"Let's give up," I growled. "I can't do this."

"Why are you giving up so easily?" Austin was mad.

"Because I'm a fricking loser!" I was angry. "Don't you see it?"

Austin shook his head. "No, I don't."

"Shut up, Kangy."

"No, stop acting this way. Like a *morrònigo!*"

I was appalled. "I am not garbage!"

"Then prove it!" He folded his arms across his chest.

"Vovo-puxhàredo!" I cussed him out.

"Just focus," Austin said, "and remember what Máurso taught to-day—you can bridge my magic. All Coaugelus do it."

"I...um...I'm not sure..."

"Yes, you can, it's innate," Austin said. "It's the reverse of what Encantreinus do in a battle with monsters. You shield your magic, and we tap into your magic. But in this case, you can tap into my magic to be stronger."

"Are you sure this will work?"

"You don't trust Ol' Kangy? You think he lies?" Anger boiled near the surface.

"But Kangy, I mean—" *If I do that, then I depend on you to be strong. To be better. To grow and be confident and succeed. Doesn't that mean I'm less than? Depending on someone else to succeed?*

"Come on, mate." Austin clasped my hand. "Just trust me."

His hand was firm, warm—no, hot. I concentrated like in the past, how I used to shield my magic from monsters. Only in reverse, I was tapping into Austin's magic. Energy surged from his fingers into my palm and down my fingertips. My body was charged.

My feet lifted off the grass. Higher and higher. The clouds floated overhead. Moonlight shone down on our faces. The bamboo trees grew closer and closer. And then we were standing softly on the boughs, our shoes touching the tops.

"Kangy!"

"Brilliant, yeah, mate?"

"Wow, we're standing on bamboo!"

"And you thought you had to have a full arsenal of magic to float again, huh!"

"Well, yeah."

"But that's what's great about this. Us. Magic. No one can take this away from you."

I could. If I slipped up. The two red dots. The wheezing and panting. Daring me to push on, to...no. Elijah. Relax. Everything is fine. Relax. You won't fail. Will you?

"Elijah," Arnulfo had said in session earlier, "just say the words, "I am gay" to yourself as many times a day as you need to."

"Yeah, why?"

"To help you accept yourself."

"I do accept—"

Stylo shot me a look.

"Okay, fine."

"Normalize being gay, Elijah. Normalize drag queens and books about boys in love and being you."

I am gay. I am gay. The words drifted through my head as I held onto Austin's hand.

"Okay, now we can run and leap as far as we want!"

"Oh, no," I said to Austin, "I'm—I'm—scared."

"Simply hold onto my hand, love," Austin said. "We'll do it together."

"But if we fall?"

"Don't you know Coaugelus always land on our feet?"

"That can't be right."

"Eli," Austin whispered, "trust me."

I swallowed my fear. My eyes locked with his. His eyes burned with love and kindness and compassion. And confidence. Austin never had to remind himself to say "I'm gay" while in class or when walking down the street when the insecurity reared its ugly head like a M'mu.

"I trust you."

In a split second, our shoes lifted off the tops of the bamboo. L'Ocle hooted and orbited overhead. Austin was lifting me higher in the air. "Let me know when you want to run and leap, Eli!"

"No, Kangy, I—I—I'm afraid."

"Don't be. Let yourself go, my Eli!"

Austin moved faster. L'Ocle flew above, her black eyes reflecting the silver light of the moon.

My heart struggled to soar, held back by the fear of two red dots, those flaming eyes. And the rasping and wheezing. Then, my heart began to beat wildly in my chest, and my lungs contracted. I let go of Austin's hand. I fell swiftly toward the bamboo and the damp earth below.

L'Ocle cried out and transformed into a golden eagle, her huge claws reaching for me. Her talons clutched me. She flew up and away from the bamboo forest, the barn, livestock sheds, and the offices of the agricultural team, depositing me on the meadow stretching past the bumblebee garden toward the lake on the north side of the property.

I lay on my back as L'Ocle reverted to being a snow owl, landing on a bough of an aspen tree nearby. Austin floated down toward me. I cried softly.

"Eli," Austin said, "why are you crying?"

"I messed up." Frustration reverberated up and down my spine.

"No," Austin said. "You did great for your first time!"

"I need to do better!"

"Relax, mate. Give it time."

"I don't have time."

"You do," Austin said soothingly. "Look, you got scared. We all are frightened the first time."

"What if I'm always terrified?"

"I don't believe that. You're strong and powerful. A fighter. My little fighter."

"Kangy—" I wanted to fall into his arms and never leave them. I wanted to travel back in time to when we were innocent. And I hadn't learned to hurt him. Me. Us.

"Eli," Austin said, "I think that's enough for tonight. You look tired."

"I'm fine!" I lied. I knew I would go home and get in bed and wake up in a panic at three AM. The red dots would be there. The tendrils of darkness would slide from under the furniture and doorways and pull me away from the light and into the void.

I was running and running as fast as I could away from the abyss. The finish line was in sight. I only had to reach the end, and then I would win, a gold medal hanging from my neck and the safety of knowing I wasn't at all like that man, the one with spit floating on his beer, my name would be in the online edition of the Daily Camaraderie and trending on social media. And in a split second, I would have leapfrogged all the uncertainty of my young life. Austin and I would be riding bikes together, fifty-five and settled.

Settled.

Safe.

Us.

A shadow crawled up from the ground along with two fucking red dots. I wasn't going to reach the finish line. I wasn't going to make it. I knew it.

And the room filled with evil laughter. Mocking me.

"Maybe give up, foolish, *Iunio*. You know you can't battle the darkness. The Shimmering is weakness, the Gloom is pure hatred and that malevolance motivates. It is all powerful. You know this. As you sit in your session, begging the world to accept you. That is weakness. Hatred is pure. Accept the power over you. Accept me."

"You told me to prove I'm not a loser."

"Maybe you are. I can make everything better. Just submit to me."

I woke up struggling for air.

I glanced at my phone.

I had a message from Austin.

"You were brilliant, mate." With two hearts and an emoji of two birds.

I smiled and put my phone back on the charger. I lay back in bed, staring up at the cherubs overhead.

"Love is stronger than hate," they whispered, as if they too were afraid of the darkness—of the cold truth that maybe love wasn't stronger than hatred.

*

I STOOD UNDER two large oak trees in Stylo's backyard while Aunt Dora sipped on a beer and Uncle Ozzie puttered around an old motáuvo, a hover motorcycle the League used when tracking down monsters. He also tricked them out. Ozzie belonged to a circuit of motáuvo enthusiasts nationwide that met up to show off their personalized bikes.

"Okay, Eli," Stylo called to me from near the back porch, "I want you to run as fast as you can and then launch into the air!"

"Easier said than done," I said, looking up at the gray roof of the house. I was supposed to leap over the house and land on the front drive-way. Ozzie had cast a gramora, so none of the neighbors would see.

"Stop being a mopey-faced fool," Stylo said. "Too much thinking, not enough doing!"

"I like to think!" I retorted. "You know, so I don't mess up."

"It's fine to mess up. What's the worst that will happen? You'll faceplant on our roof, but gravity will deposit you back here on the soft grass."

"Great," I said. "I don't want to break any arms or legs."

"Pfft," Stylo said. "You haven't grown as a Magical until you've broken a leg and an arm."

Dora chuckled, sipping a cup of steaming tea. Old school R&B played from the radio: the Stylistics, the Floaters, the Platters.

"Fine, okay." I calmed my mind, the warmth in my chest bloomed, and I tore off across the grass. In a split second, my feet lifted off the grass, and I was airborne.

"Wow!" I shouted down to Sylo and Dora and Ozzie as I neared the roof. My feet touched the shingles, and then I realized where I was. The roof shuddered under my feet. I swayed and planted my butt on the roof.

"Good job!" Stylo called to me. I stood, rubbing my rump.

"Ow, that hurt!"

"What doesn't kill you makes you stronger!"

"Quoting Kelly Clarkson?"

After lunch, we watched *the Birdcage* and *Bros.*

"Gay movies to make you realize it's normal, Eli."

"I've seen gay movies."

"Sad ones? Where gays die at the end because of course they want to see us die?"

"Um, yeah maybe."

"Yeah, well, these movies aren't about us dying. They are about us living our best lives!"

Later, we got out our skateboards and rode up Olive Avenue toward the Burbank Town Center.

"So, Eli," Stylo said as we neared the Olive Avenue Bridge, "bet you're a little tired, wanna float on your board to the mall?"

"Huh, how?"

"Easy," Stylo said. "You just squeeze your eyes. Not sure if your man taught you. It's the quick way to launch your magic. Your feet meld into the board and from there you can float along."

"No way?"

"Squeeze them eyes, bro."

A moment later, my board and I hovered a few feet over the concrete.

"This is one hundred percent!"

"Fun, huh?"

We skated over the bridge, then popped into the Burbank Town Museum, featuring an exhibit of drag costumes.

"Gays are everywhere," Stylo said. "And no matter what they try to do, we can't be erased. Trust me."

Afterward, our stomachs growled. We grabbed Chicken-on-a-Stick at the food court and skated around the plaza in front of Dirk Delomary's department store.

Out of nowhere, Dad showed up, looking wild eyed and acting a little erratic. He smelled of alcohol.

"Hey, kid," Dad said. "Can I talk to you?"

Stylo stopped doing an airwalk, watching us.

"You okay, Eli?"

Dad glanced over at Stylo.

"That your friend?"

"Yeah," I said backing away from Dad.

"He's a little short."

"He's a she, Dad."

"Oh, uh," Dad said. "Weird."

"Not weird."

"Hey, so your Mom came by. To talk. Do you know why?"

I shrugged. Because she hated you? Join the club.

"Yeah, talking all this mess in front of Florence about how I'm a bad influence. How I messed you up."

"Dad, I mean, let's leave it alone."

Stylo walked over. "You okay, Eli?"

"He's fine!" Dad snapped. "Look Eli," he said, turning his back to Stylo, "I had some investments go bad. You think you could help?"

"With what?"

"Surely you got some money?"

"I have twenty bucks."

"Maybe five g's?"

"No," I said. "I don't have that kind of money."

Dad rubbed his nose with his hand.

"Are you drunk, Dad?"

"No!" Dad said. "I'm on the wagon."

His breath betrayed his words.

"Look, I gotta go. We have dinner."

Dad ran his hands across his face. "Jesus, El. Help me out."

"Naw, Mr. Uh, I don't know what your name is—" Stylo interrupted. "We gotta go. And you know there are support groups. If you fall off the wagon."

"Mind your business!" Dad snarled.

"Okay, see you," I said hopping on my board. We took off up the hill to home.

"Yeah, so your Dad," Stylo said as we neared the gatehouse.

"That's him. Sperm donor is what Tory calls him."

"He didn't look okay."

"He has problems."

"I can tell."

"I'm just trying to move on with my life, avoid him."

"Yeah," Stylo said, "you know you're nothing like him."

"I have his DNA."

"Yeah, but you are a great person, Eli. My hero, remember?"

"Hah. I can't even fly over your house."

"Yeah, who can when they are a *Coaugeláidu*?"

"I'm impatient. I have something to prove."

"To whom? Your dad?"

I stopped in my tracks.

"Why do you say that?"

Stylo's eyes scanned my face. "Just wondering."

"Wonder a little less," I said. "He's a joke. A nothing. I'm not like him."

Sure, a voice whispered inside me.

No.

No.

No.

"Anyway, you can stay for dinner." I changed the subject. "Selena Gomez is coming over along with Sam Smith and Petra."

"Oh my fricking goodness, yes, please!"

"We wear tuxes to dinner when celebrities come. Do you have a tux?"

"Like in my back pocket?"

"Mom has extra tuxes if you need to borrow one."

"Shit," Stylo said. "Yes, let me clear it with Aunt Dora."

"Cool. We have a few hours. Want to hit the pool? Maybe a massage after?

"Oh, goodness," Stylo said, "I love being your friend."

Chapter Seven

Monochrome

AUSTIN AND I sat together in the hallway on the second floor outside of Mrs. Biederman's classroom having lunch. I bit into my bean-and-cheese burrito, chewing it thoughtfully. Austin ate two ham-and-cheese sandwiches simultaneously. He'd eat from the one in his left hand, chew, swallow, and then bite into the one in his right hand.

"So bloody good," Austin mumbled, mouth full of food. "You yanks really know how to make amazing food. Ham, cheese, God, so delish."

I laughed. "It's simply an old ham and cheddar cheese."

"Heaven if you ask me."

I sipped my soda and asked, "You ready for the decathlon, Kangy?"

Austin chewed thoughtfully. "I think so. As best as I can be. What about you, Eli?"

I shrugged. "I'm not sure, Kangy."

"You did well in the power quizzes yesterday, Eli. I think you are ready for gold."

"You think?"

"Of course, Eli," Austin said. "Though, remember it's not imperative you get gold. Silver and bronze are good too."

"I want gold."

"I know you do, but you'll still be a winner to me if you don't get gold."

He didn't understand. My goal was to prove we could be together. Winning gold meant I'd never make a mistake again. I'd never be senlàpso and screw everything up.

Austin polished off the last of his sandwiches, mumbling contentedly to himself. Then he asked, "When you win, what are you going to do?"

"Go to Disneyland!"

"Oh, God, please, can I come?"

"Duh, Kangy." I reached over and squeezed his knee. He smiled at me.

"Eli," Austin said softly, scooting closer to me. I longed for him to tuck me under his arm and rest his head on mine. To lace our fingers. And kiss. Again.

"How's session going?"

"What?"

"Session, mate."

"Pretty good, I guess."

"Yeah? That's great mate," Austin said. "I'm a big believer in therapy."

"You are?"

"Sure, mate," Austin said. "I saw a therapist for a while after I came out."

"You did?" Austin, perfect Austin. Seeing a therapist. Wow.

"Eli," Austin said, "you don't know because, well, I never told you. I didn't have it easy when I came out either."

"I thought you only told your parents recently."

"I did," Austin said, "but I told Barn first, and, well, I wasn't handling it well. I acted out at school. Got suspended. Wasn't focused when fighting alongside my parents. I almost got them killed."

"Shit, Kangy..."

"Yeah, well, Eli, know what you're going through is normal."

"I don't feel normal; thus, the problem."

"You'll be fine, mate." Austin leaned closer to me. I wanted to kiss him so badly.

"Therapy helps, mate." He leaned against the lockers. I needed him to kiss me.

"And talking. Talk to me about anything. Anything." He didn't kiss me. I sighed.

"Thanks, Kangy." I examined his face. "It's funny thinking of you needing help. You're, like, perfect, Kangy."

"Not completely perfect, but close enough, yeah?"

"Perfect." *Someday we'll kiss again. I know it.*

"Sod off," Austin said, scuffing his boots against the green-and-white tile floor, "You know I'm just full of bravado, mate."

"You are?"

"Tell anyone, and I will end you," Austin said sternly.

"Um, okay."

We sat in silence for a while. Mrs. Biederman appeared at the top of the stairs with a salad.

"Do we have a meeting I don't know about? I forget, you know. I'm sorry."

"No, Mrs. B," Austin said. "We just like to hang out here in this wing where it's quiet."

"Well, it is the English and history wing. Boring subjects." Mrs. Biederman tittered as she fumbled with her keys. "Have a good lunch, boys. See you after school. Go Aca Deca!" she said and disappeared inside her classroom.

Austin whistled a few bars from Morrissey's "The More You Ignore Me the Closer I Get."

"Kangy?"

"Yes, Eli?"

"Do you miss your gran?"

"Aye," Austin said. "She's a wonderful person. I can't wait for you to meet her. She's like me, but much, much smaller."

"I'm happy to be here though," Austin added. "California is amazing, mate," Austin said. "You have no idea how lucky you are to be here. Trust me, I've been all over the world. This is the best place to be."

"Bore-bank?"

"Brill-bank!"

I scoffed, "No way."

"Yes, way, Eli."

Austin paused to eat some chips. I sipped my cola. After a moment, Austin said, "Barn really helped me when I came out. He was my rock during that time. And then he left. It was hard, but I accepted it wasn't his choice. He had to come here with his dad who was taking charge of Wong AeroMagicals."

"And be a badass Coaugelo."

Austin stood to stretch. I watched his shirt ride up over his waistband, the fine line of hairs crawling from his jeans to his belly button.

"You do that on purpose."

"You like it, Eli."

"Kangy, Kangy."

Austin sank back to the floor, scooting close to me. "You think I'm perfect—which is pretty true—but I worked at it."

I didn't say anything, letting what he told me percolate into my brain.

"You're working at it too, Eli."

"I mean, not like you."

"Give yourself more credit," Austin said. "I see you trying. Everyday. Studying for Aca Deca, giving it your all in *Oklahoma!* rehearsals—such a small role, mate!"

"There are no small roles, Kangy, only small actors."

Austin chortled. "Well said," he added. "You're sorta short, Eli."

"I'm six feet now! Ask Dr. Hu. She can confirm."

"Still my little slimso."

"Not a dwarf!"

Austin leaned over to muss my hair affectionately. "I know you're going to get better because you are trying so hard. And you are going to win gold, In Aca Deca, the All Valley, and the 5K! I know you can do it."

"Talk about multitasking."

"It's in your DNA," Austin said. "Or you were so programmed to spend every waking minute doing something it comes second hand to you."

"Maybe I should slow down?"

"Yeah, maybe."

"I'm gonna feel so good when I win. You know. I mean I'm hungry."

Austin offered me his bag of chips. I chuckled. "No, Dáumo Máurso called me that. Means I'm determined. He's amazed I've picked up Xem Sen Ou so quickly."

"Brilliant!"

"Yeah, I feel good right now."

Austin reached in his backpack and pulled out a box of donuts. "Want one?"

"Kangy, how much food do you have in there?"

Pink spread across Austin's face. "Only these and my emergency submarine sandwich, another miracle food only found in America."

"Emergency submarine?"

"Yeah, mate," Austin said. "You never know when you're gonna get really soddin' hungry, yeah?"

I laughed.

"What are you going to do when everything is said and done, Eli?"

"What do you mean?"

"After you've accomplished all your goals. Besides taking Kangy to Disneyland? Will you feel different?"

I'll devote myself to you, Kangy, because then I'll know I can succeed in love.

I didn't respond to Austin. Instead, my mind raced back to session last weekend.

"You think love is dangerous, Belinda? Tell me more?" Arnulfo said.

"I know it's dangerous. One moment, you're ecstatic at having found the one, you're tripping the light fantastic. The world is filled with champagne and caviar. The sun never seems to set. And then in a heartbeat, it's over. It's done. And you wonder why you didn't see it coming. How could you? You wanted to believe in love, but when you did, it turns out that maybe love is too amorphous for the heart to hold."

Arnulfo leaned back. I stared at Mom. She had tears in her eyes. Stylo leaned over and handed her some tissues.

"Do you think that maybe sometimes love just ends?" Arnulfo asked the room.

"Gosh," Stylo admitted, "yes. You know, I was in love with Delma Ortega just yesterday, but today, well, she was on Insta and I realized she might be basic. And I'm not into that, you know?"

Everyone chuckled in spite of the tension in the room.

"Belinda, thank you for sharing," Arnulfo said. "Sounds like you loved hard, and that is good. You got Elijah from that love. And from what I can see he is a brilliant son. And you know, sometimes relationships end. And it's hard, but when the dust settles, you can look around and realize good comes from it ending."

Mom wiped the tears from her eyes. "Yes, maybe you're right." She was looking at me. Smiling at me.

"And I can tell you have a heavy burden from love, but maybe it's okay to move on, Belinda."

Mom nodded, staring at the pink and gray and blue carpet underfoot.

"And I'd like to suggest that coming out and dealing with being young and queer is like the experience Belinda shares. It's jubilant and amazing on one hand, you finally feel like yourself. At the same time, it's very hard. And just like love is a process, so is coming out. It can be traumatic, but you move on. You look around at what came from your journey. You're all here. That's a testament to you all. Being here means you are growing."

The warning bell rang at the end of the hall, stirring me from last week's session.

"Lunch is over," Austin complained.

"Yeah," I said, standing up, brushing crumbs from my jeans. "You asked what I'm going to do when this is all over? Well, I'm going to do nothing."

"Good plan! Kangy loves to do nada!" He considered. "After Disneyland, yeah?"

*

LATE THAT NIGHT, I lay in bed staring at the ceiling, wide awake, heart pounding, mind racing. My body hurt all over. Not possible, as Mom said, no one was tired at sixteen. I was an anomaly.

Rain fell outside. Sirens sounded in the distance. Was there a fire somewhere? A house consumed by flames, the entire world of one family gone. Or monsters lurked in the night, preying on Ordinaries. Of course. The battle never ended. I was exhausted thinking about the never-ending struggle to fight the coven. The darkness, like the vast expanse of space, a void stretching to infinity. My heart raced imagining how insignificant life on Earth was in the universe.

"Get some rest, Elijah," the cherubs urged. "We can play the harp for you. To help you sleep."

"That would be nice," I said, closing my eyes. A moment later, the plaster cherubs began strumming their little plaster harps. I relaxed.

My eyes opened slowly. I was standing in the bumblebee garden, only everything was monochromatic. The grass and flowers were black, the bees were white, the sky was white dotted with black clouds.

I looked down, white loafers, white slacks, white vest and jacket.

A woman walked toward me dressed completely in black with a veil trailing behind her and holding black roses in her hands.

"What's going on?" I called out.

"It's my wedding day, Elijah," a familiar voice said. The veil dissolved, revealing Devlina underneath, her face pale white like a Kabuki actor, mouth painted black.

"You're getting married?"

"To the most wonderful man...monster...demon...devil..."

"What's his name?" Why couldn't I remember his name?

"I know him as *Coa Tampocens*."

"The end?"

"When the Big Bang happened, at first there was light, and then from the light came darkness. The darkness was pure. And good. How do you appreciate light with no dark?"

Devlina and I walked on the black grass past the black flower beds headed to the meadow in the distance. A black pergola stood at the foot of the lake. A black orb hovered in the center.

"And *Coa Commentia* and *Coa Tampocens* divided. And the Áuqala was born and Zid'dra right after. Both had their roles. Creation, destruction. The endless cycle. What is life without death? Creation without destruction?"

"Devlina, have you been smoking the magic grass?"

Devlina said nothing. She marched toward the black orb floating over the black grass set against the white sky.

"Devlina, I'm confused. You are married to Zid'dra, but you've been fighting." I reached for her. She pushed me away. "Are you getting hitched, again?"

"Yes," she said. "And this time, I will submit to him."

"What does that mean?"

"Why fight when I should know my place."

"Devlina, maybe you have a choice."

Devlina advanced. Gray smoke lifted from the black grass obscuring the white sky. The black orb pulsed with energy.

"Elijah, Elijah..." a voice said in my mind. "You know what you can do too."

"No, what?"

"Join us, join us," the voice said. The orb grew larger and larger, rising above the smoke and blotting out the light. Two red dots appeared in the center of the orb.

I stumbled and fell to my knees. I couldn't breathe.

"You will follow her," the raspy voice whispered inside my head. "Submit to me."

"No," I said. "I am going to push myself and show the world who I really am."

The orb pulsed. The red dots bored into my head.

"Didn't you say I needed to do that?"

"I have reconsidered," the voice said. "*Havunt regardare tu.* I've been watching you. You're going to fail. It's in your genes. Just give up now."

"No," I said. "Screw you!"

The orb grew bigger. Black flames leaped and danced around me.

"*Aulare rente ada domincens adva!*"

"I'll talk to you how I please!"

"Petulant child!"

I leaped over the flames, running to Devlina's side. She stood before the orb holding a knife in her left hand.

"Devlina!" I called out after a moment. "You don't have to do this. Maybe love ends, but you don't have to."

"Shut up, you stupid boy!" a hoarse voice shouted in my head. "You will never succeed; I will stop you!"

I stood up and rushed for Devlina, pulling her back from the orb.

"Devlina, wake up! Wake up!"

"Elijah Delomary, it never rains in Southern California," she said cryptically.

And the black sky opened up, drenching me in heavy rain made of hot tar, not water. My skin burned as the tar began to smother my face.

I woke up clawing the air for breath.

"Are you okay, Elijah?" The cherubs stopped strumming. "You had a nightmare!"

"Yeah," I said. "Dreaming of Zid'dra. Random."

"You should go to sleep."

"My body hurts."

"When do you compete, Elijah?"

"Soon."

"You can rest afterwards."

I sank back into the bed. "Yes, that will be nice. Resting. Being with Kangy. Everything will be better then. We'll be solid, you know."

The cherubs resumed strumming their harps as I fell into a fitful sleep as the rain continued to fall from the sky.

Chapter Eight

Mom succumbs to love

THE NEXT MORNING Mom was reading the news on her tablet when I came down to the breakfast room.

"Where's your twin?"

"Barn's with Austin doing training for the League."

"Ah," Mom said. She stirred her coffee. "You look really tired, Elijah."

"Naw, I'm good."

Mom searched my face.

Was she reading my mind? *I am super energized.*

"I guess you are," Mom said, confirming my suspicion.

"I won't be home for dinner."

"No surprise, Mom," I said, buttering some toast. "Where to? Tokyo? São Paulo for some big dinner?"

"You're going to think I'm crazy."

"I already think that."

"Little shit," Mom said. "No, actually, Sean and I are going to dinner."

"Oh." Was that supposed to be ground-breaking news to me?

"Yes, Elijah, it's a big deal."

"Stop reading my mind!"

"Look. I thought about what Arnulfo said. And you know I like Sean a lot, and, well, we were spending time together last night."

"Ew, TMI, Mom."

"Shut it," Mom said. "We were watching *The Whale* in the theatre room, perv."

"So, what happened? He propose? You said no, right?"

"We decided to date."

I choked on my toast. "*Houtáillar*? To date? Not the fruit from palm trees, right?"

"Yes, houtáillar! Date, be exclusive."

"Mom, I'm really confused."

Mom reached over for a butter croissant, spreading jam on it. "He's a good guy, Elijah, and you know what? Arnulfo set me straight. I mean, I can keep spinning or I can stop and get off the roller coaster and just see what happens."

My stomach soured.

"Are you okay, Elijah?"

"I just—I mean, Mom, do you know what you're doing?"

Mom frowned. "Yes, Elijah as a matter of fact I do. And, well, you know, I thought you would be happy."

I wiped my hands on my jeans. "I am, Mom." I relented. "I am. I mean, you guys have been together for a while."

"Yeah, and you know I enjoy his company. And he mine. And frankly I'm ready to move on. I'm tired of being alone."

The clock on the mantel chimed the quarter hour. I glanced at the clock: 7:15 AM.

"I think that's great, Mom."

"You know I talked to your dad."

I sat down again. "Yeah?" Did I tell her about seeing him?

"Yes, I went to his apartment in Glendale. Florence was there. I said my piece. I think he understood. To leave you alone."

"That's great," I lied. I didn't want to diminish Mom's accomplishment. "I doubt I'll see him."

He had acted so strange last week. Asking for money. From me, the poorest rich boy in all of America.

"Have a good day at school, darling," Mom said, returning to her tablet.

"Yeah, have fun on your date tonight. There are condoms in the storage closet across from Barn's room."

Mom turned red. "I don't want to know why."

"Aunt Christine said she has enough children. And George also laid down the law with Barn. He doesn't want to be a grandfather while he's in his late thirties."

"Fine," Mom said. "Anyway, I'm not that easy. No matter what you think."

"I think you are like Queen Elizabeth I, married to your job."

Mom rolled her eyes. "That was old me. New me is different."

"Yeah, she's dating. For real."

"Yup," Mom said. "Don't wait up."

"Whatever, Mom."

*

I RAN AS fast as I could, arms and legs pumping, the wind at my back. Julio watched me from a bend in the track with his stopwatch and nodded in encouragement.

"Puedes hacerlo!"

A smile stretched across my face. I was close to beating my all-time best time. I was going to win the Burbank 5K if I kept this up. And why wouldn't I? The pieces were falling into place. Amanda was certain I'd win the All Valley swim competition. We had done several rounds of super quizzes in Aca Deca, and I got high scores in my subjects. And, best of all, things were good with Austin. We were in a groove. Having fun together at the Dáu Xhà, after school studying at my place or in his room, listening to music on vinyl, and going to the movies together. And no matter what Zid'dra said, nothing was going to keep Elijah Delomary from succeeding.

A drop of rain splatted on the red track, followed by another and another. I glanced at the sky. Clouds had smothered the Valley in the last ten minutes. Shit, I hated running in the rain. I pushed myself. Might as well run faster, maybe I could beat the rain.

Julio did a little dance as I crossed the finish line. He glanced at his stopwatch. Then, we both ducked out of the rain.

"*Buen trabajo, wey*," he said. "*Tan estupendo*! I'm so proud of you!"

He pulled me into a quick hug. "I hated when you gave up weight-lifting, but you are good as a runner."

"Thanks, Julio."

"You're gonna blow everyone else away, mijo."

"Hah, yeah, they won't know what hit them."

Julio stood back, hands on his hips, smiling at me. "You've come a long way, mijo. From the scrawny kid who couldn't run a few feet to this." He glowed with pride. At me. I basked in his joy for a moment. I was happy.

I went into the locker room, sitting down on a bench and pulling my shirt off. I wiped the sweat off my face with a towel, then tossed it into a receptacle for dirty laundry. Things were looking up for Ol' Elijah Delomary!

I noticed water running in the showers nearby. That was odd. No one was using the track except for me and Julio today. I preferred to shower at home, so I went to turn off the water.

All the stalls were empty in the shower room. A window stood open nearby, rain pouring inside and down the wheat-colored tile wall.

Something was off with the water... What were those? Red dots? Polka dots in water?

The water rushed to the drain in the center, the red dots spinning around and around, staring at me. I shuddered involuntarily, exited the shower room, grabbed my gym bag off the bench, and ran back to the mansion.

*

A FEW NIGHTS later, as Sean circled to clear the large earthenware plates from the farm table, which stood in the center of his dining room, he said, "I hope you liked the chicken. It was my Mama's recipe from growing up in Texas."

"I loved it," Mom said, lifting her wine glass in salute to him. He smiled.

"I don't have professional chefs here at my little house in Beverly Hills."

Sean lived in a white stucco Spanish Colonial-style mansion set among ancient oak trees a few blocks south of the Beverly Hilton. Some little house. Sheesh.

"At least you can cook," Mom said. "I can't remember the last time I cooked."

"You make a mean piece of toast, Mom," I replied to boost her ego. She had been a nervous wreck the whole afternoon before we headed to dinner. Worried about me. How I'd act being around Sean. Worry, worry, worry. The Delomary neuroses.

"This is our first official date as a family," Mom had said as we both hopped in the back of the tank-like black SUV for the ride over the 405 to the West Side. Mom was too nervous to drive, so she let Sunny give us a lift.

Don't mess it up, I told myself. For Mom. She had cried about the turmoil of her own love. The love that had birthed our little family and that had shriveled up and destroyed us in the process. Mom, Tory and me. Maybe the divorce ruined Dad too? Could it...?

Be better today, I had told myself after showering. I stared at myself in the mirror. *You can do this Elijah. For Mom.*

One of the lightbulbs in the chandelier overhead flickered. Darkness leapt from the corners near the shower and toilet. I caught my breath. The rasping, wheezy breathing. Ignore it, Elijah. For Mom...

Three golden retrievers tumbled out the front door of the mansion when we pulled into the driveway, followed by Sean, a smile stretched across his face. He was dressed casually in chinos and a light-blue button-up shirt and flip-flops. What a change. I had only seen him wearing a suit. I turned to Mom, her hair not shellacked under a helmet of hairspray or bound up in a tight ponytail, but rather falling softly around her shoulders. She wore a light blue dress, the flowy kind she used to wear in our little olive green ranch house in Reseda all those years ago. What was going on with Mom and Sean?

Sunny opened the door for me. I stepped out onto the gravel driveway and was knocked over onto the front lawn by the dogs.

"Malcolm, Harriet, Rosa come back here... Oh, I am sorry, Elijah. They are quite affectionate!"

I sprawled out on the grass in front of the rambling mansion, giggling uncontrollably while three rough tongues licked my face.

"I think the dogs like him, huh, Lin?"

Lin? Who was Lin?

Sean whistled. The tongues disappeared off my face. I sat up and leaned on my hands.

"Who's Lin?"

Mom blushed. Sean tossed a neon-green tennis ball to a far corner of the front yard, and the dogs hurtled themselves after it, bouncing off each other in the process.

"A pet name," Sean said. "I think you have one for Austin?"

Mom watched me intently.

This could go two ways. This night depends on you, Elijah.

A helicopter soared overhead. Sunny hollered to text him when we were ready, followed by tires crunching on the white gravel driveway.

Malcom tackled me, knocking me onto the grass, dropping a ball on my chest. I giggled again. Malcom was the mirror image of Boxey. My heart thumped. Boxey would tell me to breathe and let everything go...be in the moment.

"Yeah," I said taking the ball and rubbing Malcom's furry head, "Kangy, and he calls me Eli."

Mom relaxed.

"That's adorable," Sean said. "Why don't we go in and get settled? There's a fire going in the living room. And Chardonnay for the lady."

Mom curtsied for some ridiculous reason. I almost convinced myself I saw a crown of flowers in her hair.

"I have Shirley Temples for you, Elijah."

"Shit," I stammered. "I love Shirley Temples!"

"God, watch your language!"

"Sorry, Mom."

Sean's house was the opposite of our house; casual, contemporary, with the sense that the rooms opened all the way to the night sky and the Milky Way beyond. We sat around the fire, Mom and Sean stiff like boards while the dogs were on the floor chewing on dog toys.

I excused myself so they could catch their breath. I wandered upstairs to the guest bathroom where I splashed water on my face and breathed in and out ten times to calm my own jitters. Malcom pushed his way into the room.

"Hi, Malcom!" I said, squatting on the floor gently rubbing his head.

"Sean likes you!" Malcom said. I squealed and fell back.

"You talk?"

"I'm his familiar!"

"Of course, you are," I said. "He's an Encantreino?"

"Of course!" Malcolm said. "They really like each other."

"Yeah?"

"Of course."

"Do you always say 'of course,' Malcom?"

"Of course!"

I burst out laughing.

"You okay up there, Elijah?" Mom called from the bottom of the stairs.

"Yeah, sorry, yes."

"Dinner in twenty."

"Sure, Mom."

"Come with me, Elijah," Malcolm said. "I want to show you my favorite spot in the house."

I walked beside Malcolm as he padded down the hallway to a door at the end. Malcom growled softly and the door swung open, revealing stairs.. He padded into a room with arched windows on all sides.

I stepped onto the hardwood floor, my eyes taking in the panoramic view of Beverly Hills, West Hollywood, and Hollywood, the Santa Monica Mountains, and the vast stretch of South LA.

"Wow, this view is incredible!"

"I love it," Malcom said, sitting on his haunches.

"The sun is setting so you can see the lights of the Pacific Design Center! I love how they change colors."

My eyes followed the grid interrupted by red-tiled roofs, palm trees, high-rises, and jacaranda trees until my gaze fell on the semi-pyramidal glass building in the distance.

The LGBT center was a few blocks west. My mind drifted back to session. To Arnulfo. He was becoming my Gray Wizard with his staff lighting the darkness in my mind.

"This world is filled with fear and anger and darkness. And each one of you are points of light in that world. A beacon to the others and, when each of you shine, eventually the darkness gives way to the brilliance. They tell you to be afraid, but that's because they are afraid. Not all monsters come from the Gloom. Sometimes they masquerade as everyday folks."

"Yeah, right on, Arnulfo!" Stylo said. "I heard that."

"Embrace the light; lean into the good things in your life."

Austin, Barn, my friends. Mom, shit was I admitting that? I laughed. Malcolm barked. I leaned down to pet his warm, furry head.

"Come join me!"

"Sure," I said, then sat on the floor cross-legged next to him. We sat side by side as the sun faded and the night sky rose behind the Santa Monica Mountains and the Pacific Design Center glowed like a jewel in the center of WeHo.

*

"ANY IDEA WHAT that black gooey thing is floating above my pool?" Sean asked, hand raised, the muscles in his arms tensing as the blob pulsed over the blue waters. He used magic to keep the blob from moving.

"Ugh," Mom said, on her third glass of wine—she was over her limit. "Is it one of those things I've heard about made of fat and wet wipes in the sewer?"

The blob growled.

"Oh," Mom said. "I guess not."

"Elijah?"

"Well, you know—" I squatted next to Malcolm rubbing his fur. "—Mom, I think Zid'dra might be haunting me."

"What?" Mom shouted and tossed her wine glass at the blob. The glass fell onto the edge of the grass, spilling wine onto the ground.

"Yeah, I've felt his presence at home at night when I'm trying to sleep."

"Fuck," Sean muttered. "This isn't good."

"My ass it isn't!"

"Language," I whispered, too afraid to speak any louder. What was going to happen? Was this it for me, Mom, and Sean? Dinner had been a new experience. Eye opening. When was the last time Mom and I had been so relaxed at dinner? Sean was like a facilitator when our conversation seemed ready to break down, when all I wanted to do was get up and leave. Sean cracked a joke or he would simply sit back and listen to us like he was interested in what we both had to say. And for some reason, we wanted to keep talking.

"I can hold it at bay for a while, Lin, but, I mean, it's very powerful."

Mom must have been drunk because she roared like a lion and raised her arm, sending a powerful blast of pure white light out of her hand and around the blob.

"Get the hell outta here!" she screamed, snapping her wrist and sending the blob hurtling away from the pool, the palm trees lining the backyard, and toward the upper reaches of the atmosphere.

"Oh, wow, Lin!" Sean gaped, then a smile crept across his face. "I didn't know you were so fearless."

"That blob of shit was not about to ruin a beautiful night with my men."

I looked over at Sean, who scrutinized Mom. He looked speechless.

"That was badass, Mom."

Mom bowed for some odd reason. She was definitely drunk.

We went inside. Sean brought out dessert, chocolate cake with vanilla frosting, my favorite. This guy really knew how to score points with me. Sean told us about his sons, Dion and Dre. Both were overseas studying. Dion at Oxford and Dre at the Sorbonne. He showed us pictures of two tall, thin young men with their father's eyes and smile.

"I love this picture." Mom was draped on Sean. She was getting emotional. When was the last time she was this way? Ten years? More?

"Yeah, they'll love you, Lin."

"You think?"

"Sure, you snort when you laugh."

"Oh, God, Sean!"

They were laughing and whispering to each other. Mom snorted. She shot me a look. I grinned.

"I've had too much to drink."

"Two glasses is her maximum, Sean," I explained.

"She polished off a bottle!" Sean said, pointing to an empty bottle lying on its side on the dining table.

"Watch it. She may propose to you when she's in this state. Emotional."

"I'd love that."

Mom searched Sean's eyes. Awkwardness fell over the room. Okay, me, really. I left the love birds in the dining room and went to the den.

I retreated to the sofa and messed around with Malcolm, Rosa, and Harriet. *Love, Simon* played on the TV. I settled into watch the movie and cavort with the dogs. Content, a weird feeling for yours truly.

After a while, Sean and Mom pushed back their chairs and went into the kitchen to wash the dishes. The coffee machine began sputtering; the smell of freshly brewed coffee filled the room. A half hour later, Mom came out holding a coffee cup in her hands.

"You should have told me about this haunting, Elijah."

Mom was back. The booze had worn off. I sighed. "I didn't think much of it."

"Elijah!"

"Okay, fine. I was wrong."

Mom sank into one of the wheat-colored linen sofas across from me, "I worry, honey."

"I know. I worry too."

"This is serious, has he been in the house?"

I nodded.

"Not good." Mom began to look panicky.

Sean appeared in the doorway with a glass of water. He handed it to Mom, brushed her hand with his, and left.

"Christine and I will place more runes around the house. I'll research spells to keep you safe."

"Thanks, Mom."

"We're supposed to be talking to each other, right?"

"I think so."

"Arnulfo has said we need to be honest with each other."

"I'm trying," I said. "I'm not used to this."

"What?"

"Us being...normal?"

"Yeah," Mom said. "Gosh."

I heard Sean moving around the kitchen, shutting a door, and then the sound of the dishwasher humming.

After a moment, Mom stood up and went to fetch her purse, the very expensive voluminous imported leather one she brought along to meetings with heads of state, hostile shareholders, or whenever she was nervous.

"I have something for you," she said, rummaging inside the purse. She removed a flashlight, deck of cards, three protein bars, a half-gallon bottle of mineral water, chewing gum, and a flamethrower.

"Why on earth do you have all that in your purse?" Sean said, coming over to join her when she returned to the den. "A flamethrower, Lin?"

"It sprays holy water," Mom said. "You know, not all monsters are destroyed with magic. Sometimes you need a little help from the Lord above."

Sean doubled over, laughing. Mom was surprised.

"Lin, you are my favorite human ever."

Mom's face went white. Startled. Her shell broke. And she smiled broadly.

"Oh, Sean," she said, tapping the end of his nose with her manicured nail. She went back to digging in her purse for a moment, then pulled out a long, silver chain with a silver amulet on the end.

God, these two were made for each other. Mom was acting like someone else. I mean she was acting the fool around Sean. Not her usual self. The stiff one, the robot. Miss Perfect.

"Here it is!" Mom said. "I got this last week in San Miguel de Allende," Mom walked across the room to show me a small chain with a silver amulet featuring *La Virgen de Guadalupe*. "It was blessed by a bishop. I meant to give it to you. For good luck in all your endeavors coming up."

"Wow," I said like a fool. "I mean, this is beautiful."

"And it has runes on it..."

"Like, so I win gold?"

"Silly," Mom quipped. "No, to keep you safe and happy."

"Do you know me?" I caught myself. I had been happy tonight. I had been...wait for it...content! Wow.

"Maybe tonight is the first night of the rest of your life, Eli," Sean said. My heart stopped. The fire cracked and popped in the fireplace.

"Come on, let's put it on you." Mom led me to a mirror hanging near the fireplace. She set it around my neck, the silver caught the glow of the fire and sparkled.

"It's magical."

"You like it?"

"I love it, Mom."

"Good, darling."

For some reason, I turned Mom around and hugged her tightly, tears in my eyes.

"A lotta firsts tonight," Sean remarked. "Malcom, come on, boy. I gotta take out the trash. Be on the lookout for that evil blob; it might have come back."

Malcolm barked and jumped up to join Sean as he disappeared into the kitchen.

Mom and I stood by the mirror examining the amulet.

"Tonight was great, Mom."

"Yay," Mom cheered. "I was nervous."

"I know."

"You were sweet."

"Sure."

"I mean it."

"Yeah, well you singlehandedly shot Zid'dra out into space!"

"Shit, I bet he's mad."

"Too bad, so sad."

We laughed really hard.

Chapter Nine

Vampires Are Awful

"THE PROBLEM WITH how love is depicted in books and movies is the end game is falling in love. Maybe love is more complex than they tell us. Maybe we need more books and movies that show what love is really like."

Mom sipped water out of a cut crystal glass in the back of the black, tanklike SUV driving us home over the 405 back to the Valley.

"You might be on to something, darling."

"Maybe I'll write a book someday. All about monsters and love."

"Love is something that unites us," Mom said. "Whether you're gay or straight. Black or brown or white or Asian or rich or poor. Democrat or Republican. Monster or magical."

"Do monsters love?"

Mom shrugged. "I'm not sure."

"Dilemma" by Addal played on the stereo. We fell silent for a while listening to the beats and harmony of the song. I spoke up, "Tonight felt good, Mom."

"Yes, darling?"

"Yeah." I tapped my fingers against the leather on the side of the seat. "We should spend more time with Sean."

"We can do that."

"I love his dogs," I said. "Malcolm is his familiar; he reminded me of Boxey."

"I'm glad, honey."

"Maybe Austin can come next time?"

"Sean would be delighted."

"Cool."

"Slay."

"Mom, not the right use of the word."

*

MÁURSO HELD OPEN the door to the lighted cabinet containing what, to an Ordinary, were simple lighters made of brass, silver, gold, or marble.

"Go ahead, Laddie. You've earned it."

I walked closer to the cabinet, examining the contents spread out before me. This was really happening to me.

"Get a good one, mate," Barn said. "Brass counteracts evil."

I turned to face Austin. He smiled reassuringly. "It's your time, love."

"Almost didn't happen," I lamented. "Those bastards from XAQ2."

A few days ago, several agents with the Macistráuto appeared out of nowhere at the God of War Dáu Xhà asking why I was being trained in Xem Sen Ou. They waved around some paper from the Màdlinn. My stomach dropped. Fear gripped me. Máurso wasn't scared at all. In fact, he simply snatched the paper out of their hands and tore a hole in the air and disappeared into it altogether. A few minutes later, he came back with the paper and a grin on his face.

"This document has been updated," he said to the lead agent, a short man with curly black hair. "Feel free to read." The man read it, grimaced, and looked at the woman beside him.

"Me, dammit," Máurso cried. "Read the bloody letter out loud."

The man nodded and read the letter, his hand trembling.

"Per the Còngréhassa sie Estantus, after consultation with Máurso Êímpagońena, Antécallanto, adjudicator and intervenor of the law, it is decided that Elijah Coronado Delomary shall be granted status of Coaugelo within the Magicals Alliance."

The agents grumbled. Máurso growled. The earth trembled, and the sky darkened.

"What just happened?" I leaned over to whisper to Austin.

"Immortals rank just below the Áuqala and the Têrso Empras, who have a nonintervention policy in the daily affairs of the Alliance. The Immortals, on the other hand, act as arbiters of justice as necessary. All branches of the Magicals Alliance Services fall under their purview. In short, Máurso intervened on your behalf."

"Sweet."

"Aye."

Taking the document from Máurso, the short man muttered, "All right. But if anything goes wrong, then this is on you, Máurso."

"You will call me, Dáumo Máurso or Your Eminence, knave."

The man gulped. "Yes, of course. Sorry."

"Be gone," Máurso roared, "before I pound you into the floor with my fists, you numpties!"

My mind returned to the maze of rooms under the Dáu Xhà, in the *Cambra sie Ammoímentas*, where Máurso stored all his weapons along with a dozen PlasmX's for Coaugelus to receive after completing the first part of their training.

"You accomplished becoming skilled as a Coaugelo faster than most, lad," Máurso said. "Then again, you are a Delomary. And a skilled Magical. The Bane of the Gloom. It was meant to be." He put his hand on my shoulder. "I am proud of you, lad. Now go, walk to the far side of the room and hold out your arm, open your hand, and feel the energy within. You will connect with your PlasmX."

"Think brass, mate!"

"Barny!"

"Shut it, Lostin!"

I crossed the room, faced the cabinet, and held out my arm. I closed my eyes and focused on the energy in my chest. I opened my palm and, in an instant, a PlasmX nestled there. My fingers closed around the staff made of plasma.

I opened my eyes, looking down at the glowing pink and purple weapon pulsing against my palm and fingers.

"Wow."

"She's a beaut, eh, laddie?"

"She is!"

"You're one of us now," Máurso chanted. "Housà!" he roared. Barn and Austin threw their heads back and joined in. I opened my mouth timidly, then began shouting as well. Housà was the Coaugelu battle cry.

*

WE WENT TO Tommy's on San Fernando Boulevard to celebrate. Austin ordered two chili-cheeseburgers and fries; Barn got a veggie burger. Austin took him to task for not ordering a regular burger.

"Katie says I should become vegetarian," he said glumly.

"Sod off, mate," Austin said. "You need iron to fight monsters!"

"You try telling her that." Barn rolled his eyes.

"Ah, look what love has done to my wee Barny!"

"Tosser."

My chili-cheeseburger was in front of me. I was busy playing with the square silver box containing my PlasmX. The front and sides engraved with dragons breathing fire and the words "Nunma in Viacadeimo" running along the top and bottom.

"Did Máurso do this?" I asked Austin before he bit into one of his two burgers.

"No," Austin said. "That's you. The PlasmX connects with your psyche and chooses the decorations."

Austin tossed his to me onto the stone table. I held it in my thumb and forefinger. Gold with an image of a burger and fries on the front and a roaring Lion on the back and words written in Chinese characters.

"You have food and a lion," I said. "Fitting."

"Brilliant, yeah?"

"What do these characters mean?"

"That he loves food, of course," Barn said, still smarting over the veggie burger.

"What does yours look like, Barn?"

"No," Barn said. "That's private."

"Oh, come on. Really?"

"Yes!"

"I shan't." Barn stuck his tongue out at me.

Austin leaned over to tell me. "His has an image of a stuffed lion on one side cuz Barn is all cuddly like a toy. And on the other side is a mouse and a giant, symbolizing that wee folk like him can be powerful too!"

"Arsehole," Barn complained.

"I think it's sweet and very fitting!" I said.

"I can still grow you know," Barn retorted. "Up to twenty-five, yeah?"

"Don't count on it!" Austin said, laughing.

"What do the words say on your PlasmX?"

"House music forever!" Barn said. "So sod off, you two, with your grunge garbage!"

Barn got up and tossed half his burger in the trash and went to the window asking for a double chili-cheese burger.

While he waited, he typed on his phone. Austin chewed on his burgers and zoned out. The hair on my arms began to rise, and I felt a sickness in my stomach. I looked at Austin who was already on his feet.

"Monsters!"

Barn grabbed his burger from the window, wolfed half of it down, set the rest on the table, and ran after Austin and me heading to the parking lot. From the night sky, several black figures dropped onto the cracked asphalt. They were very good-looking, with jet-black hair, red eyes, and fangs bared.

Àzmadus.

"We have a message for you, Elijah." A female Àzmada stepped forward. "You were stripped of your power and now you think you can become a Coaugelo? We won't allow it. The Gloom is in disarray because of you and your allegiances. We want you dead and in the ground, worm food."

Austin summoned his PlasmX, followed by Barn

"This isn't my first time at the rodeo," I said, pulling out my PlasmX. The Àzmadus hissed at us.

"We're prepared to destroy you, Magicals," the head Àzmada said to Austin and Barn. "If you are smart, you'll crawl back to your cribs and suckle milk from a bottle and let us destroy the once-powerful Bane of the Gloom!"

"I'm still the Bane of the Gloom!" I shouted, tossing my PlasmX into the air. It spun around the Àzmadus drawing energy off them. They faltered.

"Great," she said. "Well, you don't have an Encantreinu as backup, so we shall destroy you!"

I whispered to Austin, "Do we need an Encantreinu to battle?"

"I mean it's the preferred method, but like a lot of rules in life, not a necessity," he explained. "Remember, I fought monsters with just my parents!"

"Are you two sharing secrets?" the head Àzmada asked.

"Yeah, how we are going to destroy you, slag!"

The Àzmada lunged for Austin who leapt into the air. She followed suit, grabbing his leg and pulling him back to the ground. Barn launched himself at the other Àzmadus. In a split second, the battle was on. Barn headbutted an Àzmado while stabbing his PlasmX into another. Austin was in hand-to-hand combat with the head Àzmada. I stood on the periphery, unsure what to do.

"Good night!" a voice called before something hard came down on my head.

I woke a moment later, my head throbbing, lying on the cracked asphalt staring down a horrible creature with green skin, horns, red eyes, and a mouth filled with razor sharp teeth. Àzmadus in their natural state. "I am going to enjoy sucking the life force from you, Elijah Delomary!" I searched frantically for my PlasmX. It was gone.

My mind whirred back to training with Máurso. The *Cruxamago* or "one-two punch to the chest." I pulled my hands back, then hit the monster in the chest with my fists. He yelped and flew off me. I struggled to stand when he launched at me again. His eyes turned to spinning pinwheels. He was using an *Encancto* to enchant me. *Shit, what do I do?*

Before I could figure out what to do, my body was paralyzed and my mouth forced open. The monster leaned closer to me, its fangs barred and forked tongue unfolding from its mouth. Light began to radiate from my mouth and curl toward the Àzmado

My mind was spinning images. Me at school in the first grade on the jungle gym, falling on my back, the wind knocked out of me. At Knott's Berry Farm with Grandma Smith, riding the Snoopy roller coaster. At the Temple of Magic in Hollywood, when I turned thirteen, at my initiation. I was handed the *Sepolcro Dorallen*, the holy sword of the Alliance. I hesitated. It was all powerful. If I wasn't worthy, the sword might reject me, and I would be exiled from the Alliance. I reached for it. Could I do this? I had to; it was my *desteino*. I grasped it, and a charge of electricity shot up my hand and through my nervous system.

Suddenly, black goo poured out of the monster's mouth. My body rippled. I was holding a sword in my hands, pushing it deep in the Àzmado. I had summoned a sword to kill the monster.

"Oh, shit, I'm dead!" he called before dissolving into embers that fell around me. The sword flashed and disappeared into the night sky. I sat up, watching Austin battling the Àzmadus ten feet above the ground using his fists and legs.

Barn had an Àzmada in a headlock. "I saw that. You pulled a *Lembrilla*—a "magical weapon" from your memories, mate!"

I cheered and leapt up into the air flinging myself at the Àzmadus, using my fists and head to battle them. Austin retreated and flew up and then down thrusting his PlasmX into the head Àzmada. She popped like a burning log, smoke curling into the air. Barn pulled another Àzmada toward Austin who finished her off as well. More pops and embers floated to the ground.

Eventually, we sat on the hood of Austin's car, surrounded by the remains of the coven of Àzmadus sent to off me—what else was new. Austin's cheek bled. Barn had a black eye. My hands were raw and bleeding.

"Shit," I said, "we look bad."

"Yeah," Austin said. "Did you forget to tell me that someone is mad at you?"

"Oh, yeah. I think Zid'dra is hunting me down."

"Oh, okay," Austin said, touching his cheek with his finger gingerly. A light flashed at his fingertip, and the cut healed. "Probably should've mentioned sooner."

"Would've appreciated knowing that too," Barn said, tracing his right index finger along his left eye, the black disappearing.

"Mom flung him into space on Thursday," I said. "I figured he was gone."

"Your mum did...? Oh, well, I'm not surprised."

"Maybe he has a bounty out on you!"

Austin gaped at Barn. He looked at me. For some reason, I grinned.

"Cool."

"No one can defeat us!"

"HOUSÀ!"

"Where's my PlasmX?"

"Just lift your hand up, and it'll come to you."

A moment later, I spotted a purple and pink staff whirling through the air toward me. I reached out and caught the PlasmX in my right hand.

The short-order cook from Tommy's appeared at the back door, holding a bag of trash. "You guys okay?"

"Yeah, just enjoying the night air." Austin hollered.

"Sure, okay." He dropped the bag in a trash receptacle, hurried inside, and closed the door firmly behind him.

"Barn, you better wipe his mind."

"Yeah, right." Barn stood up, brushed embers of his sweats and out of his hair then hiked over to the restaurant.

My hand began to throb.

"Shit, this hurts."

"Heal it, mate," Austin said. "Just trace the cuts with your fingers. Coaugelos have magic to heal fast."

"I never knew this."

"There's a lot you don't know, mate." Austin smiled. "Now that you're in the inner sanctum you'll learn."

Adrenaline rushed through my body. "God that was amazing. Painful. I almost died. Shit, is it always like that?"

"Yes!"

"It's so different than using magic to fight monsters."

"Aye," Austin said. "It's more raw. Mano-a-mano."

"Right."

"HOUSÀ!" I suddenly shouted and leapt off the ground into the night air. *Aveàtrano*, as Coaguelus called it, was like skateboarding using the air as your board. You first leaped a few feet into the air, then you rode the air current to any object to gain momentum, a trash can, a bush, a wall. Once on top of that you kept lifting yourself higher. A rooftop or the boughs of a tree or cruising the air current to as high as you could go.

Barn and Austin chased me up into the sky. I ran along the air, following the dips and air currents, the moon glowing high in the sky. My heart soared as my feet touched down on top of a light pole, several Jacaranda trees, and a chimney. Barn and Austin laughed and followed after me. We flew across several blocks before ending up on top of a water tower in the corner of a park nestled below the sound barriers off I-5.

"Wow that was so cool."

"See why we love being Coaugelos!"

"I mean, it is more fun than being an Encantreino."

"Yeah, right, Eli!"

"Don't get me wrong, I miss casting spells and such…hmm…" Suddenly, I was craving a candy bar. I wiggled my nose and watched a chocolate bar floating in front of my face.

"Shit, mate," Barn said. "We can't do that."

"It won't last," I lamented, waiting for it to shrivel up and disappear into the night sky. A moment later, it was still floating in front of me.

"Grab it, wanker!" Barn commanded. "I want some!"

A minute later, we passed the candy bar around.

"Shit, mate," Barn said. "You did it! You successfully summoned a candy bar!"

"And had your first kill as a Coaugelo!" Austin said.

"And I was able to leap and fly just like you two without any fear."

"Oi," Barn said. "Our little lad is growing up."

"Máurso is going to be impressed, love."

We stopped to stare at each other. Austin called me love. I smiled. He broke out into a grin.

"You should just kiss already, wankers," Barn complained.

Austin blushed. I changed the subject.

"Too bad I didn't get something to remember tonight by."

Austin laughed. "I did," he said, pulling a shrunken head out of his pocket—a gruesome, shriveled up face resembling a crabapple doll.

"What the hell is this?"

"The head of the leader," Austin said. "We can do that, you know. Make souvenirs."

"I mean, that's kinda twisted."

"What did you want, a golden cup?"

"Or her bleedin' scarf?"

"Okay, okay," I said. "But you have to show me that trick."

"Yeah," Austin said, "after we give this to Dáumo Máurso for his trophy room."

"Room?"

Barn and Austin nodded. "He has over eight million souvenirs from battles. And twenty million from his students. And this will be your contribution."

He handed it to me. I held the small, leathery head in my hand. My first kill as a Coaugelo. My first trophy.

I stood, legs a little wobbly as I looked out at late-night traffic coursing along the I-5 from downtown.

"Ladies and gentlemen, Elijah Coronado Delomary is back!"

Chapter Ten

On The Tightrope

I HIT MY stride, finally.

"Honestly," Amanda said two weeks later, "you're ready for the swim competition coming up. Swim daily, but you've got this in the bag."

Julio said the same thing. "Your running is *excelente, wey*," he said. "You're ready."

I passed repeated super quizzes in aca-deca with flying colors.

"I'm so proud of you, Eli," Austin said. "You know biology better than me!"

"No shit."

"Yeah, weird, I know, but yes, you're going to ace it!"

Everything was coming together. I was confident. I had my first, second, and then third kill as a Coaugelo. And I was able to conjure and summon small things regularly: a soda, a candy bar, and the smallest rain cloud to float over Austin and sprinkle him with a few raindrops when he was in one of his moods and acting like a blockhead.

My body continued to struggle to keep up with my mind, my will and determination. I slept less and less at night. I kept pushing myself. Only a few more weeks to go, and then I could savor sweet victory!

One night, I sat in the window seat in my room, watching the rain falling outside my window, when I heard a cry for help.

"Someone help me!"

I glanced at the clock: 3:00 AM. I padded to the door, peering outside to the long hallway stretching from Aunt Christine's suite on one end to Mom's on the other. The darkness was punctuated every few feet from the dim chandeliers overhead. Silence. The house and everyone in it were asleep except me. I returned to the window.

"Help!" a voice shouted, weaker this time.

"Shit," I complained. I returned to my room, walked over to the closet, then jammed my feet in my running shoes and headed downstairs. I grabbed my raincoat from the front hall closet and stepped outside.

Where was security? They usually patrolled the grounds at night. Maybe there was a shift change. Rain thundered down on the roof of the veranda and on the brick walkway winding down the front lawn to the main gates. I stepped onto the stairs and into the rain. I hurried to the wrought iron fence separating our property from the street. I paused, noticing a strange pink light illuminating the jacaranda trees lining the street. I turned to see where it was coming from. I gasped. The house glowed with a fluorescent pink light from the runes Mom had recently cast over the house in the Jotomoarlo Sangrancto. The ancient characters appeared as if projected on the house moving up along the façade and disappearing on the mansard roof.

"Please, help little old me!" a voice called. I looked back at the house. The house was actively fighting some evil force itself. I turned and made my way to the empty street. A half block away, I spotted a figure, shrouded in shadows between the streetlights, waving to me.

"Help! Monsters!"

"I can help you!" I called, patting my pajama pockets for my PlasmX. Puxhàredo! I left it on the dresser in my closet. I stretched out my arm and raised my hand on the off chance my PlasmX would levitate out of my room and into my hands. Nothing happened. Crap. Máurso had drilled it in my head to never be without my PlasmX. And I had forgotten that rule already. I grumbled. Okay, I would just use my fists and body to battle any monster. My Xem Sen Ou improved every week. I was a walking weapon, I told myself.

I closed in on the figure.

"Come and help me."

The stench of ashes and sulfur wafted into my nose. I gagged. Okay, a chain smoker needed my help. Mom had drilled it into my head to never smoke.

"You want yellow teeth? Wrinkles when you're eighteen? Smell like cigarettes?"

"No?"

"Good, don't smoke, ever!"

I could do this. I paused in front of a shadowy figure.

"Elijah Delomary, Bane of the Gloom, here to help..uh..ma'am, sir, they?"

The figure reached up to their hood with their hands, only the skin was blistered and black and oozing. My eyes widened, seeing rotting flesh on their arms. I stopped in my tracks. I began to back away.

"What's wrong? Don't you remember me?" A raspy voice called as the hood fell off the head of the figure. The face of an old woman with wrinkled skin and washed-out blue eyes peered at me. Fungus crusted half the woman's face.

"Come here, honey. It's me, your great-great aunt Mady!"

I turned and began to run. That couldn't be Aunt Mady. She had died when I was eight years old at the ripe old age of 102. My foot hit a rut in the sidewalk, sending me tumbling forward. I crashed onto the lawn of my friend Letitia's house. I sprawled on my back, rain beating down on my face. My heart lodged in my throat. I wanted to cry out for help. I wanted to run, but for some reason, every muscle in my body was paralyzed. I heard the sound of Aunt Mady's walker clacking on the sidewalk.

"Come and give me a hug, honey!"

I closed my eyes. *I should have woken Barn, called Sunny. Security.* No, I— Stop, Elijah. You didn't know any better. You meant well. *The path to hell is lined with good intentions.* No, stop. Stop. Stop beating yourself up.

The clacking stopped. Aunt Mady, or whoever she was, stood over me. I was helpless. Thunder rumbled. Our twelfth atmospheric river of the rainy season. The vernal equinox passed weeks ago. Springtime. It never rained this much in Southern California. Something was wrong, someone was trying to drown the land of milk and honey. Drown La La Land and wash California into the sea.

Wheezing filled the air. I pressed my eyes closed as a hand reached for me. A vision bloomed in my head. Two pinpoints of red light that grew and grew and grew filled my mind.

"You proved yourself quite capable," the voice said. "I was hoping you'd run yourself ragged, trying to prove to yourself you're not some piece of crap like your father. I hoped to watch you collapse and die. You didn't. Then I was sure you would give up. You surprised me. So now I am here to destroy you, so Devlina is weakened, and I can grow stronger!"

I heard a snap followed by a crack. A screech and howl. My muscles twitched. I opened my eyes. The figure was gone.

The sun blazed high overhead set against a vibrant blue sky. I sat up, facing Mom and Aunt Christine on the sidewalk. They glowed with a golden light; Mom's arms and hands released a dazzling light. I squinted, watching a half circle ray blaze from Mom's hands. A burst of luminescence fanned out in all directions, illuminating the houses, trees, and the desolate street.

Another inhuman, bloodcurdling screech filled the air, then silence. The light faded, and the sun melted away. The sky turned dark. Rain began to fall again.

"Let's get you inside, darling," Mom said, leaning down to help me to my feet. As we approached the house, I noticed the pink light surrounding the contours of the old mansion. The runes held strong, ensuring our safety.

Inside, Christine embraced me and Mom, and slipped upstairs to her suite. In my room, I kicked off my shoes and hung my wet coat on a hook in the bathroom.

Mom sat on my bed, awash in the soft yellow light from my lamp.

"Am I in trouble?"

Mom's shook her head. "No, why?"

"I should have known better." Mom's favorite line.

"No, darling."

"Come again?" Had she forgotten her favorite line?

"You're okay, hon."

I sat in the wing chair by the fire.

"That figure was Aunt Mady! She was calling for help."

"That wasn't Aunt Mady," Mom said.

"Mom, I was sure I was going to die."

"Yes, that creature had powerful magic."

"I think it was Zid'dra."

"One of his minions, like the blob at Sean's house."

"Oh, I thought that was Zid'dra."

"He has an army of monsters."

"Are you sure we're safe?"

"Of course, darling." Mom sounded confident, but why did her face show concern?

"That light thing. How...? I mean, what was that?"

"A *Luminabo Immenso*."

"Wow, that's a powerful incantation! You turned the night to day."

"The only thing that would purify and destroy that creature."

"That was pretty cool." I laughed.

"You know, I'm spending more time practicing magic. I forgot how fun it is." She stopped herself, then looked at me. "Are you okay?"

"I'm fine," I grinned. "I've had three kills as a Coaugelo."

"Oh, wow."

"Yeah, I'm feeling really good these days."

"That's great," Mom said, but a look of concern crossed her face. "Elijah, what were you doing up so late?"

"I told you. I heard a scream."

"You look very, very tired. Do you want to stay home tomorrow? Take a mental health day? Maybe we can go to the spa?"

"No, I'm fine, Mom."

"We can see a movie!"

"Naw," I said. "I got this, Mom."

Mom opened her mouth but then stopped herself. "Okay, darling, you're the boss." She stood. "Get some rest." She walked to the door. "The rain will end, you know? Seems like it might not, but it will. And the sun will shine again, and it'll be hot, and we'll complain that it's too uncomfortable."

"Thanks for the reminder, Mom."

"Night, darling."

*

I WALKED THROUGH heavy, black smoke, hands out, trying to find my way. My eyes stung, my lungs heavy from smoke. Bright orange flames erupted in front of me. A shadow appeared as the thick, black clouds retreated: a tall woman wearing black stilettos and a black miniskirt and bodice with black hair framing her face.

She had this very large *armedellae*, a plasma weapon that monsters were fond of using against Magicals.

"Devlina?"

Devlina glanced over her left shoulder at me. I gasped. Half her face had melted off, revealing the muscles and veins in her face, her left eyeball hanging from the socket.

"Elijah? What the fuck are you doing here?"

"I was battling a monster near my house and almost died."

"Yeah?" she said, preoccupied. She lifted her *armedellae* and began firing rounds up in the air.

Black, flaming objects fell all around me. I squinted through the heavy smoke, trying to figure out what she was battling. I looked down at the ground, smoke stinging my eyes. The objects were dead black crows, flames licking over their lifeless bodies.

Corbenstae as they were called in the Dark Language or *Corbenmala* in the Old Language, Zid'dra's feared legion of attack birds.

"Why are you shooting down Corbenmalas?"

"I'm a little busy right now, Elijah," she said, pumping the weapon, shaped sort of like a plastic super soaker, up into the darkness all around us. The red light from the plasma blazed into the sky, momentarily revealed thousands of Corbenmalas swarming overhead cawing and crying out. One grabbed her eyeball with its beak.

Devlina pumped the armedellae, and red plasma hit the bird. It burst into flames, falling at my feet.

"Your face is half melted off!"

"Yeah, well, you know that Zid'dra tried to compel me to reunite with him—force me to submit to him like I am a beta. Beta! Can you imagine me a beta?" She laughed, and her eyeball shuddered. "You saved me. Strange how that keeps happening." She winked at me.

I grumbled, "We're not friends, Devlina."

"Sure," Devlina said. "Anyway, after I woke from the trance Ziddy cast on me, I stomped over to him, and well, I took him to task!"

"Watch out!" I cried as a Corbenmala darted out of the thick black clouds over head, claws out lunging for Devlina's face. Devlina lifted her weapon, spun around, and toasted the bird.

"Zid'dra had a temper tantrum. No surprise there. Anyway, he told his second wife, Máu Rabetica, to deal with me."

"No, shit."

"Yeah, that heifer set fire to my mansion in Beverly Hills while I was taking my nightly beauty nap on my bed of nails. I was burned alive."

"Oh, crap. Are you okay?"

"Never better," she said, pumping rounds directly into the smoke in front of her. "I forgot how invigorating it is to be burned alive. Happened to me several times in Europe . I really freaked out those uptight witch haters when I'd twerk as I was roasting."

"That didn't happen."

"It did!" Devlina said. "Then I smote the fanaticals who hunted down witches and cursed them with little—um, well, you know."

Devlina spun around firing her weapon at the birds. Flashes of red and orange and blue.

Devlina paused to wave her hands over her *armedellae*. "Reloading," she said. "Anyway, now I have progressed in my war with Ziddy. The War of the Roses has nothing on us, y'know?"

"Yeah?"

"Yeah. First, I wiped out many of his legions of hellions, and now I'm moving on to destroy the other Máus. The wicked wives of Ziddy. I will win. And then Ziddy will have a reckoning coming. Can I get an amen?"

"Amen?"

Devlina noticed I was gawping at her face. She snapped a finger. Her face bubbled back into place, and her eye returned to its socket.

"Better?"

"Uh, yeah."

She fired some more rounds above.

More Corbenmalas fell around me, melting into the black obsidian floor peeking out through the smoke. "Devlina, I was attacked by my great Aunt Mady just now."

Devlina paused, turning to look at me. "Nothing more fun than a battle with family! Did she kill you? Is this the new and improved, reincarnated Elijah?"

"No, I didn't die," I explained.

"Too bad," she said. "I've been tortured, burned alive, drawn-and-quartered and murdered and generally killed multiple times and always come back better than ever. I highly recommend it."

"You don't understand," I said. "Aunt Mady is dead."

"Shit, well, that's gothic."

"Yeah, terrifying."

Devlina gritted her teeth, pumping red plasma into the sky. She said, "You know that Ziddy likes to play mind games like that."

"Mom said it was a minion of Zid'dra"

"Probably, but hey, at least you're popular.

"With the wrong people."

"There's no bad attention."

"I almost died?"

Devlina said, "Shit, I'm sorry Elijah. I'm sorry you're involved."

"Not entirely your fault."

"That's the spirit."

"Well, I'm a Coaugelo now. And I can use magic! Here, I can summon another weapon for you."

Devlina paused as a black, three-headed pterodactyl-like creature circled overhead.

I wiggled my nose. A puff of smoke rose from my hand. As it cleared, a cupcake appeared.

"Um, well, thanks for the thought."

"Shit, it's not working too well."

"Don't sweat it," Devlina said. "You need to celebrate you!"

A three-headed Corbenmala swooped down at Devlina pecking her forehead before she aimed her armedellae and turned it into a smoldering mass of flaming feathers.

"Look at how far my boy has come. From the sniveling mess at the lake at summer camp after being kissed by a boy to a Coaugelo."

"Okay," I said.

"Don't diminish yourself," Devlina said. "You're like me now. A survivor. They tried to defeat you, break you but you rose like a phoenix from the ashes..."

Devlina lifted her right arm and pushed her armedellae sideways, pumping the trigger. A flash of red light filled the semi-darkness around us before the sound of shrieking and smell of burned feathers.

"I'm a survivor," I repeated.

"And just like Ziddy can't keep me down, you need to believe in yourself. Remember his first rule. He can't destroy you, Elijah. You are getting stronger and stronger."

"You're right!"

"Of course, I am," Devlina said, then added loudly, "I am the Queen of the Gloom!" The earth shook; lightning flashed in the clouds.

"Now are you going to allow yourself to love Austin?"

"Wait, what?"

Smoke swirled around me. My eyes teared up profusely. I coughed. More Corbenmalas dropped around me and melted into the ground.

"I get you because we are linked, boy-o. You fear giving your heart to Austin because of insecurities. But stop being afraid and just love him."

A black creature, spewing flames from its nostrils, swooped down from the sky, claws out, heading straight for me. I opened my mouth to scream.

My alarm clock buzzed, 5:00 AM. I sat up in bed, body aching, head spinning. Where was I? Home. I glanced out the windows. Drizzle. Had that all been a nightmare?

I padded to the bathroom, turned on the water in the shower and stripped off my pajamas. I coughed. Black smoke curled out of my mouth. My eyes darted to the mirror. I gawked at a black feather stuck in my hair.

Chapter Eleven

So Much Winning

DRIZZLE FELL AS I stood with Amber Rustyn and Tomiko Fukada waiting for the bus to take us to Costa Mesa for the Academic Decathlon.

I shifted foot to foot listening to "Sex & Candy" on my headphones. And there he was like "disco superfly," looking beautiful in his red raincoat, his long hair tucked behind his ears, sunshine pouring out of him. Austin. Sauntering over, sipping a coffee.

"Morning, loves," Austin said to Amber and Tomiko, who giggled whenever he spoke to them in his posh accent. "Quite a lovely day for a sporting event."

"Good thing it's inside, Austin," Amber said.

"Aye," Austin said. "Good thing there's no outside event. Imagine that, a sprint while reading *War and Peace*, yeah?"

"Gosh, that would be hell!" Tomiko giggled.

"*War and Peace* or the rain?" Austin winked at them. God, he was so smooth and charming and amazing.

"Both," Amber said.

"But the sprint would be fine then, lass?"

"Nooooo," Tomiko said.

"Austin, you are too much sometimes." Amber played with her hair, rocking back and forth. God, she had a thing for him.

"I'm smashing the sleet!" he said. Amber and Tomiko laughed.

Amber said, "No, it's breaking the ice."

"Oi, these Americanisms." He winked again at them. Then he walked over to me, eyeing my shirt and tie, letterman jacket, the sky. "You look great, though you need a slicker. I think that's the word in America."

"You look good too, Kangy."

Austin beamed. "I wore a shirt and tie. I know you have a thing for preppy Asian boys from Hong Kong."

"Kangy!"

Amber and Tomiko giggled.

Austin loomed over me, chuffing.

"You look tired, mate."

"Had a long night."

"Studying?"

"Battling monsters."

Austin frowned. "You didn't invite me?"

"I was ambushed."

"Hmm," Austin said, "maybe I should move in with you. Be your round the clock bodyguard."

"I'd love that."

"You would?"

Devlina's words came to mind. Growing stronger. Be true to myself. Give my heart to Austin.

"Being around you all the time."

"More than now?"

"Yeah." I looked up into his warm brown eyes. He smiled broadly. A horn bleating interrupted our conversation.

We spun around. Mrs. Biederman hit the brakes hard on her

sports car inches from Austin, Amber, Tomiko, and me.

Amber screeched.

"Who's ready to...umm...slay queen?"

Amber groaned. Tomiko shouted, "No, Mrs. Biederman, no."

"The rest of the team is coming!" she said, taking off running as five cars pulled into the parking lot. We all laughed. Mrs. Biederman, wiry and energetic, looked wild with her giant hair flying around her hair.

"Here's the bus!" Beiderman screamed, flagging down the white and gray bus. "Costa Mesa, here we come to win the GOLD!"

Eventually on the bus to Costa Mesa, I sat by the window, Austin next to me. His right leg was pressed close to mine. He chuffed. He was content.

Happy.

Safe.

"Tired, mate?" Austin whispered.

"Yeah."

"Take a nap, long trip."

I closed my eyes, leaning against the window listening to "Under the Bridge."

My breathing slowed, became more regular.

I stood on a bridge, the Sixth Street Viaduct peering toward Downtown. The Santa Ana winds blew fiercely. A baby cried from a stroller across the street. A man screamed. I shuddered. Perspiration dripped down my face. The temperature soared to ninety degrees. Smoke obscured the San Gabriel Mountains looming far in the distance; wildfire burned out of control devouring homes and trees and lives. These fucking devil winds. The bridge moved violently. Everything shook. I struggled to maintain my balance. I looked up and saw Austin. I had pulled my heart from my chest and handed it to him. He shook his head. The ground gave way beneath me. I tumbled into oblivion.

"Austin! Please, I swear it's your heart this time! I won't mess up!"

The bus lurched, and my head banged against the window. My eyes flew open. The noise of the engine disturbed the quiet of the bus.

"You okay, mate?"

"Yeah, I fell asleep."

"You were snoring, mate."

The darkness clawed at me. I was *so* tired.

"November Rain" started playing through my headphones.

Jesus. *It doesn't mean anything, Elijah*, I told myself.

We arrived an hour later at Costa Mesa High School, a typical Southern California school, low slung, with classrooms assembled around a grassy quad. Mrs. Biederman gave us a stirring pep talk.

"You guys are ready! Ready for this! Let's go and kick butt!!!"

Austin looked at me. He tucked his hair behind his ear. His fingers brushed mine. He was so close... We were so close...again...

"Take your headphones off, Elijah," Mrs. Biederman told me.

"Don't make her mad, mate," Austin whispered.

"Elijah!" Mrs. Biederman shouted. "You have speech first. Get going!"

I nodded and began walking across the grass staring at a map of the school to find the classroom. After a few minutes, I found the right place and took my seat in the back, waiting for my turn. My speech was on nuclear disarmament, and I gave mine last.

My competitors presented amazing speeches on climate change, cyclical poverty, animal rights, and on and on. The darkness hovered, but I forced it away.

My turn came. I ignored the fear building in my stomach and presented my speech to the proctors, being sure to pace myself, enunciate clearly, and make eye contact.

"Well done," one of the proctors said. I was encouraged.

After I finished my speech, I wandered outside to find my team. The rest of the day became a blur of tests culminating in the Science Super Test in the gymnasium. The bleachers were filled with teams from all over LA, friends, family, even journalists from the local TV stations. I took my seat on the floor.

I stared at my desk. Puxhàredo. My body was wracked with nerves. This wasn't the darkness—this was different.

I spotted Austin in the bleachers. He had helped me study for this. He nodded to me, giving me two thumbs-up and smiling like a dork.

A horn sounded and we began the test in earnest. As each question came, I found myself knowing the answer.

To

Every

Question.

I wrote the answers as fast as I could. I smiled. I was going to ace this. The crowd cheered me on. Austin stood waving a sign that read, "Go Eli!" with a peace sign scrawled next to the block letters. The buzzer sounded. I jumped up, elated. I did it.

The judges tallied the results. The gymnasium fell silent. All eyes were on the judges.

A woman stood up.

"The gold goes to Elijah Delomary, Burbank High School."

Oh

My

Fricking

God!

I jumped up and down and cheered!

Mrs. Biederman ran down the bleachers and onto the wood floor to hug me. The rest of the team swarmed me. Amber thrust my hands up.

"WINNER WINNER, CHICKEN DINNER!"

Austin slid close to me. "I'm proud of you, Eli."

His warm breath tickled my ear. He reached for my hand.

I was so fucking excited. I won the science competition. I had never won anything. I brushed his hands with mine. We squeezed pinky fingers. I looked into his eyes and saw *home*.

I was like a hurricane-ravaged galleon desperately seeking safe port.

You won gold! You won gold, Elijah!

On stage, one of the judges slipped the gold ribbon over my head. All my hard work had paid off. The darkness. Maybe suffering pushed me to succeed?

Afterward, Mrs. Biederman waved for us all to stand together for a team photo. I'd later see that, in the photo, Austin stood behind me, blowing a kiss toward my ear. I guess he was like me: he never gave up. I guess I wasn't like him: I had given up—*on love*. I was like my mom that way. No, I knew better than that. Mom made love work—*now*. With my win, I became a better version of myself.

My mind wandered to Dad. He had approached me that day with Stylo, and he wanted something to make himself better while taking from me. He had taken Austin from me. And I had refused to give Dad anything. No, Dad was gone from my life.

"I'm so proud of you, little Eli," Austin said, pulling me in for a hug.

"Thanks, Kangy," I said.

Austin, you see, was like his Dad. He believed in love. Austin Sr. adored Cecilia. Their love was *effortless*. There was a song about this, but I couldn't remember. I sagged into a seat on the bus, completely fatigued.

Tomorrow, I competed in the All Valley Swim Competition. Another win and I would set myself apart from the little "sniveling" boy as Devlina called the old me. Rain hammered the top of the bus as we pulled out of Costa Mesa High School. I fell asleep on the bus, my hand on Austin's knee as we returned to Burbank.

At home, after the competition, I went straight to my shower, stood under the hot water, and pulled energy from the water. I hadn't slept at all last night. I had pushed my body for months, running like a hamster on a wheel, but I couldn't give up. I was so close to my goal.

Mom waited for me in my room.

"Elijah!" she said, holding up a bottle of champagne and two glasses. "You won gold at the competition!"

"Mom, I'm naked!" I slammed the door on her.

"Elijah," Mom called through the door. "I've seen you naked. I changed your diapers!"

I sat on the toilet, dripping onto the fluffy white bathroom rug, water running down my face. Why didn't I feel proud of myself? My mind rumbled back to Aunt Mady. The two pinpoints of red light growing and growing and growing. Those words. Telling me that I would fail. *I had to fail.*

No. Stop.

My body hurt all over. My engines ran on fumes.

"Elijah?"

"Yeah, Mom, I'll be out in a second."

"This deserves a celebration. You're allowed to drink tonight!"

"Yay!" I deadpanned.

"Elijah, aren't you happy?"

"I don't like drinking, Mom. Makes my head hurt."

"It's only a little bubbly. Get dressed and have a glass with your old mom in the front parlor. Barn is here and Kevin and April. And Austin."

"Is it a party?"

"Yes, Mrs. Singh made an ice cream cake too. Chocolate. Your favorite."

"I can't eat cake. I have to swim in the All Valley tomorrow."

"And?"

"Mom, carbs make me fat."

"Elijah." Mom laughed through the door. "You are not fat!"

I stood up and examined my body in the mirror. When stressed out, I scrutinized my body. I hated how I looked.

"Honey, are you all right?"

"Yes, Mom!" I snapped. "God, let me get dressed already."

Silence. I glanced over my shoulder. A few months ago, I would have smirked and given myself a point for hurting Mom. Don't be a jerk, Elijah.

"Sorry, be out soon."

"Okay, darling," Mom said. I heard her footsteps retreat across the room. My door opened, closed.

*

ADRENALINE FROM MY win at the Academic Decathlon powered me as I walked out to the pool at the All Valley Competition held in the state of the art Pauloni Swim Center at Winchester University in West LA. Hours swimming with Amanda. Multiple competitions throughout the Valley to get to this moment. I had a gold medal already. I proved that I was nothing like Lawrence Eugene Smith. A loser.

The crowd cheered. Mom jumped to her feet wearing a T-shirt with my face on it emblazoned with the words: "GO ELIJAH!" Aunt Christine and George and Aunt Lisa and her fiancé, Patrick, wore T-shirts reading #TEAMELIJAH. Mom covered her mouth with her hands, something she did only when particularly anxious.

I turned and spotted Austin, Barn, Austin Sr., and Cecilia sitting below Mom. They cheered and whistled.

I smiled broadly.

Austin mouthed, "You look hot, mate!"

I blushed.

Out of the corner of my eye, I noticed a figure. I recoiled. The red dots! I blinked. Dad. Sitting beside Florence. Both looked upset.

Pull it together, Elijah.

"You can do anything you want," Arnulfo told us two weeks ago. "Each and every one of you can go out there and be the best. You have it in you. They can't take that away from you. Be proud of yourself."

I breathed deeply, waved to my family, and stepped onto the block. I wanted to finish the competition so I could take off this ridiculous bathing suit. I worried that I looked fat. Why did I feel like this? Mom said I looked great. Austin called me his little muscle boy. So why couldn't I see what they saw? When I looked in the mirror I saw my flaws. When Austin looked at himself in the mirror, or window, or anything reflective for that matter, he would smile and see his perfection. Could I someday casually glance in a mirror and see someone I liked? Not someone who repulsed me, no matter what?

I shook my head to stop the thoughts. I hated Dad for showing up. The darkness was slithering around the pool reaching for me.

I bet I looked like one of those sumo wrestlers I saw on a documentary with Mom last night. Big and soft. "That's your Dad if he lost weight!" Mom joked sitting next to me munching on popcorn. "I don't know why I fell in love with a fat guy. I always dated svelte men before. Pedro, who I dated in college, was a soccer star. All muscle. Wow."

"Mom, I don't want to talk about the bodies of the men you dated."

"Don't be a killjoy." Mom tossed popcorn at me. "He had an eight-pack. He was a master sailor too. I mean we almost made it across the Pacific before the typhoon blew us off course, and he ended up in Manila, and I ended up in Minerva."

"When you became the first Queen of Minerva?" How many times had she told me this tale of how she unwittingly united all four regions of Minerva to fight together to vanquish an army of Máunadas determined to conquer Old Earth. Afterward, Mom was crowned as the first Queen of Minerva.

"Yes," Mom said, "I had quite a few suitors too you know. The Vana'a are all tall, muscular and hu—"

"Stop, Mom!"

Mom chuckled. "I raised a prude," she said. "Must be from your dad. He's uptight. I should have travelled to Manila and tracked down Pedro and married him. I deserved his body. Your dad was fat and gross.

"Pedro was good and built. Too bad he decided to join a reclusive order of celibate Mùn Táis who dedicated their lives to the pursuit of scientific ways to use magic to heal."

Good and built. Be good and built, Elijah. Mom hated "fat and gross Dad." Shit, I ate cake last Saturday. I had a cheeseburger yesterday. Or was it a week ago? I couldn't remember. "A moment on the lips..." Mom and Aunt Christine joked all the time.

Pull it together, Elijah. Concentrate on swimming. Not your body. Or this ridiculously tiny swimsuit. Who designed this? Some pervert?

I looked over my shoulder at Amanda. She mouthed, "You can do this, Elijah!"

Two short buzzes sounded. My stomach turned. My toes tingled.

Shit, this was the moment. Four years training with Amanda to learn to swim competitively as Mom wanted for me.

When I first moved into the mansion with Tory, years ago, Aunt Christine hired Amanda to teach me to swim.

"I can't have you drowning," Christine had said to me that first week. "This pool will draw you in. It's magic you know."

"It is?"

"Sure, like the rest of the house. Magic and pools can be dangerous, hence you need to learn to swim properly. I have a friend from college. She'll come by tomorrow to teach you."

"Really?" I was so excited. "I've always wanted to learn!"

"Aren't you glad you're here, then? With your favorite aunt. You can do whatever you want. Swim, learn Magic, sleep in late, stay up late, eat ice cream for breakfast. Anything."

Anything seemed possible before I travelled to Minerva and found Mom and brought her back and things changed because she was different and she made me into someone else. And now, she had transformed again. She was a chameleon. A new version lived with me; this version liked to smile and wear sundresses and believed in love.

I stood in position on the platform and slipped on my goggles. One buzz and I dove into the water. A charge of electricity circulated through my nervous system, pushing, forcing my arms and legs to cut through the water. To breathe. To keep going forward. Propelling myself in the water where freedom lived. Either in the Pacific or in chlorine, water liberated me.

I touched the wall, flipped around and swam back. I was a dolphin, like the ones who stuck their heads above the water when I was on my surfboard waiting for a wave. Dolphins were the dogs of the ocean. Their heads rose from the water and they smiled and cackled at me. Dolphins laughed at the world. If the earth had a sense of humor, dolphins were its voice.

When I left the pool, I stood staring at the concrete floor, listening to "Wrecking Ball" by Miley Cyrus on my headphones, and waiting off to the side with the other swimmers. Chad Lo strutted around, certain he won. He shot me a look meaning, "You lost. I won. Deal with it."

Puxhàredo. Water dripped down my neck. I opened and closed my hands. Please, please, God, all my hard work and sacrifice. Let me win. I pleaded with God or whoever dwelled in the heavens past the Áuqala.

"Dreams," by the Cranberries, played on the playlist on my phone. *Please let these dreams come true so I could be someone entirely new. I've been running so hard. I need this.*

"Elijah Delomary wins the All Valley Swim Competition!" A voice called over the PA. Cheers erupted. Chad shot me this evil look. I was sorta confused momentarily, like maybe Mom cast a spell to make it seem like I won or something until I saw the swim times. My name flashed at the top of the list. *I came in number one. Holy fucking pux-hàredo, médedo. I did it! Elijah Delomary did it!*

Mom pushed down from the stands and ran toward me, almost slipping and falling into the pool on her way. She cursed, regained her composure and pulled me into a tight hug.

"My baby boy!" she said, then whispered in my ear, "I am so proud of you Elijah. My God, you were like a dolphin in the pool zipping back and forth."

"I really won?"

"Yes, darling," Mom said. "I always knew you could."

"Oh, my goodness." I kept saying over and over.

Austin and his parents and Barn and the rest of my family came down to congratulate me.

"You never fail to amaze me, mate," Austin whispered in my ear. "You should be so proud."

I leaned up on my tippy-toes and planted a kiss on Austin's cheek. He beamed. I paused. Shit, Dad. I scanned the bleachers. He and Florence were gone. Why did I care if they had seen me kiss Austin? This was me. They had to accept me.

We went home, where Mom organized a pool party, of all things. I wasn't in the mood to swim, but my friends were there waiting for me.

"You're awash in gold!" April said, floating on an inflatable unicorn. "You're like the next Tom Daley!"

"I knew you could do it, bro," Tyrone said after splashing water in my face. "You're always worrying about things. I'm not good enough at this or that."

"In other words, we knew you were going to kill it, Elijah!" Tyrell added.

Later, Mom put on a show using magic to cast fireworks over the house that only we could see. I noticed Sean standing next to her, his arm around her waist. Mom turned and kissed him on the lips.

Austin sauntered over to me. "Eli and Kangy were like fishes."

"Thought you said we were like cats?"

"Whatever," Austin said. "There's nothing we can't do together."

He pulled me close. I rested my head on his shoulder. This Saturday, I would run the 3.7K marathon from City Hall to Disney Studios and win again. And with my third win, I'd have the confidence to say to Austin, definitively, "Will you take a chance and love me again?"

Chapter Twelve

The Rain In Southern California

"RAIN IN SOUTHERN California is both a blessing and a curse; on one hand, the rain brings life to the desert we live in. Too much brings flooding, death, and misery. Long ago, Angelenos paved over the rivers of Southern California, the once revered Rio de Los Angeles, that brought life to the dry soil one moment and the next destruction was contained. We lost something when she was paved over."

I ended the stream from Los Angeles Valley College, a weekly podcast of California history. I hadn't slept all week. I spent my nights in my room trying to distract myself from the darkness clawing for me. I struggled to slip into sleep. When I fell asleep, it was like I was awake the whole time. At four or five every morning, I woke up terrified. Of what, I couldn't guess. I had a premonition that something terrible was going to happen to me and maybe the world. The darkness smothered me. Space was a vacuum. Devoid of sound or warmth.

The night before the Burbank 3.7K I closed my eyes and saw

Devlina spinning around and around me, holding her armedellae in her hands, pumping red plasma at the Corbenmalas attacking her. I looked up and the darkness gave way to fiery skies. A huge monster with eight legs rose high above the flames, opened its mouth, and released locusts, swarming Devlina and me.

"You're going to lose, Paràsàfàna!" Máu Rabetica, known as the Goddess of Wrath, cackled while hovering over us.

"You can't beat Zid'dra, and you can't beat me. Give up."

Máu Rabetica aimed her own armedellae at Devlina, pulled the trigger. Devlina burst like a water balloon hitting the pavement. Smoke enveloped me. I stood on Austin's front lawn in driving rain waiting for him. Dad stood nearby, holding a glass of beer with spit in it. "Drink up, boy!" He tipped his beer to me. I looked away. The red door to Austin's house opened. In a flash, the house was gone, replaced by a carwash: go in gay, come out straight.

I woke up screaming. Barn appeared in the doorway. "Mate? Are you okay?"

"Nightmare."

"Again?"

"Every night."

"Want me to stay with you?"

"It's okay; only a few hours and everything will be okay," I said, holding Ocho tightly against my chest. "Only a few hours."

"The marathon?"

"Yeah."

"Are you sure you're up to it? You've looked so tired this last week."

"I can do it."

"You don't have to," Barn said.

"I want to." I lay back down.

"Why isn't Austin here? He can stay with you. Your Mom won't mind."

"I'll mind."

"Come again?"

"I have to... I mean... What if I?"

"If you what?" Barn leaned against the door. "Elijah, have you cooked up some wild plan to prove yourself to Austin?"

I gulped. Was he able to read my mind like Mom?

"Yes, if I do everything right, I can banish this darkness in me and love Austin."

I didn't say that.

"Someday maybe you'll get married to Austin. And you'll become a Kang. And then you'll be gentler on yourself," he said, walking over to squeeze my arm. "You're going to do great tomorrow."

He closed the door. I heard him pad back across the hallway to his room and close the door softly. I lay in bed waiting for the morning to arrive.

*

"YOU ARE ALWAYS On My Mind" by the Pet Shop Boys poured through my headphones. I shivered against the cool and damp air. My breath curled out of my mouth like smoke as I exhaled. Unseasonably cold weather had settled over Southern California, the temperature in the low fifties rather than high seventies, low eighties. It had rained for two weeks straight. It was almost as if God was trying to wash away my imperfections. Rain for the last five months of being sixteen. I made a deal with God, that once I won the marathon he'd give me Austin. I was not religious, but when we went to Mass last Sunday, I asked him to help me. He understood better than anyone how to battle the darkness.

In a week, I'd be seventeen years old. No longer a boy. A man who listened to Arnulfo when he said, "Gay is Good. Gay is who you are!"

I searched the clouds pregnant with rain. *Please wait until I'm done*, I pleaded with nature. God, whatever. Thunder rumbled. What if the rain wasn't caused by God, but someone else, someone more sinister?

Mom came over to me. "You sure you want to do this?" She had her hair pulled off her face and wore a thick jacket, T-shirt, and jeans, looking relaxed and... Was that possible? Happy? Sean stood near the fountain in front of City Hall, talking to George and Aunt Christine. They laughed like old friends. Mom and Aunt Christine's war was in the rear-view mirror. I passed them in the hallways lost in conversation. Sitting in the garden drinking tea and huddled together laughing at inside jokes, or in the game room playing *Mortal Kombat* together on the PS5. Like they reverted to being teenagers themselves.

"Yeah, I'm really excited!" I exclaimed, jogging in place. "I have a good feeling about it." I sorta lied. The darkness fell over Burbank, covering the city and mountains in a pall. *No, I am ignoring the darkness. I am going to be triumphant.*

"You don't have to, you know," Mom said. She held a can of cola in her hand.

"Mom! That's not diet!"

"Oh, I didn't notice. Oh, well. No biggie." I thought about Rule Number One. We loved cola. I was determined. I was gay. I was proud. I accepted who I was. The whole world could judge me and call me names and try to pass laws against me and criminalize me, but I was me. I was free to be who I was born to be.

"I want to, Mom," I added. "I'll have great legs after this." I laughed and then Mom laughed too.

"Okay, well, maybe you can take it easy after this."

"*Oklahoma!* starts tomorrow."

Mom paused. "That's a lot. You've been pushing yourself for a few months now."

"I know. I want to"

She looked at me. "Is it my fault?"

A shadow fell over her face. I recognized it—the look of failure.

"No, well, yeah, originally but now, well, you're different and so am I. I want to do this for my own brand."

We discussed my brand last weekend. Arnulfo said, "It's not uncommon for people to create a persona for themselves to protect themselves. You're high profile, and I can see why you would do that.

"Not only do high profile people create brands, so do many gay people. A way to interact with a hostile outside world to fit in. Feel safe."

Arnulfo added, "Maybe you can let go of the brand. You have a supportive family, Elijah. You have supportive friends. You don't need a brand anymore. And teenagers make mistakes. That's how we grow. Maybe a brand was to appear perfect. But no one is perfect. That's what makes us human. That's what separates us from the monsters. We are flawed. Monsters ignore their flaws. We accept them. Right, Mom?" Arnulfo looked at Mom, who breathed deeply and agreed, "You're right. Mistakes help us grow. And no, we don't need to hide who we are anymore. I love you, Elijah! All of you, in fact."

"See?" Arnulfo said. "And, Elijah, remember when you are open and vulnerable you let people in. Let people love you."

Let.

People.

Love.

You.

The buzzer sounded, and I took off running from City Hall, following the flow of bodies down Olive Avenue toward the overpass across the I-5 freeway and Disney Studios.

At the crest of the overpass, a sensation of flames, smoke, and darkness filled me with fear and anger and destruction. "You will fail!" voice chanted from the black monster with eight legs rising overhead, below the clouds. The monster wanted me to fail. I glanced up into the clouds. Two red eyes burned like supernovas.

"No, no, fuck you!"

The supernova grew bigger and bigger and blinded me momentarily. I stumbled, regained my balance, and pushed on. *I'm a teenager. Maybe failing is okay. Maybe what happened to me and Austin was okay. Maybe I'm learning from my mistakes.*

I paced myself for the long run to the Walt Disney Studios. I focused on my breathing. Inhaling—*whew*—exhaling. *Hàlar* is the Magicals word for breathing. *Imhàlar, echàlar*. Inhale and exhale. *Whew*. My legs moved and arms pumped. I glanced over and saw Stylo and Aunt Dora and Uncle Osvaldo outside St. Finbar's clapping and cheering and waving me on.

A few blocks ahead, I saw Barn—he had his hands cupped around his mouth, cheering me on.

"Come on, mate! You can do it! Almost there!" He was full of energy, jumping up and down, urging me on. He jogged on the sidewalk, past the barricade separating the runners from the spectators. "You got this, Elijah!"

I smiled at him and grabbed some water from a woman handing cups out to runners, downed it then looked back at him and almost stumbled and fell again. Tory appeared from behind Barn, jogging and whistling and screaming. "Come on, Cory," she said, using her pet name for me. "You can do it. Make me proud."

My eyes were so wide. "Tory!" I shouted.

"Elijah!!!! I love you!"

I wanted to cry.

Oh

my

fucking

God.

Tory was back. She looked good! Her red hair was long and shiny and fell past her shoulders. She looked thin and sad and also, strangely, happy too. *Did I look like that?*

My legs were jelly. My side hurt and my head was ready to burst. I didn't know how I was still running. Thunder rumbled; the supernovas flashed in my eyes and then the sky opened up. Puxhàredo. Of course. As the water streamed down my face, all I could think about was the podcast. The rain brings life to Los Angeles but can also wreak havoc and destruction in the land of the Queen of Angels. How can she bring life and death?

"We contain multitudes," Arnulfo said, looking around the room. "Elijah." I watched him, holding my breath.

"Making mistakes is how we learn and grow and for you to become a man."

"Dad made a lot of mistakes. I can't forgive him."

"Can you forgive yourself?"

The rain was falling hard. We needed the rain to alleviate the drought, but mudslides blocked highways and slid down mountainsides in the night. Creeping fingers, smothering its sleeping victims. Houses fell off cliffs, hugging the coastline, dropping into the sea. Maybe the rain needed to stop.

I spotted the finish line. I tasted another win in my mouth.

"And if I can't?" I said to Arnulfo.

"You matter, Elijah. You're a son, a brother, a friend," Arnulfo said. "They labelled you to make you hate yourself. But they are not who define you. You define yourself. You matter without gold medals or whatnot. Do you understand?

"Your struggle from boy to man has less to do with your Dad than maybe the world. No one makes movies about straight guys struggling with their identity. They can be anything, superhero, villain, the boy next door. No one pauses when they kiss a girl. Men like your Dad don't have to accept themselves. They are who they are born to be."

Arnulfo's words rattled in my head. I was no different from anyone else. I wasn't the only gay boy in the world. I was one of many, all over the world.

I was not alone.

I was not alone.

Thunder boomed. Rain continued falling on me. I squinted through the rain, feeling the darkness edging closer and closer. I spotted my reflection in the window of an insurance brokerage through the rain. I recoiled. Puxhàredo, did I really look like that? The fucking cheeseburger I ate last week. That ice cream cake!

Thunder rumbled.

"You think you can intervene like that? *Iunio malum,*" a voice whispered behind me. "You are going to die, foolish boy. I have summoned all the rain to destroy you. *Iunio malum desi mortens.*"

No, no, it couldn't be. The darkness and the rain and the fear and loathing inside me coming together like a tsunami.

"Elijah! LOOK OUT!" I heard Devlina shout. My vision turned away from the window. My eyes grew big.

"Oh, fuck!" I couldn't stop in time. A guy stumbled and fell in front of me onto the street. He brought down another runner who stumbled toward me. I crashed into him, and then I went flying. Airborne, hands stretched out in front of me.

It rained harder. Lightning flashed.

"When it rains in the desert, all the paint and makeup covering the mountains and plains and beaches melts away, revealing the intricate plan from long ago. They came for one reason, fame. A mirage. All life is a stage, and we're nothing but sand, man."

The poem from Ansolanderr Càstronevès flashed before my eyes. The rain washing away the paint and makeup creating me. And then my entire body crashed into something firm and unmoving, and I spun head over heels, and just before everything went black, I heard thunder and the rain and then screaming and then sirens. I kept thinking of the fucking poem. It never rained in fricking Southern California until this year.

*

SLOWLY, THE HOUSE lights came up, revealing the cavernous expanse of the Million Dollar Theater in Downtown LA. I swiveled my head around at the rows of seats, the boxes on the sides, the balcony seats that stretched into the darkness above. I was seated in the middle of the orchestra section when an organ rose stage right. Mom appeared from a side door wearing white makeup on her face and a black outfit. Why was she dressed like a mime? Was Halloween early this year?

She took a seat at the organ and stretched her fingers, paused to push her hair off her shoulders and began playing in earnest. The lyrics to Melissa Manchester's "Don't Cry Out Loud" played all around me as the red velvet drapes on stage pulled back, revealing a silver screen. A movie played in that shaky, sepia tone of long ago. A title card announced:

"Cor Assundra Sie Elijah Delomary dé Cãe Naqoboèst Hêgo Hava Tubo."

The Life and Times of Elijah Delomary Who Almost Had It All. I craned my neck around. Why was I here? What was this?

An old-time villain appeared, wearing black boots, pants, cape, and black mask. He dragged a flailing boy to the train tracks. The boy struggled. Cut to a train racing toward the villain and the boy, steam billowing toward the brown sky.

The villain tied the boy to the train tracks and pointed to a maiden dressed in white and lashed to an old, gnarled oak tree.

A card read: You knew I had to stop you. A spell cast by your mother did this. Now in order to win the war, you must go!

The movie faded before the train reached the boy. Cut to a modern pool. A boy swimming laps. Lights flickered. The water bubbled and spun counterclockwise. The boy struggled. A man, the boy's father, walked around scoffing and holding up a sign: Why Ask For My Opinion?

The scene changed again. The boy ran down a street in the rain. The boy's sister held up a sign that read: "Being the Best Totally Erases All the Mistakes You Made, Cor!"

The music changed to "Under the Bridge." The screen darkened. My gaze fell to my hands, which were growing into the armrests. I wanted to leave. I needed to get out of here. A drum roll. The screen lit up, and I was in April's house a few days after breaking up with Austin. April loved to have parties at her house. Her parents worked long hours. The big, old house felt lonely. Parties livened it up. April leaned against the sink and sighed, "Oh, Elijah, why did you do that?"

I put on my sunglasses. She took them off.

"You're not Bono."

"Yes, I am," I said. "A gay Bono."

"I don't even know who Bono is," she confessed. "Must be some weird guy who messes things up just because."

"He's like the greatest rocker of all time."

April shrugged, handing me lemon-lime soda with grenadine in it. A Shirley Temple in a red plastic cup. She knew I hated drinking. April handed out cups of beer to some strangers streaming through the kitchen heading to the backyard to smoke weed.

"You broke up with Austin, but what I don't get is why you didn't just talk to him?"

I stared into my cup watching the pinkish liquid bubble.

"You know I can't talk to people about what's wrong with me."

April reached into a cupboard for more vodka. She handed it to Tina who was giggling. She was buzzed. "Eli, stop doing this to yourself."

"What am I doing?

"Sabotaging yourself."

I laughed. "It's not my fault."

She looked at me. "It's not? You're terrible when you're alone?"

I nodded, staring at the copper pots hanging from an iron rack over the center of the island. She reached into another cupboard and handed Tyrell a bag of chips. She looked back at me, frowning. I looked at my Shirley Temple.

"Maybe you just don't understand, April."

"Understand what?"

"Coming out. Being gay. The pressure and the anger and the sadness and how it all fucks with your mind."

"You're right, I don't," she said. "But you know, I come out, in a way, every day. Being biracial: Asian and White. People look at me and ask me where I'm from. Why I look the way I do."

I thought about that. "It's different, April. People make laws against us. Just last weekend Monsignor O'Reilly preached that gays were going to burn in hell. Mom stormed out."

April sighed. "I'm sorry Eli," she said. "I guess I don't understand."

"I snapped, April," I told her. "I couldn't take the heat. I hurt Austin and I'm afraid I'll do it again."

She looked out the window. I followed her gaze. Kevin dancing. He waved to her and me.

"Love hurts sometimes, Eli, but you have to talk. You can't bottle it up inside."

"Maybe it's easier to love someone when you're straight. You never question who you love. You don't have to accept that about yourself first. You don't have to learn to love yourself and *then* love another person."

She looked at me.

Silence.

The plastic clock ticked over the door to the dining room.

"I know it was hard for your parents to love each other. But that doesn't mean it has to be hard for you. Austin adores you. Just talk to him. Okay?"

Kevin appeared at the sliding glass door. "April, come on. It's "Beautiful People"! Our song!"

April patted my hand. "It's going to be okay."

I leaned against the counter, staring at the clock for an hour. The hour hand read 2:00 AM. I turned to the windows over the sink. April and Kevin leaned against each other outside. I wandered around the house. The karaoke machine flashed and glowed in a corner, urging me to pick up the mic and sing something, anything. April's grandma, the chaperone of the party, snored away in a recliner. Puxhàredo. April would have her deaf grandma chaperone the party!

I stepped up onto the makeshift stage. I made my selection, waited for the numbers to count down, tapped the mic, and inhaled.

I finished the song and put down the mic. Someone clapped. Someone shouted, "Faggot, shut up."

I hated *that* word. The F word. Like a knife tearing into my flesh every time someone tossed it at me. I dismissed it. I had to, but over a lifetime, wouldn't all these little cuts add up? Maybe people hurled it at us so we would die, go away, their problem solved.

I opened the front door and stepped outside. I was in the desert. Joshua Tree. The stars a riot of light and color. I caught my breath, *gosh this was beautiful.* Lightning flashed in the distance. The summer monsoon rains. Every summer heavy rains fell in the desert of Southern California, Arizona, and New Mexico.

Thunder rumbled. Clouds smothered the stars and burst over the desert. I was perched next to a raging torrent of water. A flash flood. The desert was notorious for dry, rocky arroyos turning into raging rivers during the monsoon rains.

A flash of lightning lit up the darkness. Austin appeared across the stream. No. He was in the raging river, clinging to the top of his car He must have been caught on the road when the flash flood hit.

"Austin! Austin!" I screamed. He screamed back at me in Cantonese.

I didn't understand him. I was screaming in the Old Language. Reaching for him.

He didn't understand me. I pronounced his name *Ow-stihn* in the Old Language.

A wave washed over him, and he disappeared.

"AUSTIN!"

Lightning flashed. I was blinded momentarily. The scene changed. I floated in the ocean off Malibu. Sunny held a phone to his ear by the white limo in the parking lot off the beach. My fucking family, we had a security detail.

"Richer than God."

The water dipped. Seagulls circled overhead. I scrambled onto my board; only a shadow fell over me. I turned just in time to see the tsunami hurtling toward me.

Fifty feet high. I was going to die.

"AUSTIN!"

I plunged underwater and struggled for air. A flash of light. My lungs filled with air. I ran as hard as I could and my side hurt and my legs were like jelly. A torrent opened over me. A runner stumbled in front of me.

"WATCH OUT!"

Too late. I flew through the air, hit something immoveable and spun over it.

I crashed to the pavement headfirst.

"Elijah, don't you know it's human to make mistakes. It's how we grow as people." I heard Arnulfo's voice on the periphery. "Please, accept that you made a mistake with Austin. You don't need to do all this to prove your value. You're worthy to be loved and to love; ignore what they tell you. You matter and your love matters. Let go of the past and grow, honey."

And then I heard another voice, "Stay with me, Elijah." It was Sunny. "Come on, laddie, come on…"

Part Two

THE GRAVITY OF ELIJAH AND AUSTIN
COR DOLORIMENTA
—THE HURTING

All I see through the dirty windshield is darkness,
I'm heading nowhere at 100 miles an hour.
We're all dying inside,
Why can't we find the light?
Are we running in circles?
Waiting to feel good, feel good, feel good?
At the sleazy fuel station, hot wind blowing sand in my face,
Sandstorms bearing down on us,
They never promised us happiness,
Back in the car and turn up the radio,
Block out the pain.
Drive all night,
When the sun rises,
On your doorstep, I catch my breath,
Ignore the fear bubbling inside.
A knock,
Oh my,
You smiled,
Maybe we can move past the hurting,
Because you and me,
Can turn dark to light,
We're all made of light.

Xeimei du Cascàdayez
Poems of Modern Minerva Vol. 2

Chapter Thirteen

A Human Octopus

MY EYES FLUTTERED open. I focused on the room looming around me. All white. Machines beeping. A nurse held my wrist, taking my pulse. Tubes were inserted into my appendages. I realized I was a human octopus. I checked the window.

Rain.

"I heard Máurso intervened," a white-haired man said to the nurse in purple scrubs.

"I know that's right," a young nurse replied. "He was behind the boy after the accident and caught Zid'dra, and, well, sent that mother-fracker packing."

"I blame the Còngréhassa," the man said. "Leaving the boy almost defenseless."

"Heads will roll, Doctor," the nurse said. "He's a Delomary. The Bane of the Gloom."

I choked.

"Welcome back, hon." The pretty Black nurse smiled. Her smile lit up the room. "We've been worried about you."

I tried to talk. My mouth didn't work.

"It's okay. You just rest. I'll get you some water."

She patted my hand and exited with the white-haired doctor. I closed my eyes.

Heavy footsteps echoed in the hall. My brain whirred and rattled slowly. I wrestled to reengage my brain. Who was outside? I flipped through images in my mind, trying to place the footsteps with a face. A hand touched mine. Strong, yet tender. I opened my eyes.

Austin towered over me. He peered at me through his thick black glasses. My heart soared on seeing his ridiculous glasses. He tucked his hair behind his ears.

"Eli," he said. *Eo echàlluno.* I exhaled. He held my hand. I closed my eyes. I was with Dad at the club house. The server handed him the beer with spit in it. I grabbed it before he could drink it. I set it down and told him: "Dad, you don't have to drink that. Just relax, will you?" And then I was in the desert. The river ran backward. Austin's car emerged from the river and ended up back on the highway. Austin's face appeared in the open driver's side window. He honked. "Get in, love." I reached for the passenger door, and he grinned. "Austin, there was a car wash— I wanted to go in and come out clean, but I'm not dirty, it turns out." I cried...

I woke up. The sun set long ago; the overhead lights burned brightly. I panicked. Where was Austin? Was I dreaming? Oh no. Where was I? Mom peered around the open door. "Elijah? Are you awake?"

I nodded. A surge of happiness rushed through my body.

"What happened, Mom?"

"You had an accident when you were running. You were pushed over an unused news rack and hit your head hard on the curb."

I touched my head.

"They put you in a coma. To reduce brain swelling."

"That's scary, Mom."

"You also broke some ribs and your left arm. In two places. And your right leg.”

"So, you’re saying I lost the race.”

Mom laughed. She squeezed my arm.

"You’re ridiculous, darling.” Tears ran down her face.

"Fuck, Mom, I was so close.”

"Language.”

"Puxhàredo!”

"LANGUAGE!”

"Um, Mom, if I broke my body, why do I feel awesome?”

"Morphine, sweetie.”

"Gotcha,” I said. "Can we keep some at home?”

"No, way,” she said. "I love you, Elijah.” She added, "I was so worried. Everyone was worried. Thank God you’re safe. Maybe close your eyes again.”

"Mom, I had a dream about Dad. I told him to ease up.”

"Close your eyes, darling.”

I agreed and fell asleep. No dreams. I woke up. Weak sunlight spilled in the window.

Austin read to me from *The Cat Who Played Post Office*, the hardcover version we bought together at Books and Things on San Fernando Boulevard after Chinese New Year. The city had a parade. A blur of red and gold. Dragons with furry eyelashes. The beating of drums. Firecrackers. We had been holding hands. I loved the Lunar New Year. Families come together from all over the world to eat, drink, and be together. Family. I loved my family. I closed my eyes as he continued reading with his perfect King’s English.

He stopped reading.

My eyes opened. "Don’t stop, please.”

Austin cheered, "Oi, mate, you’re awake.” He came over, holding Little Ocho in his hands. "I was so worried, mate. Ocho needs his papa!” I grinned and chuckled. My side burned. The morphine masked my broken ribs.

"Austin, I am sorry.”

He peered at me through his glasses.

"Eli, it's okay."

"Austin, I mean…"

He squeezed my hand. "Eli, I promised I'd never leave your side. I'd always be with you. And I am always going to be with you."

Fat tears burst from my eyes.

"It's okay to cry, Eli. You know that? To make mistakes. We're still boys."

"The only two gay boys in the world."

"Not really. But you are my Eli, and I love you."

"Austin, I was stupid. I'm sorry."

He held my hand, and I fell asleep.

My eyes drifted open slowly. I spotted Barn standing by the windows. Austin held my hand. "Eli, were you doing all those things to prove to me that loving you was worth it?"

I shot a look at Barn. He rolled his eyes.

"No, I mean. Well, maybe."

"Eli," Austin said, squeezing my hand tighter, "you are one daft cow, you know that? That brain of yours. *Destes cavananjas retoreisa rien tro bien.* I think you need a new brain. You don't need to win gold for me to love you."

"My brains do work okay," I repeated the phrase to Austin. "I…uh…"

"You two should just be together, already," Barn said, turned to face me, then leaned against the windowsill.

"Do you want to be with me, mate?"

I watched him. My stomach was sour.

"What if I…?"

"Well, you dumped me twice," Austin said, "but we can leave that in the past. Do you love me?"

I concentrated on his beautiful face. He wiggled an eyebrow.

I laughed. "I love you so much it hurts."

Austin beamed. "Yeah, more than Little Ocho?"

"Hush."

He howled.

"Do you promise to not turn your back on Ol' Kangy again?"

"I do."

"Swear?"

"Pinkie promise!" Barn said. "So it's a binding covenant, mates."

We interlocked our pinkies.

"I think you've learned the errors of your ways, Eli."

"Yeah?"

"Yes, life is better with Kangy. Yeah?"

"Yes."

"And you know Kangy is tired of seeing his Eli doing all these bleedin' extracurriculars. Can we just chill a little?"

I glanced at my arm hanging beside me in a sling. My leg in a cast.

"Yes, I think I can do that."

"Kangy and Eli, together forever? I scrawled it on a tree."

"Yes, Kangy."

"Don't forget me!" Barn interjected. "I want to spend time with my best mates too, yeah?"

"You're too short, mate!"

"Shut it, Lostin!"

We all laughed. Until my ribs hurt. And then my eyes were heavy.

I woke up hearing a terrific crash, glass shattering, and a deep voice cursing. My eyes flew open.

Máurso stood at the foot of the bed, a frown stitched on his face.

"I tried to open the door and sneak in, but I forget my own strength, laddie."

A cat hopped on his shoulder. Another jumped onto the bed.

A nurse walked in and glanced at the smoldering door.

"We can't have this mess, sir."

"I'll take care of it," Máurso grumbled. "I'm a god, you know." He snapped a finger. The wall flew back into place, the shards of glass rearranged themselves in the window that looked out into the hallway. The flames and smoke vanished.

"Wow, cool, Your Eminence," I said.

"Aye, well if you can't fix your mess, what kinda god are you?"

Máurso sat in a chair, but it crumpled under his weight, and he fell to the floor. He cursed up a storm before summoning a chair made of concrete; he took a seat and reached for his cats. He hauled one onto his lap. Another climbed up the leg of his track pants.

"Well, looks like you didn't win the marathon."

I gulped. "Were you hoping I would?"

"No, laddie," Máurso said, reaching for a cat who had appeared out of thin air and was now climbing his dreads. "I want you to focus on Sem Xen Ou! You are becoming a valiant Coaugelo. You have destroyed many monsters and shown great teamwork."

"I don't think I'll be doing any fighting any time soon," I squeaked. "Am I out of the Dáu Xhà?"

"Don't be daft!" Máurso roared, leaning down to rub the back of a black cat who had slithered from under my bed. "Ach, you Delomarys and your incessant need to be number one. You get better. You always have a place with me at the Dáu Xhà."

"Really?"

"Aye," Máurso said. "And I'm a god, so you better believe that's a command!"

"Okay, Dáumo." I paused. "Um, is it true? Zid'dra was at the marathon?"

Máurso leaned down to pet the black cat at his feet. "Aye," he said. "Seems he was preoccupied with you. Hurting you."

"Yeah."

"But you're alive," Máurso said. "He's one twisted, monster." Máurso said, "He likes to play games. Mind games. Say one thing, mean another. You need to stay away from the darkness."

"I know."

"Anyway, he won't be bothering you."

"Really?"

"I got him in a headlock, then pretended he was a discus and I was back on Morra Êímpagońena at the *Collosseo*, and I spun around and around and sent that devil flying. He'll be ricocheting off the tops of mountains all over the planet for a while."

"Thanks, Dáumo."

"Well…" Máurso wasn't into thank-yous and emotions. He stood. His cats scurried up his body, sitting on his shoulder. "You take it easy, lad. And come see me when you're better."

"For sure!"

In the blink of an eye, Máurso and his cats disappeared.

*

I SPENT MY seventeenth birthday in the hospital. How awesome was that? No, it wasn't great at all. Trust me. Nurses coming and going in and out of my room all night long to check on me, waking me abruptly every time I finally would drift off, so I couldn't really get a good night sleep. Other times, I woke up, panicking, heart racing, body drenched in sweat, struggling to breathe. The darkness still had its clutches on me. Along with my newly broken bones. Perfect way to usher in seventeen.

Mom, the aunts and uncles and Barn and Stylo and Tory came to celebrate. Tory brought me a cake shaped like a penis—colored pink.

"I heard you came out," she said, walking in with the cake. "I mean, I'm not surprised."

"You're not?"

"Um, no. Your teddy bears, all those damn scented candles you used to hoard."

We laughed. Barn hugged me and wished me a happy birthday.

*

MOM STAYED WHEN the others left. The nurses said visiting hours were over, but Mom reminded the nurses that our name was outside the front door. Great-Great-Grandpa had donated money to build the hospital.

The darkness settled around me, like a blanket slowly smothering me. My heart raced. I thought I was calm, but I guess I wasn't. The darkness stalked me during the day now. Mom held my hand. I was better for a moment. I opened my mouth to talk; only I stammered. I was trying so hard to force my tongue to work, I needed to break free from the darkness and talk to Mom. Mom could help me. I knew she could.

"Honey, is something wrong?"

I kept stammering.

"Do I need to call the nurse?"

I shook my head.

"Mom...I need...um...um."

"Pee-pee? Poo-poo?"

I laughed, which made her smile. "MOM!!!" We looked at each other. "Mom, I need your help." I can't believe that laughing made it easier to talk.

"What's going on, Elijah?"

"There's this darkness that hurts me. I can't sleep, Mom. I can't relax. I'm scared all the time.

"I wish you had told me sooner."

I contemplated the tubes sticking out of me. I was a human octopus.

"The Octopus of Death." That's what everyone jokingly called our family and our corporation.

My family. Puxhàredo. Not perfect, but my family. My octopus.

"Elijah," Mom said, "this isn't the end of the world."

I looked at her. "What do you mean?"

"There's a solution to everything, darling."

"Really?"

"Yes."

"We'll get rid of the darkness and get you better."

"You think?"

"I know."

"Mom, you look so relaxed right now."

"I feel more relaxed. Happy almost."

"Wow, I never thought I'd hear you say that word."

"I feel like I have a new lease on life. With you. With Tory. Things are going to be better. I know it. And I've learned a lot in our support group. I can help you.

"I was talking with Arnulfo and Stylo, and, well, Arnulfo has his own practice and works with queer youth. I'd like for you to see him one-on-one. I think seeing someone who went through coming out and being gay will really help you."

"I thought you said I was better."

"Honey, you are better, but I think you need more help. A lot has happened to you these past few years. I have a suspicion the darkness is part of that trauma."

"Trauma?"

"Yes, darling. I didn't recognize it before, but I do now. You need some help."

"Am I like Tory?"

"Too much pressure." Mom grimaced. "From me. I'm sorry. This is my fault and I'm going to fix it."

"What about the support group?"

"I think you will get better with one-on-one help with a therapist without me in the room."

I couldn't believe this. I had never thought about that. I felt a sliver of light in the darkness.

"You're going to be okay, Eli," she said, squeezing my hand.

"Mom, I'm worried..."

"You don't have to be."

"Yeah?"

"I think talking to a gay therapist will help you navigate through all the feelings you've had that have made you stuck."

"Stuck?"

"You're stuck, Elijah," she said, "between being your old self and your new self. And then you fell in love with Austin while navigating a big transition. That was a lot to bite off."

"I hate myself."

"No," she whispered, "I love you. You are strong and brave and kind and love so deeply." Then she added, "I know what it's like to be sixteen. I was once."

"One thousand years ago?"

"Behave yourself!"

"Okay, Mom."

"You have a choice, Elijah"

"I do?"

"You always have choices."

"What do you mean?"

"We both have always had choices, even though I made you think you didn't, and that's my fault. You have a say in your life."

She held my hand for a while. I closed my eyes. Then I thought about Austin.

"I really worry that I'll mess things up with Austin."

Mom shook her head. "No, way," she said. "Don't be negative. You can fix this."

"How do I do that?"

"By being there for him," she said. "Being a boyfriend means you stick together no matter what. You talk to each other about problems, feelings. You work together to navigate life. I didn't do that with your father. I was part of the problem too. Elijah, you should know that. Sure, Dad walked out. But maybe I left him no choice."

"Mom!" I screamed, "Mom!" *Why was she saying this?*

"No, Elijah. Our marriage was complicated. We're very different people. I think a part of me was drawn to your father because of how my parents reacted to me marrying him. He was no one like they wanted me to marry. I felt rebellious. But then, it turned out that marrying him hurt me not my parents. And that's the thing, Elijah. Love is a gift, not a weapon or something to be used to hurt others. I've learned that."

My body ached. The machines whirred and beeped.

"I've been talking to someone, you know."

"A therapist?"

"Joyce, the family therapist. She's helped me see what I did wrong."

"Wow, Mom... Wait, are you okay?"

"Sure," she said. "I'm fine. Look, what I'm saying is that love is work. You have to work on being a good boyfriend. You can't just run away when the going gets tough."

I stared at the blanket. "I did do that. Like Dad."

"Who knows, but Elijah you were going through a lot."

"Too much pressure?" I shook my head.

"Yes," Mom said. "And now it's time for you to just relax. Summer is starting early for you. You'll be in the hospital another two weeks, and you can't go back to school before summer ends."

"My classwork…"

"You'll do it at home. I've set everything up."

I leaned back against the pillows, closing my eyes.

"We're going to get through this together, darling. We'll sort out this darkness business and get you on the right path. I'm here for you, okay?"

I leaned back. Mom was going to help me. Mom was going to help me get better.

"Mom," I said after a while, "I heard there was a commotion at the Còngréhassa. Do you know what happened?"

Mom pursed her lips. "Yes. I flew to London and called for a *Cáuro*."

"A quorum?"

"Of all the heads of the families," she said. "And I read them the riot act. The *Estàntus*. You almost died. It was because of them! You shouldn't have had to make the decision you did. And I heard how they were going to penalize you for studying with Máurso," Mom said. "Well, I used my political capital thanks to my allies and friends and half the Estàntus resigned. There are going to be elections now. No more of the same people running the show for ages. The Alliance has calcified. We desperately need change. So, we can meet the demands of the future. The coven is stronger. We have to be prepared."

"Um, Mom?

"Yes, darling?"

"Are you saying you fired some Estàntus?"

Mom chuckled. "You look tired; get some sleep."

I closed my eyes. Mom went to bat for me. That made me happy.

Chapter Fourteen

The Gravity of Austin

TWO WEEKS CAME and went. Dr. Hu came by and checked my vitals and cleared me to go home. A nurse came and detached me from the many machines I was hooked up to. I was no longer an octopus. Mom signed off on my release, and Austin helped me out of bed and into a wheelchair.

"Finally free from this prison, love," he whispered in my ear, "and soon you'll be in love jail with Kangy, where you're going to get all better."

Sean poked his head in.

"How you doing, Elijah?"

"Better, Sean."

"Good to hear, sport." Usually I'd hate a nickname from someone dating Mom, but Sean was different. Sean was becoming like family. Mom glowed around him.

"Is it okay if he stays at my place, Belinda?" Austin asked. "My parentals and I wanted to celebrate his birthday."

Mom chewed on her lower lip. Sean came up behind her, putting his arm around her shoulders. "I think it'll be okay, Lin. Promise to have him back tomorrow? We would like to have him home."

Austin smiled. "Yes, I promise."

"Then have a good time," Mom said.

A few hours later, I was propped up in his bed, arm and leg in casts, sunlight filtering in the picture windows overlooking the Verdugo mountains. Ocho tucked under my arm, Meow-Meow and several other stuffed animals arranged on my lap.

Austin turned on his record player slipping "Violator" by Depeche Mode on. Then he ran downstairs to get us mango ice cream and lemonade. We lay in his big bed eating ice cream and listening to the music. My heart pounded. My anxiety crept back.

"It's not darkness, as you call it," Arnulfo told me when we had our first session in my hospital room. "You are suffering from an anxiety disorder."

"A what?"

"Anxiety. You have anxiety."

"So, I'm nuts, then?"

Arnulfo shook his head. "Anxiety is a normal thing. Mental health is important, Elijah. Don't diminish it by calling it names."

"I'm sorry."

"It's fine," Arnulfo said. "How long were you following that schedule of your Mom's?"

"Four years."

"And when did you come out?"

"Almost a year ago."

"And you came out to three hundred of your peers?"

I nodded.

"And you spent the most time with your dad in years? And you fell in love with your one and only gay best friend?"

I saw where he was going with this.

"That is a lot."

"Did you have any time for yourself?"

I laughed. "Come on, Arnulfo, my family is "richer than God." We don't have time."

"You're not your family. You're seventeen. Still a boy."

"I may be a man."

"Yes, you are becoming a man. But the pressures you've been feeling are not normal. You don't need to carry the burden for your family. Your mom can do that. And she knows that now."

"I mean…"

"No, Elijah. You are seventeen. You can start living your own life. And that means you can do whatever you want. Well, maybe when the boot is off and the cast."

We laughed. My eyes opened. I was in Austin's room. The record player hissed. I looked around. It was dark outside. Where was Austin?

"AUSTIN!"

I heard something outside in the hallway. A song. It sounded familiar. The door opened, Austin's face glowed from the light of white candles on a white frosted cake. He sang "Happy Birthday" to me in Cantonese. His parents beamed from behind him.

I blushed.

"Happy Birthday, love," Austin said, setting the cake down on the table he pushed over next to the bed.

I started crying. His parents looked at each other. Austin said something to them in Cantonese. They nodded and left the room. Austin stood over me, rubbing my hair with his hand.

"Let it out, love," he said over and over again, softly and gently.

Austin was, in essence, the blue ski parka he bought me when it got really cold last fall, durable on the outside, warm and soft on the inside. When I stopped crying, he sat beside me. "Tell me what's going on, love."

"I've been doing too much for too long and it caught up with me, Kangy."

"No kidding."

"When my powers were taken from me, I sort of lost who I

was...and I guess a part of me pushed myself to be a winner."

"What do you mean?"

"I figured that if I won Academic Decathlon and made the Olympic team and won the race I would finally be someone. A boy who had a purpose. I wanted recognition that I was someone."

"You did win."

"I lost the race to Disney Studios."

"You tried though," Austin said. "Besides, you have a purpose. To be you, that's all. Elijah Delomary."

"What do you mean?"

"You do everything for everyone else, without question. You followed your Mom's soddin' plan and that daft brand of hers. You sacrificed time to spend with me. You were there for me when I was confused about what it means to be who we are. You helped me come out. You tried so hard to be the perfect boyfriend. And when everything you did caught up with you, when the Còngréhassa found out about what Boxey was doing so we could be together, you accepted punishment to save Boxey. That showed me who you really are. You know what is right in every fiber of your being. You love deeply, Elijah. And I feel that love. And I love you."

I looked at Austin, sort of speechless.

"Elijah," Austin said, "I believe in you. I see you for who you are. And to me, you are a wonderful boy. The boy who, even without a plan or a brand, is everything I need to be happy. Just you. That makes Kangy happy."

"I'm happy with you too, Kangy."

Austin wrapped me in a big hug.

"Kangy, I have anxiety."

"Okay. A lot of people do."

"Arnulfo calls it an anxiety disorder."

"Okay, well, it can be treated?"

"Yes."

"Good, then I will help you."

"Kangy..."

"You are a wonderful, kind, and loving boy," he said. "You give everything to everyone else. Your family, that soddin' Alliance. Even that slag, Devlina. You listen to her even after everything she did to you."

"I trust too easily."

"You see the good in people...monsters. Remember the M'ma you let go from the backyards? How many Encantreinus would spare a monster in their own backyard?"

"I mean, it didn't do anything wrong. It was hungry."

"See?" Austin said. "You know right from wrong, you see beyond titles and roles and do what is fundamentally right."

"And you pushed yourself to become a Coaugelo. You didn't just give up. You never give up. You are brave and strong, and I see who you are, someone who sees past all the others have covered you up with, and that is the boy I love."

"Kangy, I love you."

"I love you too."

"I have a broken arm and leg and ribs. Maybe I should have given up."

"No way," Austin said. "It's not in your DNA."

"Arnulfo explained that I'm having panic attacks caused by severe anxiety over the last year. I call them the darkness. I'm afraid that you might get—"

"Eli," Austin said, taking my hand, "I am here for the good, the bad, and the ugly. Got it?"

"But the panic attacks. I'll keep you up. They happen at night, mostly," I explained. "I freak out and can't sleep. Start losing my shit."

"That's what I'm here for."

"But I don't want you to suffer."

"*Aietto*," Austin said, "I am here for you. Everything. You can wake me up, and we'll deal with the panic attacks together. I am here for you, no matter what." Austin then added, "I have nothing to do really."

"School!"

He shrugged. "Without my best mate, my love, with me at school, it doesn't really matter, yeah?"

"Kangy, I don't—"

"I want to help you, Eli."

"It's terrifying, Kangy. The darkness, the panic attacks"

He rubbed my head. "I'm here for you. I want to help you through this."

I sighed, and I cried again.

"I don't deserve you."

He shook his head. "Stop saying that, Eli. You are a beautiful boy," he said. "We deserve each other. We found each other. I love you, Eli." I leaned on his shoulder.

"Have some cake. It's devil's food cake with vanilla frosting."

"My favorite." I sat up and watched the candles flicker.

"Make a wish, then blow them out, love."

I knew what my wish was. It was coming true. Like a cherry blossom unfolding as winter receded and Spring arrived. And then, in an instant, anxiety barreled at me like a speeding train in the old sepia tone silent movies at the Million Dollar Theater in Downtown LA. My arms and legs were tied to the tracks. It was coming. I closed my eyes. I couldn't stop it.

Austin's mom made chamomile tea and came in, and she sat next to me and she chanted softly. Slowly my heart began to beat normally, and the numbness in my arm went away. Austin held my hand the whole time.

After a while, Austin helped me downstairs to the family room. We sat in front of a roaring fire.

Austin Sr. and Cecilia sipped wine and listened to a famous Cantonese diva on the stereo. They were talking shop, about their day tracking down a new coven in Newhall. Serving a cease and desist letter from the League. Having to battle with the not-so-happy Àzmadus in the new coven. Almost being sucked dry of their life force.

"Good thing we brought along fluffy," Austin Sr. said. Fluffy was their new feline assistant, currently curled up in a random box in a corner near the fireplace. Monsters didn't like cats. "Once she appeared, they all started getting hives and sneezing and easily gave up."

They laughed. Austin laughed. I laughed. I battled new monsters, in my head.

Austin Sr. talked about the night Austin was born. A meteor shower glowed over Hong Kong. It was a good omen. Cecilia shrugged. "I was in labor for twenty hours with him; not so good."

Austin commented, "I didn't want to leave your womb, Mum. It was so comfy."

We all laughed. As the fire began to burn low, and the wine bottle was empty, I realized I had to go to bed soon. I felt a jab in my stomach.

"I'm scared to sleep," I whispered in Austin's ear.

He nuzzled my face.

"I'll be with you."

Austin carried me upstairs. I couldn't take a shower with my arm and leg in casts, so Austin helped me to wash my body with a washcloth and shampoo my hair in the sink.

"I'm scared, Kangy. Sleep is the worst."

Austin knelt beside me as I sat on the toilet seat, my hair dripping down my neck.

"What happens at bedtime, love?"

"I don't know how to sleep anymore."

"What do you mean?"

"It's like a door. I can't figure out how to get inside to sleep."

Austin stood up to dry my hair with a towel. "Fortunately, you have thousands of years of evolution on your side, love."

"What do you mean?"

"Your body is built to sleep."

"But I don't know how to sleep anymore."

He kissed me on the top of my head. "You will."

Afterward, Austin helped me brush my teeth. (Technically, I had a hand to brush my teeth, but he offered, and I was following Arnulfo's advice, allowing myself to be taken care of.)

A few minutes later, we were in bed. I lay there as he breathed softly, already on his own voyage into the land of Nod. My heart pounded; my head felt warm. My throat closed up.

"You should consider taking anti-anxiety medicine, Elijah," Arnulfo had said at session. "I can talk to your mom."

"No," I said. "We don't take medicine in our family."

"Why?"

"We're Delomarys."

"What does that mean?"

"We have an image to uphold," I said. "*Nunma in viacadeimo. I'm not a victim.*"

"Surely some of your family take medicine."

I shrugged.

"I'm scared of taking medicine, Arnulfo," I explained. "I pore over side-effects, and I'm convinced that something terrible will happen to me."

"That's part of your anxiety. I think you've spent so much time worrying about bad things happening and this 'brand,' as your mother calls it, 'becoming tarnished' that you're always trying to predict things. But you don't have to. Let's be positive. Medicine could help you. Help us work on treating the root of your anxiety."

I must have fallen asleep, but then I woke up, my heart racing.

"AUSTIN! AUSTIN!"

Austin sat up rubbing his eyes, "Eli?" he whispered. "Are you all right, love?"

"AUSTIN! My heart—it won't stop pounding. I'm going to have a heart attack and die."

He wrapped his arms around me. "No, no, you are not, Eli."

He sat up and leaned against the wall. I laid my head on his lap. He held me.

"Close your eyes, mate." And he sang to me. "Sometimes I feel like my only love is Eli Delomary, my Eli Delomary. Lonely as I was, together we fly."

"That's...ama...zing."

After a while, I fell asleep.

Chapter Fifteen

La Biscayne, Minerva, 010010

I WOKE UP suddenly, my heart pounding. The anxiety disappeared for a few hours, but it roared back once my eyes opened. A cacophony of bells rang outside the blackout drapes pulled across the windows. Odd—without any churches nearby.

Austin splayed out on the other side of the bed fast asleep. I sat up, watching him. He was adorable when he slept. And peaceful. Wait—I swore he was smiling. His arms were tangled up with Foxy while Ocho was plopped on top of his head. I glanced at the clock. It was almost seven—he was going to be late to school! I shook him gently. He grumbled.

"Kangy, you have to go to school."

"I'm skiving off today, love."

I scratched my head.

"Playing *hooky*!" He flattened his voice into an American accent. I broke out laughing. He was so cute when he translated his slang words for me.

"And," Austin said, slipping out of bed, Ocho and Foxy falling onto the rumpled sheets behind him, "I have a surprise for you."

My body hurt. With a cast on my arm and leg, I struggled to sleep in my favorite position, on my side, curled up in a ball like a cat. I had to sleep pretty much sitting up. Not that I did much sleeping with my anxiety simmering below the surface.

"Surprise?"

"Yeah." Austin grinned. He paused to stretch, then crossed the room to the drapes. "You are so going to be awed and amazed."

"What's outside? Is it another sunny day? If so, I'm already happy. Too much rain this year."

"Better."

"Really?"

Austin pushed the drapes apart. Sunlight poured over him and into the room. I squinted.

"Here, let me help you to the window." Austin crossed the room to the bed, leaning down to help me up. He held out his arm. "Lean on me, love."

We crossed the room slowly. Near the windows I noticed the plate glass was gone, replaced with leaded glass windows with a diamond pattern at the top.

"Did you replace your windows?"

"Nope."

He pushed the windows open, and warm, moist air buffeted my face. The sound of bells peeled outside, and the heady scent of jasmine and orchid wafted in my nose.

"Wait, we're not in Burbank?"

Austin shook his head. "No, mate, that is just a gramora." He waved to the room. The air rippled, and his bedroom disappeared, replaced by a huge space with a vaulted ceiling painted with gold leaf and studded with...rubies? Emeralds?

"Are we in the Tàcqo Paláujo?"

Austin nodded. "Yeah, mate. While you were asleep, Asmàra, the

Queen's Maiden, came, and we whisked you here to La Biscayne!"

I didn't know what to do or say. Instead, I turned and faced the open window. My eyes drifted from the towering Canary Island palms rising above the formal gardens several stories below, bursting with irises, roses, mums, dahlias, and birds-of-paradise. Fountains, studded with diamonds and emeralds, tinkled while courtesans wearing elegant robes of red and purple strolled among the sycamore and elm trees.

"Oh my God, Kangy!" I shouted, turning and falling into his arms.

He planted kisses all over my face. "The queen is expecting us for brunch soon."

I turned again and leaned against the window seat, tears in my eyes. Fat white clouds drifted over the city, magnificent buildings made of marble and granite and decorated with jewels or painted in bright reds or soft greens or warm yellow and gentle terracotta with red tile roofs, towers, parapets, and domes stretched across a wide valley divided by the meandering Reo Calargo Dêtillo, named for the reclusive Purple Dragon dwelling among piles of gold and jewels in the bowels of Morra Êímpagońena. In the distance, Mount Olympus loomed over the city, its summit shrouded in fog and clouds.

"Austin, I mean, I can't believe…"

"Love, I know you missed being here in La Biscayne. Queen Minerva reached out to your mum a few weeks ago. She invited us for a retreat with her as a gift for all your hard work."

"Oh, shit, no way. But I mean, I didn't win the marathon, and I'm supposed to be in *Oklahoma!*"

"Relax mate, the show will go on. Barn, it turns out, is a wee bit obsessed with the stage. Katie suggested he fill in for you, and apparently, he's super into it."

"No way."

"Yes, he's tried to grow a moustache and got elevator shoes so he's taller. To be a judge, you have to be tall, or so he thinks."

"Ah, Barn…"

There was a knock at the double doors, covered with gilt. I eyed the door. Austin winked and walked across the room filled with overstuffed, formal chairs and marble-topped tables, several uncomfortable sofas set around an immense green, marble fireplace. Two chandeliers with emeralds, rather than crystals, glowed above the four-poster bed set among gilt-framed paintings of what appeared to be famous figures in Minervan history. I noticed a king on a rearing horse slaying blood-thirsty Orgmas. Magic coursed through the room.

Austin opened the door.

"I'm here too!" A familiar voice said. Stylo walked in the room wearing a green suit and boots. "Excited to see me, Eli?"

"Stylo!" I tried to get up and run to her, but I merely toppled over onto the window seat.

"Easy, brother," she said, walking in, her eyes scanning the room. The wallpaper featuring vines slithering from floor to ceiling, white flowers blooming.

"This place is sick," Stylo said. "You know, I've never been to La Biscayne or Old Earth or, for that matter, anywhere other than to the Philippines to see my grandma."

"The Tàcqo Paláujo is enormous," I said.

"And there are freaking jewels everywhere." Stylo lowered her voice. "When I was given a tour of the gardens, while you two were sleeping and doing who knows what—" She winked at Austin. "I was getting intoxicated from all the magical flowers. I tried to use my pocket knife to pry a few rubies from a fountain before Àsmàra stopped me. She's the queen's main chick. Her Chief-of-Staff, and she is drop-dead gorge. Holy crap. Skin the color of cinnamon, green eyes, and tall. I can climb her!"

"Enough of the sex talk." Austin waved a finger at her. "You're here as a guest, not to bang the Queen's Maiden."

"Oh, she ain't no maiden," Stylo said. "She's too hot to be celibate." Stylo paused. "Is she?"

"I don't think so," I said. "I think that's just an archaic name for the chief of staff."

"Good." Stylo sat on a green silk settee near the bed. "Oh, not comfortable; anyway, maybe I'll invite her to drinks. We're legal to drink here, and there's a sick dyke bar just outside the gates. They have Drag King shows and play heavy metal. My kinda place."

"We need to get ready," Austin said.

"Go ahead." Stylo moved to an overstuff chair, sticking her feet up on a green ottoman. She pulled out a magazine titled, "*Ravolta Santuagu!*" or Minerva's version of *People* magazine. She began flipping through it while Austin and I went to the bathroom.

A half hour later, we lounged on several green upholstered chairs in the antechamber of the Queen's Salon, a breathtaking room with a vaulted ceiling decorated with a fresco of Immortals and Magicals battling monsters.

A bolt of lightning crashed onto the thick green Persian rug at our feet. I looked up. Cupidêro sent bolts of lightning at a battalion of Máunadas. Áucúitus rushed down at a group of Coaugelus running toward a group of Àzmadus. Fire breathing elephant-like monsters circled in the corners, smoke drifting from the fresco into the room and swirled around the eight chandeliers illuminating the vast room.

"They're really fighting up there!" Stylo exclaimed. A flaming spear rushed by her; she ducked.

"I don't know if I like this room."

Propped up in a chair, I tried to figure out how to move around the city. My casts limited my mobility. I bit my lip, taking in the bank of elaborate, gilded mirrors in front of me reminding me of my trip to Versailles with Mom and Tory two years ago. My eyes wandered over gilt-framed paintings of dour looking royals riding on unicorns or scowling on thrones floating among the stars. One seemed to be gawking at me. I looked away. My red hair.

Àsmàra, tall, slender, wearing all white, which set off her dark skin, her hair piled on her head and decorated with jewels, frowned at the green marble clock on the mantle.

"She's punctual," Àsmàra said. "She only has a half hour to brunch with you."

Irído, the Queen's Secretary, also dressed all in white, poked his finger on a tablet. "She knows she has a tight schedule today. Meetings with the historical society of La Biscayne, the Association of Architects and Alchemists, the Press Club of Greater Biscayne..."

"Maybe she's dithering in her closet... She never can decide what to wear."

"Something sensible," Irído said. "I tell her that. Every time. You go to her room. I'll speak to security and have them fan out across the palace to look for her."

Àsmàra disappeared through a secret door hidden behind a bookcase while Irído crossed the room and exited into the gardens.

"Uh, well, maybe no brunch for us?" Stylo frowned. "I was looking forward to *Itzpatchelès et Comardo* for breakfast. Floating flapjacks made from corn flour drenched in syrup from the magical Comardo tree. You can walk on your head after eating a few bites!"

"Does it heal broken arms and legs?" I lamented.

Stylo scratched her head. "I dunno."

Austin glanced at his watch. "This is odd, innit?"

A tapping sound stirred my attention. I scrutinized the bank of mirrors lining the wall across from me behind several potted palms.

A short, stout woman around twenty-eight with light-brown skin, green eyes, and dark, curly hair pulled into a ponytail rapped a large ruby ring on the glass. From the inside.

"Queen Minerva!" I gasped. She raised a finger to her lip, waving for us to come to the mirror.

"Wow! Wow!" Stylo shouted. "Holy moly is she a snack. Thick. I like it!"

Austin helped me up out of the chair. We walked over to the mirror. The glass rippled like water.

"*Dêpinin!*" Minerva whispered. "*Hava porr escondarr jaco nevo deseêja imféleiz ina delloma divêrsoallen!*"

Stylo slipped through the rippling glass, followed by me and Austin.

Queen Minerva, usually decked out in either flowing gowns studded with jewels or her military outfit in red and purple, was wearing a black and gold track suit, hoop earrings, and running shoes. "We have to sneak out," the queen said. "They have me on a loop of endless meetings. Everyday. Damn constitutional monarchy. I'm a figurehead."

"I'd love to be you," Stylo murmured.

"And you are?"

"I'm sorry," I said. "Mina, this is my friend Stylo."

Stylo dipped low to the floor. Minerva glanced at me.

"*Acenta la compleńuno?*"

"You don't curtsy here," I whispered to Stylo. "Just hold your hands together at your face and nod."

"Oh, I'm sorry, Your Honor...er..."

Minerva rolled her eyes. "Let's not," she said. "I'm not in the mood for that."

Austin placed his hands to his face and nodded to the queen.

"Austin Kang Jr.," she said, lifting up on her toes to embrace Austin. "How's your Nan? It's been too long since I saw her. Battling the monsters as usual?"

"Always, Mina."

The queen turned to me. "Oh, Eli," she said, "whatever happened to you? Monsters? Máunadas, I'd guess. They are a deplorable lot."

"I tripped, actually."

Mina laughed out loud. "Stop joking." She turned to Stylo. "This boy loves to pull my leg. In public, I have to be dour, unemotional. The living embodiment of the enduring legacy of Minerva, and this boy always cracks jokes and makes me lose it for a moment."

"I'm not joking." I frowned. "I tripped during a marathon."

"I'm pretty sure Zid'dra had something to do with it," Austin said. Stylo agreed.

"He's caught up in a marital spat between the Prince of Darkness and the Queen of the Gloom."

"Oh, Gods," Minerva said. "Those two wankers."

"Yeah," Austin agreed.

"Well, look, I have everything planned out," Minerva said. "We are going to play tourists. See the sights, pretend we're nobodies. Have some good food and drink and merriment. You deserve it, Eli."

"Wow," Stylo murmured. "The queen calls you Eli."

"I didn't catch your name?"

"Oh, um, I'm Stylo Gutierrez, Coaugela, Ma'am."

Minerva nodded. "*Enxhànctuno.*"

Stylo turned red. "Oh, me too."

Minerva's attention moved to me. "Well, you're certainly a mess, aren't you?"

"Can't you use some magic and just heal me up?"

"Unfortunately, looks like you have broken bones," Minerva said. "We could use magic to heal your bones, but when you crossed back into your dimension the magic would dissolve and you'd be back to square one. Spells and enchantments get mixed up in the transition. Might make it worse.

"Of course," she said, summoning a silver kaftan out of the air. "Magic can help you today. Put this on. It'll make it so you don't have any broken bones so we can travel unencumbered."

Austin helped me wrap myself in the kaftan. Once on me, a bright light flashed, and my casts disappeared.

"I can move my arms and legs!"

"Sick," Stylo said. "Can't you take it home?"

"I'm afraid it won't work past the early evening. This kaftan is a work in progress. My team of Encantreinus haven't worked out all the kinks yet," Minerva explained. "Now, come on, we have to escape the palace before Azzei finds me. And she always does."

Minerva snapped her fingers. In an instant, we stood on a square of grass under towering palm trees swaying in the warm, humid breeze. A tall, beaux arts-styled building rose above the square.

"This is Placa siec Pamas," Minerva explained. "The best street food is there on *Alladra Vazcáíno*. Who wants some *Itzapatchatelès* or

Mutùcoauqas?"

"Me! Me!" Stylo shouted. "Take me to the food!"

She grabbed Minerva's arm. Minerva raised an eyebrow and looked at me.

"She's enthusiastic."

"And friendly," Austin added.

"You have spunk," Minerva said. "Usually, I'd request they have your head for touching me, but I like your moxie." They took off walking toward a small alley set between two towering apartment blocks.

We spent a few hours stuffing ourselves with food from the many stalls lining the alley serving exotic and delicious dishes from all over Minerva. Dishes like *Lépoveitqa*, a noodle soup; *Ximplaràra*, eggs and cheese tort; *Áucolada*, meat, rice and veggies baked in a *Tlàmpoco*, an earthenware dish. Magicals mingled with Ordinaries. Taxadérmunus with Humboldtus.

"I can't believe I'm really seeing talking and walking stuffed animals. Look at that bear eating a burger!"

"The burger is made of cotton batting," Minerva said. "Taxadérmunus have a delicate system."

"Right," Austin added. "Meaning their insides are made of felt and yarn."

Several trees rose nearby, standing in pails of liquid, shaking their arms and talking animatedly. Leaves drifted to the ground.

"They're drinking their brunch," Minerva said. "Sparkling water, they love it."

A dozen alpacas wandered by, talking quickly about whether to have organic grass or organic alfalfa for lunch.

"Talking, living creatures," Stylo said. "I love it here! Why don't the alpacas at home talk?"

"They do," Minerva said. "Only on your Earth you can't understand them. Not advanced enough."

"Not enough magic, yeah?"

"True," Minerva agreed sipping a *Màclata*, a drink made from yogurt, pineapple and various spices. "*Es êtrango*, how your Earth is ten thousand years ahead of us and you have to plug in things to power them. And you don't have floating skyscrapers."

"What?" Stylo said. "The skyscrapers float here?"

"Child," Minerva said, "you really haven't been here before?"

"No."

"Well then, come on, let's go!"

We left the *Alladra Vazcáino* and trekked across the vast city, which resembled the grandeur and epic architecture of Paris or Barcelona or Rome, with the modernity of Tokyo or New York.

We rode on the bullet train to Càrrasola Rioja et Morra, home to the city's financial district, packed with skyscrapers hovering a hundred feet over blocks of low-rise stucco and tile buildings housing boutiques selling everything from jewelry to high-tech electronics to haute couture on streets shaded by massive jacaranda trees.

Minrva held up a green plastic card. "Shopping is on me!"

"Yes!" Stylo exclaimed. An hour later, we had accumulated several bags each.

"I don't want to carry these." Minerva handed them to Stylo. Stylo struggled for a few steps.

"Okay, you look like you're going to collapse." Minerva waved a hand. The bags disappeared into the air. "They'll be in your rooms."

We went sightseeing with the queen. We took an elevator to the top of the four hundred story *hmStabl Emprallen et Trijabutei sie La Biscayne* Building, Minerva led us to a private deck overlooking the city and pointed out landmarks to Stylo:

"The city stretches across the valley with the *Cáus sie Empras*, the Hills of the Queens—named for yours truly," Minerva said,"or, rather my ancestors, but anyway, on the other side is the semi-temperate rainforest called the Tàcqo Ollimbado, Stylo."

"Wow, the forest stretches all the way to the horizon."

"That it does," Minerva said. "It's dark and dense and magical, and a little bit scary and frightening too. We don't go there"

"Point taken."

Afterward, we visited museums, historic churches, palaces, and parks.

"Do you own every one of those palaces?"

"Yes," Minerva said. "I am a queen; it's what I do—own palaces."

"And?"

"That's all, girl," Minerva said. "And I wear fancy clothes and I open and close the Cáuro and, every once in a while, when all hell breaks loose, I intervene to right the ship."

"Does that happen a lot?"

"Not usually," Minerva said, "but the Cáuro is made up of Magicals of all sorts and sometimes they don't see eye-to-eye and things get heated and they call me in. I have to become the mom and bad cop and order everyone around."

"I feel like you enjoy that," Stylo said.

"Is it that obvious?"

"Yes, Your Majesty."

Minerva giggled. "Let's ride the floating roller coaster at the Parcòn sie Tivolla next!"

We ate too much *máyez minervantu* corn slathered in chili sauce at the *Emprallen Jardins*—yeah, I puked in some bushes—and as the sun set, watched fireworks over the marina on the Calargo Dêtillo in the *Càrrasola Camtchàtqa* near the Tàcqo Paláujo.

"Today has been awesome, Kangy," I said, leaning my head against Austin's shoulder as we sat on the grass sloping down to the *Embancadêro* lining the harbor.

"I'm glad you enjoyed the surprise, love."

"I haven't felt my anxiety all day."

"Yay!" Austin cheered, then chuffed. He sniffed me, then kissed me. He had a thing about sniffing. Like he was a real cat.

"I've enjoyed the day as well," Minerva said. "Having a gramora up all day and looking like any other regular *Biscañistu* has been a treat. You know how tiresome it is having people make a fuss and bow all the time?"

"I'd love it!" Stylo proclaimed.

Minerva eyed her. "Why don't you shadow me tomorrow? I have a bunch of boring royal affairs to attend. Sorry, boys."

"I'd love to!"

"You'll see how dull it is," Minerva yawned, "But I think your enthusiasm might rub off on me."

"I think we'll be by the pool tomorrow," Austin said.

"In the shade?"

"Of course!"

Minerva laughed. "Smart." She rose to her feet, as red and green and blue light illuminated her face. "Well, we better get back before Irído and Àsmàra send out the Mezclantus to hunt me down."

The next few days were a blur of sitting by the pool in the gardens or showing Stylo around the vast city. Attending balls and galas in our honor. Meeting dignitaries, including Cupidêro, or Jupiter, the *Monir Antécallanto*, or the First Immortal. He was the lead god by day and DJ by night, spinning trance music. We went to a music festival in the *Jardins Tàlacapotoàl* in the *Càrrasola Inmirado* one night, took a little *Qauixa Ecstracto* to enhance our mood and danced the night away or at least until the clock chimed three and we had to make a mad dash for a hovermobile to take us back to the palace before the spell wore off my kaftan and my arms and legs stopped working.

In the vast city, we mingled with Xymlantus, the wise, powerful creatures from the Fifth and Sixth Dimension who floated rather than walked, and who had red or orange or yellow or blue hair and who talked telepathically. Or we attended lectures hosted by talking stuffed lions who were famous intellectuals at the *Umnavesseo Emprallen sie La Biscayne*, the Royal University. We even went to the *Valledra Volqenhorigo Sie La Biscayne*, the folkloric ballet featuring dancers who were talking trees. It was something else to watch redwood and birch trees soaring through the air to music.

"Never thought I'd see a redwood tree have so much grace, yeah?"

"Right, Kangy?"

"This is fricking trippy," Stylo muttered. "I feel like I've been high the whole time I've been here."

"Shhh," Minerva said. "We are supposed to be stoic, remember?

Stiff upper lips and all. I told you this, Stylo. You are my protégé, and I expect you to return someday and do your part."

"No, shit."

"Langra!"

"Sorry, yes, will do."

We all burst out laughing.

"*Dáumnanabo*, Eli!" Minerva quipped. "You made me laugh!"

We continued giggling until Àsmàra intervened.

"*Pudo ea vovo lembra aqeva cor Empra?*" she said sternly.

"Yes, Azzei, I know I'm the queen. Now go away, before I have you beheaded." Àsmàra rolled her eyes and retreated behind us. Minerva tapped me gently with her silk fan. "Eli, you're making a mockery of the queen. Please behave!"

On our last night, after a grand party, with an abundance of food and entertainment, Austin and I strolled the gardens under the three moons of Minerva, named for the Têrso Empras or the Three Sprite Queens who presided over realms of Minerva: Balama in the far north-east, Amistala in the far south east, and Cataraña in the central west.

"I swear my anxiety is gone, Kangy."

"Incredible."

"But when we get home...?"

"We'll deal with it together, love."

"It's so awful though."

"I know, Eli."

A bush trembled nearby. Austin pulled out his PlasmX and held it in front of him.

"*Lloroha manitáuru! Sema in Coaugelo!*"

A tiny fleck of light floated from the top of the bush and drifted toward us. Austin put away his PlasmX. The light floated to the grass. Green smoke arose, and Queen Minerva stepped toward us.

"I had to sneak away to bid you farewell," she said softly. "I have to travel to Morinth-M'am-Raq'or tomorrow to host a conference attended by several Immortals and Cataraña herself. More like I'll be the great peacemaker. The Immortals are gods and act as such." She covered her mouth. "They act like their poop doesn't stink."

We laughed. Minerva continued, "Amistala can be rather uptight and ornery when she's not the center of attention. And when she's in a room with the Immortals, well, it's a given she's not the center of attention."

"What do you do? I mean, you are the queen?"

"I just watch the mess and try to make sure no one gets killed when they start using magic against each other."

We all laughed.

After a while, Minerva said, "I hope you had a good trip, Eli?"

"I did, Mina," I said. "I'll miss your magic giving me the use of my arm and leg, if only temporarily."

"The magic is stronger here," Minerva said, "but don't despair, Eli. You will get better back on Earth. In due time."

"You know I'm impatient."

"I know," Minerva said. "Tapping your foot at dinner as if signaling for Irído to hurry up and move on to dessert!"

"Was I that opaque?"

"Yes!" Austin and Minerva said in unison.

We walked to a wooden bench under a willow tree along a meandering stream with water glowing iridescent pink. Purple fish zipped around the water.

"What if I begged to stay?" I said suddenly. "I've become a Coaugelo, trained by Máurso himself."

"Máurso is the best of the best," Minerva said. "The most sensible of the Immortals."

"Me and Austin, we can join the *Qénocqus sie Minerva*, maybe?"

"You are too young to join the Knights of Minerva, unfortunately."

"But we're technically knights because we are Coaugelus," I said.

"Yes, that is true," Minerva said, "but, Eli, you need to go home to be with your family."

"My mom would be okay with it."

"No, she wouldn't," Minerva said. "I know your mother too well, careño. She'd miss you too much. She adores you."

"I guess you're right."

"Of course, I'm the queen! If you disagree with me I can have you dunked in batter and deep-fried and served to monsters."

We laughed again.

"And what about you, Austin?"

He dodged my glance. "I miss my folks already."

"Kangy!"

"They're my best mates, love!"

Minerva put her arm around my shoulders and squeezed. "Eli, you are always welcome here. Where would I be if you hadn't come to help me battle Devlina and Caligrula years ago? I am eternally grateful, but when I see you, your arm and leg in casts, I see that you need to heal."

"I can do that here! I feel better already."

"You have to face the real world, Eli," Minerva said. "You can't hide from your problems here."

"I'm not hiding."

"You have to go back and get better, Eli."

"Please, I can stay here. I'll be your butler or valet or wallet or whatever it's called, please?"

"Eli," Minerva said, "Magicals from Earth must live on Earth and vice versa. It's a rule of the universe."

"Fucking Còngréhassa!"

"No, the universe, Eli," Minerva said. "You and I exist in two different planes—"

"The multiverse, love!"

"Exactly," Minerva said and added, "Besides, your family needs you, sweetheart."

"So, you don't want to help me," I grumbled.

Minerva squeezed my arm. "No, Eli. You know it's not like that. It's just it's time for you to go back to reality..."

Suddenly, the air around us rippled.

"Your time has come to an end, dear," Minerva said, standing up. "Come on give me a hug."

"I don't want to go! I'm not ready."

"You'll be fine, Eli. You have Austin, he's the greatest boyfriend ever. And a poweful Coaugelo. And your brother Barn. Your Mom! And Christine of course. Máurso as well. You are surrounded by wonderful people, Eli!"

Minerva began dissolving like ashes drifting from a burning piece of paper.

"Take care, Eli! I'll be watching you!"

Chapter Sixteen

Burbank, CA 91501

IN A FLASH of green light, I appeared in my bed at home in the big, rambling mansion. I looked around, dazed and confused. The mantel clock ticked above the fireplace. I could hear Barn singing "Oh What A Beautful Morning" out in the hallway.

"You sound great, babe," Katie replied to him from the other side of my bedroom door.

"Like Michael Bublé, love?"

"Well, not quite..."

"Oi, come on, lass. Don't be cheeky!"

My arm throbbed. My leg, propped on the bed, ached. My heart pounded wildly in my chest. I searched the room. Where was Austin?

"KANGY!" I shouted.

Barn stopped singing. I heard footsteps outside. The door opened.

"Oi, when did you get back, mate?"

"Just now. But where's Austin?"

Katie and Barn exchanged glances.

"We haven't seen him."

A *whoosh* filled the room, followed by a burst of light under the door to the walk-in closet. Fingers of green smoke slithered into the room.

"Oi, bloody hell!" Austin shouted, busting out of the closet. "That saucy minx put me in the closet. No one puts Kangy in the closet!"

"Serves you right, mate," Barn said. "I'm glad to cover for you in *Oklahoma!* and my mate here, but couldn't you have invited me and Katie for at least one day and night to see the queen?"

Austin scratched his head. "Oi, didn't know you would want to go."

"Bleedin' dense monkey," Barn said. "See the queen! Roam La Biscayne. Go to the food stalls in the *Alladra Vazcáino*. Attend the *Valledra Volqenhorigo* with the Her Majesty. You know I love the folkloric dancing with the Humboldtu trees; they wear the best costumes and are, well talking AND dancing trees! Bloomin' arse, yes, we wanted to go."

"Sorry?"

"Darn right you are."

I lay on the bed, my anxiety barreling toward me like a train.

"Eli?" Austin called. "You look flushed, Eli."

He scrambled to the bed as my eyes closed, and I gripped my duvet as the darkness swept over me. I struggled to breathe; my arms were numb; my throat closed up.

"I think I'm having a heart attack!"

Austin picked up the phone by my bed to call the emergency medic on duty. Barn went to get my mom. Katie stood by the door, freaking out.

"Elijah? Are you okay?"

I couldn't speak. The room turned upside down. I closed my eyes and held onto the duvet.

A light flashed.

A siren screamed in the distance.

"Zid'dra almost killed you."

"Devlina?"

"Yeah, but the spell your mother used against him that night on the street weakened him and your amulet protected you and Máurso came to your aid."

"You shouted my name."

"I was warning you."

"The rain—was he causing all the rain this winter?"

"One of his many tricks. He was getting into your head. Elijah, you have to fight the darkness…"

Thunder rumbled.

No more rain, please. God, please.

A gust of wind hit the windows. Was Zid'dra trying to get in?

Two eyes. I couldn't get the image of the burning blood-red circles of light out of my head. My heart… Was it stopping? No. Would it pop? That can't be right. A seventeen-year-old having a heart attack.

"Heart attacks mean you don't feel loved," April remarked one stormy day last December. "I love my dad. Mom loves him too. We tell him we love him. How could he not know?"

"It was a mild heart attack, right?"

"Yes," April said, setting the book on metaphysical causes to illness. "So maybe he knows he's loved?"

"Tell him, again?"

"Yeah." April's face was gray. "I mean, Elijah, he's my dad. I'm scared."

Rain hit the windows of the Central Library where we had sought shelter when the rain burst over us halfway to Foster's Freeze. We were *senlàpso*. The only two people in our friend group who loved ice cream during the winter.

Winter ended long ago.

A match flashed. Phosphorus tickled my nose.

"Elijah," Nurse Hatzuko said my name, his hand holding my wrist to check my pulse. "Can you hear me?"

I blinked. The lights came up in my room. Had I been in the Million Dollar Theater downtown? I looked around the room. The blue-and-white wallpaper in the room decorated with galleons plying the oceans set among anchors, compasses, stars, and octopi. Mom loomed over me, concern played out on her face. Austin was at the foot of the bed, stroking my feet. Barn and Katie were in the hall, talking to Aunt Christine and Uncle George.

"You had a panic attack," Nurse H. said, looking down at me through his round, gold glasses, his moustache moving as he spoke.

Moustaches moved when we talked.

Crazy.

"I thought it was a heart attack."

"Your vitals are perfectly fine," Nurse H. said. I couldn't stop staring at his moustache. Should I grow one? Would I be different? A man. Yes, I would be a man then.

He looked at Mom. "Here's some medicine he can take to calm down."

Mom nodded, her face strained, like the time I fell off my skateboard and busted my ribs.

"Please don't die!" she had said, holding me and screaming for Tory to call 911.

"Twelve-year-olds don't die," Aunt Christine said later at the hospital after the doctor prescribed medicine for Mom's nerves. "You're indestructible, sweetheart."

The medicine had soothed Mom's nerves.

"This medicine will calm you down, Elijah."

Shit, I had bad nerves like Mom.

Austin fetched some water from the bathroom. I stared at the small, cylindrical white pill in the palm of my hand. Freedom from nerves? Two red circular dots? Will it end the rain? Please, God, please.

I swallowed the pill. A few minutes later, my toes tingled.

"The medicine is working, love," Austin said, scrambling up the bed to sit beside me. Mom and Nurse H. spoke in hushed tones in the hallway.

Arnulfo, his therapist. Talk to him. Needs attention. Medicine will help. Central nervous system overwhelmed. Needs to heal. He'll be fine in time.

"Simply indestructible," Aunt Christine had said leaning over to brush the hair off my face. "And medicine for the pain. Bet you'll be on your skateboard in no time."

Austin's powerful arms wrapped around me. He pulled me close to him. His heart beat, *thump-thump, thump-thump*, reassuring, like the sun rising after the darkness.

*

THE CRESCENT MOON hung high over Homer's Peak. Sunny grumbled as he drove the golf cart up the brick path from the Olympic Training Center, through a grove of Coastal Live Oaks to the Equestrian Center, home to a dozen thoroughbreds. Mom was passionate about horses and racing. In her downtime, she came to the stables to care for the horses and release tension.

The stables were quiet except for the crunch of alfalfa or the soft whinnying of the horses.

"It's late, you should be asleep, Beta2." Sunny called me Beta2, my code name for security, when he was in a mood. Being woken at 3:00 AM put him in a mood. "If your mom finds out..."

"I'll take the heat."

Sunny glanced at my arm in a cast. And leg. He shook his head. "I'll be outside walking the perimeter, yeah?"

I nodded and stumbled along the slate floor down the main aisle lined with stalls. I found Aristantzea, Mom's prized blue mare, named for the warrior queen of the tribes of Minra, who battled the *Plaga sie Ornbullos,* a horde of ogres who decimated and subjugated much of Old Earth until the young queen, blind in one eye, led an uprising that freed her people.

I looked into Aristantzea's brown eyes. She whinnied and chuffed. I ran my hand along her soft fur.

"When was the last time we rode?"

Artistantzea leaned down to munch on some alfalfa.

"Three years ago? Before I had all those things to do? Do you remember? We used to race across the upper pastures."

The horse lifted her head and chewed the alfalfa thoughtfully.

"As you can see, I can't ride anymore," I said. "I mean, maybe someday when my body isn't broken anymore."

After a while, I went outside. A meteor shower lit up the night sky over the mansion, mostly dark save the lights on the first floor as the overnight crew worked to clean the rooms where Mom conducted business running our octopus of death.

A meteor blazed toward the house, a red tail trailing behind it. Wind rustled through the boughs of the oak trees dotting the stone plaza outside the stables. I trembled. The meteor turned into two circles of red light as it hit the house. The mansion glowed pink for a moment, the meteor bursting into a million specks of pink light. In a heartbeat, the lights flickered out. The mansion glowed for a while before the light faded. The runes had protected the house.

The wind died down. The horses inside stopped braying and whinnying.

My amulet glowed warm against my skin. I reached inside my shirt, pulling it out.

I was scared. I had broken bones and a fried brain. Literally, a mess. Seventeen and having a crisis.

"Medicine will help," Arnulfo told me. "It's the only way, really."

"To do what?"

"For us to get to the root of the issue and help you get better."

"Look at me."

"I can see you have some broken bones."

"And my mind?"

"It's a little overwhelmed. It happens."

"Not to me."

"It can happen to anyone."

"But medicine, well, you know my family. We don't like medicine."

"Says the boy whose family owns one of the major pharmaceutical companies in the world."

"Why do you think we don't trust medicine?"

Arnulfo laughed. "Funny, Elijah." He leaned back into his green chair. "Look, Elijah, like you have casts to help set your bones, medicine will help your brain get back on track."

"I read about the side effects of antidepressants. Scary."

"They have to list any side effect, even if only one person had it. That doesn't mean it'll happen to you."

"Have you met me? My luck?" I nodded to the casts on my left arm and right leg.

"You'll be fine," Arnulfo said. "Don't you want to feel normal again?"

Normal. *Somàl. Somàl. Somàl.*

Once upon a time, I was normal, sharing a cabin along with five other Magicals at summer camp. Then I made a choice while floating on the water of Shasta Lake that changed everything for me. Everything.

"Trust me. The medicine will heal your mind. The casts will help your body."

"So, I'll be the boy next door again?"

"Do you want to be?"

I shrugged. "I want to sleep."

"You'll be able to sleep," Arnulfo said. "The medicine will help treat your underlying anxiety and that will help you sleep at night."

"Are you sure?"

"Would I lie to you?"

I shook my head.

Arnulfo's office faded into the night sky along with my memory. I gazed back at the stables.

Sunny appeared around the corner smoking a cigarette. "You ready to head back, lad?"

"Yeah."

"You find what you were looking for here with the horses?"

*

FOR SOME ODD reason, "Bohemian Rhapsody" played softly over the speakers in Dr. Hu's office as I sat on the edge of the examining bed.

"Mama, just killed a man..."

Dr. Hu perched on a stool across from me, her long, black hair falling over her shoulders as she tapped into a smartphone.

"Mama, ooooh..."

"Did you pick this song for some reason?" I whispered. Mom had her back to me, staring out the window at the thick fog hanging over the valley.

Dr. Hu looked up from her smartphone. "No, it's just some random playlist the nurses like."

"Okay."

Dr. Hu brushed her hair off her face and looked at me. "Okay, Elijah we're going to start you on ten milligrams."

"Okay."

"This is the dosage to see if you can handle the medicine."

"Can I?"

"Of course."

"Are you sure?"

"...Just got to get out, just got to get right out of here..." I stared up at the speakers embedded in the drop ceiling over the sink. Dr. Hu smiled.

"I swear it's just a coincidence."

I shrugged, pulling on my index finger with my thumb and forefinger.

"Don't be nervous."

"I'm afraid."

"You don't have to be."

"Arnulfo says it's part of my anxiety."

"It is," Dr. Hu said. "After two weeks, we'll evaluate how you're handling the medicine, and if all goes well, increase your dosage to twenty milligrams. That's considered the therapeutic dosage. It takes a while to build in your system and work fully. About eight weeks—"

"Shit," I grumbled. "Two months?"

"Yes, but in the meantime," Dr. Hu said, "you'll take this. It's an emergency pill for when the panic attacks come..."

"At night," I whispered, "the darkness..."

"Think of the pill as light."

"Yeah?"

"Yes, Elijah," Dr. Hu said reassuringly. "And soon you'll be better."

"I hope so."

"You are working with Arnulfo. You're going to take medicine. You're going to rest. You're going to be fine."

Mom turned, the gray light from the window creating the effect of having halo.

"We're going to take it easy, darling."

"What's that?"

"Do nothing for a bit."

"Us?"

"Yeah, I deserve a vacation too."

"But the Octopus... Who's going to feed it?"

"It'll be fine."

Dr. Hu tapped into her smartphone. "Okay, the prescription was sent to pharmacy. Any questions?"

Will I die? Will I slip into a coma? What did it mean that my personality could change drastically? Suicidal thoughts. I was susceptible because I was a teenager, or so the internet warned me.

"Darling." Mom read my mind. "No, you'll be fine."

"If you notice anything, call me. We can try something else. There's a solution for every problem. Understand?"

Why had no one ever told me that before?

*

LATE THAT NIGHT, silver bars of moonlight streamed in the windows of my bedroom. I lay in bed, my heart beating wildly, my breathing shallow, my toes tingling. I clutched Ocho to my chest. I didn't dare look toward the door to the walk-in closet and bathroom. What if two red circles of light glowed menacingly in the darkness? Austin stirred next to me.

"Love?" he whispered. "Are you okay?"

"I'm having trouble... Well, I mean..."

Austin slipped out of bed, and faced me . His hair stood up in every direction. He rubbed the sleep from his eyes. "Time for the emergency pill."

He walked around the bed to tousle my hair and walk to the bathroom. I closed my eyes. He'd have to walk past the red circles to get the medicine. What if... I mean, anything could happen to him. The darkness could devour him. My pulse quickened. How could I survive without him?

The room glowed with pink light. The runes?

Austin hummed a few bars from "All These Things" by the Killers. The floorboard in the threshold to the bathroom sighed under his feet. He opened the cabinet and closed it softly, the latch clicking. A moment later, the tap squeaked and water gurgled into a glass. The floorboard groaned again.

My eyes followed him across the room from the danger of the darkness. He stood above me, his face filled with love and compassion.

"Down the hatch, love."

"Are you sure?"

"Of course," he said. "You'll feel better. I swear."

"How do you know? I mean, really."

"I know everything, right, love?" He kneeled in front of me, rubbing my right knee with his hand. "I'm a Leo—you know this. Come on, don't dither. Time for you to get back in my strong arms. We can slip off to the land of nod together. Me and you, flying on a magic carpet."

I stared at the small, white pill. My eyes turned to his. He smiled, motioning for me to put the pill in my mouth.

A moment later, I opened my mouth, popped the pill, and washed it down with water.

"What happens now?"

"The first night of the rest of your life."

"Haven't I heard this before?"

"Yeah, I think I repeat myself," Austin said, standing over me. He tumbled into the bed. "You know you love it, yeah?"

"Ever notice how you are your biggest promoter?"

"Someone has to do it. Why not me?"

I sank into his arms. The sprinklers clicked on down below in the gardens. A fire truck's sirens bleated somewhere far away. I listened to the beating of Austin's heart. The vice around my chest began to loosen. I could breathe again. We slipped under the covers, laying side by side, holding hands. The darkness faded as the silver moonlight grew brighter. The sirens in the distance faded.

Chapter Seventeen

Survivors

THE TEMPERATURE HOVERED near ninety degrees. The first signif-icant heat wave of the year. I was propped up in a chaise, under an um-brella, slathered in sunscreen, holding onto Ocho.

"This is odd," Mom said next to me, sipping a piña colada. "I don't think I've done nothing since I was your age." She set down the glass. "I think I might go crazy. We should practice M'am Sáu Eu to quiet our brains."

"Our brains aren't meant to be quiet, Mom. You know this."

I conjured a hummingbird, purple and yellow. It flitted over the cast on my leg.

"Your magic has returned!" Mom exclaimed excitedly. A second later, the hummingbird dissolved into the hot air.

"Barely."

"Enough."

"Should be better."

"You're fine just like that."

"Really? That sounds odd coming from you."

"A whole new mom."

We sat in silence for a moment. Mom sipped her drink. I sank into the chaise lounge. I had slept well after taking the pill. Such an odd feeling getting a full night sleep. I needed so much more.

"I see you're shirtless."

"Yeah," I said. "New me."

"I'm glad you're removing the layers."

"Same," I said. "I like that you stopped shellacking your hair with hairspray and epoxy."

Mom chuckled.

Austin and Barn sparred with each other, in matching fire-engine-red racing briefs above the sparkling water of the pool. Their cousin Mason, down from San Francisco for the summer—he could be their twin, same dark hair, lanky body, high cheekbones—pulled lightning from the air and tossed it at them.

A bolt singed Austin's hair.

"Oi, what the soddin' hell, Mase?"

"That was supposed to shock you, not set you on fire," Mason said in his flat, California twang. He was a Mùn Tái. He used his magic in healing, but he was an accomplished fighter in his own right.

"Bloomin' hell, Mase," Barn complained. "How about less shocking? We're doing *escrimàgos*, not trying to die."

"You two complain too much."

"Says the lad always sulking because his girlfriend doesn't pay him enough attention."

"Erika spends more time taking selfies with her friends than with me. I have a big heart," Mason quipped. He summoned a waterspout out of the pool, sending it heading toward the boys. "And if we're dating, doesn't it seem right we'd spend time together?"

"He's right," Barn said, dodging the waterspout.

"All right, Mason," Uncle George said, stepping out of the pool-house where he and Christine had been sucking face or something.

"Don't kill my son and nephew, please."

"Come on!" Mason grumbled. "I can reincarnate them!"

The waterspout twirled around the edge of the pool.

Christine appeared from the shadows of the poolhouse, her lipstick smeared. "Reincarnation is too painful." She eyed the waterspout and snapped her fingers. The spout collapsed and washed into the pool. Austin and Barn flew down toward Mason. Barn waved a hand at him. Mason's body tensed.

"Not a darn *Flummoxo!*" Mason shouted. "Uncle George, now they've paralyzed me with their magic and are trying to kill me!"

"All right, enough," George said, soaring up to meet the boys. "How about you three come down and have some bleedin' lemonade and food already."

"I can eat!" Austin did some flips in the air over the pool, landing on his feet near me.

Barn drifted down to the surface of the water and did a somersault before landing on his feet near the BBQ.

"Oh, that's a nice move, Barn," Sean said from where he stood turning hot dogs.

"Thanks, Sean."

Mason's body disappeared into the sky.

"Oi, bloomin' hell," Austin complained, "Mase is sulking again. Sure, become invisible. You Wongs are too thin-skinned."

"Piss off, Kang," Barn said, holding a plate out for Sean who placed a hot dog on a bun and set it on the plate. "Wongs are stronger than Kangs."

"Surely you jest, Barny!"

Mason reappeared behind Barn, snatching the hot dog off his plate.

"Hey, what the hell!"

Mason's body disappeared again except for his lips, which continued chewing.

"You puxhàredo Encantreinos!" Barn complained.

Mom chuckled. I looked over at her.

"I guess we have some entertainment." My hands loosened around Ocho.

"Doing nothing is okay..." Her voice trailed off. "Right?"

"Sure."

"We'll get used to it?"

"I think so."

"Sure," Mom said. "One can feel fulfilled doing...nothing."

We looked at each other. I gulped. I would have to get used to this.

"Why are you eating three burgers, Lostin?"

Austin's face reddened. He held a burger in each hand while another floated above his right shoulder.

*

THE FOLLOWING DAY, Tory and I had a picnic in the bumblebee garden. Early morning fog burned off, and the temperature soared into the high eighties. Bumblebees drifted from snapdragons, sunflowers, lavender, and bee balm. Our first time alone since my accident. We needed to catch up. I was propped up on a bench next to Tory, eating a sandwich.

"What happened, Tor?" I bit into to my sandwich. Salami, mortadella, and black forest ham with provolone and brown mustard. My favorite.

"I thought everything was fine," she said, her sandwich beside her, mozzarella and tomato on a baguette, untouched.

"I was working at Puzzles Corporate part-time and just started school. I was living in the dorms and thought everything was fine."

"It wasn't?"

She shook her head. "I felt this pressure in my head everyday. My left eye kept twitching."

"Someone put a curse on you." I laughed. Tory shook her head.

"That's an old French-Creole wives tale."

We fell into silence. I focused on the buzz of bees and a lawnmower growling in the distance. *Tejana* music blared from a speaker in the back gardens. Water gurgled in the fountain set among the flower beds.

A hot breeze lifted the poplar trees that acted as a wind break between the bumblebee garden and the rose garden. A sea breeze kicked up at the beaches right now. In a few hours, the marine layer would drift over the Santa Monica Mountains and slide into the valley and bring relief from the scorching heat.

I leaned into the bench, scrutinizing my half-eaten sandwich.

"Tor?"

"Yes, Elijah?"

"Then what happened to you?"

"I don't exactly remember. I went to class. It was one of those lectures with a hundred students in a huge room. A class the size of a theater—can you imagine that?"

I shook my head.

"And then everything went black. And when I woke, I was in the hospital. Three days later. That's when Mom said I should go stay with Tante Charlotte and Toncle Rivolier in Switzerland."

"I thought you were in a hospital or something."

"Delomary PR said that," Tory explained. "But I was with family, recuperating."

Tory sipped her sparkling water. A bumblebee droned over us, mumbling about pollen. The wind picked up. The bee drifted away.

Tory scanned the garden around her. She whispered, "I'm sorry I never believed you. I went to Minerva."

My eyes grew big. I'd been to Minerva five times. Every time, Tory, the pragmatist in the family, said it was all a figment of my imagination. She wanted nothing to do with Minerva, the Seventh Dimension, Old Earth, the Old Language, or the Alliance. She claimed my powers were fake. I was fake. That really hurt.

"I'm so sorry, Elijah," Tory said. "I met Queen Minerva, my best friend was a talking cat named Orangina, my guide was a Némezda..."

"A what?"

"It's a rabbit that has wings and talks. They're so fun to be around."

"And then what happened?"

"I stopped a revolt, braved a coven, and fought the Dark King. I might even get a statute for bravery in Clockwork Square in La Biscayne in front of the queen's palace."

Tory explained how there was a portal to Old Earth in a pool in the gardens behind Tante Charlotte's and Toncle Rivolier's chateau. "I dove in one day and came up in a lake in the middle of the Tàcqo Ollimbado. I thought I was hallucinating until Orangina the cat came and told me where I was. And, geez, it was wild and so fun."

"Yeah?"

"I mean I had a talking cat for a guide and a flying rabbit. Man, we had a blast. It was kinda scary, you know. But after battling a few covens and the Dark King, well, I felt different about myself. About who I was. What I could do." She bit into her sandwich. "I don't know. I feel different these days."

"How so?"

"More complete. Like I know who I am."

"So, can you do magic?"

Tory laughed. "No, I took after Dad, I guess. No magic. I mean, some I suppose, since I could go to Minerva and such. But I'm not like you."

"Was."

Tory put her arm around me. "That was BS. We all know it."

"Yeah, I'm really mad at the whole thing."

"Me too," Tory agreed. "Barn told me you made lemonade out of lemons."

"How so?"

"You're a warrior now."

I chuckled. "Yeah, I guess so," I said. "It's fun fighting with Austin and Barn. I can do some magic." I summoned a soda out of the air, handing it to Tory.

"Diet cola," Tory said, cracking it open and taking a sip. She gagged and spit it out. "Prune juice!"

"Yeah, well, my point; my magic isn't the same."

"You're trying!"

"I guess."

"Don't be hard on yourself, Cory," Tory said. "Anyway, don't worry," Tory said, patting my hand. "Give the medicine time. It takes a while to start working. Right now, your brain is so fried from everything, it's just out of control. The fears you have, that's your brain misfiring."

I concentrated on her. "You had a nervous breakdown and so did I."

I looked into her blue eyes. I watched waves crash on the breakwaters off Long Beach. Heard the crashing surf and smelled the salt water. Tory reminded me of the ocean, beautiful on the surface with so much swirling beneath the waves. Had I ever swum out in the ocean that made her? No. I realized that. I didn't know my sister. That made me sad.

She pushed her long red hair off her face. "Our family is a mess in a lot of ways." She said, "There's all the pressure to succeed."

"I hate it, Tory. It ate me up inside"

Tory squeezed my knee. "I know, kiddo."

Sean called me kiddo as well. From Tory, nineteen, it sounded a little weird. Both of us teenagers. Tory lived on the adult side of teenager. The great divide between child and adult. In one year, I would live on the same side as Tory.

"We're lucky though, Elijah," Tory said. "We live in that big house, have everything we want, we never go to bed hungry. Our family is Magical. We sleep at night knowing we're loved."

"Now, I guess."

"Mom has gotten better recently. I can tell. I guess you changed her."

"What do you mean?"

"Mom is different. Not only how she dresses and looks these days—like a normal mom not some corporate robot in a pantsuit. She is relaxed. She smiles! She tells us she loves us!"

"Sorta weird, yeah, Tor?"

Tory giggled. "Yeah, we're not used to it. Yet."

"I guess me and Mom changed together."

"You have." Tory said, "That is because of you and Mom doing the work."

"The work?"

"Therapy, counseling, *talking to each other.*"

A green-and-yellow truck emblazoned with the words "Delomary Household Services" drove slowly along the gravel road leading to the greenhouses and operations center up the hill.

Tory brushed her hair off her face, squinting up at the sun. She glanced back at me.

"We have to count our blessings, Elijah. We are lucky to have Mom and our family. And each other."

She reached for my hand. I let her lace our fingers. We had never held hands. Ever. It felt good to do it now.

"We had a schedule. Our lives planned out," I said.

"Don't get me wrong, what Mom did to you with that crazy schedule and her five-year plan for both of us was insane. Normal parents don't do that, but, you know, while I was away, I realized that at least Mom loves us enough to be a helicopter mom and create that schedule.

My mouth was open. "I don't know if I'd go that far. I like the new mom!"

"Me too," Tory said. "Mom came to see me a lot while I was in Switzerland. We'd spend long hours just talking. It was nice."

"Mom can be fun to talk to when she's chill."

"She's chill now," Tory said.

"New year, new Mom?"

Tory laughed. "I know, I guess I just have some friends whose parents didn't pay them much attention or seem involved in their lives. It messed them up too, you know?"

She continued, "I know people with no love. When people aren't loved they do terrible things. We're loved. I love you, Elijah"

I smiled at her.

"Tory?"

"Yes, Elijah?"

"I feel like I don't know you."

She nodded. "Same. I mean I come back and hear you came out to three hundred kids at BHS. That's fricking bonkers, Elijah. Why the heck did you do that?"

I shrugged. "I had completed one of those chain letter things you pass around. Saying I was gay. I meant to give it to Tyrone. Only it disappeared. Someone must have found it. I didn't want to be blackmailed. I figured I had to come out before whoever it was who had it could use it against me. *Nunma in Viacadeimo.*"

"*Nunma in Viacadeimo.*" Tory nodded, squeezing my hand. "I guess you were smart to do that." She leaned into the sun, closing her eyes. "And now you have a boyfriend, who is really cute and sweet, as it so happens. And you've been going through a lot with Dad."

"He's pretty awful," I said. "I took out what I felt about Dad on Austin."

"That's what Dad does. He brings out the worst in us, and we don't even realize it. It's his personality. Corrosive."

I disappeared in her eyes again: the waves, the sound of the surf, the spray of salt water.

"Am I going to get better?"

Tory smiled. "I promise. And when you feel your heart pounding and your throat closing up and you get out of bed and pace and you feel crazy, take the emergency pill. It'll help."

"I'm scared to."

"No, Elijah. Don't be."

"Part of me likes to suffer."

"We're Catholic—it's how we were raised. Suffer here and now, and then when we die, go to Heaven."

We both laughed.

"Don't suffer. Jesus would want us to be happy."

Happy.

Happy.

Happy.

I listened to the buzz of the bees all around us. The gurgle of the fountain and the poplar trees rustling from the breeze coming from the west.

"Tory?"

"Yes, Elijah?"

"Um, can you scratch my arm. The cast is itchy as fuck right now."

She snickered and picked up the long-handled scratcher we brought. I closed my eyes in ecstasy as she scratched my arm.

*

I BATTLED THE darkness all night long. The medicine helped; the black faded to gray at the edges. I woke up past noon and spotted Austin's side of the bed was empty. The last week of school. I missed him already. I had planned to get up with him, but my body lacked the energy to move this morning.

"I'll do it tomorrow," I told myself.

I went to the bathroom, put on my cast covers, and showered. After stepping out into the muggy room, I stood examining myself in the mirror. A bulb flashed. The moon cracked in two. I heard a scream. My eyes glazed over. I peered into the mirror at myself with loathing. Gravity tilted. A slow burn spread in my stomach. The darkness. I was so fucking huge. *Sideways turn, please. Jesus, look at the side. I am the size of a whale. Like Dad, who's disgusting because he's blubbery and stupid and ridiculous. I don't want to be disgusting like Dad.*"

"You want to be good and thin, Elijah," Mom always said. "Not fat and gross like your father."

Take your pill, Elijah, it's time. Take the pill.

"Nunma in Viacadeimo."

I pushed my hand to open the medicine cabinet. My hand trembled. They say the fat cells instructed your brain to eat more when too much is lost from working out or from an illness.

The darkness did the same thing. It conjured up hatred and fear and loathing to fill the space. Nature abhorred a vacuum. I swallowed the pill.

My head filled with fog. I glanced at my watch: 3:00 PM. I told Austin I'd meet him at school. I wore a boot now. I could walk, with crutches, very slowly. I sighed. It's hard to dress when you're wearing a cast—one on your arm and one on your leg. *God, Delomary, you really took a tumble. You're a mess.*

Stop.

Stop.

Take a breath.

Why was it easy to live in Minerva? Right out of the hospital and I was able to do anything—wearing my "Jesus kaftan" as Barn called it.

Maybe the light? Golden rays drenched the city, making the buildings, parks, plazas, and tree-lined boulevard glimmer. Some houseplants, I overheard Mrs. Singh say one time, can survive in low light. "But they thrive in bright light."

"Weren't there palm trees lining Passêo-siec-Antécallantus?" I had asked Queen Minerva one day as we toured the dense city center, the queen in disguise looking like a contestant on *Ru Paul's Drag Race*. I guess drag queens are common in the capital. Why not?

"Sure," Mina said. "The palm trees like sunshine, so they sometimes pick up and go a few blocks south near the river to sunbathe. Oak trees switch places with them. The light is better here than on your Earth. Brighter, more healing. You can thrive in the bright light, Elijah. It's magic in its way."

Thrive. I needed to flourish.

"The cure to what ails you is light, which cleanses our wounds."

I pulled out a tank and shorts. Easy access for getting into with my current situation. Wait, is my chest hair getting wilder? Can't it stop growing?

I put on the tank, managing to stick my cast through the arm. Rockets fired in my brain. A war raged between the medicine and the darkness rendering me nothing more than a spectator.

No, I'm the grass on the fields of Shenandoah, where the Civil War raged.

I met Austin outside school. Austin beamed like the brilliant midday sun over La Biscayne. He leaned in to kiss me on my cheek and reached for my hand.

I refused. I pushed it away. Cannons fired. Austin's smile faded.

Rockets exploded. He talked animatedly at me. He let go of holding hands for a moment. My puxhàredo fear. Internalized homophobia and the darkness. That was one helluva care package from the world of bigotry.

Austin, when he walked, made funny sounds. He'd make this meep-meep sound, soft, gentle. He'd cheer unexpectedly and sing half songs. He sometimes skipped, then turned and looked at me. He always smiled. *I don't deserve him.*

"Why do you say that, Elijah?" Arnulfo said at our last session.

"I don't know. Have you met him? His love is as great and limitless as the gases fueling the sun. What am I? Look at me. I am overweight and hairy. I'm becoming a Sasquatch. People who look like me don't deserve love."

"Elijah, you are just as deserving of love as anyone else."

"But look at me!"

"Elijah, have you thought that how you view yourself is not how others see you?"

I laughed at him. Arnulfo was funny.

"Elijah, I think you are used to attacking yourself because you blame what happened to your parents on yourself."

"No."

"Elijah, how you look is not what makes people love you. They love you for who you are within."

I burst out laughing. Arnulfo sounded ridiculous.

The cannons kept firing within. They wouldn't stop. My ears burned, hurt from the onslaught of artillery in my own private war.

We walked home—slowly, since I had to use a cane. Lean into the hill.

"I can drive you lads back," Sunny had said.

"I have to prove to Austin I am willing to sacrifice for him."

Sunny gripped the steering wheel; his head turned to look at me.

"Elijah, I think coming to pick him up is good enough."

"No," I had said firmly.

"Your mother won't be happy."

"I don't fucking care."

Shit, I was an asshole.

As we trudged up the hill to the mansion, Austin sang one of his little made-up songs. He turned down the wrong street. He became lost easily. He depended on me to lead him the right way. I hated him for not knowing how to get home. He had lived here a year, almost. *He is so brain dead.* The darkness burned in my head. I kept walking. *He is senlàpso. Why can't he figure out how to walk home?*

I pushed myself up the hill. My brain throbbed. Medicine ebbed and flowed. My heart quickened. My own private war.

Austin's boots stomped loudly on the concrete underfoot.

"Elijah!"

He reached for my arm. I pushed him away.

Boom! A cannon exploded with smoke and gunpowder.

A car blasting "Bad Guy" by Billie Eilish whooshed past us. Kids laughed and screamed as they ran through the sprinklers on the front lawn of a house across the street. The temperature hovered in the low nineties. Welcome to summer in La La Land.

"Elijah, I am talking to you!" Austin towered over me. His eyebrows furrowed. His voice raised, filled with rage.

I stopped. No, it wasn't the magic or the light in Minerva that made me feel normal, but rather the lack of routine. In La Biscayne, on the streets lined with oak trees that had swapped places with palm trees, surrounded by talking stuffed animals and where drag queens hid an actual queen spending a day with her friends, I found freedom. No plans or brands or schedules. In the sprawling capital, spreading under mist-shrouded Morra Êímpagońena, existed a version of me who lived to experience life.

I didn't need to be ten thousand years in the past and in another dimension to live that boy's life. I simply could push down the walls surrounding me and reach out to Austin.

Austin waved his hands around erratically, his eyes gigantic, burning with anger. The hot, heavy air stirred around us. The boughs of the jacaranda trees spread over us and lifted in the slight breeze. Tears sprung in his eyes. He leaned forward, his long hair falling over his face. He sobbed with his face obscured by his hands. Oh, fuck. A couple walking a dog gaped at us as they passed by. Startled. Why was one boy crying and the other just standing in front of him doing nothing?

Was he heartless? Frick. Puxhàredo. *Am I this heartless?* Gotta do something.

Please, medicine, please work harder!

I kicked the cardboard walls. I pushed the box open. I fought the darkness holding me down. The medicine had to work. I had to reach out to Austin. *Fuck. Come on. He's red-faced and bawling. My heart is breaking*. I broke bones to prove to Austin that I was different. I had to show him I changed. *I wouldn't give up on us.*

"Austin! Austin!" I held onto my crutches, desperate to wrap my arms around him and pull him close to me.

He looked at me teary-eyed. I had never seen him cry. Not once, even when I stopped talking to him at school. Breaking up with him in a rainstorm. He never cried, at least in front of me. He removed his glasses. *Oh my gosh, he's naked without them.*

"Austin!" I said his name over and over again under the spreading jacaranda trees while kids played across the street.

Kids were filled with so much love. Love came easy to them. Love can come easily to me. *Try harder, Elijah.* I balanced myself with the crutches and reached for him to tuck his hair behind his ears.

"I promise," I had said that to him. I chiseled it into diamond that I tucked into my heart. I would never push him away again. I chose to stand with him on the side of the line he had drawn in the sand. On one side, I was with him; on the other side, I was alone in the darkness.

The sun in La Biscayne was brighter because the mantra of Minerva was "*Tobo aqel importa veo Minerva es amora.*"

"Austin." I came closer, whispering in his ear, "I'm sorry. I am so sorry."

His head fell against my shoulder.

"I am so sorry I didn't hold your hand, and I snapped at you."

I stepped back and looked at Austin.

I was shocked.

In this moment, under the fragrant jacaranda trees above us, in the middle of June, I realized I was looking at a boy. A sixteen-year-old boy with long hair. I thought he was something else. He seemed like a warrior, an emperor, an unflinching Immortal like Máurso or Ammara, also known as Venus. The fucking pop star.

Instead, he was a boy just like me, filled with his own insecurities and fears and sorrows and pain. He wasn't any different than me, really.

Maybe he just knew how to function better than me. Maybe, while I gravitated toward negativity and self-loathing, he had mastered leaning into happiness, keeping his darkness better locked away than I had. Maybe, he had chosen to ignore his demons so he could live in the present.

He started sobbing again. I took his hand and held it tightly for a moment. I balanced my crutches, so we walked and held hands along the sidewalk shaded by ancient trees, past a Mexican man wearing a cowboy hat and selling *helado* from a push cart to smiling kids, past girls from our school sunbathing on their front lawns, listening to Tove Lo singing out from their phones, and past a snarling dog lunging for us from a fenced-in yard.

Thank God the dog was on a leash. Halfway home, Austin stopped sobbing. The street became quiet. A car drifted by us. The hot air languished around us. Austin's black boots clunked along. He hiccupped. We stopped. He grabbed my hand and squeezed. His hands were so warm. *Meep-meep*. A song. A snippet.

He sang a snippet about a boy in a tree.

"There's a boy in a tree, oh my, oh me. Why is he in a tree?"

He giggled.

"No one knows why, little Eli."

I squeezed his hand.

"Can you scratch my arm when we get home, Kangy?"

"Right, yeah," Austin said skipping a few steps.

Meep-meep

Mum-mum

"Look at that flower!" I pointed to a hydrangea bush studded with purple flowers, bordering the sidewalk.
"Brilliant, love, brilliant flowers."

Chapter Eighteen

Birds and Bees

A FEW DAYS later, Austin pushed a cart around our favorite home fur-nishing store. Mom disappeared to look at a room set up to be a yoga studio. She was suddenly into yoga and practiced everyday with Chris-tine in her own yoga room on the first floor. But that wasn't good enough for Mom. She wanted her own place to practice yoga. Then again, when you live in a house with forty-eight rooms there was space for two yoga studios.

Austin paused the cart in front of a display of duvets. "This will look perfect for your bed, mate." He pulled the duvet to his face, rubbing it and closing his eyes, "Soft," he said, "and looks so clean."

I frowned. "What about when we, you know?"

Austin paused rubbing the duvet cover peering at me through his glasses. "What?" He smiled mischievously.

"You know!"

"Say it."

"Sex," I hissed.

A woman turned to look at us with a disapproving look on her face.

"*Puno, puno, puno*!" Austin chanted the word for sex in the Old Language, which he knew she didn't understand. She mumbled something about speaking English and pushed her cart away from us.

Austin just laughed. "Americans," he announced loudly, "are very uptight when it comes to puno! Sex!" His eyes fell on an elderly Chinese woman who said something to him in Cantonese. He frowned, turning to me.

"What did she say?"

"That I should spend more time studying and less time thinking about sex. Sounds like my gran." He chuckled. "Anyway, mate." He lowered his voice. "We can wash these after...you know...someday... puno...you and me," he said, placing the duvet set in the cart, then taking my hand and shouting for Mom to meet us in the restaurant for Swedish meatballs because, of course, he was hungry. Austin was always hungry.

"Do you think I'm weird?"

"Define weird," Austin said, as he he reached over and snatched a donut from behind the glass separating the food from the line.

"Me. Prude. You think I'm Puritanical."

"You're American," Austin said. "It's not your fault."

"I do... I mean...well..."

"Easy, Eli," Austin said. "It's fine. I'm not a sex-obsessed teenager," he said, but he looked directly at a man behind the line who was slinging fries.

"Thanks for sharing that info, kid." The guy rolled his eyes.

"Thanks for listening."

"Fries?"

"Yeah." And then he eyed the plate and the meager amount of fries. "Surely, you can do better than that?"

The man grunted and heaped on more fries.

While we waited in line to pay, I reflected on my session with Arnulfo.

I was scared of having sex. Of the risks. They always tell us that when we have sex, we'll catch something.

"HIV is a scary thing, but it's a manageable condition these days," he said. "And there are things you can do to be safe. Use protection. Take medicine like pre-exposure prophylaxis. Be monogamous."

"That's me," I told him. "I want to be monogamous with Austin."

"Then why are you worried?"

"I'm not ready for that step. I mean, when we do that, have sex, I'll definitely be a man."

"That's a good thing."

"What if I want to be a kid forever?"

"That's impossible."

"Why?"

"You have to grow up, Elijah."

The last year taught me growing up was painful. Arnulfo looked at me. "If you are worried about taking your relationship to the next level, tell Austin. It's that easy. Talk it over with him. That's what adults do."

Later that night, Austin helped me bathe, one of the perks of having casts on my arm and leg. We were both naked in his huge walk-in shower, with a bench, and steam from the sauna setting swirling around us.

"Kangy?"

"Yes, Eli?" he said, gently washing my back with a washcloth.

"I was talking to Arnulfo about sex."

"Yeah?"

"Yeah," I said. "And my fears about it, and he suggested I talk it over with you."

"Good," Austin said. "Eli is learning to talk to his Kangy rather than running from him."

"I'm afraid of having sex because they say it's dirty between two boys."

"They are stupid," Austin said, gently washing my left arm. "I think it's better. Neither one of us can get pregnant, and we love each other, and that is how we'll share our love."

"Call it lovemaking? Yuck."

Austin laughed, his guttural laugh. "We can call it something else. Puno?"

"Barf."

Austin laughed some more. "Eli cracks Kangy up."

Now he was washing my hair as I leaned my head back to keep my arm and leg dry.

"Kangy?"

"Yes, Eli—keep your eyes closed tight, love."

"When we have sex, will we still be us?"

"Of course, we will, love. I mean, we'll be different but still us."

"Different?"

"Well, not virgins." He laughed. "You are still a virgin, right?"

"Am I ever." I laughed. "I mean, I worry. What if we feel so different and it affects us?"

"We'll feel different, but we'll talk through it? Okay?"

"And we'll be safe?"

"Of course."

"You won't do anything weird?"

"Define weird, love."

"You know, drip hot wax on my face."

"Maybe something else."

He whispered in my ear.

I looked at him. I didn't understand what he meant.

He just laughed, peering at me. "Eli, you are really one of a kind, and that's why I love you."

He dried my hair and kissed me on the lips.

Later, in bed, I remarked, "We're so close to being men, Kangy."

"Yes, but we still have a lot of growing to do." He added, looking at me laying shirtless in his bed, "Though you've turned into a man, body-wise, Eli. You have this line of hair going from your belly button to your chest, and it's so sexy."

"Really?"

"Yes," he said. "I have very little hair. I wish I had hair like you."

We laughed a little. "We can trade if you want!"

"After we trade scalps?"

"Sure," I said, rolling over to grab Ocho. "Austin?"

"Yes, mate."

"Will you be with me? When we grow older?"

"Always," he whispered. "And you?"

"Always, Kangy. Always."

And he pulled me close to him, and told me to relax, close my eyes, and sleep.

I woke up like clockwork screaming, "Austin! Austin!"

"Let's go and see the day start, Eli," Austin said. He helped me up to the roof and we watched the sun rise over the Verdugo Mountains. The brown mountains turning from dark-gray to purple to burnt sienna, covered with splotches of dark-green chaparral.

We huddled close together as the morning chill dissipated and the sun gently warmed the roof around us.

"Thank you, Kangy."

"For what, Eli?"

"For this, last night."

"You're welcome, Little Eli."

"My panic attack wasn't so bad this time."

"Eli's healing."

Chapter Nineteen

Out of the Rabbit Hole

AS JUNE DRIFTED on, Southern California's famous June Gloom—coastal fog—gave way to warm weather in the afternoon, my leg healed, and I no longer needed to use the boot or walk with a cane. I woke up in my bed, curled under the new duvet and bedding I bought with Austin, looking up at the leaves of the Monstera plant arching over my bed from its perch on my bedside table. I wiggled my toes comfortably.

I scanned my room, admiring the vintage REM, U2, and Red Hot Chili Peppers posters Austin and I put up on the walls last night after buying them at the newsstand on San Fernando Boulevard. Mom rummaged around the attic and found boxes of my stuff that she had banished in her fit of rage during the winter of my discontent. My plastic building blocks, my collection of toy cars, and even my dollhouse, a perfect replica of the mansion. We set it up on a table in a corner, near a fiddle leaf fig tree growing toward the ceiling.

I lowered myself onto the floor and sat cross-legged, staring at the house, three stories with a tower on one side, lit from within. I used to spend hours playing adventures in the house. The boy who lived with his aunts battling monsters. I had missed the dollhouse so much when Mom took it away. Now, months later, I didn't know what to do with it. I guessed I forgot how to play with toys in the last few months.

*

A FEW DAYS later, Mom and I walked along San Fernando Boulevard eating ice cream and talking.

Mom's red hair was pulled into a ponytail and she wore her giant hoop earrings and aviator sunglasses and she looked amazing.

"You know what, Mom." I said, struggling to put into words what I had discussed with Arnulfo last session.

"What?" Mom said lazily, enjoying the afternoon sun, the ocean breeze blowing into the Valley from the coast.

"Remember when you called Dad a fat piece of shit?"

"Did I?"

"Yeah."

"Okay."

"Remember when you said I shouldn't be like Dad..."

Mom stopped. "Wait, you didn't think I thought you were fat?"

I nodded.

"I'm sorry, Elijah," Mom said. "Shit, I should have known better. I know you've been having body issues lately. No matter what, I love you. I've been a bad parent." Mom grimaced. *Was she going to cry?*

"At least you stuck around."

"You're my son. Of course, I stuck around."

I licked my ice cream thoughtfully. "It's weird, Mom, but I really thought he was some superhero that was actually doing cool things. That's why he wasn't around."

Mom didn't say anything.

After a while, she said, "Well, he was a superhero once. He

changed. We changed. Life happens.”

Mom finished her ice cream and rubbed my arm. “The best thing that I got from your dad was you.”

I blushed. I didn’t have poker face.

“Mom, that’s sort of gross.”

Mom laughed. “It’s true!” She added, “Sex isn’t gross, darling.”

I should not be having this conversation with my mom.

Mom looked at me. “I’m serious, darling.”

“You’re being ridiculous, Mom. I’m never having sex.”

I said that too loudly.

A few people turned to look at me.

Mom chuckled.

“This is awkward,” I said.

I mean, I shouldn’t be talking to Mom about sex.

“When you love someone, like Austin, sex just happens. You shouldn’t worry about it so much.”

“Would you be mad if we did…well, you know?”

“Yes.” Mom deadpanned. “I’ll beat you with a wet noodle.”

“Funny, Mom.”

“You and Austin are very close; that’s easy to see. And when you have a strong relationship, sex just increases the intimacy you share.”

“What do you mean?” I was still sorta gagging over this conversation.

“Well,” Mom said, “you feel closer to them. You share your love physically, and that’s a beautiful thing.”

I thought about her and Sean. I know, that was a gross thing to think about. I changed the subject.

“You’ve been serious with Sean for a while.”

Mom nodded.

“Do you think you’ll marry him?”

“Maybe…someday. We’ll see.”

“No way!”

"Yes, it's crossed my mind."

"You vowed to never marry again."

"Arnulfo helped me to understand things about myself. And I'm not afraid anymore." Mom paused." Don't get any ideas, we're not planning on getting married anytime soon."

"Are you having sex?" I said a moment later. I couldn't resist.

Mom laughed and laughed. She was slyer than me.

"None of your business! Now, let's go into this candle store. I know how obsessed with candles you are."

*

A WEEK LATER in the bumblebee garden, Austin leaned back on his elbows, shirt off, revealing his eight-pack and well-defined physique.

I sprawled out on a red and blue beach towel reading *The Cat Who Played Post Office* aloud to Austin. Ocho rested on Austin's chest, his black glass eyes catching the late afternoon sun filtering through the leaves of the sycamore and poplar trees shading the edge of the garden.

"I love Jim Qwilleran."

I finished the page and flipped to the next one when Austin patted the grass near him while grinning mischievously. "Come here, love."

"Kangy?"

"Come and sit on Kangy's lap."

"Kangy!"

He peered at me through his sunglasses." Come on, love. Let go, let Kangy"

"I don't want to be the little spoon!"

"Eli, it's okay." Austin explained," Someone has to do it. Why not you?"

I rolled my eyes at him. "Being the little spoon means I'm weak."

"Yin and Yang," Arnulfo told me during session. "You can't have big spoon without little spoon. You fit together perfectly, so just go with the flow, Elijah. And stop worrying about what the little voice in your head says. When you're in love and together with someone, there are no rules as to who you have to be. Just do what makes you feel good."

"I heard some guys saying that if you do one position you're not even gay."

Arnulfo laughed. I mean, he howled loudly.

He knocked over his cup of tea.

As he was wiping it up, I said, "So, if the person likes the other position does that make them gay?"

I shrugged. Arnulfo chuckled." No, Elijah. That's the talk of people who don't know better. Don't listen to that at all. Men love a person, and everything about that person and those differences, the ones you're talking about, are what make a relationship work."

"I've heard in some languages the words for those positions equate to tough or weak. I mean, I don't think I'm weak at all."

"That's just the nuance of language," Arnulfo said. "And how many times have I told you it's okay to be weak. To show your vulnerability, to ask for help?"

I shrugged. "Every time we have session you tell me."

He tapped his head. "Do you see a pattern?"

I shrugged again. "I just worry about being weak to Austin."

Arnulfo chuckled. "I think you're way past that stage. He knows you have weaknesses and strengths just as he has; remember, being vulnerable, which is what I prefer to a loaded word such as weak, shows your partner that they can be open with you too. Revealing your true self to Austin makes you grow stronger as a man."

"Men are vulnerable?"

"Of course, Elijah. Real men, not the toxic masculinity the media wants men to model. Be you, and Austin will love you."

I sighed, thinking about that session. That really stuck with me. That conversation. About being vulnerable. Especially to Austin. I guess I had revealed my whole self to Austin and he loved the 100 percent of me he saw. And that was a sign I was becoming a man.

Austin was staring up at the sky with Ocho tucked under his arm, singing something in Cantonese.

"You look so sweet," I said, crawling closer to him. "And hot."

"Yeah?" Austin pulled me down onto his lap. "Kangy's Biggie is happy to see you, love."

He snatched off my sunglasses, lifted my shirt, and began running his fingers along my chest.

"Kiss me!" I murmured into his ear.

Austin pulled me toward him.

"You should be practically naked around Kangy all the time, love," he muttered in between nipping on my lower lip. "I love how you trimmed your fur."

"I think you're the only one who likes my chest hair."

Austin chuckled. "I doubt that, but needless to say, I'm the only one who gets to rub my hand in it, love."

We kissed. The juices flowed as we rubbed and petted each other. We rolled over onto Ocho, smooshing him into the towel. Eventually, we came up for air. Austin lay on his back, gasping, his hair sticking up in every direction, his glasses crooked on his nose.

I smoothed my hair, leaned down to kiss him again, and began to read aloud. Soon, Austin mumbled to himself and made chuffing sounds. I plopped onto my back next to him.

"I love the bumblebee garden. This is where I really went bonkers over you. Do you remember?" he asked and rolled over so he was leaning over me, peering into my eyes. "That day, when you were having your bloomin 'tea party with Little Ocho, I knew I had to be with you. I needed that side of you in my life."

I quipped, "It wasn't a tea party. We were sunbathing and discussing current events."

He tickled me. "Is that so, love?"

"Besides, you've told me this, many times. Ow, that tickles!!"

"Is that so? So Kangy is repeating himself, yeah, love?"

"Yes."

"Get used to it. Kangy loves to repeat himself."

He went for my weak spot, tickling me under my knees.

I screamed out loud. Bumblebees continued to drone around us, and the fountain gurgled nearby.

"You jolly well know it was a tea party, Eli. You and Little Ocho and these bleedin 'bumblebees."

I squealed as he kept tickling me.

"Say it was a tea party!"

I resisted. He tickled me more.

"FINE!" I shouted. "It was a tea party, Santa!"

"Santa?"

"You said jolly."

Austin peered down at me through his glasses." Jolly right I did!"

After a moment, he rolled onto his back, panting, staring up at the sky.

"You're such a romantic, Kangy."

"So are you, Eli."

"I am not!" I countered, not wanting to admit my affinity for romance since I equated that with weakness.

Blah.

Blah.

Blah.

Arnulfo would tell me to embrace my romantic side.

"I'm a fighter, Kangy!"

"Sorry, that's bollocks, love."

"Maybe."

"Not maybe, you love love, admit it, mate."

"I guess," I said. "You know I've cried more in the last year than in my entire life. Arnulfo says that's a good thing."

"I agree with him," Austin said." You're becoming more confident the more connected to your feelings you are, Eli."

"Like it or not, Elijah," Arnulfo told me during our last session, "you're on the verge of being a man. It's happening whether you like it or not."

I paused, mulling that over. Arnulfo held a steaming cup of tea in his hands.

"What does that mean?"

"It means you deal with things that happen to you, and sometimes they are good and sometimes bad but you get through it and make decisions for yourself on your own."

I sighed looking at him drinking his tea. The guy was always drinking tea. Herbal tea. I was surprised herbs don't sprout atop his giant mane of gray hair. Finally, I grinned.

"I think I'm okay with that, Arnulfo."

Arnulfo smiled. "Good."

Chapter Twenty

Last Day of School

TODAY WAS THE last day of school. I met Austin at his house to walk with him. Austin didn't bring his soccer gear but grabbed his backpack, and we walked together under the spreading jacaranda trees. The last day of school had its own energy, a sense of the year winding down as another class of seniors graduated, leaving behind their past and opening a door to their future. Everyone else bid farewell to another school year and welcomed three months of bumming around, no studying, no tests, no homework.

I had tried to convince Mom to let me return to class, but she and Dr. Hu wouldn't be dissuaded. I completed all my coursework, and my body continued to adjust to the medication.

"We don't want you to have a panic attack at school," Mom told me. "Besides, you should be happy to not be at school."

"The last day of school is like Christmas to kids. There's an excitement in the air. The present is summer break!"

"You walk Austin to school, then come home, okay?"

"Mom, I'm missing out on kid Christmas."

"You'll survive," Mom said, leaning against the counter in a quiet corner of the kitchen, watching videos on her phone.

"Please?"

"I'm watching cat videos," Mom said dryly. "You should too when you come home."

"I got you hooked, Mom," I said. "So maybe..."

"No, come home. That's an order."

"Yeah, okay."

"Besides, your cast comes off today. That should make you happy." Mom set her phone down on the counter next to her.

"Hell yes!" I said, "I'm tired of this thing!"

Ten minutes later, Austin and I were holding hands on the way to school.

"You're content, Kangy."

"How can you tell?" Austin asked.

"You're making your chuffing sounds."

"Mum-mum-mum," Austin replied.

"That's the sure sign right there."

As we walked along, under the sunlight filtering through the canopy of the Jacaranda trees, Austin pointed out flowers growing along the borders of lawns.

"This is rosa borealis. That's Latin."

"Real Latin or Kang Latin?"

"You decide." Austin grinned mischievously.

"I better say real Latin or I have a feeling you'll get mad."

"Not mad," Austin corrected. "Disappointed."

We giggled.

"What creates fog, mate?"

"Heat in the inland valleys rises, pulling in cold air off the Pacific which causes condensation at the coast..."

"Wow, so smart, Eli," Austin said. He paused to pick a daisy and presented it to me.

"For my lovely Eli."

"Thanks, Kangy." I tucked the flower behind my ear.

"I love our walks, Eli."

"Me too."

"I'm happy you're holding my hand."

"Of course," I said, "I'm glad to hold your hand to make you happy."

"Mum-mum-mum," he muttered contentedly. "How are you doing with the medicine?"

"Good," I said. "The brain fog has receded. I'm not blurry-eyed anymore, and the darkness isn't black anymore. More like twilight or dawn just before the sun comes up."

"Brilliant, mate." Austin squeezed my hand. "I'm glad you're feeling better. And how is session?"

"Better," I said, "I'm more relaxed. And I no longer break down in tears or end up shouting at Arnulfo."

"That's great, mate," Austin said and added, "Are you excited to get your cast off?"

"You don't know," I said. "I hate the punisher, as I call it. I can't wait for Dr. Hu to saw it off, blow it up, or whatever she's going to do."

We snickered while birds sang in the boughs of the ancient trees shading the street.

Devlina's appearance was different. More opaque. A part of me missed hanging out with her in real life, arguing over her destroying the world and me affirming I'd stop her. Her telling me to lighten up and me telling her that was rich coming from a Malevolent called the Queen of the Gloom.

When I dreamed of Devlina, she was in her house of horrors in Beverly Hills, only the walls were no longer rotating panels of black obsidian, but rather made entirely of flames. Only not real flames, more like fire licking out of the windows, up the sides of a house as if on an old VHS tape. The images flickered and appeared wavy and distorted.

In one memorable dream, Devlina came to me, her face melted off and turned into red wax on the floor.

"I killed *Mäu Anveddia*," she explained, and her skull shimmered with flecks of glitter. "She's Zid'dra's second wife, the Goddess of Envy. Ha. I offed her by being better than her. She died of envy. Imagine that."

She doubled over with laughter while her face spun around and around like water circling a drain.

"Devlina, maybe you can just stop. You know what kind of husband Zid'dra is. Accept it. Why keep fighting him?"

"You're adorable, babe."

"Devlina! Be sensible, stop your battle with Zid'dra. Leave him be! He's weakened and not hurting anyone anymore."

"Revenge is mine!"

"I heard Mom talking to Simon Tong from XAQ6. The coven is uniting against you. You can't win this battle."

"Killjoy," Devlina said, before disappearing down the drain in a swirl of red wax.

I peered down the dark drain. "Devlina," I whispered, "be careful."

I shook the latest dream from my head as I walked back home after escorting Austin to the gates leading to school. Mom honked the horn of her cherry-red sports car.

"Hey, you! The boy with the red hair!"

I turned slowly. "You talking to me?"

"You're the only redhead here."

I grinned and opened the passenger side door.

"You ready to lose that thing?"

"You don't know," I said. "I am over the Punisher."

"Goodbye, punisher, you fucker!"

"MOM!"

Mom hit the gas, and her sports car leaped off the pavement and roared down Glenoaks Boulevard to the red granite high-rise with bands of black windows on the border of Glendale, home to Dr. Hu's practice.

Dr. Hu wasted no time sawing off the Punisher. And like that, I was free.

"How does that feel, Elijah?" Dr. Hu asked, depositing the pieces of the cast in a trash receptacle.

I stared at my arm, pale with swirls of dead skin.

"Wow," I said, "good. Glad to be done with casts."

"Maybe keep in that way for a while?" Dr. Hu said to me but looked pointedly at Mom.

"What? I didn't make him trip!" Mom said, reaching in her purse and fishing out some chewing gum and unwrapping it. "Anyway, I'm a cool mom now, right, darling?"

"I guess." I laughed. "You call me darling now. Not sure if I like that."

"Prefer honey bunny or sweetie pie?"

"Mom, no."

*

LATER, I SAT in the sand in front of the trendy El Mar hotel located on the beach in Santa Monica. A fire burned in a pit on a large patio behind me. Fog hovered on the horizon. Mom surprised me with an end of the year party, inviting all my friends.

"Hey, Elijah." April came to sit next to me. "This is so awesome." She sipped something out of a red plastic cup.

"Glad you are having fun."

"How are you doing?'

"Better," I told her. "I'm starting to sleep normally again. Haven't had a panic attack in a week."

"That's awesome,"she said. "Look, I'm sorry that this happened to you."

I shook my head. "April, it just happened. You've met my mom. She's intense. I'm intense..."

"Neurotic too."

I laughed hard. "Okay, true."

"Prone to being a perfectionist, dramatic."

"Okay, I get it April."

She broke up and squeezed my leg with her hand.

The ground near us trembled and sand began collapsing into a hole. April and I crawled away. A second later, Máurso appeared in front of us.

"I heard there was a party!" he said, wearing a Hawaiian shirt, khaki shorts, flip-flops, and a purple-and-red lei. An orange tabby cat sat on his shoulder.

"That was quite the entrance, Dáumo."

Máurso stepped toward me. "I am a god, remember? I have to make an entrance."

Mom glanced over at us. She smiled and waved to Máurso. "Hiya, Marsy. I'm glad you came."

My mouth dropped. "Marsy?"

Máurso grunted, "You didn't hear that, lad." He stomped across the sand toward Mom, demanding a pitcher of mead mixed with soda.

Mom summoned a pitcher out of the air and handed it to him. In a moment, they were talking and laughing like old friends. It had never occurred to me that Mom had her own relationship with Máurso.

Kevin ambled over to us, wearing khaki shorts and a blue Dodgers jersey. He fist-bumped me and sank into the warm sand. We talked for a while about the end of the school year, me missing the last day of school, the casual banter of best friends. After a while, April and Kevin began talking in their twin speak, whispering and rocking in the sand. They paused to kiss. I loved seeing my best friends in love. When the sun went down, Austin and I watched fireworks, holding hands. Santa Monica had fireworks every night in the summer.

It sounded so great to hear my friends happy. I made a toast at the hotel restaurant earlier thanking them for being there for me the last year.

"We're your friends!" April said, somewhat indignant that I was toasting her. In her world, friends were family. Maybe she was right.

Mom grabbed her glass of champagne and stood, clinking it with her knife. "I have some announcements to make. First, my son, known lovingly as Beta2, my darling Elijah, is cast-free and ready to terrorize monsters and pedestrians equally, as he rides around with his skateboard. He's also decided he wants to study architecture when he goes to college. I'll be your first client. I'd love a cozy, modern cottage to retreat to when I'm tired of the drafty, maze-like mansion we live in!"

"Really?"

"Yes, Beta2."

Then Mom lifted her glass to Tory, sitting next to April—they had become quick friends in the last month—turned out both had a passion for fashion.

"Second, I'd like to congratulate Beta1—"

Mom's voice was interrupted by Sunny, who growled, "Those are their secret security names! For the love of haggis!"

"My apologies to the security team," Mom said. "Anyway, Tory has decided to study business administration at Winchester University, and she is going to intern with me at Dirk Delomary Global Holdings."

Tory beamed.

"She's going to study business because she's shown an interest in running our little family vocation." Mom winked at her. "And she will study the theory of applied arts and sciences."

"I'll never be able to conjure anything," Tory interrupted, grinning. "But I'd like to better relate to my family since I'm the Marilyn in our little Munsters family."

I shot Tory a look, mouthing: are you sure?

She mouthed back: heck yes!

Mom continued, "Finally, there was an election at the Southern California chapters of the Temple of Magic, and well..."

Aunt Christine, sitting beside her, stood, "What B is trying to say is she was named an *Estànta Áussenta*. That means, to all our ordinary friends and family, she'll be calling the shots at the Còngréhassa, helping to bring the Alliance into the twenty first century."

I stood, clapping really hard. Austin whistled, and the restaurant buzzed with conversation and more applause.

Mom stood with Christine. "I'll be handing over my role as head of the Temple of Magic for the Southern California Chapter to Chrissy here. We will all be in her capable hands. Not only is she one of the best teachers of magic, but she's got real spunk. She'll make sure the Alliance in LA shines again!"

Christine curtsied because she was a fool like that. "Also, I plan to redecorate. The *Miami Vice* theme in the lobby is so dated. And we are not going to wear togas anymore. Yuck."

Everyone in the room chuckled. Máurso stood. "To the Delomary family." He scanned the room making eye contact with Tory, Mom, Christine and Uncle George, Barn, Austin, and me. "Me, I love your bloomin' family. I hope you all consider this lowly God of War a part of your kin." And then he began to get weepy—nine-foot-tall Máurso began to cry! The room filled with mist and the sky darkened and his many cats slinked over to him and began rubbing against his legs.

"Máurso, of course, you're one of us. You like cats. You're intense and have a temper and you are so, so kind even though you don't want anyone to know it."

Máurso became more weepy, and then he changed into a hawk and flew out an open window.

"I'm afraid," Mom said, "he doesn't want anyone seeing the God of War in this state." Mom raised a glass. "*Levas Continua Festar*!"

After the speech, Austin and I trekked out to the sand to be alone. I watched the light from the fireworks play on Austin's face. Red and blue and green and yellow.

"Are you glad it's summer, Kangy?"

Austin nodded. "I'm excited to spend everyday with you, my Eli.

"Are you feeling better?"

"Yes," I whispered. "I think I feel kind of high from the higher dose. I mean I feel really happy and mellow right now."

Austin shook his head. "That's not high, that's Kangy. My cuddles and kisses are making you ecstatic, yeah?"

We giggled.

Austin looked at my arm. "You glad to have your arm back?"

"Yeah," I responded. "I'm looking forward to battling monsters at some point. First, I want to have adventures with you."

"What sort of adventures?" He threw me this wicked smile, dripping with sexual innuendo. I was certain Austin was ready to take our relationship to the next level.

"All sorts of adventures," I said ignoring his innuendo, watching the fireworks overhead.

"Maybe without trousers and pants, love?"

"Trousers and pants? Are you using weird British slang, Kangy?"

"Trousers are PANTS," he intoned. "And PANTS are underwear, yeah, love?"

"What the hell does that mean?"

We both laughed really hard for a while as red, white, gold, orange, and green fireworks exploded overhead.

After a while, Austin and I wandered into the hotel, which was part of our family's many real estate holdings. We stopped at the bar to order some Shirley Temples, then poked our head in the lounge, packed with people drinking and dancing to alternative hip-hop. We played darts for a while in a courtyard by a fire pit, then went up to a room to give ourselves facials.

Austin pulled his T-shirt off and sauntered around the suite saying, "Look how sexy I am, mate!" Only he was walking strange, head out, arms akimbo, walking bow-legged. We retreated to the bathroom. I smeared a cucumber and lemon peel mask on his face and mine and some blackhead removal strips on our noses. Then we went and sat holding hands and sipping our drinks.

We must have fallen asleep. I woke slowly, hearing the whoosh sound of the gas fireplace, my eyes adjusting to the shadows leaping and falling on the bamboo ceiling. I touched my face; the mask had dried and was crunchy and tight. I turned my head. Austin had his mouth open, drool dripping from the corner of his mouth.

I stood, crossed the room, and went into the bathroom to wash the mask off. I switched on the light, and then, well, I screamed like crazy.

In the mirror, behind me, near the shower, appeared the most frightening monster I had ever seen. A phantom composed of shades of gray and white and black. She had long, stringy black hair and black eyes. An unseen breeze winnowed her hair.

She opened her mouth and shouted like a banshee, then lunged for me and floated through the glass separating the shower from the rest of the bathroom. I screamed. She shrieked.

Maybe it was the medicine. Perhaps it surged right when fear set in. Or maybe, I was just annoyed and needed my mask off my face. Either way, I instinctively pulled a sword out of the sky and impaled her in the torso. Wait, I was supposed to use my PlasmX. Oh, crap. What was going on?

"What the hell!" she gasped in shock, her eyes flickering.

"I am trying to take my mask off and have a delightful evening with my boyfriend."

"I am here to destroy you," she stammered, the sword stuck in her torso. Her whole body flickered and quivered like a hologram. "I am the ghost of this hotel, a ghoul who has haunted this spot for fifty years, preying on twentysomethings and party animals, scaring the bejesus out of them for fun."

"Well, you got me on the wrong night."

"That's not cool," she said. "You are supposed to be terrified." She frowned. "You're a fricking kid for God's sake. I love scaring little creeps like you!"

"I'm a Magical," I said. "This isn't my first time at the ghoul rodeo. I kill your kind so that other creeps, as you call them, aren't traumatized for a lifetime."

"Oh, for crying out loud," she said. Her body flashed for a moment, revealing a skeleton. "Why didn't you wear a shirt or something to warn me?"

"According to the Pàcifimenta, you are not supposed to haunt or prey on Ordinaries at hotels."

"The—uh, look, I died here unexpectedly. I drank too much champagne and tripped on a rug and hit my head. Then I awoke, and I was here, floating around."

"So, you're not part of a coven?"

"Oh, no," she said, "but I was in a cult. You know, we sacrificed and worshipped the devil."

"Bad idea."

"Judgmental."

"Look," I said, "I need my sword back and you have to be gone."

"Says who?"

"Me, Elijah Delomary, Bane of the Gloom."

The ghoul mouthed the words of my name, then scratched her head, confused.

I rolled my eyes and wrinkled my nose. The air rippled. A breeze picked up, rustling through the toilet paper nearby.

"Look," I said, "I'm supposed to report you to the Anti-coven League. They are the police for monsters like you. They can pick you up and haul you away. They might even call the *Macistráuto*—they're the fuzz, you know—and they'll send you to the *Màdlinn* in London to face trial. You don't want to go to trial."

"Madeleine? London, trial? I'm confused."

"The Màdlinn has jurisdiction over monsters."

"I'm not a monster, honey."

"Look in the mirror."

A second later, she shrieked, "What is that?"

"You," I said. "And the Màdlinn will find you guilty of terrifying Ordinaries—humans—and recommend you be sent to the *Excelà*."

"The Accenture?"

"Excelà—the void. You'll dissolve into nothing."

The ghoul touched her quivering face. "Rid the world of my beautifully horrific face?"

"Or," I said.

She raised her eyebrows. "Or?"

"I can let this slide. I mean, I'm not into having to deal with Agécendrus from the League tonight, so I'll give you a choice," I said, pointing to two rippling circles in the air. "Go to the pretty place with harps and white light and clouds to your left or the Gloom, where it smells like farts, feet, and is inhabited by terrible monsters. That'll be to your right."

The ghoul's appearance shifted, quivered, and flickered in and out.

"And you're sure I can't stay here and jump out from the closet at toddlers? Hover over couples on their honeymoon scaring the living daylights out of them? Haunting the staff in the laundry room?"

"No," I said. "Look, my sword is disrupting your magic. The League is a short call away. I have a mask to take off. Can you decide, please?"

"I'll take the smelly place!" she said, pulling the sword out of her torso, handing it to me and flying into the tear in the air leading to the Gloom. I wrinkled my nose and closed the tears behind her.

"Oi," Austin said. He stood in the doorway, hair standing up every which way, his mask shriveled on his face. "You defended yourself from a phantom!"

"She jumped out at me!"

Austin smiled. "You weren't even scared."

"Did you see the whole thing?"

He nodded. "Yeah, it was amazing how you just reached up toward the sky and pulled that sword out of the air!"

"Yeah, it was instinctual," I said. "But I didn't summon my PlasmX."

"You used magic, intuitively," Austin said. "Your magic is getting stronger!"

"Shit, you're right!"

"As you get better, so does your magic."

"Cool!"

"And you bent the law a little to show compassion for a ghoul."

"I know. I mean she was scary AF, but, you know, I think she just got lost when she died unexpectedly."

"And she just needed a push to the fiery place we call the Gloom."

"Exactly."

"My Eli, doing right in the world while getting better every day!"

Austin pulled me into a hug and tried to kiss me, but our masks stuck to each other, so we had to separate, then wash our faces with hot water. Afterward, we were both feeling frisky, so we began to make out. Good thing that ghoul was gone or we'd probably have given her quite the show.

*

"I FEEL CRAZY," I said to Austin at breakfast the next day. Mom was still in her room, asleep. So were Kevin and April. Máurso was outside reading to a half-dozen cats on the beach. Sean was sitting across from us, reading the news on his tablet and drinking coffee.

Austin bit into a croissant. "Why do you say that, mate?"

"Last night, how I handled myself."

"You mean, calmly?"

"Yes."

"That's good."

"I'm not used to it."

"It's a process, Elijah," Austin said. "You can't expect to change immediately."

"I'm impatient."

"You're too hard on yourself, my love." Austin chewed on a piece of bacon.

The battle inside me was a struggle of the two faces of the Gemini, one happy, one sad. One hopeful, the other fearful. One strong, the other weak. I was bifurcated. The medication acted as a bridge. Helping to soothe my nerves.

"You were pushing yourself too hard," Arnulfo said at session last week, leaning back in his chair, sipping one of his herbal teas.

"My mom," I clarified, wanting to deflect.

He shook his head. "You know that you were pushing yourself too. Remember the All Valley Swim Competition, aca-deca, the marathon?"

Damn, game on, Arnulfo.

"Give it time, Elijah. Don't push yourself," he said. "Go with the flow. Learn how to just relax."

I rolled my eyes.

Arnulfo was a hippie or something when he was young. Now, at thirty-five, he seemed old to me. I feared that time spreading between seventeen and thirty-five. All that growing up to do. My body was tired at seventeen. Geez, how would I feel at twenty? Twenty-two? Anxiety bubbled inside.

"Don't dwell," Arnulfo said, seeming to read my mind. "Stop thinking about things."

"You're right, Arnulfo," I said. "When I stop dwelling, my anxiety dissolves."

"Exactly."

*

A FEW DAYS later, Austin and I went to Razz-ma-Tazz, an ice cream shop where April and Kevin worked. Early in the afternoon at one o'clock, the large shop, with bright red booths and a red counter running along the left side, was empty.

April grinned when she saw me and Austin walk in. "Well, if it's not my favorite two boys."

We climbed onto the black-vinyl-topped stools next to the counter. Fans spun overhead.

Kevin wandered over, high-fiving Austin and me.

"What's up, fellas?"

"Enjoy the party?" I asked.

"So fun!"

"I got drunk!" April whispered very loudly.

"You drank?"

"You didn't?"

"No," I said. "You know I don't like booze."

"Geez," April said. "Anyway, I had fun."

"I had to help April when she got sick. I had the best night ever."

"Shut up, Kev!"

We all chuckled. After a while, I asked, "How was the show, *Oklahoma!*?"

"Awesome!" Kevin said. "After the performance, I think I want to be an actor."

"I want to be a professional singer!" April added.

They stopped, looked at each other and groaned. "We have to be doctors."

"Neurosurgeon."

"Anesthesiologist."

They both laughed again.

"The musical was a hit," April said a moment later.

"Thanks to us," Kevin added.

They stopped and kissed.

"Get a room," someone shouted.

I looked around. We were the only people in the place.

"What the heck?" I said.

We all looked at each other, confused. A moment later, I said, "I'm sorry I couldn't be in it."

April leaned over the counter and squeezed my hand. "Elijah, there's always next year. We're going to do *Hair*."

"Oh, well, I have plenty of that."

"Dude, you don't have to force yourself to do things you don't want to do. You were on this hamster wheel trying to please everyone else when you really just needed to stop and take a long look at yourself in the mirror. Get comfortable with what you see. The hamster wheel just distracts you. Trust me, I know. For the longest time I was trying to be something I wasn't to prove who I was."

April wiped the counter down with a red cloth. Austin leaned on the stool, eating his ice cream and nodding as Kevin continued.

"I thought I had to listen to one kind of music to prove I was Black, or like a certain food to prove I was Korean."

"What happened?"

"I went with you and April and Barn to Old Earth. I saw trees that walked, stuffed bears that talked; I was turned into a toad and was super into eating flies. FLIES! And then you turned me back to a human. That's when I realized nothing mattered anymore. I could just be me."

April stopped wiping the counter and leaned over to throw her arms around Kevin. His eyes were misty.

"I love you."

"I love you too, babe."

"Wankers," Austin mumbled. "I'm crying into my bleedin' butter pecan and pistachio sundae!

"Float On" by the Floaters droned from the jukebox in the corner. April went back to cleaning the counter. I focused on my ice cream melting. Chocolate peanut butter. My favorite.

After a while, Kevin began humming "People Will Say We're in Love." April sang softly while Austin tapped along with his fingers on the red countertop.

My toes tingled. My heart beat faster. Goose bumps rose on my arms. The room in front of me became distorted. Wavy, like a video stuck buffering.

"ELIJAH!!"

Devlina shouted across the room.

"Elijah! Another day another dead Máu!" she said. "Ziddy is mad; the coven is aligned against me; fuck them all!"

I shook my head, trying to break up the clouds in my brain.

"People Will Say We're In Love." Kevin pulled April in and kissed her again.

Austin clapped enthusiastically. *What just happened?* I saw Devlina. Was this a side effect of the medication? Imagining Devlina talking to me?

Later, in bed, as we watched the moonlight stream in the huge windows facing the Verdugo Mountains, I told Austin about seeing Devlina.

"I wouldn't worry, love," he said. "That daft cow seems hell-bent on getting you to help her but you have choices."

"Yep."

"Do what you want." He traced his fingers on my forehead writing L-O-V-E.

"And you have me, now," he said. He wore only a pair of pajama bottoms, the moonlight casting shadows on his firm stomach and chest. "I am a proficient Coaugelo. Fierce in Xem Sen Ou and good with my PlasmX."

"You like swinging your PlasmX around?"

"Saucy minx," Austin retorted.

Austin chuffed, bringing Little Ocho over to me. "I love my Eli."

I laughed.

Austin, without his glasses on, squinted at me in the moonlight streaming into the room, moving Ocho's little tentacles and throwing his voice, low and soft like an octopus.

"Don't you feel connected to the universe with magic, Kangy?"

"Aye," Austin said, "magic is like surfing, only instead of water you are riding on the power of the stars."

"Connecting to something that's bigger than you."

"Greater than us, connecting all of us," Austin-as-Ocho said.

I lay in his bed, falling silent. After a while, I said, "For the first time since that horrible day at the Edificea sie Dêtillus in London, months ago, I feel connected again to the universe, Kangy."

Austin leaned over and drew the moon and stars on my side using his fingers. A chorus of crickets drifted into the room from the windows opened to the front yard below. After a while, I drifted off to sleep.

Wavy.

Distorted.

Static. I saw Devlina going up, up and then spinning around and around, her black hair flying around her face, which was pale white, tinged with green.

"Elijah! I am so alive!" She held up the disembodied head of some monster, orange goo dripping from the severed veins dangling from its neck.

She waved the head around in front of her body, trying to get my attention. In a split second, she was doing the puxhàredo Charleston on the water in the pool after Austin and I came out.

"Elijah! Watch me!"

God, Devlina, my connection to Old Earth, however accidental. Mom used Malac Malactańena to summon her from where she was entombed in a watery grave beneath the Oceana sie Tranqauilimenta.

Devlina and I were caught in a tug of war. Back and forth. What she wanted, what I wouldn't let happen. What she needed, what I couldn't let her have. And now… No, I could just stop thinking about her. Stop worrying. I had choices. A life to live. My casts were gone. My magic was coming back. I was a warrior, a fighter, and a lover. Why bother myself with her?

Chapter Twenty-One

Red Flowers Falling On Concrete

THE MEDICINE WORKED by healing the synapses in my brain, rewiring the circuitry, and soothing my body. I guess I needed a lot of sleep. I had averaged ten hours every night the past two weeks.

I stayed up with Austin, and we'd swim in the pool until past midnight on the warm, balmy summer nights, or we would goof around his house, practice fighting with our PlasmXs, listen to U2 or Turandot on vinyl on his record player, sit up on his roof and watch the stars, watch Wu Xia movies with his parents until late, late at night.

Wu Xia movies came from China, usually Hong Kong, a mix of mystery, magic and martial arts. The actors leaped and flew around using cables and appeared to be a lot like Coaugelus.

I tried to learn Cantonese, so I could talk to Austin and his parents in their native tongue. I could count to ten:

Yut

Yee

Sam
Say
Mm
Lok
Chut
Bah
Gao
Sap

Austin told me to sing when I pronounced the words. I was a total weirdo walking around his parent's house, barefoot, singing the first ten numbers in Cantonese, but his parents were pretty impressed.

"Not too many white guys want to learn Cantonese," Austin Sr. told me. "Too many tones."

To be honest, I fell in love with the language. Counting to ten in Cantonese began to remind me of *home*.

I slept late most days. Austin, Barn, Stylo, and cousin Mason would gather to play soccer on the field at our house. When I would finally awaken and shower, I would meet them and we'd go and battle some monsters then get dim sum or sushi or tacos at the mall down the street from the mansion.

When we'd be out, I would always hold Austin's hand. Always. I was beginning to crack. I mean, I actually *liked* cuddles, hugs, and kissing him on the lips. Even in public. Sometimes people would stare, usually ugly women with mullets or perverted looking old men that probably spent their teenage years killing little animals and burying them under their houses. I didn't care anymore.

One night, Austin, Barn, Stylo, Mason, and I went to Max's of Manila, a famous fine dining Filipino place in Glendale. Stylo ordered tons of dishes for us including pancit, adobo, lumpia, and ones I've never had like kare kare, meat in a peanut sauce. We all dressed up. I mean, all five of us wore suits. Stylo looked really sharp in a white suit.

"This way, boys," the maitre d' said as he whisked us into the dining area.

"See?" Stylo said, hitting me in the chest playfully. "I look like one of the guys; that's awesome."

We gorged ourselves on the amazing food. We all asked for tooth-picks after dinner, then unbuttoned our pants and leaned back in our chairs after we ate, like how Sean and Uncle George did after a big meal at home.

Austin paid the bill, and we went outside once we could move again.

"Let's go to Heavenly Billiards," I said. "It's gay night!"

Barn groaned.

"I am going to get attacked!"

"You wish you were that dishy, mate."

"Come on, Barnhard," Mason said. "Go with the flow, dude."

A half hour later, at Heavenly Billiards, we let loose. I threw up my hands and shook my hips to the beat of the house music playing.

"Soddin' house music," Austin grumbled.

"Come on, Kangy," I said, pulling him toward me. "Loosen up."

"I am quite loose and quite the dancer, you know?" He shot me a gregarious smile and began shaking his rump. "Do you like me dancing like this, mate? Am I twerking?"

"No." I shook my head. "You're not twerking. You're dancing like a stick figure."

"Do you not like it, love?"

I pulled him to me, leaned up on my tippy-toes, and planted a kiss on his lips.

He wrapped his arms around me, chuffing contentedly in my ears.

"While you're necking," Barn, across from us, announced, "I'm dancing with my thumbs up, which is a brilliant way to dance. And, more importantly," he said, "I'm staring at the ceiling because I'm quite dishy, and I know the gays want a piece of this arse, but you know I don't want to give anyone the wrong idea."

"Drink your beer," I said. "Leo Tolstoy Chan. When you get buzzed, you get frisky."

"Yes, I am Leo Tolstoy Chan according to my fake ID," Barn ex-plained. "That totally sounds legit, right?"

"No, Barny."

"I got it, right?"

"Drink up, mate," Austin said. "You know you want to be the center of attention on the dance floor."

"'Tis true, mate," Barn said. "You know you got it going on when chavs and birds want to get up on your grill, yeah?"

"Chavs?"

"Never mind, Eli," Austin said. "The King's English is hard for you to understand."

I stuck my tongue out at him. He grinned. Stylo sauntered by us.

"I'm working a circuit, boys," she explained, "talking to as many hot girls as I can. Look at that group of tall Asian women over there. Wow! The taller the better."

"I suppose you and Eli are similar," Austin mused, his arm around my waist, sipping a Shirley Temple in his other hand. "He, my little dwarf, likes tall men too. Tall Asian men."

"I'm not a dwarf!" I protested. "I'm six feet tall!"

"So short compared to me, your giant."

"I like scaling tall things," Stylo said. After she sipped her beer, which had been acquired with her fake ID.

"I'm going to scope out those hotties in the back of the dance floor." Stylo disappeared into the squirming, moving bodies.

Austin and I wandered outside to get some fresh air. We leaned against the brick wall of Heavenly Billiards in our slacks and dress shirts and black ties. Austin chuffed and mumbled to himself, then stared into my eyes. He leaned over me, his hands touching the wall. He straightened and pulled me by my black tie to kiss me. We must have been really going at it. Our juices were flowing, our male parts struggling against our pants. I was really in love with Austin and also very horny, which was new for me.

Usually, the darkness stopped that. But now, well, I had a stonker, as Austin would say, and so did he.

"Is Kangy the Biggie coming for a visit?" I laughed.

He pushed my hand onto his crotch.

"Kangy the Biggie loves his Eli"

Wowzers.

Someone coughed nearby. We stopped kissing. Austin turned his head.

"We got some fags here, huh?"

A group of drunk frat guys wearing red ball caps circled us. One of the boys held a bat. Did they always carry bats for a night on the town?

"Is there a problem, mate?" Austin asked. He straightened and towered over all of the posse of haters.

Barn wandered outside to smoke a joint. Stylo was with him. My stomach dropped. If my powers were stronger, I could mow these closet cases down with my magic.

"I think many people that hate gays turn out to be gay," I had told Arnulfo during our last session. "Republican senators sponsor bills against us and then are caught with some young boy in Aruba. "

"When we suppress ourselves, there are all sorts of unexpected consequences, right, Elijah?"

He had been right. Look what I had done to myself suppressing myself.

I tuned back in...

"Where the fuck are you from, mate?" a boy said derisively to Austin. "The United Fagdom?" He turned to his friends. "England is full of queers."

"I'm from Hong Kong, you sodding *barmy chavs*." He made fists. "Now bugger off."

They looked confused. His slang didn't register. He had called them "white trash" in English, which was funny because they failed to comprehend. I shook my head. The scene unfolding in front of me was serious.

The boy with the bat stared at Austin, then he grinned.

"Time to beat you little pussies up."

Little did these morons know that Austin and Barn were both red belts in Xem Sen Ou. Stylo loved kickboxing. And, well, with my training from Máurso, I was getting very good at using my fists.

The boy with the bat swung at us.

"Puss—" *Crack*! Austin snatched the bat from him, kicked his legs out from under him, and tossed the bat up in the air. It never came back, so for all we knew it was probably still floating around somewhere above Heavenly Billiards.

"Who's a pussy now?" Barn said, lifting a boy up with one hand then flinging him like a rag doll into an open dumpster nearby.

"Hey, that was our leader!" another boy said, lunging for Barn. Austin intercepted him, using his left leg to kick the boy into the wall. Austin and Barn were shouting in Cantonese and flying around using Xem Sen Ou, like actors use Kung Fu in Wu Xia movies.

Flying through the air, feet kicking the haters, Barn and Austin's fists pummeling their faces and sides. *Bam*, a fist connected with Austin's face. Blood spurted from a cut over his right eyebrow. He flew back, hitting the white stucco wall behind him. He touched the bleeding wound over his right eyebrow, examining the boy who hit him. An evil smile spread across Austin's face. He motioned for the boy to come at him.

"Come over here, little piece of shit!"

Pow!

Bam!

Crash!

Bodies fell to the ground. Austin stopped to kiss me on the cheek. Then his fists flew past my ears.

Zoinks!

Crash!

Two boys collapsed behind me. I closed my eyes, fear pulsing through my veins, desperately wishing I had Little Ocho with me to cuddle. My anxiety exploded inside me.

"Reach deep inside you and touch the magic within, love."

Evangeline whispered to me, her beautiful face glowing with a wavering white light before me. The medicine surged. I opened my eyes. Austin's left leg connected with the boy with the bat. The boy stumbled sideways. Stylo punched him into Barn, who then kicked him. He sailed over a planter, landing on the hood of a car parked at the curb.

Mason appeared holding a can of cola he had snuck out of the bar, along with his familiar, Genghis Wong, a red panda. His mouth dropped, and he let go of the can, which crashed on the pavement, spilling its contents.

"Are you guys kicking ass without me?" In an instant, he was airborne, lunging toward the bigots. Genghis morphed into an eagle and launched an air attack, his claws lifting one screaming bigot into the night sky and carrying him away from us.

Austin flew over me, somehow managing to kiss me on my forehead. He used his hands to connect two heads, knocking the boys unconscious. Stylo took out two muscular dudes with one kick that sent one into the other and then both face-first into a wall.

I thought about Dirk's motto "Nunma in viacadeimo." The medicine surged. I felt strong. Screw these assholes. I was going to use Xem Sen Ou too! I clocked some lanky guy who punched me in the stomach, sending him face first into a planter.

Another guy leaped at me. I did a flying kick to his head. He stumbled backward. A guy Genghis had lifted off the ground and tossed onto the the awning of the newsstand slid to the ground, jumped to his feet, and lunged for me. I placed my hands in front of me crossed, a technique called *Solja Brillar* or Sun Shines. I pulled my hands back and thrust them forward. A blast of magic sent him up into the air.

"*Morpheima Ãe Auzo!*" I shouted. "Transforming the Bird." Another technique Máurso taught me.

Silence. I could feel the energy of the homophobic frat boys dissipate into the night air.

A breeze lifted the leaves of the Persian silk trees spreading overhead. Red flowers drifted around us. I scrutinized the sky. The moon peeked through the leaves. My fist pulsed, burned. I grimaced, looking at the scene before me. Ten boys sprawled out on the sidewalk. Three gays, two straight guys, and a familiar had cleaned up the floor with them.

Barn, his left eye blackening, his nose bleeding, smiled triumphantly. He hugged Austin. Stylo cheered. I couldn't believe us, myself.

I thought of Arnulfo,

"Haven't you realized, Elijah," he had told me, "when you believe in yourself, you can do anything."

I closed my eyes. I heard the soft rustle of the flowers falling around us.

"We are Family" drifted out the open windows of Heavenly Billiards.

I heard laughing, singing. I opened my eyes. Barn, triumphant, Austin smiling amusedly. Stylo, grinning ear to ear. Mason fist bumped Genghis who morphed back into a cute and cuddly red panda.

One of the boys groaned. Another cursed.

I looked at them.

"How does it feel to get bigot-bashed, losers?"

"Hey, what's going on over there!" someone down the street shouted.

"We got to go, boys!" Stylo said ducking up the alley, turning and urging us to hurry up. Austin wiped blood off his split lip while Barn was totally charged screaming in Cantonese and waving his arms around.

"I bloody love destroying haters!!!"

"Barn." I grabbed his arm. "We have to go"

A woman wearing daisy dukes with frosted hair looked at us. "Shit," she said. "You really wiped the floor with those assholes."

Two police officers hurried toward us.

"You guys get out of here. I'll explain what happened. Fucking homophobes." She pointed to the boys groaning and squirming on the sidewalk.

Another man joined her. "They fucking deserved it. Fucking trash."

I was on adrenaline. We battled monsters. It's what we did. However, this time we battled human monsters. I mean, they had a fucking bat with them. Who the hell walked around on a Saturday night with a bat other than a baseball player? Obviously looking for trouble. Shit, that was scary. We piled into Austin's black luxury sedan.

"I can't believe you turned a guy into a dove," Stylo shouted. "That was so cool!"

"Yeah," I said. "Felt so good!"

We were too charged to go home. We drove to Watanabe's Market on Glenoaks Boulevard on the border with Glendale city limits. The sleepy security guard at the door stood up as he saw us come in bruised, bloody, and a little shaken.

Punching someone repeatedly, in case you didn't know, hurt a lot. Shit, my fist was throbbing. Stylo picked up the latest *Tetas* magazine saying, "I'm celebrating by drooling over my favorite things."

"Mine too," Barn said, peering over her shoulder at the centerfold.

I followed Austin who pulled a fluffy white lamb off the toys rack.

He cuddled it in front of me. "I need this right now, love." He frowned, still shaken up.

"Of course." I leaned on my tippy-toes and pecked him on the cheek and squeezed his hands. He leaned forward to kiss the lamb. His long hair fell over his face. I tucked it behind his ears. He smiled broadly at me. Connected. We were connected.

I got colas and cheese snacks.

"What's rule #1, Kangy?"

"No bleeding lemon-lime soda ever, love."

Barn sauntered over to us, picked up a bag of cream-filled chocolate sandwich cookies from a shelf near us. We looked at each other. We looked like shit.

Stylo laughed at the end of the aisle.

"We look fucking crazy!"

I think we laughed for five minutes straight. The five of us, in our disheveled suits, beat up and bloody: five teenagers plus a red panda in Watanabe's Family Markets past midnight howling at ourselves.

"I can't believe we did that!" Stylo said.

"We're powerful!" I added.

"That was fun, master," Genghis said to Mason, who leaned down to scratch him behind his red furry ears tinged with white.

"You were a hero, Genghis. Thank you for all your help."

Genghis chittered merrily.

We headed to checkout.

"Rough night, eh?" the Asian woman said, scanning cans of soda, a box of cookies, bags of chips, some frozen peas and several apples for Genghis, while searching our faces.

"Midnight Mass," I said. "Man, they take penitence for our sins seriously these days."

She stared at me; then she blinked before she continued to scan our purchases. She looked like she had no idea whether to laugh or call for security.

We ended up on the stargazing rock in Homer's Glenn, the heat from the afternoon sun still emanating off the granite. Here, on the rock, with only faint light from the crescent moon, the stars exploded above our heads. The gravity of the universe tugged on me. I was under the sway of Austin. I was his moon now. And he was mine. We were stuck in orbit around each other, and we'd never leave each other. We sat in silence for a long time, listening to the sounds of creatures rustling in the chaparral around us. A star burned across the night sky. Puxhàredo, this world we lived in, filled with so much hate and so much beauty.

Mason and Genghis Wong watched the glimmering lights of the valley below. Mason rubbed Genghis's fur, eliciting content chittering from his familiar. Austin sat near me and ran a finger over the cuts on his hand, healing them with a faint pink light.

"That was crazy," Barn said, munching on a cookie while holding a bag of peas to his face.

"Welcome to the wonderful world of being gay and being affectionate," Stylo said, holding a bag of peas on her hand.

"That's fucking bollocks."

Barn cursed. His face burned red. He was so mad.

Stylo set down her bag of peas and walked over to Barn. "I can heal your wounds."

"I'll conjure something for the pain," Mason added.

Barn pushed Stylo away. "I can't fucking take it." He continued,

"Who the bleeding hell did those chavs think they were? They can go around and beat you up for being in love? I'm fricking going to lose it. Elijah, you suffered before you came out, then suffered some more because of other people's 'morals' and feelings. Well, if someone thinks being in love is immoral, I'm telling you that person is the immoral one. We live in a twisted and sick world. Sometimes I really wonder if we're fighting the wrong monsters. At least with Àzmadus and such, you know they are bad. But those people, they pretend to be so righteous and good and they are just hurting people for no real reason. People just living their lives and harming no one. Those people are the real monsters. They are the real demons on this Earth. Give me a red-skinned demon with yellow eyes and ten horns any day."

We didn't respond. The crickets began chirping in unison around us. Austin hugged his stuffed lamb. Mason rubbed Genghis Wong's shiny, brown and orange and white fur.

"I'm not going to allow it, mates," Barn said defiantly. "I'm going to tell Dad that I'm going to take some money, and I'm going to travel the country seeking out justice for queers."

"You don't have to roam the country, Barny," Austin said after a while. "You just filter out the noise and you pay attention. You join the cause, mobilize, and vote. That's the American way."

"You're some expert now, Lostin?"

"Wee, Barny, you can't fight every bigot."

Barn stood. "I'm going to try!"

"Relax," Stylo said. "Someday you'll have kids, and you'll teach them to be open-minded and accepting. The more people like that will turn the tide."

Barn sat down. "Sure, you're right, but my fists hurt," he quipped. "I fucking hate everyone."

"How about some pain relief?" Mason said, placing a hand on Barn's. A pink light emanated from his palms, then flashed out.

"Feels better, mate."

"It'll last a little while," Mason said. "You'll need some more later."

No one spoke. I turned my eyes to the Big Dipper overhead. What

I was seeing now existed thousands of years ago. Someday, will Barn's great-great-great-great-grandkids see a night sky without the Big Dipper? Will they live in a world where people aren't attacked for the color of their skin, whom they love, where they come from, the language they speak, who they worship or don't worship, or for their gender?

Puxhàredo, life sucked. Being gay sucked. Getting beat up for having a tender moment with your boyfriend. Too bad there weren't roving gangs of drag queens taking down straight couples. I imagined straights running terrified while the drag queens screamed: "Stop wearing black dress shoes with jeans, you fashion victim."

"Stop dating ugly straight guys, girl."

"Stop pushing your agenda to have kids you won't raise, spreading hate and bigotry while feeling smug and entitled."

Or, I heard in some countries, goons go around beating up straight people for holding hands. We needed those here to teach them a lesson. I sighed. *No, shit no. No one should cower from love. That's fucking bullshit. I don't want that.* I was mad. I leaned back, looking at Cassiopeia glowing above our heads. Austin chuffed and kissed his lamb.

"He's named Lammy Poo," he whispered in my ear. His warm breath tickled my ear. I chuckled, feeling better. I squeezed his hand.

Then I looked into his eyes. He had a defeated look. A weary look, like he was almost traumatized by what he had done. The thing with Austin was his rage was deep inside him. He knew when to go to his rage and use it, to let it power him, to shape and mold it, and swing it like a sword.

His rage was a means to an end. Mine just boiled below the surface, mostly hidden. I never knew how to reach it until it burst forward, and I couldn't control it. Austin controlled his rage. He understood its terrible power. He only used it when he had no other choice. Even then, he terrified himself with his power. I saw it in his brown eyes. He was horrified with himself.

"You protected me," I said, "and that was brave and heroic and I love you, Austin Kang Jr."

A tear fell from his eyes. I wiped it off his cheek. I tucked his hair back behind his ear.

I kissed him. After we parted, he sighed. He looked up at the stars.

Glowing, the light here was from ten thousand years ago, when it left the stars deep in the galaxy. I thought about the drag queens pummeling smug, entitled straight white guys while singing "YMCA."

I was glad we stood up for ourselves, but I realized that no matter what, the world would always suck. Who you loved, how you looked, how you dressed, what you did for a living or not. Being mixed race. Being Magical. Being a Monster. People sucked.

Maybe, though, the answer was that we could choose to be different. We didn't have to let them bring us down to their level. We could be better to each other. Was I making sense? I wasn't sure.

I hugged Austin, who was muttering in Cantonese to Lammy Poo.

"Mum-mum."

"Feeling better, Kangy?"

"Yeah."

"You want to go home and cuddle tons?"

He nodded, then pushed Lammy Poo toward me. "We'll cuddle Lammy Poo too, Eli."

"Sure, Kangy, whatever you want."

*

THAT NIGHT, I dreamt of Devlina. She was distorted, wavy, and static pulsed behind her head that floated without a body in the center of a black-and-white TV.

"I told you the world sucks," she shouted. "Ordinaries. I have no idea why your family and the Alliance guard them like they are precious diamonds when they do terrible things to you."

Devlina's face scattered into the static. She fought to reassemble herself.

"Ordinaries are awful, remember?" she said. "They made you come out. They make you think being in love with Austin is weird. Why do you defend them?"

"This isn't about Ordinaries."

"It's not?"

"Devlina," I said. "You have to stop. What you're doing with Zid'dra. The Gloom. You can't win."

Devlina's face disappeared, then exploded into hundreds of little faces all circling around me.

"He made his choices. He stopped loving me," she said. "We were happy. We were in love and then he got greedy."

"I know, Devlina," I said. "But you need to step back and think about what you're doing."

"Purifying."

"No, Devlina."

"I want to be appreciated. I want to be worshipped. Not for what I do, but for who I am."

"Devlina, you've done bad things before."

"Shut up."

"Devlina, you can change."

"What do you mean?"

"You can stop what you're doing, and let him be."

"NEVER!"

"If you keep doing what you are doing, you'll destroy all of us."

She screamed. The sound pierced my ears. I covered them protectively, cringing.

"I hate this misogynistic, racist, homophobic world!!!"

"DEVLINA!"

"Come on, be part of my war!"

"No, Devlina, I can't. I've already fought enough battles for other people. I'm different now."

"Look," Devlina said, "in the past, what I did, that wasn't me. I mean, I was drunk."

"Fuck you. You don't drink."

"Adderall?"

"No way."

"Steroids." And she laughed and laughed while the sound echoed in my brain.

"You're not a body builder," I said. "Why would you take steroids?"

"I'm a fucking new world builder."

"What does that mean?"

"It means I will create something beautiful from the wreckage of this world."

"Devlina, look, I forgive you for what you did to my family and me. Maybe you can forgive Zid'dra and let it go?"

Devlina just flashed and quivered and kept repeating "New World Builder" over and over and over.

I woke up. The medicine surged. My heart thudded in my chest. An owl hooted outside. The sprinklers turned on in the garden. I exhaled, looking around as moonlight streamed into Austin's room. He was clutching Lammy Poo and mumbling in Cantonese in his sleep.

I lay back down, cuddling into him. I didn't dream the rest of the night.

Chapter Twenty-Two

Temple of Red and Purple

A LIGHT FLASHED. A hand hit a horn. Alarms sounded.

Screaming. The moon cracked in two. I hated myself and disappeared into my insecurity.

Austin called to me from the greenish-blue water in the Olympic-sized pool where I trained with Amanda before the "Fall," as I called it. He brushed his hair back off his face.

"Come on, love," he said. His hands floated on the water. He was glowing. The water shimmered. I hesitated, standing on the wet tile floor surrounding the pool. I was sinking into the quicksand of my insecurity. Was I ready to get back in the water? Was I ready to start training again?

"I can't do this, Kangy."

"Yes, you can."

"I'm afraid," I said. "What if I can't swim?"

"Don't be afraid," he said. "The water is warm and soothing."

"Are you using magic?"

He laughed and laughed. "The little magic I have." He closed his eyes, and the water flashed purple and orange.

"Do I have to get out and push you in?"

I couldn't talk. I stared at the water. My tongue didn't want to work.

The gravity of my self-loathing dictated that it spin counterclockwise indefinitely. How could I breach it? The medicine surged.

"I'm broken." I lowered my eyes, then stared down at my toes. "One minute I feel better; the next I feel worse."

"You're getting better every day, love. You know it!"

"You don't have to be broken," Devlina said, her face floating in the water. "I am getting stronger. There will be a reckoning. This world. It's breaking.

"I'm a fucking new world builder!" Her phrase rattled around in my head.

In an instant, it was me and her in the main hall of the Temple of Magic in Hollywood. Among the red and purple columns, candles flickered in rows along the sides of the walls. A fountain tinkled. A bell chimed. A fresco of the universe painted on the wall glimmered.

Devlina wore a purple Qi'Xhè. She unsheathed a red sword.

She bowed to me.

"Prepare for war," she said.

"I can't."

"The war has started," she said. "You have to pick a side."

I felt the steel blade against my face, cool to the touch.

"Remove your *Sopulcro*."

"My sword?" I glanced down. There was one in my hand.

In an instant, she was airborne, flying around me. The blade touched my shoulder, which erupted into flames. The sword was touching me, slicing into me, burning into me.

"See that? Fat." My shoulder burned. I blinked. Austin floated in the pool before me.

"Oi, love." Austin shook his head. "No, no. Where did you get that idea about being fat?"

I blinked. I mean can't he look at me? See what I'm seeing?

I thought of Arnulfo.

"You need to stop seeing the world through your fear."

"Is that a joke?" I said glaring at him. "Something they teach you in therapy school?"

He shrugged. "What if they do? It's still valid. See yourself through hope. Compassion and love."

"You're twisted, Arnulfo." *That didn't make sense at all.*

Devlina's Sopulcro hit my body again. I wasn't in Arnulfo's office. I was in the Temple of Magic with Devlina. She lunged for me. "I said, I forgive you, Devlina! It's okay to forgive, you know that."

"Forgiving is for the weak!"

"Maybe it's okay to be weak then." Her sword flew toward me.

I shook my head. I was standing along the pool. Austin's eyes were focused on me. He was concentrating. The water bubbled, and steam rose into the air. Austin glowed. His aura, golden.

"Elijah, the war is here, and you have to decide whose side you're on." I heard Devlina's voice. The pool disappeared into the steam.

My eyes opened. Another voice filled my head: "Reach deep inside you and touch the magic within, love."

I picked up the sword on the stone floor of the *Rocotomo sie Qu'el*, the Temple of Magic.

I flew up toward Devlina and met the blows of her blade with my blade.

"I'm not fighting you or getting dragged into your battle," I said, "but I will fight to save my home. This world isn't perfect, but it's mine. And if I'm weak and you win, then so be it, at least I tried.

Wheat fell all around me. I lunged for Devlina. The sopulcro plunged into her.

She stared at me. "I knew the fighter was still in you!" she said. "Look at you, after all you've gone through and suffered, and you're a...*aquenta paletans*? What is the word? You're sort of a 'badass'!"

She laughed. A moment later, she burst into a million stars that sparkled in the air of the dome high above me.

"Elijah," Austin called to me softly, "dive in the water. Swim to me. You can do it."

Steam billowed around me. I stepped forward. I felt the sides of the pool with my toes, breathed in the scent of chlorine. Austin floated, kicking his legs under the water and urging me to come in the pool.

"I'm coming!" I said and leaped into the water.

Water splashed. Austin complained.

"Warn me before you cannonball into the water, mate!"

Immediately, I was surrounded by the warm water. My body was alive and filled with light. My head rose from the water. Austin swam to me.

"I knew you could do it, love."

His arms enveloped me. I was safe.

"I love you, Kangy," I said and leaped up in the water to kiss him on the lips. He giggled, and then he kissed me back.

"And I, you," Austin said. "My Eli."

The horn stopped blaring. The two pieces of the moon fused back together. The alarms fell silent. I looked down at my body. I wasn't this ugly monster.

I was simply me. The boy in love with Austin Kang Jr. The boy who believed in himself and who stopped hurting himself because of fear and loathing.

"Don't you feel good in the water?" Austin said. "You're a swimmer!"

Austin floated in the pool smiling at me broadly. The heat of the water seemed to seep into my soul.

*

MOM HOSTED WEEKLY parties at the mansion.

"I'm not happy about this, Miss Delomary," I overheard Mrs. Singh saying to Mom at breakfast. "We have a budget, and these parties are busting it!" Mom walked out of the kitchen. Mrs. Singh looked at me. I shrugged.

"I'm just as surprised as you that she's having all these parties,

Mrs. Singh."

"Your mother only hosts parties for three reasons: a fundraiser for someone running for office, for a famous charity, or as a mixer to wine and dine powerful people into doing whatever Dirk Delomary Global Holdings wants them to do to make your family richer."

"That's not true," I said dryly. "She throws herself a big birthday party every year."

"Yes, to support her charity du jour." Mrs. Singh tapped onto her tablet. "We can write those expenses off. I need to stay under budget or Delomary Fiduciary Trust will call me. I don't like talking to bean counters, do you?"

"Let Mom talk to them. I'm sure she'd have a blast telling them about how important fun is."

"You're funny, really funny." Mrs. Singh walked toward her office mumbling under her breath in Hindi. When she spoke English, things were okay; when she spoke Cantonese, things were getting iffy, but Hindi? Well... I got up and went to find Mom.

I found her in her study—with Sean. They were moving furniture around.

"What are you guys doing?"

"Rearranging furniture," Mom remarked.

"Why?"

"So, I can work here when I stay over," Sean said. He'd started staying with us a few nights a week. Mom ordered him his own monogrammed clothes: pajamas, slippers, bathrobes, swim trunks, casual pants, some polos and flip-flops. He lucked out—no knee-length socks.

"Wow," I said. "Mom, you have a man living here!"

Mom shot me an evil look.

"I don't see you complaining," Mom said as Sean pushed her desk parallel to the bank of windows overlooking the rose gardens. "I hear you guys talking about skateboarding, surfing, swimming, running, and your favorite architecture gods."

"I was a professional skateboarder, Lin," Sean said, clearing a lamp off the table and pushing an ergonomic chair toward the desk.

"And a surfer in college. I wore puka shells and was quite a catch."

"He was!" I said. "He had a new girlfriend every week."

"And I had abs."

"You still do."

"Of course, I do, Lin." He was getting frisky. Mom rolled her eyes. He grabbed her by the waist and pulled her in for a kiss. She glanced at me. I looked away. I heard them smacking lips.

I coughed. "I'm glad he's here," I said. "Mom, I think he should move in permanently. He makes you happy, and when you're happy, the rest of us are happy. Especially Mrs. Singh, who, by the way, needs you to turn tonight's party into a charitable event so she can deduct it or something and keep the goons from Delomary Bean Counters Trust from showing up with guns or something."

"What are you talking about?"

"I dunno," I said. "But Mrs. Singh started muttering angrily in Hindi."

"Shit."

"I'll talk to her," Sean offered. "Smooth things out."

"Thanks, baby."

"Sure, honey bunny."

"Uh, gross."

"Elijah, how about you go and hang out with your boyfriend and leave us adults alone?"

"So you can adult?"

"Now!"

A few hours later, after the sun set, the back meadow was transformed into a festival. With booths offering various games such as ring toss, dart fling, and flaming-knife-hurl. Bizarre. There were booths selling crafts, paintings, macramé. A huge, white pavilion with dancing and another with a buffet. There was a Ferris wheel and carousel. No wonder Mrs. Singh was muttering in Hindi.

"Well, lad," Máurso said, appearing out of a fissure in the ground behind a booth selling pottery. "This looks fun."

I jumped. "Where did you come from?"

"The ground."

"Why?"

"Why not?"

A half dozen cats crawled out of the fissure and chased after him as he made a beeline for a booth offering soft drinks.

Austin waited for me by the gazebo. He wore black slacks, black shoes, a white shirt and black skinny tie with his long hair slicked back. He looked so beautiful.

He flashed me the peace sign.

"You look dashing!" he said, pulling me in for a kiss. "Look at you with your linen slacks, powder-blue dress shirt, linen vest, and blazer. And designer sneakers, of course."

"Of course."

He put his arm around me, and we headed around the pavilion to the lake to watch live music.

"Is that Beyoncé?"

"Of course, it is," I said. "Do you like the steamboat glowing with ten thousand lights she's performing from?"

"Holy shit," Austin said. "How much did that cost?"

"A small fortune."

"I'm going to love being a part of this family."

"Sure," I said. "But I'm still becoming a Kang."

"And giving up the surname a million people would kill for?"

"Gladly."

After Beyoncé performed, Sia took over. She wore a giant teddy bear onesie which caused a hullaballoo with some of Máurso's cats. During a break in the music, Austin and I went to the pavilion to have dinner and listen to Sergio Mendes croon as we had surf and turf washed down with Shirley Temples.

We wandered around the festival for a while, browsing among the booths, playing a few games of flaming-knife-hurl (Austin narrowly missed setting fire to the burly guy managing the booth), rode the carousel, then went to watch Sweetie's band, Vengeance and Lace.

"Hello, Delomary family and friends!" Sweetie shouted, his voice booming from speakers hidden in boulders set around the lake. "This one is dedicated to Elijah and Belinda. Let's fun!"

"Let's fun!" Austin shouted as Vengeance and Lace began playing "Love in a time of destruction," his number one hit currently playing everywhere. He told me the song was a denunciation of the backward politics of hate.

Austin jumped up and down, hands in the air, having a blast.

"So much fun, mate," he said, pulling me closer to him, wrapping his arms around me. We began to slow dance for a while.

"I can still have your baby," a familiar voice said. My blood cooled. "If you want."

I turned. Wearing a slinky, form-fitting, black body sock masquerading as a cocktail dress, covered in sparkling diamonds, holding hands with a gorgeous boy from school named Damien Tavashjan, was Blair Winchester.

"Security!" I shouted.

"Oh, hush," Blair said holding up a white, engraved envelope. "I was invited."

"You conjured that," I said. "You use magic however you want."

"So?" She said, "Jealous?"

"All right, Blair," Austin intervened.

"Relax," Blair said. "Your Mom has been talking to my mom. I guess they're trying to smooth things out between our families."

"She would never!" I blurted out. Would she?

"She's dating Sean Barnett," Blair continued. "You know he's one of the most influential and powerful tech CEOs on earth?"

"Sure, Blair." This girl would never change.

"And he's friends with my mom."

"Hi, Elijah. I'm Damien."

Blair's face reddened. "I'm sorry, bae. I have no manners."

"It's fine." Damien brushed her hair off her shoulder then said to me, "What you did, Elijah, was brave."

"What did I do?"

"The harvest game?"

"Shit, yeah."

Damien stuck out his hand to Austin. "And you too. Hi, I'm Damien."

"Austin Kang, Junior. Pleasure."

"Same."

"Anyway," Damien said, "you inspired my kid brother to come out to my parents."

"How did that go?"

"Shit show. We're Persian," he added. "But good. My folks happened to be watching the prime time show on Global News and saw the feature about being gay in America."

"Yeah," I said, "Mom ordered the news division to run those."

"Great timing!" Damien laughed. Blair looked left out.

"Damien might be richer than you, Elijah."

Damien rubbed Blair's arm. Her face shone. She took a deep breath. She was relaxed. She was glowing like the puxhàredo Madonna in all those renaissance paintings at the Huntington Library in San Marino.

"Blair here," Damien said, "gave a big speech on acceptance to my folks. She lectured them. In Farsi."

I gaped at Blair. She demurred.

"Wow, Blair, are you changing?"

"Are you?"

"Guess not," Austin quipped.

"Calm down, bae."

"Sure, bae."

"Anyway, we're allies," Damien said. "Good to see you!"

"Bye, Elijah!"

"Uh, bye, Blair?"

After a while, the pop star Venus took to the stage. She wore a pink leather jumpsuit, pink boots, and had pink woven into her braids.

"Oi, Delomary family and friends!" she shouted. "This one goes out to Elijah!"

I think I turned three shades of red as the people near us turned to gawk. She began playing "Gravity of Love," which was currently battling with "Love in a Time of Destruction" for the top spot on streaming.

Máurso appeared, with his cats, out of thin air.

"Hi, Dáumo," Austin said, squeezing my hand.

"Boys," he said. "This lass is pretty good."

"Great," I said. "I love her."

"So did I."

"Come again?"

"Long ago," Máurso reminisced, "we were lovers, fighters. We were inseparable." His voice cracked. I glanced at him. He rubbed a tear from his eyes.

"I think he moved from soft drinks to the hard stuff," Austin whispered.

"Then everything went wrong. Romans stopped worshipping us. She got angry. I got angry. I started a few wars. She stirred up hatred—she's the Goddess of Love and Hate, you know. And, well, that was that."

"Did you date anyone else?" I did the math. Was he single for almost two thousand years?

"No."

"No one?"

"There was a lass, a lesser goddess," Máurso said, "Tilcomedea."

"Tilcomedea?" I asked. "Isn't she the goddess who lost it and caused the potato famine?"

"Well, it wasn't my fault, if that's what you're implying!" Máurso grumbled. His cats scattered. The ground trembled. Lightning flashed.

Mom and Sean walked by us. "Oh, hey, Mom, it's your buddy Máurso!"

"Hi, Marsy! Having fun?"

"Aye," Máurso said. "Quite the party. I meant to talk to you both about news I heard from the Alliance. About the coven..."

They stopped talking to look at me. I used that as our cue to head back to the food pavilion.

*

LATER THAT NIGHT, Austin and I were curled up in his bed watching *Cocaine Bear* on his flat-screen TV.

"The bear!" Austin was losing it. "Snorted coke and is going crazy, Eli!"

"Yes, I know."

"Eli, bears don't do coke!"

"I hope not."

"But, Eli, look at how cute the bear is...and then it snorts coke!"

My phone vibrated. We both stared at it. I picked it up. A new email from Áurmiddo.

"Oh, been a while, yeah, love?"

"Ages."

"Want me to pause it... Oh no, don't bleedin' run! Never run from bears!"

"It's fine."

I went into his bathroom and closed the door behind me:

Careńo Elijah,

I'm sorry I haven't written. I mean, I did, but I didn't send anything. I guess I found myself thinking about you a lot. More than I wanted to.

I'm studying Magic at the Umnavesseo sie Qu'el Antigo in Eustantinoplo in Sujo-Cujo. One day we were doing picturing work. I wanted to see you. I have been worried about you since your last email. And then I saw you with the beautiful boy with the long black hair and glasses. You were sitting on the beach, huddled into him watch-ing fireworks.

He must be your boyfriend. I hope so. I want you to be happy.

I am. I met someone here. His name is Moàxantchl. Named after the famous poet. He has reddish hair like you. He's from Menotha—apparently red hair is common there. Sure your ancestors aren't from there? LOL. He laughs just like you do. I love him very much. We do everything together. It's so nice to have someone again after you. It broke my heart not being with you every day after last summer.

Please tell me you are well, and write me back ASAP.

Love,

Áurmiddo.

I returned to bed. Austin was squishing a pillow with his hands. "The bloody cokey bear is awful, Eli!"

I sat next to him. He glanced over. "Everything okay, mate?"

"Yeah," I said. "Áurmiddo has a boyfriend."

"That's brilliant, mate."

"Áurmiddo had opened me up to the world. He unlocked the dusty vault buried in my sub-basement that contained *My Secret*."

Austin paused the movie and laced our fingers together. "I'm glad he did that, Eli. I'm glad because if Áurmiddo didn't help you, I wouldn't be with you now. My beautiful red-haired boy." He added, "You were different back then, mate, and now you're growing up. We both are."

"And Mom's changed too."

"Yeah. Did I tell you I saw Sean moving boxes of stuff into the house?"

I laughed. "Yeah, he tried to sneak them in through the service entrance."

"You okay with that?"

"I love Sean," I said. "He's fun to talk to. Sometimes, when I get home late from practice he'll sit with me in the kitchen and we'll talk about all sorts of stuff. Sometimes, Tory comes and we have a great time.

The three of us."

"Like you have a...dad?" Austin paused. "Sorry, I shouldn't have said that."

"No, it's true," I said. "Uncle George is busy with his own kids, but Sean is around. And he's easy to talk to. And when Mom gets going, he knows just how to deal with her."

"Sounds great."

"And he's been super supportive," I said. "He and Aunt Christine bought a pride flag and hoisted it over the house. Did you notice it?"

"Yes, I love it. Dad is thinking of getting one too."

"I guess one of the security guards made a comment," I said. "Mom lost it and was about to turn him into a toad, but Sean went and talked to him. I mean, I think he really bawled the guy out. Sunny came and said he apologized to him and asked to apologize to us as well."

"Jolly brilliant," Austin said. "Maybe you don't need magic all the time to fix things. Maybe talking is good, right, Eli?"

"Right, Kangy."

"My Eli."

"My Kangy."

Austin glanced at the TV. "Okay, let's get back to the strung-out bear!"

Chapter Twenty-Three

War Looms

THE TEMPERATURE HOVERED at a hundred degrees. The century mark. Austin took a swig from a metal water container. We were standing under an ancient magnolia tree, past the gazebo, practicing Sem Xen Ou.

"I think we've had enough, mate," he said, pulling his shirt over his head. "It's too hot!"

I stared at his body. "Hubba. Hubba!"

We both laughed.

"Let's get into the air-conditioning."

We headed toward the house. Austin's phone vibrated.

"An alert from the League."

"Really? I didn't know you got alerts. I thought only agents got those."

"I'm interning, yeah?"

"Cool," I said. "I want to intern. How do I do that?"

"Play your cards right with a certain, sexy Kang?"

"Who is this certain Kang?"

Austin burst out laughing. "ME!"

Inside the house, we headed to the solarium, rinsed off, then jumped into the pool. Tory was sitting nearby, her head stuck in a book, laptop open.

I swam to the surface. "Getting ready to go back to school?"

"Yes, but I have to catch up," she said. "Hot out?"

"Too hot."

"That's why I stay inside from June to September."

"That's a change," I teased. "You used to like to slink around in a bikini when you were younger. Sit by the pool. Pose for the male staff."

Tory rolled her eyes. "I was young, naïve."

"Yeah," I said, floating by the edge of the pool. Austin swam past me, lifted himself out of the water, grabbed a towel, and looked at his phone.

"You were still better than your friends. What did you guys call yourselves?"

"The Burbank Bitches Club." Tory shook her head. "We made Blair look like a saint."

"Ah, but you were nice to me."

"You're family."

"You could have been mean."

"I was acting back then to fit in."

"You were too smart for them."

"And too stupid to realize that back then."

I kicked my feet. Tory set her book down.

"You're looking better each day, Cory."

"So are you," I said. "You don't look like a tweaker anymore."

"Rugrat," she said, laughing.

"I'm glad you're back."

Tory smiled. "Me too, Elijah."

Austin pushed his phone down. "Bollocks!"

"Something wrong, Kangy?"

"A bunch of joggers were were found dried up like prunes at the LA River."

"Àzmadus."

"Aye," he said. "They suck the life out of Ordinaries."

"And they found a bunch of decapitated bodies in Griffith Park."

"Malloupus?"

"They feast on souls."

"That's crazy," I said. "Àzmadus and Malloupus know they can't go on killing sprees. Raise the suspicions of the Ordinaries."

"Exactly."

"What do you think is happening?"

"I think Devlina is disturbing the balance," he said. "We should talk to Uncle George. He'll know what's happening."

George Wong stood by the cold fireplace in the library, an enormous room lined on three sides by floor-to-ceiling bookcases filled with leather-bound books, from romance novels to history books to magic books.

"The coven has called a meeting of all the Gloom."

Aunt Christine lounged in the brown recliner with her eyes closed. Mom leaned against a bookcase, arms folded across her chest.

"Devlina has gone crazy."

"She is a Máu, the Goddess of Lust of our dimension. And when she killed Máu Anveddia, the Goddess of Envy in another dimension and attempted to kill Máu Supervia, Goddess of Pride on Other Earth, that raised flags."

"Can someone explain what a Máu is exactly?" Austin said.

"A Máu is simply a goddess who turned to the Gloom and became a Malevolent. Formerly, they were goddesses of things such as wheat for Devlina, or of herbs and medicines, in the case of Anveddia, and bees and ants in the case of Supervia," George explained to Austin.

"Zid'dra, after marrying each one, gave them dominion of a coven in a part of the Gloom throughout the universe. And named them Máu."

"Which means Dark Queen in the Dark Language."

"She's always been a total crazy," Christine said. "I battled her multiple times," she said.

"Your favorite time was when you turned into a thirty-foot panda and fought her mano a mano in the parking lot of St. Joseph's Hospital during a thunderstorm."

"She was thirty feet too," Christine said. "We destroyed half the area."

"Which the League had to recreate at considerable cost and with a lot of magic."

"Oh, magic doesn't run out."

"Only an Encantreina would think that," George quipped.

"So, what's the plan?" Mom said, filing her nails with an emery board.

"The League and XAQ2 are investigating. They have XAQ6, the secret service of the Alliance, tailing Devlina."

"Shit," Christine said. "XAQ6. They're super secret. The Ninjas of the Alliance. This must be serious."

"We think Devlina plans to attack the coven and Zid'dra himself."

"That could destroy the universe," Mom said.

George nodded. I stared at the fireplace. I knew Devlina's plan. Did I say something? I was honor bound to tell. To protect the Alliance. What had the Alliance done for me? I heard Arnulfo in my head.

"You did what you did. You have to own it."

I owned it. Fine. I embraced the whole thing. Still, I didn't say anything.

I didn't want to betray Devlina. I wasn't sure why.

*

"YOU SURE YOU want to do this, love?" Austin leaned into the driver's side window, peering at me through his neon-green sunglasses.

I gripped the steering wheel. "Yeah," I said. "I have to do this."

I thought about Devlina. I understood her. The betrayal. She had been a carefree Antécallanta, the goddess Persephone roaming the world helping with the harvest; then Zid'dra emerged with his golden chariot and carried her off to the Gloom. To be his wife. And then he broke his vow and married other Antécallantas that he turned into Malevolents. The dark version of their former selves. No longer living in the Shimmering, the light.

Dad. I had to confront him. I had to tell him my secret. He had taken me to my own darkness. The medicine flowed into my body giving me courage. I had to do this.

"I should come with you," Austin said.

"I have to go alone."

Austin stood up, stretching. "I worry about you, Eli."

"I'll be okay." I pulled Ocho out from under the passenger seat. "He's coming."

"Little Ocho." He smiled. "Okay, well, text me if you need me."

"I will."

"I'll be staring at Friend Finder the whole time," Austin said. "So I know where you are."

"You have training with Barn and Mason and Máurso."

"I can be there in a snap." Austin laughed. "You know me, yeah?"

I laughed. "Okay."

"Enjoy driving this barmy car."

He peered at Christine's hot pink sports car. "You are really making a statement."

"Exactly."

Fifteen minutes later, I pulled up to the curb of the massive, boxy apartment building Dad and Florence lived in on a tree-lined street near the Glendale Galleria.

A Black woman walking a dog paused and said, "Is that your car?"

I nodded. "Shit," she said. "I need one of those." She grinned. "The other Encantreinas in my book club would love to take a spin in that."

Magicals, well, we're constantly outing ourselves to each other. There's gay-dar. And then there's mag-dar.

I laughed. "You want to take it for a spin now?"

Her mouth dropped. "Really?"

"Yeah," I said. "I'm Elijah."

"Delomary?"

"Yeah."

"The one and only Elijah Delomary, Bane of the Gloom?"

"Yeah, that's me."

"Fuck the Alliance," she said passionately. "What they did to you—"

"It's okay," I said. "Really. I found a new groove."

"Yeah?"

"Yup."

"I heard there was a big shake-up in London," she said. "Fired half them assholes!"

"Pretty much."

"They deserved it," she said. "I'm Ebony. Waller."

"*Encantruno.*"

"*Comesmo.*"

"I'm going to come out to my dad," I said. "He's an ordinary."

"Oh, Lord have mercy."

"I mean he knows I'm Magical. I'm going to tell him I'm gay."

"Work it out, boy."

"I'll need the car in an hour."

"I'll be here," she said. "Good luck, Elijah." She looked down at her chihuahua. "Come on, Venus. Let's go for a ride."

Soon, I huddled on the edge of a black faux-leather sofa in the living room in the two-bedroom apartment. Dad was frying ground beef making "ethnic food:" tacos. Puxhàredo, Dad and his backward thinking. Florence sat outside on the balcony, smoking. They had a cat they named Felix. Clever, huh? Only, Felix had white fur. He looked sad, like he didn't understand why he lived with my dad. He ambled up to me and licked my hand, and when I petted him, he seemed to sigh.

"Take me with you, please?"

Dad's back was to me. Florence was outside, quiet. A breeze stirred the sheers on both sides of the sliding glass door. Mom said the war changed Dad. Arnulfo didn't buy it. Arnulfo had served. He had a husband, Will, and two beautiful kids, a boy and a girl named Antonio and Maria, who were shown smiling in every single picture on the wall behind his desk.

"Maybe," Arnulfo explained to me, "your dad doesn't know what family is?"

"How the fuck not?"

"It happens, Elijah. Remember what I've taught you."

"Be open-minded."

Open-minded.

"How's your girlfriend?" Dad snickered from the kitchen.

Florence puffed out a cloud of smoke. Felix licked my hand.

"Please save me from these people!"

I rubbed Felix's fur. "She's not my girlfriend."

"She has big knockers."

"Jesus," I said. "Don't talk like that, Dad."

Florence shifted in her seat, pulling on her cigarette.

"You can be her boyfriend while still dating other girls. Don't get attached. Stay away from love, Elijah."

He laughed. Knocked back a soda in one gulp. Then belched. Felix strutted out of the room.

Florence kept smoking.

"Dad," I said, standing and walking over to the counter separating the kitchen from the living room. "I have to talk to you." My heart was in my throat. The medicine surged. *I could do this.*

"Yeah?" he said, smoothing his comb-over with his hand. The one that had been touching raw beef. "'Bout what?"

"Me, Dad," I said. "Me."

"I saw your pink sports car." He snickered. "Your fucking family. Richer than God. Fucking too much, man."

"Dad..."

"I mean, they love to rub it in the faces of us mortals. That we're nothing."

"Dad."

"That Frenchman, your great-great-grandfather comes over a hundred years ago and cheats and swindles and does God knows what to make them so rich…"

"Dad."

"I fought in the war…"

"Larry!" Florence interjected from the patio.

Dad stopped. He looked at me.

"What?"

"I'm gay," I said softly.

Dad froze. Florence coughed. Felix peered back into the room. His eyes seemed to plead, *please take me home with you.*

"Oh, well." Dad was flustered. His hands trembled. "I mean. So. Um. I mean."

"It's fine," Florence said, flinging the cigarette butt over the railing. "Good for you, son."

"Dad," I said, "I don't need your acceptance or your love, really."

Florence lit another cigarette and rattled the ice cubes in her glass of iced tea.

"I can't believe you just walked out on us like you did. And then you never came around. And then, when I do see you this year, you tell me all this crazy shit about how to be a man. You made me question who I was, being gay. That hurt me. A lot."

Dad was silent. The sound of beef sizzling on the stove and the dishwasher humming behind him next to the sink filled the apartment.

"I listened to that shit," I said. "I almost lost the best thing that ever happened to me."

"That Asian boy," Dad said."I knew it. He recruited you."

"Shut up, Larry," Florence said.

"No one gets recruited, Dad," I said. "I was born this way. Just like I was born an Encantreino. A Magical. It's who I am."

"That magic mumbo jumbo." Dad rolled his eyes. "Your mom was always going on about it."

"It's who we are, Dad."

"It's how them Delomarys got rich"

"That was through hard work. Dad."

"Your Mom was handed everything."

"No, Dad. Mom worked hard. She still works hard."

"You should get a job, Larry," Florence said.

Dad fell silent. A moment later, he asked, "So what does this mean for you and me?"

I looked at him. "Whatever you want."

He looked past me, out to Florence on the balcony and the trees screening the apartment from the pool out back. Kids were laughing and splashing in the water below. Someone older told them to stop trying to drown each other. *Please, God, please.*

"I am your son," I said. "I want you to be my dad. To do that, I need you to own what you did."

"What do you mean?"

"Say sorry, Larry," Florence said.

Dad's face flushed red. He made a fist, bringing it down hard on the counter. Beef sizzled. The dishwasher hummed. Felix disappeared down the hall. Dad closed his eyes. We stood across from each other, in a standoff.

"Dad?"

Dad was thinking, staring at the meat sizzling in the pan.

"Well, hello there," Florence said a moment later. I turned. Austin's head appeared over the railing.

"I'm checking on my boyfriend."

"Oh, you're the recruiter?"

"Fuck, yes," Austin said. "Look how cute he is. That red hair."

"Quite the catch."

"Mind if I scale over and join you?"

"Be my guest." Florence waved her cigarette toward an open seat across from her.

"What the hell is going on?" Dad said.

"That's my boyfriend, Dad."

Austin climbed over the railing, nodded his head in Dad's direction, then slid into a chair across from Florence. She poured him a glass of iced tea from a green glass pitcher.

"I'm sorry," Dad said abruptly. "About it all. Your mom told me...I should've... I... Look, son, I've had some... Well, look. I have this man I talk to."

"He's cleaning up his act, Elijah."

"Yeah," he said. "I'm not good with love. Or relationships in general."

"He's lucky to have me," Florence quipped to Austin. "I know all about love. I'm an expert."

"Oh, can I have your number? In case I need advice?"

Florence laughed, handing her phone to Austin.

"Your mom, though, she's a—"

"Shut up, Larry," Florence said. "What happened was long ago," she said. "Elijah, they weren't the right fit; that's all"

Dad looked away.

"I get that man," Florence said. "He drives me crazy. Do you feel me?"

"Oh, yes, ma'am," Austin said. "Eli tries my nerves too."

Florence chuckled, raising her glass to Austin. They toasted each other. Of course, they did.

"Larry, bring over those tacos. Elijah, come join us. What's your name, son?"

"Austin Kang Jr."

"Pleased to meet you. You a Magical too?"

"In the League, ma'am."

"Oh, I dated an Agécendro in college. Hottest men join the League." She grinned. "Women too."

I sat next to Austin. He gripped my knee. He had scaled the side of the building—three floors to come be with me.

I mean, how awesome was that?

"Austin, you look okay," Dad said. "You the marrying kind?"

"Yes, sir."

"Oh God," he said, placing a tray of tacos on the glass-topped table. "Marry a Delomary? You must be very patient or a little crazy yourself."

"Both, sir," Austin said, reaching for a taco.

"God bless," Dad said. "Now, boy, go get me a root beer."

"Say please, Dad."

"Fine. Please. Jeez. Stop getting all woke."

Florence glared at Larry. A horn sounded below. Austin peered over the railing.

"Why is there a woman getting out of your car with a chihuahua?"

"That's Ebony. She's an *Encantreina*. She wanted to go for a ride."

"Oh," Austin said. "Perks of being in the Alliance."

I thought about that. Being in the Alliance meant I had another family, a larger one.

Fuck. What about Devlina? Should I tell my family her plans? My head hurt. I was hungry. I'd think about that later.

"I want to drive it next," Dad said.

"Shut up, Larry," Florence said. "You'll drive too fast and crash it, dear."

We all laughed. Like really hard.

I looked at Dad. Maybe, just maybe, something good could come out of our relationship.

"By the way, Dad," I said, "I came out to a quarter of my school at the Harvest Game. I shook things up."

"Damn right, you did," Dad said. "That's the only way to do it, son," he said smiling broadly.

*

"I'M SHOCKED," MOM said the next evening after dinner as we unwound in her study. "Your father actually apologized." One perfectly circular shaped piece of ice clinked in a tumbler. "Did you record it for proof?"

I shook my head. "Too bad," Mom said, "I'd love to have seen that."

I clenched and unclenched my hands. I was stalling.

"Mom, I wanted to ask you something."

"Sure." Mom closed her eyes. She'd had a long day dealing with the fallout from right-wingers boycotting a burger chain we owned in the South because they put up pride flags. Mom refused to relent to them. The stock of the subsidiary was down. Investors weren't happy.

"I know you didn't have a good day."

"That's what you get when you're in charge, darling."

"I appreciate you supporting the community."

"Of course, those haters can go to another burger place if they don't like it."

"Yeah." I fell silent.

Mom opened one eye. "Elijah, what do want to ask me?"

"Um, so you know, I've been training with Austin and Barn with Máurso at his Dáu Xhà, and I'm good, Mom. Really good. I love slicing and dicing monsters."

"I'm sure." Mom sighed. "I would prefer for you to be an En-cantreino…" She paused, setting down the tumbler on the edge of the coffee table between the sofas we sat on. "What I mean is I'm glad you found something within the community again."

"Mom, trust me. I miss using magic. And I can…barely. But here's the thing. That's over. And this is now, and anyway, I have this letter."

I produced a red envelope sealed with purple wax with an imprint of the symbol of the Anti-coven League—a witch's hat in a circle with a line through it.

"What's this?"

"Read it."

Mom opened the letter, paused. Stood, walked to her desk to fetch her reading glasses. "Getting old sucks," she said ruefully, putting on her glasses. She hovered behind the ivory-colored sofa as she read the letter. I studied her face, my heart in my throat.

Mom folded up the letter. "Join the League?" Mom rubbed her temples. "You can't join the League, Elijah."

I stared at the fire crackling in the fireplace behind Mom. "Why not?"

"You're technically not a Coaugelo."

"I am," I said angrily. "Máurso talked to the Còngréhassa himself. He ordered them to accept me."

Mom looked surprised. "When did this happen?"

"A while ago."

"You didn't tell me?"

"I uh..."

"It's fine." Mom softened, coming around the sofa and sitting beside me. "I'm glad Máurso did that. He's such a sweetie, you know. Tough on the outside, yada, yada."

"Yeah, he let those Estàntus have it!"

Mom smiled. "That's why we have Antécallantus like him around, to appeal to when the Còngréhassa are being foolish."

Mom glanced up at the painting of Evangeline and Dirk over the mantel, Dirk holding a cigar in one hand, Evangeline clutching Dirk's arm. Smoke circled from the cigar, Evangeline apparently saying something.

Mom folded her arms across her chest.

"Austin is already interning with the League," I said. "I want to do this with him. I love him."

"It's dangerous for you, honey," she said. "The coven knows all about you. Our family. Our position in the Alliance."

"I know," I said. "I'm seventeen, Mom. Almost an adult. I am going to do this."

"Without my blessing?"

"Yes, Mom," I said. "I have to do this."

The fire flared behind her. In the painting, Dirk tapped his cigar into an ashtray and said something softly. Thunder rumbled. The green-shaded lamp on her desk flickered.

"Fine, you guys," she said to the painting. "You got their blessing," Mom said, "and mine, honey. I know you'll do the right thing."

I jumped off the sofa. "Shit. Really?"

Mom glanced at me, unfolding her arms to step forward and embrace me. "Yes, darling."

"This is big, Mom," I said. "You trusting me."

"I know. I'm growing up. Don't you love it?"

I made a heart with my hands. Thunder boomed. Mom's tablet on the coffee table lit up.

"That is Agécendro Simon Tong with XAQ6," Mom said, reaching for the tablet.

"XAQ6!" I said "The Áuqala's Secret Service."

I surveyed the image of Simon Tong—he was very handsome and also looked to be about twenty-two.

Mom nodded. "I have to take this in private. A lot of dangerous stuff is happening."

"Okay, Mom."

"Have a good night sweetie." She tapped on the tablet. "Good evening from rainy LA. How's London?"

"Oi, same, actually. Good to talk to you, Belinda."

"Same, Simon."

Mom mouthed, "Say hi to Austin for me."

I grinned at her. "I will," I mouthed back.

I lingered by the door. "Simon, this is serious. Let's discuss in the Old Language."

"The Gloom have been learning the Old Language; better use a spell."

"Certainly."

I ducked into the hallway, which glowed with the light of the sparkling chandeliers, then turned left to go see what Barn was up to.

I found him in the conservatory, picking at some green bushes by the doors to the back parlor.

"Good news."

"You're in?"

"Exactly!"

Barn and I fist bumped. "Let's go share the news with Lostin'—" He paused. "—after I help myself to these new snack plants Aunt Christine created."

"Snack plants?"

"Sure, this one has chocolate bars, that one string cheese, and the other one bags of jelly beans and crisps."

"No effin' way!"

"But you gotta grab something quick; the branches like to slap away hands."

Barn held up a bag of chips and his hand, now featuring an angry welt.

"Aunt Christine probably did that because she knows your dad likes to snack."

"Right, and Dad is trying to drop ten for our family vacation to Bora Bora at the holidays."

We went on talking for a while. I snatched a piece of string cheese without getting slapped on the hand. Then we went upstairs to call Austin to share the news.

Chapter Twenty-Four

Moritz/War

"GANG WARS HAVE erupted all over LA. People are overdosing at a never-before-seen rate, and a serial killer is stalking us, LA. Hello and welcome to Channel Seven News at Eleven," a plastic-faced anchor announced on the local evening news.

"The Macistráuto's press office is doing brilliant work covering the escalation of the coven's attacks on the Shimmering," Austin said, huddled next to me chewing thoughtfully on popcorn.

"It's scary, mate," Barn said, digging in the red plastic bowl. "It's never been this bad."

"Usually a few killings here and there," Mason chimed in.

The large screen TV hanging over the fireplace in Austin's media room flickered. We watched Alliance-affiliated press spin the recent bout of Ordinaries getting killed by Àzmadus. Their bodies deflated, their life force drunk by the monsters found along the LA river, in parks, on the beach, in parking lots of malls and colleges. Ordinaries were freaking out. The air in LA was thick with tension. The City of Angels was on edge.

"It feels like the end of the world," Mason said.

Stylo nodded. "I'm not usually scared, but right now, yeah, a little."

"Àzmadus usually know to feast off of criminals, real gang members, terrorists, white supremacists," Barn said. "Now they're attacking families and even kids"

"Bloody vile," Austin said, pulling me close to him and kissing my neck. "Stay close to me, Eli."

"Always."

He chuffed contentedly.

Later, lying in Austin's bed, listening to his heart beat through his chest, I said, "Shit is scary now, but I'm excited to be an intern of the League."

"You'll love it," Austin said, leaning over to kiss my cheek. "Little Ocho is very happy, yeah?"

He picked up the stuffed octopus and made his little head nod happily.

I fell asleep dreaming of sitting on the sofa at Arnulfo's office watching the rain fall outside the windows facing Santa Monica Boulevard.

Devlina's face appeared, spinning around and around behind Arnulfo.

"Think positive," she said. "Embrace the good."

"What the hell is happening, Devlina?"

"I told you," she said, her face dripping off her skull and falling like white wax on a frozen Arnulfo's shoulder. "I am at war. With the coven. All the Gloom. Zid'dra."

"Ordinaries are dying," I said. "The Alliance is getting serious about this. They called in XAQ6."

"Oh, I'm so scared." Devlina laughed maniacally. "I don't care," she said. "I am doing what needs to be done. I was Pàràsàfana, the Goddess of Wheat. People adored me. Worshipped me in temples all across the world. I was all powerful! And I gave that all up for Zid'dra." She said, "And now we are locked in battle, but I will turn the coven against him, and then I will show him who's boss…"

"Devlina, I've told you: just let it go. Stop doing what you're doing."

"Too late."

"Not too late."

She laughed. "Oh, look at you. You are good with your mom. Fine with your dad. All lovey-dovey with that boy."

"What does that have to do with you?"

She growled, "I gave up my life! I have nothing!"

"Devlina," I said, "you're the Queen of the Gloom. All the other Malevolents are not the ruler of the Gloom."

"I am going to cleanse the filth—"

"Devlina, you're powerful. Zid'dra knows it. You two can work things out. That should be enough for you."

"Was being the heir to the Delomary family fortune enough for you?"

I paused. Her face slipped off the skull. She looked fucking ridiculous, a talking skull.

"They're not the same thing."

"Aren't they?"

I woke up suddenly. The rain had stopped. The moon flooded Austin's room with silver light. I felt this deep sense of unease. There was no reasoning with Devlina anymore. She was spinning out of control. That scared the shit out of me.

*

A FEW DAYS later, Austin and I had dinner with Dad and Florence at a Thai restaurant in the Glendale Galleria after Xem Sen Ou training. Dad and I were trying to figure things out. But it was hard because we were two very different people. Dad had his corrosive moments. I retreated behind walls. I won't lie, it was hard spending time with him after all that happened, but he was trying. Maybe that's all sons and fathers need from each other, understanding.

After dinner, Florence and Dad clasped hands and headed away from Brand Boulevard to walk the few blocks to their apartment. We waved goodbye to them; I reached for Austin's hand. He squeezed tight, leaning over to kiss me.

"You okay?"

"Yeah," I said. "I mean, Dad is Dad."

"Yeah, but I can tell he's trying, Eli—" Austin's voice was cut off by bloodcurdling shrieking. People began imploding all around us. Àzmadus flew overhead. Heads began to pop off their necks. Malloupus attacked people on the street, knocking them down, then cuddling them tightly as they slowly drew the life force out of them until the bodies lay lifeless on the ground.

Austin pulled out his PlasmX. "Stand behind me, love," he said, pushing me behind him protectively.

Ordinaries ran around us screaming, shouting, pushing into stores, restaurants, anywhere to get off the street. Cars crashed into each other on Brand Boulevard. A bus collided with a truck, spinning around until it hit a streetlight and toppled over. The streetlight sparked and crashed to the ground. Ordinaries climbed out of the bus, bleeding and dazed.

Among the confusion and chaos, monsters preyed on people. An old man deflated next to me as a pretty Asian Àzmada sucked his life force out of him with her fingers. Flickers of white light dripped from her mouth, the last of his essence.

"We got to do something," I said to Austin.

Áucúitus flew out of the sewers, shrieking and flying after Ordinaries, mouths open and fangs bared, ready to wrap their luminous bodies and devour them.

"Oh, my God!" a woman in a pink tracksuit shouted to us. "We have to run!"

I opened my mouth to tell her to get behind us when an Áucúitu enveloped her, bit her head off, and then consumed the rest of her body.

I gagged. Blood and guts littered the street.

"I got this, Eli," Austin said.

Austin was nearby, swinging his PlasmX at various monsters, slicing and dicing them and ranting like a madman over the screams from Ordinaries and sounds of cars crashing and explosions rocking the buildings nearby.

Glass from broken windows of the high-rises lining the street rained down around me.

"Mortens, Macicens!" A raspy voice shouted in my ear. I turned quickly as the fangs of an Áucúitu dug into my arm. Red-hot pain exploded over my body. My head spun and stars erupted behind my eyes.

"Eli!" Austin shouted from several yards away. He was surrounded by a pack of Malloupus that circled him, ears erect, growling at him and ready to cuddle him until they sucked out his soul. "Eli!" His hand reached for mine before I saw him disappear into the pack of golden-furred monsters.

"Kangy!" I jumped into action, leaping up into the air and spinning rapidly, sending the wraith flying off my arm. I didn't need a PlasmX. I was magical. I was still an Encantreino in my heart. I was going to pull magic from my soul and summon a weapon. And, by God, it wasn't gonna be something wrong, like a feather pen or a candy bar. No, no, no. Nunma in Viacadeimo!

I hovered over the street. Chunks of concrete flew past my head. I winced as they landed on burning cars and bodies littering the street.

"Let's get a weapon!" I shouted out loud, concentrating hard to connect to the magic within.

A puff of pink smoke surrounded me. As the haze dissipated, my eyes settled on a very large flamethrower in my left hand.

"Oh, wow, fricking yeah!"

I clasped it with both hands and aimed for a dozen Àzmadus racing toward a group of Ordinaries scurrying to get out of the street. I pumped the trigger. Pink plasma shot out the end, arced over the street, singed a few palm fronds from the trees lining the street, then connected with the three Àzmadus closest to me. Their eyes grew big before, with a loud pop, they turned to black goo and dropped to the cracked and burning street.

"MACICENS MAL!" shouted several Àzmadus rushing toward me. I growled and pumped the trigger, atomizing the rest.

I floated back to the sidewalk. That was pretty awesome! Where was...oh shit. Austin, I lost sight of him. Where was he? I looked around. The Malloupus were gone. Pools of orange and red blood mixed on the curb, dripping over the side and toward the sewer.

"Kangy!" I shouted, leaping into the air and looking around desperately.

"I'm here!" Austin called, standing in a large crater in the middle of the street surrounded by burning fur. "These fricking devil dogs got a taste of Ol'Kangy!"

I flew toward him, arms outstretched. I crashed into his body, sending him falling backward. He landed on the ground. I landed on top of him. I covered his face with kisses.

"Ah, my Eli."

"My Kangy!"

"What's that?" He motioned at the weapon in my hand.

"Oh, something I conjured to destroy monsters."

"Did you forget your PlasmX again?"

I hung my head.

"I told you to say the spell so that the PlasmX finds you no matter where you are."

"I keep forgetting."

"We'll do it at home, later!"

"HELP!" someone screamed, jolting us into action. I stood; Austin followed me. He glanced at my arm, covered in blood.

"You're bleeding, mate!" Austin stretched a hand out. "I'll heal you."

"No time, we have to help the Ordinaries!"

"Okay, okay," Austin said.

As we raced to find the voice calling for help, the top of a luxury hotel nearby exploded, sending glass and concrete raining onto the street, smashing cars and a man standing in the middle of the street.

"Shit, Kangy that man—"

"Too late for him."

"No, but Kangy."

Flames erupted from a manhole under the debris.

"Duck into that arcade!" Austin said.

"I'm going to heal you," Austin said, passing a hand over my shoulder. As the pain disappeared, I noticed a huge concrete container filled with green catnip next to me. A sign flashed Petso-Rama Pet Store on the wall next to us. Monsters, and particularly Àzmadus, were deathly allergic to cats and catnip. The dander in the fur of the cats and the oil of the catnip caused the negative ions holding monsters together to explode.

"Grab that catnip!" I called to the Ordinaries. "I heard those monsters hate that stuff. Fling it at them as you flee. Take as much as you can!"

Austin and I pulled clumps of it out and handed them to the panicked men and women who took off running down the colonnade and away from Brand Boulevard.

"Shit, we have to find Dad and Florence!"

"Okay," Austin said. "I'm sure they're fine though—"

Before he finished his sentence, an explosion across the Brand Street Bridge lit up the night sky, sending Austin and me tumbling backward. Red flames burned above a series of abandoned cars, buses, and police cars on the bridge. Smoke circled from the flames smoldering in the wreckage of the cars.

Out of the smoke rose a tall woman wearing a gold-and-black leather dress, black stilettos, with her black hair piled high. The woman's hands were raised above her head. Dark clouds appeared above the smoke. Thunder drummed in the distance. The ground quaked.

I noticed what looked like small, golden pellets raining down from the clouds. Malloupus reared back on their hunches, hissing. Àzmadus screamed. Áucúitus began floating back into the sewers.

"Monsters hate wheat as much as they hate catnip and Magicals!" Austin shouted, pulling me close to him. Thunder boomed again. The building above us lurched forward. Plaster rained down on us.

"I call on you to stop this war," the woman said, hovering over the burning cars. "I am your queen. Paràsàfàna! Wife of your Lord and Unholy Spoiler, Zid'dra! I am the Queen of the Gloom."

A tall woman dressed in black, looking like an origami doll, rose from between two smashed planters.

"I am Auhaqa," she shouted up at Devlina, "Princess of the Coven of Àzmadus."

"Auhaqa!" Devlina said, "Cease this war. Submit to my reign!"

A small Black man, looking suspiciously like he wore a dog costume, joined her. "I am Prince Fido of the Coven of Malloupus."

"Prince Fido." Devlina reached for him. "Cease the war. Submit to my reign."

A green blob floated overhead. Soon it became a large doll resembling the character Gumby.

"I am Prince Màdàmaxo of the Morpheimus"

"Submit to me!"

Finally, a beautiful woman, resembling a Persian princess from a movie about a genie in a bottle, pushed past Auhaqa, Fido, and Màdàmaxo.

"Well, well, well," she said, "did you forget me, Miss Thing?"

Devlina gasped, "Rabetica?"

"In the flesh, boo-boo," she said. "You thought you killed me."

"It was all a misunderstanding."

"No misunderstanding, Paràsàfàna," the woman shouted angrily. "You had me hung, then quartered, and when you weren't satisfied that I was dead, you had me baked into a very large donut that you fed to your troll friends!"

"You survived that?" Devlina squeaked.

"Yes, you monster!" Rabetica was hovering over the cracked and smoldering street. "I HATE YOU!"

"It was just a test!" Devlina laughed.

"Some joke, you vile has-been."

Devlina's left hand grew five times as big as normal and stretched toward Rabetica. "Accept my apology!"

"Fuck you!" Rabetica said, "Never!"

"Call me Devlina," she said. "Rabetica, Auhaqa, Fido, Màdàmaxo, let us put war behind us. Let us work together to make this dimension better for the covens of the Gloom!"

Devlina winked at me. Fricking Devlina. She was crazy, a lunatic, but, God, I loved her.

"Never!" Máu Rabetica said, "You are merely a queen. We take our orders from our true Master. Lord Zid'dra."

Cheering erupted from the Àzmadus, Malloupus, and Morpheimus filling the street around us.

"Fuck him," Devlina said. "What has he done for you?"

Auhaqa, Fido, and Màdàmaxo, began talking quickly among themselves.

"HE HAS DONE EVERYTHING FOR US!" Rabetica screamed at the heads of the covens. "He is our master. The Magicals follow the Áuqala, we follow Zid'dra," She said, "Not some pathetic Goddess of Lust, of wheat. A has been. Ordinaries gave up on you. Stopped worshipping you. All the Antécallantus were glad to see you go. You're nothing. Nothing." She floated around Devlina, looking at her condescendingly. "And Zid'dra is making me Queen of the Gloom. You're no longer wanted anymore.You are being phased out entirely! All worship me, the new Queen of the Gloom."

"Hey, wait a second there!" I said standing and running into the street suddenly. "Devlina is a queen. She is strong and powerful and loyal."

Devlina looked at me, surprised.

"Hiya, kid!"

"Hi," I said.

"And who the hell are you?" Máu Rabetica loomed over me, at least ten feet tall. She sniffed the air. "Do I smell a Magical?"

She motioned to the Àzmadus, Malloupus and Morpheimus circling me. "Take him!"

Austin lifted his PlasmX, and the monsters paused their advance. "Over my dead body."

"Have it your way, Coaugelo," Rabetica shouted. With a wave of the hand, Austin went flying.

I watched him disappear behind smoldering wreckage nearby.

"Kangy!" I leaped for him. Rabetica jerked her head to the left. I froze midair facing her.

"I know this smell. It smells like Cassiopeia. Of Volqeńus. The fucking fair folk." She looked at me. "I smell a wretched Delomary, a descendent of that white magic whore, the Áuqala."

I tried to shout a retort, but my face muscles were paralyzed.

"Stop what you are doing, Rabetica!" Devlina shouted.

"Why? Because you say so?" Rabetica jerked her head to the right, sending Devlina spinning head over heels twenty feet above the street.

Rabetica laughed cruelly. "I hate that sumbitch over there. She is NOT LOYAL to Zid'dra, our Glorious Dark Lord and Destroyer of Ordinaries." Rabetica floated toward me, her coal black eyes reflecting the flames licking up the sides of the damaged, smoldering high-rises lining the street. "I especially hate you and your kith and kin, boy." She summoned a black ball of flame in her left hand. I watched it hover over her palm. "Elijah Delomary, the notorious Bane of the Gloom," she screamed, "you and your fricking family think that the universe belongs to you. That it is yours to protect."

I desperately tried to summon magic from all parts of my body. Nothing happened. Rather, I could feel the magic drifting out of my body.

Thunder rumbled overhead. More explosions boomed around me. Rubble tumbled into the cracked and wrecked street.

"I am going to enjoy killing you, red-haired freak," Rabetica said, her right hand caressing my face. "And when you are nothing more than a bad memory, I will turn around and I will destroy Paràsàfàna. Bye, bitch!"

Maniacal laughing surrounded me, bore into my head. Auhaqa, Fido, and Màdàmaxo and their covens of monsters crawled over the rubble of downtown Glendale and began chanting in unison as they advanced toward me.

"Die, Delomary. Die!"

"Redhead Freak!"

"Richer than God!"

"Kill the Magical!"

"Destroy Elijah, Bane of the Gloom!"

I concentrated, searching for Austin's heartbeat. There it was. And then...yes, his own glimmer of magic. I connected to him and summoned waves of purple light from beyond the clouds. The purple light rained down on the monsters. They shrieked, hissed, and scattered into the smoking debris lining the street.

"Oh, you think you can pull magic from your boyfriend?" Máu Rabetica laughed. "I am draining magic from you as we speak, and that makes me stronger. To kill you, Paràsàfàna, and then when I finish, I will gobble up your little Glimmerer. When I am done, I will rise up and be the new Queen of the Gloom!"

She reared back, flinging the black ball of flames at me.

"Enjoy dying, Delomary!" Then flames encircled my body. My body convulsed. My mind shorted out. I couldn't see anything or feel anything. Oh, puxhàredo. This was not how I was supposed to go out.

"Die, Delomary. Die!" chanted Máu Rabetica.

I was about to be killed by monsters in Glenndale. The nickname, Glenn-dead, was never so accurate. I braced myself as I heard Rabetica muttering words in the Dark Language, followed by thunder rumbling and the crackle of electricity. A wave of energy crashed into my body. My skin burned. *Puxhàredo, why was this happening to me? Seventeen and facing death too many times.*

Part Three

A MILLION STARS
PROMO ONTAŃO PERNAMBUQÒCO VENTRAS?
—FROM "WHERE DOES THE WIND BLOW?"

Skipping through the flames,
Of my despair.
One, two, three,
The clock strikes the hour.
Three, four, five,
Into the rabbit hole I fall.
La, la, la,
Spinning toward the Gloom,
I tumble, head over heels,
Six,
Seven.
Did you know that the universe is a circle?
Eight,
Nine.
Searching, searching, searching,
In the darkness,
Pierced by the flicker of diamonds in the night,
Ten.
You appear before me,
I can't believe it,
You're made of a million stars...a million shimmering stars.

Coàxantchl Pujo, *"Collected Poems of the Second Great Age"*

Chapter Twenty-Five

L'Auberge

I STOOD ON the patio of *L'Auberge*, a trendy restaurant on Melrose Boulevard in West Hollywood. Reservations were booked a year in advance. The line was fifteen-deep, an hour wait, minimum. We were going to brunch here.

"Come on, mate!" Barn called to me from the street. "Let's go to the Oak; there's no line."

Forget it, I was Elijah Delomary. My family was important. My mom practically lived at this place, bringing important people to wine and dine. My name meant something. I was somebody.

"I'll get us a table," I called to Barn, Mason, Katie, and Austin. Okay, Elijah, you got this. Think of the poised boy who lived in the mirror back in your trailer the night of the opening of the Keith Haring exhibit at the Delomary Art Museum of LA. He would breeze up to the maître d' and simply ask for a table. *I can do this*, I told myself.

I cut the line, ignoring the glares of the other people jockeying for a seat so they could see and be seen. The maître d' watched me push past the line, observing me.

"Elijah? What are you doing here? Is your mom here too?" The pretty, young Chicana woman named Juana grinned and then stepped around the podium to give me air kisses. Air kisses!

Someone grunted. A girl snapped a picture. Another poked a guy dressed in a white faux fox fur suit and whispered, "Is that Elijah Delomary?"

I ignored the crowd. *Use your status and position to your benefit, Elijah. Not to the benefit of your rumbling stomach.*

"I was curious if you could squeeze me and my entourage in?" I shot Juana my million dollar smile. Juana glanced at the tablet in front of her, scrutinized my group, the line, then the tablet.

She smiled. "You don't have a rezzie do you?"

"Juana, I won't tell if you don't."

"We're fully booked, Elijah."

"Please?"

Juana glanced at the tablet, the line, then back at me again. "I love the black-and-white theme you're rocking today. Black baggy trousers, skater shoes, white checkered polo. Very chic. Who's the designer?"

"Calvanno Coulanno. Doing a special collab with my Aunt Christine and the Puzzles brand she manages."

"I love Calvanno; he's amazing." Juan nodded to Katie. "I love your friend's black-and-white checkered tennis skirt, black stockings, black tank, and cut-off jacket. You wouldn't... I mean...couldn't?"

"I'm pretty sure Aunt Christine could messenger the outfit to you if you want to wear it out tonight. I'll text her."

"Wow." Juana grabbed several menus. "I love your família. This way, Elijah."

I waved to the others, then followed Juana through the french doors, across the terracotta floor.

"How's Belinda? She was in with a group of Europeans last week. Suits. They looked *aburrido.*"

"Probably some investors she has to wine and dine."

Juana showed us to a table in the center of the patio, usually re-served for famous stars, directors, producers, studio hotshots, and even the president.

"Brunch is on us," Juana said. "Thanks for being a loyal patron. And for posting the pictures of our food on your Insta!"

"We can pay," I said. "Really."

"*Tú dinero no es bueno aqui*, got it?" Juana winked and floated back to the front of the restaurant.

I loved having food comped. The perks of Mom spending lavishly on food and drinks when she brought investors or visiting executives from the far-flung satellite offices of our family company. The pux-hàredo Octopus of Death.

"Someone has his mojo back," Austin whispered to me as we set-tled in to the white wicker chairs. "Look at my cat being charming, char-ismatic and making people feel special."

"I'm practicing using soft power."

"Good, Eli," Austin said, squeezing my hand under the table. "Soft power motivates people."

"It's how my family stays in power."

"Oh my God!" I heard a familiar voice call out my name. "If it's not my favorite Delomary."

I turned my head. Blair Winchester, radiant in a white sundress and stilettos, holding hands with her drop-dead gorgeous boyfriend, Da-mien. I stood. Shook hands with Damien. Blair stepped close to me.

"You saved me, Blair," I whispered in her ear as she leaned in to air kiss my cheeks.

"Whether you want to admit it or not, you are a *Patrician*."

"I'm in the Alliance."

"We have our own Alliance."

"You can join the real Alliance."

"And give up our freedom?"

I sat down. "Join us for brunch?"

"I can't," Blair said. "We're on our way to London. For a confer-ence of *Patricians*."

"What do you mean?"

"There are *Patricians* the world over."

"Magicals who aren't part of the Alliance?"

She nodded. "We protect our own," she whispered. "We can still have a baby someday." She laughed.

"You're crazy." I laughed back at her. "But honestly, thank you."

My mind raced back to Glendale. I had squinted when the flames encircled me. I was praying to God that I didn't die. I was on Brand Boulevard, my head spun, blood ran down my cheek, where a piece of shrapnel lodged itself. I stared down a pack of Malloupus circling me, intent on tearing off my head and feasting on my soul.

I looked around in a daze. Devlina lay on top of a smoldering luxury sedan, her body lifeless. Malevolents weren't supposed to die like that. Killed by another monster.

"Get the fuck away from Elijah!" Blair had screamed. Three Malloupus, snarling and dripping saliva, nearby turned. Blair stood above me, hands on her hips, twisting her nose.

"I said, get off my fucking bestie!" A bolt of white light shot out of Blair's well-manicured hands, hitting the Malloupus in their haunches, sending them flying into the air.

Blair leaned over. "Are you okay, Elijah?"

"Yeah," I said. "Are we really besties?

"Sure," she laughed. "You can still become a Patrician and have protection!"

"I think I'm okay," I said. "But thanks for offering."

She twisted her nose, sending catnip and wheat raining all around us. The various covens began retreating. Disappearing into the night sky, the shadows, down alleys, and into the sewers and cracks in the pavement. Sirens erupted on the freeway below. Helicopters appeared. Agents for the League and XAQ2, in their trademark black suits, moved among the wreckage of Brand Boulevard. I leaned up on my elbows. Red hot pain burned in my legs and my head. Blair smiled, placed her tiny hands over my head, and closed her eyes, whispering in the Old Language. White light poured from her hands onto my head, legs, body. I felt instantly better. Like drinking a sports drink after a grueling run.

"Blair!" I said, "I didn't know you had that level of magic."

"There's a lot you don't know about me." She winked.

Damien appeared. "Hey, babe," he said, "is he okay?"

"He's alive," she said.

Damien peered down at me, holding her hand. "Dang, you look bad, Delomary."

"Don't tell me you're another *Patrician*?"

He laughed. "No, my family is in the Alliance," he said."I'm forbidden to date Blair, according to my parents. Screw them."

Wow, I wasn't the only Magical bound to stupid rules. I looked over at several overturned, smoldering cars. Austin stood and was dazed and confused.

"Bleedin' hell!" he shouted. "Where is that Goddam slag, Rabies, whatever her name is?"

"Kangy!" I called to him, waving my hands in the air.

"Eli!" Austin shouted, jumping over the planter. "Thank God you live! I was worried about you." He came over and pulled me up into a tight hug, running his hands through my hair. I snuggled into him. He kissed the top of my head and made cooing sounds.

Blair frowned. "God, can you two get more fucking cute?"

Agents began swarming the scene. "We got to get out of here," Damien said, waving two fingers. A blue bubble appeared and expanded into a portal. "Come on, boys, let's get out of here. Before they start asking questions about why a Delomary is here among a war between the covens."

I looked over. Devlina was gone. Did the coven get her? Poor Devlina.

The sun filtered down on me through the boughs of bougainvillea curling around the wood pergola overhead. Soft house music drifted from speakers hidden in the planters, barely audible above the din of conversation, plates clattering, and occasional laughter.

"See you around, Elijah," Blair said.

"Have a great day, Delomary," Damien added.

Barn watched her go. "I can't believe she saved you from those monsters."

"We were almost toast."

"Blair to the rescue." Barn shook his head. "I wish I had been there!"

"Me too," Mason said. "I want to kill monsters."

"Trust me," I said. "Be glad you weren't there; it was terrifying. Glendale is still a mess. The news says a gas explosion caused all the death and destruction."

"When it was really monsters going crazy, and Devlina battling Zid'dra's other wife."

"You know I have very little knowledge of the coven. My branch of the family isn't really into magic or the Alliance or anything," Mason said.

"Devlina was there," I said. "She was trying to get the covens to join her cause."

"What is her cause, mate?"

I looked at the bacon and eggs on my plate. Listened to the murmur of diners around us. A fountain tinkled nearby.

"She wants to be loved."

Barn, Mason, and Austin burst out laughing.

"That cow wants to dominate the world," Barn said, buttering a piece of toast.

"All Malevolents can't be trusted," Austin said.

Mason glanced at his watch. "Shit, I have to go. I have to get some things from the Marchého Imradomensanabo downtown before I meet with my parents tonight. We're going to Disneyland tomorrow then back to San Francisco the day after."

I thought I had it bad. I mean, my family carried a heavy burden for the Alliance, Ordinaries, the Universe. At least I knew who I was. Mason? He knew magic but not much about the Alliance.

"How's Erica?" Barn asked Mason as he drank some water.

Erica was Mason's on-again, off-again girlfriend. He didn't really like her. It was obvious.

He shrugged. "Fine. I guess," he said. "Sorry to run and miss hair-cuts."

I flagged down Juana, determined to at least tip her and the waiter.

"No, esta bien, Elijah!"

"Okay, thanks as always, Juana."

"Anytime, Elijah. Stay magical." She winked at me. My eyes widened. She sauntered away.

*

"TA-DA!" BARN SAID a few minutes later in front of a gray stucco store-front with huge glass windows.

"What's this, mate?" Austin said, peering in the windows through his aviators.

"A salon," Barn said, "to get your hair cut!"

Austin frowned, running his hands through his long hair.

I squeezed his hand, whispering, "You don't have to cut your hair."

He shook his head. "No, love," he said, "I'm ready for something new."

We both needed new haircuts. Mine was shaggy now. We both had started to grow our hair out at the same time this spring. Our little moment of rebelling against our parents.

I glanced over at Austin. He smiled at me in amusement. "I want to look hot for you, love!"

"You already are hot, Kangy."

Austin leaned in for a kiss. I leaned on my tippy-toes and closed my eyes as our lips touched.

I had a plan for Austin. I was surprising Austin by taking him to Hong Kong to see his grandmother for his birthday. Austin adored his grandma, and it had been six months since he saw her when she was sick. Barn helped me plan the trip. I was taking advantage of my family's octopus-like tentacles of resources for this trip. I mean, my family some-how owned an airline and had several 747s for use by executives to travel between North America and operations all over the world.

I surveyed the trendy salon with black leather chairs, chrome furniture, black marble counters, and stylish men and women milling around in tight black T-shirts and jeans as they cut hair.

A haircut cost an outrageous five hundred dollars.

Austin pulled me close when he saw the prices.

"Too dear, love!"

"Dear?"

"*Expensive!*" he intoned.

"Oh." I laughed. "But you're worth it."

Soon, he was frowning at an oval mirror hanging on the wall in front of him, as his shiny black locks tumbled to the floor. After a wash, dry, and some product fingered into his hair, he peered at himself in the mirror. He raised an eyebrow and looked at me.

"Awesome," I said. "You look beautiful, Kangy. Beautiful."

Austin beamed at me. His hair was longer on top, and spiky, while short on the sides. He looked trendy, stylish, and sexy.

"You look like a bleedin' model, mate." Barn laughed.

Next, it was my turn. Austin hovered over me, consulting with the stylist in Cantonese. Barn added his opinion too. The woman smiled.

"I get it, sounds great." She smiled, patting me on the shoulders. "Just relax."

I was like a sheep being sheared as a shower of red hair rained down around me. When the stylist was done, she, Austin, and Barn surveyed me. I sat nervously. They grinned.

"Damn, love," Austin said, "you look brilliant."

"Not like the slacker surfer dude," Barn added. "Great, hot, amazing." I glanced at myself. My hair was tousled, like I just stepped out of the water at the beach. I actually loved the look.

"I wish my hair had your texture, love," Austin whispered in my ear.

"You look great, Kangy. Our next stop is at a tailor to get fitted for new suits. For the birthday bash at the house," I lied.

"Oi, right mate." Barn played along. "In the ballroom. You have to be a real ponce to have a party in the ballroom."

Austin grinned. "That's going to be great."

Little did he know the suits were to see his grandmother. Barn told me his grandmother Au Yeung was at the top of Hong Kong society, where it was important we dressed up for her. After my fitting, it was Austin's turn. Katie joined us. Soon Barn and Katie were staring into each other's eyes, mumbling how much they loved each other, so I slipped outside to get iced coffees.

A blast of hot air buffeted my face as I stepped onto Melrose Boulevard. I slipped on my sunglasses and headed to a coffee bar nearby. I passed an alley and heard this hissing sound. I tried to ignore it. *Probably nothing, some kids hissing at each other for fun*, I told myself, the hair on the back of my neck standing. I kept walking. Something hit my back. I turned around slowly. My eyes grew wide.

In the shadow of a clothing boutique on one side of the alley, Devlina stood in her usual black stilettos, black leather mini-skirt, and black bodice.

"I thought you were dead!" I said, walking over to her. "The battle in Glendale. I was sure Máu Rabetica offed you."

"I'm invincible, remember?"

"I guess," I said. "So, what are you doing here in this crummy alley?"

"I'm doing some light shopping."

"The fuck you are."

"The fuck I am," Devlina said. "And watch your language."

I noticed Orville Conry and his puxhàredo Plebeians holding very large swords made out of some gleaming green material.

They formed a line across the alley, facing Devlina. Hissing at her.

What the hell was Orville doing here with his Plebeians? Were the rumors true? Had he joined the coven?

An Àzmado knelt on the roof of a skateboarding shop. I shaded my eyes, scanning the roof. There were several Àzmadus baring fangs at Devlina. (Really quick note about Àzmadus—they could go out in daylight as long as they drank some wheat grass. Weird, I know. Catnip and wheat killed them. But, wheat grass protected them from the sun. Random.)

"What's going on here, Devlina?"

"What do you think?"

"Looks like you're in trouble."

"Hey, is that you, Delomary?" Orville steps forward holding his green sword high over his head. "You come for a chop yourself?"

"Just had one."

"You look cute, Elijah." Devlina smiled.

"Thanks."

"Get the fuck outta here, Delomary," Orville said. "The Plebeians are here to deal with this fucking traitor."

"So, what, Orville, you've joined the coven along with your Plebeian toadies?"

I glanced over my shoulder toward the end of the alley. People walking by us on Melrose were totally oblivious to what was happening in the alley.

A gramora.

Clearly.

"Hey, fuck you," I shouted to Orville.

He growled, "This isn't your fight Fag-gina"

"You want me to come and kick your ass, Orville?"

Orville rolled his eyes. The Pleibian toadies tightened their grip on their swords.

"Yes," Devlina said, "just go over there and kick his ass, Elijah, baby."

"That turd knows I can."

"Fuck you, Delomary!"

Orville waved his sword, and the Plebeians rushed Devlina.

She kicked them with her stilettos, summoned birds to attack them, and sent wheat down on the Àzmadus. They hissed and screamed as the wheat hit their faces and arms, burning their skin.

They bared their fangs at Devlina and me.

I was supposed to stay out of her mess. I had promised myself only last night that I was done being sucked into other people's troubles. Ha. I was a sucker for drama. For that reason, I was beside Devlina kicking, punching, ducking swords, and backing her up. Orville tumbled backward, fell onto the cracked pavement, and passed out.

"Why do you look sorta transparent?"

"I'm not fully charged, man."

"What do you mean?"

"Apparently, when you broke your leg and arm last summer you affected my powers."

"You sure that's not from your battle with the covens last night?"

"No," Devlina explained.

I paused to punch a Plebeian in the face. A fist hit me in the arm. I turned, kicking a Pleb in his side.

"I told you we're connected. Thank your mom for that," Devlina said.

"All these months you were using my magic?" I growled. "I knew you wanted me around for your sinister plans. Not to help you smite this homophobic, racist world."

"I mean, I like having you around."

"I knew you were using me. You never change. Never."

An Àzmada fell from the sky, landing on my shoulders, growling, "I am going to end you, Elijah Delomary!"

"Fuck off!" I spat, flipping into the air, sending the monster airborne. I spun around and kicked its chest. It flew across the alley, hitting a peach-colored wall hard.

"Wow," Devlina said, "your Xem Sen Ou is really good."

"I've been training with Dáumo Máurso."

"Don't make me barf," Devlina said. "I am not a fan of his. He once sent a thousand legions to hunt me down."

"Bet he had a good reason."

"I thought you forgave me!"

"I did," I said, "until just now."

"I'm sorry," Devlina said, her face turning inside out on her skull, then reverting.

"That was scary."

"Do you accept my apology?"

"Fine."

"Good," Devlina said. "We gotta clean the alley with these clowns."

"Devlina, I've told you to leave Zid'dra alone. Look what he did to you in Glendale."

"That's more of a reason for me to keep up the fight," Devlina said. "He's not getting the last word."

"You never learn."

"Neither do you."

"You can't let go."

"Can you?"

I headbutted a Plebeian. Devlina turned one to stone.

"Look at you: new haircut, new attitude."

"Yeah, well—" I was cut off by the sight of a huge elephant-like creature lumbering down the alley, its red eyes shooting orange laser beams at Devlina and me. A beam hit my arm, burning my skin. I yelped, jumping into the air. Puxhàredo, an Orgma, kills and eats Magicals. Even Malevolents like Devlina.

"Shit," Devlina shouted as her semi-transparent arm smoked. "Daddy isn't playing."

I stopped. *What the hell am I doing? Why am I helping Devlina? I cannot help Devlina. We are not one and the same. I needed to get out of her drama.* I closed my eyes, focusing on my breathing, my magic. Electricity charged through my nervous system. I heard an explosion. A crash, followed by hissing and sparking. I opened my eyes. Devlina was gone. Orville and the Plebeians were retreating down the alley. The Orgma had vanished.

Austin appeared at the end of the alley, holding an iced coffee. "Eli? What are you doing?"

I turned. "Oh, nothing. You know, I like to explore alleys."

"Yes, one of your quirks."

"Did you get me a cold coffee?"

"No," Austin said. "Do you want one?"

"Yes, Kangy, obvi."

Austin lumbered toward me."Obvi, yeah?" He stood over me, peering down at me through his thick glasses. "Obviously, like my love for my wee Eli?"

"Yes, Kangy."

Chapter Twenty-Six

Mile High Club

THE OUTSIDE OF the 787 double-decker plane read Delomary Global Holdings Corporation in red and purple. I sat by a window, in a white-leather lounge chair across from Austin as we hurtled at five hundred miles per hour over the Pacific, headed to Hong Kong.

"This place is posh!" Austin said an hour earlier as we entered the private lounge reserved for my family, outfitted with chandeliers, leather sofas and chairs, a full bar, and private restaurant, at the terminal for Global Airlines.

"Oi, I love that your family owns an airline and has a separate terminal for you," Austin said, sinking into a white recliner. A waitperson in a blue-and-red uniform circled with a tray holding flutes of champagne for Austin's parents. Another server brought two Shirley Temples, handing one to Austin and one to me.

Austin sipped his drink. "This is the life for a me."

A plate appeared with a burger and fries. "Oh my God," Austin exclaimed, "food!"

He dug into his burger, closing his eyes and chewing contentedly. Austin Sr. and Cecilia clinked their flutes. After a moment, Austin paused chewing. "But, you haven't told me where we're going?"

His parents grinned at me.

I smiled. "Surprise! We're going to Hong Kong!"

Austin's mouth dropped.

"To see your gran."

Austin shook his head. "You're shitting me, love"

"I am not shitting you, love."

"Mum, Dad, where are we going?"

"Hong Kong!"

Austin's face lit up. He mumbled something in Cantonese. His parents nodded.

"Happy Birthday!" I said a moment later. Austin's face flushed, meaning he felt emotional. Leos—big cats filled with emotions simmering just below the surface.

Austin stood and pulled me into a tight hug. 'Thank you, love," he whispered in my ear. "You are amazing."

"Happy seventeen," I said. "And thank you for sticking by me."

"Was never in question."

A half-hour later we were at 35,000 feet in the posh lounge on the second level of the massive plane. Cecilia and Austin Sr. lounged in a corner sipping champagne, arms draped across each other's shoulders talking quietly in Cantonese.

I said to Austin, "So, you want a tour or what?"

Austin looked up from the bags of chips and candy in his lap that he had been munching on. Austin loved snacks. "I thought you'd never ask, love!"

I grabbed Austin's hand and led him past his parents, out of the all-white lounge, and into the hallway.

"Mr. Delomary, Mr. Kang," one of two stewards said to us.

"I feel like royalty."

"You are Kangy, my Prince Charming."

Austin beamed.

We slipped through a door at the end of the hallway.

"This is the formal dining room. Seats eighty."

Austin gaped at the long table lined with white leather chairs and the two crystal fixtures set above the table. I pushed into the next room.

"This is the casual dining room filled with small tables and seats for intimate meals."

"Two dining rooms," Austin said. "Your family knows I love to eat."

We zigzagged through the plane past the yoga studio and spa and library featuring a gas fireplace and five thousand books, a bowling alley, putting green, movie theater, Olympic-sized pool and gym.

"How do you do bench-presses if there's turbulence?"

"We never have turbulence on this plane."

"How is that possible?"

"The marvels of Delomary Corporate engineering."

He grinned. "Or magic?"

"Probably both."

We ended our tour in the lower level.

"These are the suites," I said, waving my hand at a series of double doors around a central vestibule.

"Suites, love?"

"You know, for sleeping?"

Austin peered at me through his thick glasses, then grinned.

"Oh really?"

I opened the double doors to our suite. Austin stepped inside, mouth dropping. "King-sized bed. Plush white comforter and bedding. Leather headboard and wall coverings. Soft lighting. A chandelier!"

"We have our own living room."

"Another fireplace!"

"Perfect for flying over the Arctic Circle.'"

"The bathroom is bigger than my room back home!"

"Heated floors, towel warmers, deionized water."

"Why are there four shower heads, mate?"

"Uncle Teddy designed this plane. He was a bachelor. And recently came out. I guess he had wild parties on this plane," I said.

Austin frowned, looking at the tile floor.

"It's clean, weirdo."

"You never know, some gay men like to make a mess everywhere."

"Is that so?"

We laughed some more.

"We can have breakfast in bed or here in the lounge by the fire."

Austin pulled me close, peering down at me.

"How lucky am I? I meet the richest boy in the world, who whisks me in absolute luxury to see my gran in Hong Kong."

"I'm the lucky one, Kangy."

"Of course, couldn't you just open a portal to Hong Kong?"

"Against the oath," I said. "And my magic isn't that strong. I don't want to get us trapped somewhere else."

"Yeah," Austin said and pulled me closer to him, "I'd hate to get trapped with you somewhere unexpected."

Well, clearly, we made out a little. Hands all over, kissing, moaning. The works. Then there was a knock at the door.

"Dinner is served in the dining room, Mr. Delomary, Mr. Kang."

"Thanks, Theresa," I said to the steward. "Can you send a round of drinks to Mr. and Mrs. Kang while Austin and I freshen up? We need ten minutes."

The pretty young woman nodded. "I'll have the kitchen send out the appetizers as well."

"Thanks, Theresa."

I closed the door behind me. Austin peered at me through his thick glasses. "This is a whole new Eli. One I've never seen before."

"I'm feeling better every day."

"It's ace, love. You're poised and confident."

He pulled me close again. "It's very sexy."

We made out some more until I pushed him into the bathroom, where we laughed as we washed our faces, buttoned our shirts, fixed our ties, and combed our hair.

"We look awesome," Austin said, looking in the mirror. He towered over me in his bespoke black suit. I scrutinized the boy in the mirror. I recognized this one. He was poised and confident, the boy next door. The one Karla created long ago at the Delomary Art Museum of LA.

After dinner, Miriana, the main steward, asked us to retire to the library for port for the adults and Shirley Temples for Austin and me.

"That fireplace is something else," Austin Sr. said, sipping on a glass of port, and slouched into a brown leather arm chair. "On an airplane."

"Your family certainly know how to travel in style," Cecilia said. "I usually abhor flying. Packed like a sardine in a smelly, hot plane."

"That's because you fly economy class, Mum." Austin laughed. "We can afford first class!"

"Waste of money, son," she said.

"Chinese mums never want to splurge. When we travel, we stay with family. I have to sleep on the floor."

Cecilia shrugged. "You're seventeen. It's good for your back."

I laughed. "We stay with family too."

"See!" Cecilia beamed at me.

"But Delomarys always live in mansions. Even our poorest cousins in Dallas have a seven thousand square foot house. With ten guest rooms."

Cecilia sighed. "Your family really is richer than God."

A while later, Miriana dimmed the lights and supervised as a team of men in suits pushed in an elaborate three-tier white sponge cake covered in whipped cream frosting and covered in candied mangoes, pineapples, and strawberries.

Seventeen candles flickered on top. Austin waggled his eyebrows.

"I love sponge cake!"

"I know, silly. I told Pierre, the chef."

While the stewards sang "Happy Birthday," I leaned over to Austin and whispered, "Make a wish, love."

"But it already came true," he said. "I met you."

"Surely you have another dream?"

He shot me this wicked grin, then blew out the candles. We gobbled down cake, guzzled three Shirley Temples each, and polished off a couple of bowls of freshly made gelato.

Austin Sr. and Cecilia shook their heads. "Ah, to be seventeen again."

Austin Sr. rubbed his stomach. "I could eat like that when I was seventeen."

Cecilia laughed. "You still eat like that. Only it stays with you."

They laughed and cuddled and talked softly in Cantonese to each other.

All that sugar went to our heads. We raced around the plane chasing each other. We returned to our suite, changed into our swim briefs, and hopped into the pool.

"Finally embracing that slinky swim brief that shows off everything, huh, Eli?"

I shot him a wicked smile. "I figured you'd enjoy seeing me in this."

"Very much, love."

I floated in the pool while Austin did handstands. After two hours of frolicking in the pool, we returned to our suite, dripping wet in our swimsuits. Austin dried me off with a towel, staring at my body.

"So, bleeding hot, love." He smiled, then began to tickle me. "That sexy V-line leading straight to your..."

"Kangy," I said indignantly.

"You love it."

We laughed some more and chased each other around the room in our bathing suits, jumping on the bed. Finally, we collapsed onto the bed, giggling and panting.

Austin loomed over me, pinning my arms to the bed over my head.

"I love you, Elijah Delomary."

Kangy the Biggie stood at full attention. I was electrified. "Kangy, I think we should...you know," I whispered.

"I'll never hurt you, Elijah."

I nodded. "I know, Kangy.

"I'm ready, Kangy."

"Are you sure, love?"

"I'm ready because I feel safe with you."

He leaned down and kissed me with his pillowy soft lips.

And it happened at 35,000 feet. Somewhere over the middle of the Pacific Ocean. We both become members of the notorious Mile High club. The experience started like the first day of school, scary, awkward, painful. Then slowly turned into the excitement of Christmas and New Year's and finally the thrill of the Fourth of July, with fireworks exploding everywhere.

Afterward, Austin leaned over, peered at me worriedly, and asked, "Are you okay, love? I didn't hurt you?"

"Yeah, I mean, I think I'm dead." I laughed. "I might walk funny tomorrow."

Austin frowned. "I'm sorry, love."

"Kangy, relax."

He smiled. "It was fun though. Right, love?"

I grinned. "Weird, honestly, but yeah fun, but only because it was with you."

Austin wrapped his arms around me, chuffing contentedly, kissing my face all over. We drifted off to sleep, our naked bodies intertwined. My eyes opened slowly. The phone buzzed next to me. Austin leaned over me to pick it up. He spoke in Cantonese to his parents. Sounded like something was terribly wrong. Puxhàredo, did they hear us? Uncle Teddy told me the rooms were soundproof.

Austin hung up the phone. "My parents are having breakfast in bed," he said. "They said we should too. And they want to steal the robes and slippers."

"Um, they are free for them to take." I laughed.

I lay in his arms.

"You all right, love?"

I had a mix of emotions. On one hand, I felt so close to Austin, closer than I ever felt to someone, and yet, I also felt he was very far away.

Of course, being raised Catholic, I also was battling guilt.

I told Austin how I felt.

"I feel the same, love," he said. "Weird, but without the Catholic guilt, of course."

We laughed at that.

"If we get married, you have to become a Catholic," I told him.

"Kangy is not an organized religion type."

"Mom will never agree to us getting married."

"She'll never say no to Kangy."

We both laughed.

"I'm hungry. I'm going to order for us." Austin picked up the phone and began talking in Cantonese. He hung up and said, "Your kitchen staff are exclusively Chinese; did you know that?"

I shook my head. "Well, good thing you came along to order breakfast for me."

There was a knock at the door. "We're two hours out of Hong Kong. Mr. Delomary."

"Thanks, Miriana. We're having breakfast sent in."

"Perfect," Miriana said, adding, "The limousine will be ready at the gate to take you to Mrs. Kang's estate in Causeway Estuary. That will be 9:00 AM Hong Kong time."

"Thank you, Miriana. That will be great."

Austin sat up in bed, shaking his head. "I am so not used to this Delomary. Who are you, where is my frightened, lost Eli?"

I laughed. "I think he's gone. Replaced by a man."

Austin looked at me. "I guess we're men now. How does it feel?"

"Awkward," I said. "I mean, I am not giving up Little Ocho or Meow Meow or daydreaming in the bumblebee garden now that I'm supposedly an adult."

"Who said you had to?" Then he patted the bed beside him, throwing me a mischievous smile. "Now, come and sit next to Kangy. I'm afraid my biggie misses you."

I rolled my eyes. "Have I created a monster?"

*

THE KANG ESTATE sat at the end of Causeway Road, hidden behind ivy-covered walls and set on the top of a low hill. The elegant brick Georgian mansion reminded me of the house Uncle George and Barn lived in when they first moved to Burbank, only much larger.

Au Yeung "Victoria" Kang stood at the end of a long hallway waiting for us, her hands folded elegantly in front of her. Austin spotted her and took off running . He wrapped her in a warm hug. The usually restrained woman hugged him back, laughing and talking to him in Cantonese.

"Go ahead; don't be bashful," Cecilia said to me.

I was nervous meeting new people. Austin pulled away from her, before leaning down and whispering in her ear.

She smiled at me. "Welcome, Elijah Delomary, to my home," she said in flawless English with the same regal accent as Austin, his parents, and Barn.

She was a beautiful, diminutive woman in her early seventies, well-dressed in white slacks, heels, a lavender blouse, and her hair cut in a fashionable bob that strangely reminded me of the one Devlina favored.

"I am most pleased that you have brought my son and daughter-in-law and my beloved grandson to visit me here in Hong Kong. Ever since they left me, I have been heartbroken."

Austin and his parents began talking animatedly in Cantonese.

"I am grateful for the invitation," I said. Yes, of course, I called and asked if we could come. Well, I didn't call. One of Mom's assistants called one of Victoria's assistants, and they set the whole thing up. This happened with rich families—assistants interface with assistants to plan meetings.

"I am glad you are well," I said.

"Oh, I simply had a cold last winter; everyone always gets worked up when "Gran" gets sick."

Everyone laughed. Austin and his parents began arguing with her again in Cantonese. She muttered something back to them while proceeding to take my arm. "Let me show you around my little cottage."

Her home had fifty rooms on thirty acres on the edge of Victoria Harbor. Not such a cottage, with breathtaking views of Central Hong Kong, Kowloon Island, and the South China Sea.

We ended up in a rose garden on the side of the house.

"This reminds me of the rose garden we have back at our house," I said, leaning over to smell one of the enormous pink roses bending over the brick walkway.

"The house—" She laughed. "I know all about your family, Elijah. The second tallest building in Hong Kong belongs to your family. Delomary Asia Tower."

"I guess Austin told you about me."

She shook her head. "No, my dear, I know your grandmother. Very well in fact."

"You do?"

"We studied at Winchester University."

"You did?"

"Why, yes, I did my undergraduate work at Oxford and Cambridge, then got my PhD in Applied Hygenic Sciences at Winchester University."

"Holy, moly, that's cool!"

"Your grandmother has a PhD in Applied Arts and Sciences. We fought monsters together, long ago."

"No way." I was speechless. "I can't imagine my grandmother fighting monsters. She's so uptight."

"Not always," Victoria said. "She was young once. We both were."

"I'm sorry, I shouldn't—"

"You're fine, dear," Victoria said. "I understand. Your family has a burden. You do, your mother does, your grandmother." She added, "I sit on the Còngréhassa sie Estàntus"

"What do you mean?"

"I voted against you being stripped of your powers," she said. "And not because you are dating my grandson, but because it is wrong to do what they did."

"I'm sorry, I don't understand."

Victoria looked up at the old mansion.

"Let's go inside and have some tea. I'll tell you everything."

Soon, we were in her private library, a large room overlooking the garden with red damask wallpaper and two walls filled with floor-to-ceiling bookcases stuffed with books, mostly in Chinese.

She waved me into a floral print armchair by the fireplace.

"Hong Kong was once part of the Mã-Lo kingdom. When the Mongols invaded, the Yellow Emperor and his subjects set out to sea to escape and ended up on Old Earth."

"The Mã-Lo settled alongside the Vana'a, Minra, and the tribe of Romans called the Passonians. There was a war instigated by monsters who didn't want Magicals to unite as one, and eventually Minerva was founded.

"Hong Kong is a special place. As such, the Gloom have always wanted control of it and its people. Warlords, witches, demon kings, hellions, and various covens have all swept through Hong Kong. That's why the Anti-coven League was founded here centuries ago."

"Austin says by your family."

"Yes," she said. "The Au family. My ancestors. The League passes through the female lineage."

"Delomarys are matrilineal too," I said. "Me being a male raised some eyebrows when Mom decided for me to be the heir."

"Gender is all an illusion."

"The world is obsessed with gender roles, and sexual orientations."

"Simple-minded people," Victoria said, "divide and conquer. The oldest strategy to maintain power.

"The League," Victoria continued, "almost vanished during World War Two. The coven became very powerful. Hitler, Mussolini, Emperor Hirohito, all aligned with the coven and various monsters within the Gloom."

"What do you mean?"

Victoria laughed. "There's the Shimmering, where Magicals such as ourselves and Ordinaries live. Everyone else lives in the shadows, the recesses of the Gloom. Tyrants are always born of the Gloom, not the Shimmering. Take that politician of yours, the one who left recently left office. A Malloupo. Soul sucker.

I sat there shocked.

"You didn't know?" Victoria laughed. "I thought Delomarys know everything."

"My mom doesn't involve me much with the Alliance."

"She is wise," Victoria said. "It is a burden."

"I took the Oath. I know my family's place in the Alliance."

Victoria nodded, poured me a cup of tea, added a lump of sugar and some milk, then passed the cup to me. "Do you know why I voted down the resolution to destroy your Familiar? To strip your powers?"

I stared into my cup.

"Because you are a boy," she said. "The punishment didn't fit the crime. You are young. You deserve to live the life of a teenager. To be free to make mistakes."

I looked up into her wise, kind eyes.

"Your family has always carried a heavy burden," she said. "More so than most of the three hundred Corpos Sangrancto. However, it isn't a burden for just you to carry. That's why there's an Alliance."

"My family would disagree."

"That's still not your burden," she said. "And you have support."

I thought of Austin. She smiled.

"The League wasn't always part of the Alliance," she said. "Coaugelus are warriors. There was a time when the League wanted nothing to do with the Alliance."

"Really?"

She nodded. "Politics. Astroístus, Encantreinus, and Antécallantus weren't always natural allies."

"That doesn't make sense."

"Magicals looked down on our skills, our powers. Or lack thereof."

I thought of George, Barn, Austin. Saving my ass too many times.

"Dirk and Evangeline changed that. They met with my ancestors. They pushed the Còngréhassa sie Estàntus to embrace us."

I never knew any of this.

"Good thing too. For when the Last Battle loomed, it was the partnership between our families that saved the Shimmering. Created the Pàcifimenta, and frankly even saved the Gloom. We were the victors. Most Magicals wanted to banish the covens and the Gloom."

"That isn't possible."

"You are right. How do you get rid of night? Darkness?" she asked. "You can't."

She stirred her tea. "You were the one who fought Devlina, were you not? Who forced her into the portal, where she was captured by the Áuqala? The Queen of Queens, Evangeline, your great-great-grandmother?"

How did she know this? No one knew this story. It was a well-hidden secret of what I had done. No one in our local Temple knew this story. No one.

"I know because I saw what happened."

I dropped my spoon. It hit the table loudly before tumbling to the red Persian rug below us.

"You don't need to worry, Elijah," she said, reaching for my hand. "We are sworn to protect you."

I stared at her earnest, dark-brown eyes.

"What are you saying?"

"What they've told you isn't quite true," she said. "The thing is, Elijah, you have great power."

"No," I said. "I am not very good with magic."

"You are mistaken. When you traveled to Minerva and fought bravely in Tyne, where you foiled Devlina's attempt to take over Old Earth, don't you know she wanted to slit your throat so she could drink your blood and become more powerful? She wanted to become the Máu of Old Earth."

"I don't follow."

"Each dimension has a Máu that reigns over the Gloom of that dimension. Except Old Earth in the Seventh Dimension.”

"So Devlina wanted to be Queen of the Gloom here and there?”

“That's right,” she said. “She is Máu Licuria, the Goddess of Lust. She lusts endless power.”

“I still don't know what this has to do with me.”

“Devlina needs your power to be stronger.”

“Yes, I know,” I said. “My mom linked me to her when she summoned her.”

“Is that so?” Victoria looked at me worriedly.

“Yes.”

“You have to be careful, Elijah,” she said. “The Gloom covets your power. Your place in the Alliance. Your soul. You are inherently good. You know the difference between right and wrong deep down inside you.”

“I was raised to do what's right.”

“You do what's right because you want to.”

“Maybe I just do what I have to.”

“And that's why some voted to take your powers.”

“What do you mean?”

“We think there was a conspiracy. An infiltration of monsters into the Alliance that conspired to strip you of your powers. So you'd be harmed.”

My blood chilled. “What are you saying?”

“With you out of the picture, the coven would be stronger.”

“No, I mean, how could there be monsters within the Alliance?”

“The Alliance was weakened, neglected. Magicals became distracted; Ordinaries grew comfortable. Monsters emboldened. What better way to destroy the Alliance than by removing you from the equation?”

I was scared. “Maybe I should talk to my mom.”

“You're safe here,” Victoria said. “No one dare harm you at this place.”

I tried to quell the panic rising inside.

“Your family and mine worked to root out the rot in the Alliance, remove the threats internally, and clean up the Còngréhassa. You no longer need to worry."

"It wasn't an accident that George and Barnhard came to live in Southern California five years ago," Victoria said a moment later.

I looked at her. "What do you mean?"

"The League knew of the danger facing your family. You."

"And Austin?" I asked. "Was he sent to look out for me?"

She looked at me. "What do you think?"

I shook my head. I had an awful feeling in my stomach. Had he been pretending all along? Did he love me, or was he only with me to protect me?

Victoria reached for me. "No, Elijah, my grandson truly loves you."

I stood. "I need to lie down. Can someone show me to my room?"

"Elijah," she said, "I didn't mean it that way."

"I'm really confused," I said. "I'm jet-lagged. I need some rest."

Victoria's eyes scanned my face. She bit her lower lip, then pressed a button on a table next to the sofa. A man appeared in the doorway.

"This way, Mr. Delomary."

Upstairs, I lay in a soft four-poster bed overlooking the gardens and Victoria Harbor.

Filtered sunlight poured over the harbor and the Star Ferries plying the waves. I was unsettled. Last night, Austin and I connected. Mom was right. Having sex changed things. I wasn't right. I was confused. Did Austin love me, or was he merely on the payroll to look out for me? Someone knocked softly at the door.

It opened, and Austin's head appeared around the door. He peered at me. "Everything okay, love?"

I frowned at him. "Why exactly are you with me?"

He appeared stunned. "What do you mean?"

He stepped in the room, closing the door quietly behind him.

"Your grandmother told me your family protects my family. Are you on payroll or something? Did she set this up?"

Austin shook his head. "No, love, it's not like that at all."

"Than what is it like? Because I'm feeling very confused right now and, frankly, used."

Austin sat on the bed, staring out the window.

"Are you mad about last night?"

"Maybe."

"Why?"

"I let you do—that. And now I wonder if it was some sort of initiation. Hazing. Sick ritual. Deflower the Delomary."

Austin turned and looked at me, anger and hurt in his eyes.

"Is that what you think? I'm just some asshole that goes around deflowering boys?"

"Honestly, I don't know anymore."

Austin's eyes flashed.

"Are you pushing me away...again? You promised me, Elijah. You promised me."

I could see his eyes misting over.

Puxhàredo. *Don't do this,* I told myself, *the Darkness is gone.*

I reached for him. "I'm not pushing you away."

I could sense the destruction waiting inside him. He was good at controlling his internal rage until he wasn't.

A few weeks ago, I had pissed him off, acting like a fool. He had gone into his bathroom and begun slamming the shower doors until I heard a terrific crash. He came out holding one of the shower doors that had broken free from the enclosure. He'd stared at me sheepishly that day. Austin was weirded out by his own strength.

Now, Austin was by the windows, trying to control his rage.

"It's me, Austin, not you. I'm confused. Your gran was telling me stuff..."

*

I CLOSED MY eyes. I had to get away. Not push him away, but I needed a moment to think. My eyes opened. Water lapped on the sides of the pool. The snow-capped San Jacinto mountains rose above Palm Springs. A storm raced over the Coachella Valley the night before flooding the desert and blanketing the mountains in thick snow.

Uncle Teddy stepped out of his rambling midcentury house.

"Elijah?"

He was surprised. I gawked at him. "Can you see me?" He bobbed his head.

"I mean, really see me?"

He walked to me, placing his hand on my forehead, his hand warm. He was real.

"How did you get here? Did you drive down from LA? And why didn't you just ring the doorbell instead of sneaking in?"

"Because I'm not here. I mean, I'm in Hong Kong right now."

Teddy laughed. "Oh, you're doing a multiverse hop, aren't you?"

"A what?"

"We Encantreinus can hop between dimensions."

"No, that's not true. We can't do that."

"Well, not all of us. The strongest of us can."

"I'm confused. About the League. What they want from our family."

"They're the good guys," Teddy said. "You know that."

"Are you sure?"

"Don't you know that?" Teddy motioned for me to come inside the house. A young man, wearing only a bathing suit, lounged on a pink sofa.

"Danny, this is my nephew, Elijah."

The handsome young man opened his eyes and gave me a lazy look. "Nice to meet you, kid. You're a looker just like your uncle."

He closed his eyes again.

I followed Teddy to the kitchen. "You need a Bloody Mary."

"I hate alcohol."

"Virgin, of course." He laughed. "You're not a virgin?"

I shook my head.

"You're dating that Kang kid, right?"

I nodded.

"Oh. Wow. My boy, it's that serious."

"Yes, I love him. But his grandmother—"

"How is Miss Vicky? I love her. She is such a hoot."

"You know her?"

"Of course. Jesus, that mom of yours has been keeping you out in the provinces in that mansion in Burbank. You need to spend more time with the rest of us. You need to open your eyes to the real world."

"What does that mean?"

"It means that things are not quite as you thought."

"I still don't understand."

I was getting mad like I stepped into an alternate universe. Nothing was making sense anymore.

"Eli," Teddy said, handing me a tumbler filled with tomato juice, "being a Magical is more than what your mom has told you. And she was right. You're just a boy—"

"I'm a man now," I said angrily.

Teddy paused. "Okay, look, there's a whole world you know nothing about. You're going to learn about it. And probably really quickly, but what you need to know is who you can depend on. Us, your family and your friends and Austin."

"But Victoria said he was sent to protect me."

"Not directly," he said. "I mean, yes, they moved to Burbank for many reasons. There's a darkness forming. War is raging within the coven. Zid'dra is moving against Paràsàfàna. She's battling him. Old allegiances are crumbling; new threats are on the rise. There are monsters fighting for supremacy over the coven and Earth itself."

The lights flickered off. We looked up at the sloped ceiling.

"You need to go, now."

"I don't understand."

Rumbling sounded in the distance. What was that? A truck, an out-of-control train? The whole house started shaking violently.

"Elijah Delomary," a horrible voice filled my head. A hoarse voice. Two red dots appeared in front of me. No, no, they said Zid'dra was weakened! He couldn't harm me.

"Things were accomplished on my behalf to strengthen me. I am coming for you. *Suium venrant pro destruiat!*" The two dots grew and merged into a blinding red light that enveloped me.

My eyes fluttered open. My body was drenched in sweat. My heart pounded in my chest. Runes glowed pink on the wallpaper on the walls around me. The medicine surged inside me. I caught my breath. Soft voices sounded outside in the garden. I swung my legs over the bed and peered out the window. Austin's grandmother was hosting a party. People milled around in suits and cocktail dresses. A band played under a tent.

I glanced at the clock. It was ten o'clock. What time did I fall asleep? A knock sounded on the door. The man from earlier entered the room

"Mrs. Kang wonders if you would like to join the party in the garden?"

"Yes, let me get dressed. Do you know where my clothes are?"

"We laundered and pressed your suit. We also took the liberty of filling the closet with several other suits. We hope they are to your liking."

I padded to the closet. Several bespoke suits waited for me with matching black shoes.

"These are perfect. My compliments to Mrs. Kang."

The man closed the door behind him. I turned the water on in the shower. I sat on the toilet. I felt the gravity of the universe again. The Alliance, the coven were at war. Austin. Okay, I had to do the right thing. I stood and glanced in the mirror. *Yes, you know what to do, Elijah. You know how to handle the mess you made.*

Chapter Twenty-Seven

The League

AUSTIN STOOD ON an embankment tossing rocks into the waters of Victoria Harbor. Hearing me approaching, he turned around and glared at me through his thick glasses.

I wiped my sweaty hands on my slacks. The air was thick with humidity.

"Hey, Kangy," I said, touching his arm. Austin pulled away.

"I'm mad at you," he said. "You turned last night into something dirty. Like I just go around doing that."

Mom was right. Things changed. They became vastly more complex between us. I reached for him.

"I'm a total nutter? No, ponce. Hmmm, chav?"

"I think the word you are looking for is bleedin' wanker."

"Yes, that's it. I am a wanker. Total wanker."

"Soddin' bastard."

"Yes, that too."

"Bloomin' arsehole."

"Yep, that too." I stood beside him, reaching up to pet him on his head. He closed his eyes and grumbled.

"I'm sorry, Kangy. Honestly," I said and stroked his head.

Austin's face softened. He reached for my hand.

"You're the only one I'd ever share that experience with."

A moment later, Austin asked, "What did my gran tell you, love?"

"All about the League and my family and our connection—between our two families. And my powers. That they are very formidable. Even if they are bound deep inside me."

"So, you assumed I was assigned to you like a special agent? A bodyguard, perhaps?

"Look, love, when I first saw you with Barn the day we moved in, I knew I had to meet you."

"Really?"

"There was this voice in me."

"Random voices?"

He pushed me playfully. "No, love! Don't be daft."

He took my hand. "No one assigned me to you. You're such a silly bloke.

"My parents are Agécendrus with the League. We moved to Burbank because tensions were rising within the coven in Los Angeles. They were assigned to do surveillance of the situation. There were fears that the Gloom might try to overturn the pàcifimenta and a war would break out between the Alliance, the coven, and Ordinaries."

"Looks like it came true."

"Aye." Austin pulled me close. "My assignment was to be a student. That's all. I fell in love with you."

"You are brave to date me."

"Love you," he said firmly.

"Fine, but it's still true. I am like an onion, Austin. I have layers."

He laughed. "An onion, huh? Is that like a reference to your heritage?"

I looked at him quizzically.

"French onion soup!" he explained in a flat American accent. "You're French, right? Just like the *soup*."

I rolled my eyes. "You are such a dork."

"That's why you love me." He strutted around me. "Speaking of... There's a buffet inside. Let's get out of the heat and have some Cantonese delicacies. Things you've never had. I can't wait to share with you."

"Nothing weird though," I joked.

"Come on, love, ox balls in oyster sauce are brilliant, yeah? I'm joking!" He laughed pulling me up the grassy lawn toward the house.

*

THE STAR FERRY pushed through the waters of Victoria Harbor headed to Kowloon Peninsula to go to one of Austin's favorite hole-in-the-wall noodle places.

I was drenched in sweat even though it was cooler on the water. The heat and humidity of Hong Kong reminded me of summer in New York City. Maybe hotter though. I wasn't sure which was worse.

"Are you going to be okay, love?" Austin said, standing beside me holding onto the railing, the wind whipping his black hair off his face.

"If I faint, just take me somewhere cool and quiet."

He shot me a wicked look. "Ooh, and then what?"

"Cool me off!"

We both laughed. We watched the view of the harbor, the city all around us, the forest of skyscrapers, the huge mountains rising above the city. I spotted Delomary Asia Tower rising like a white pinnacle above the skyline of the city.

"Your grandma said she voted against the Còngréhassa taking my powers."

"Jolly right," he said. "Gran is smart."

"She said there was a conspiracy against me."

"That's right, Eli," Austin said. "It wasn't your fault. Do you see? Some traitors conspired to hurt you."

"Shit, that's scary."

"Yeah, but they've been dealt with."

"Yeah?"

"Yup," Austin said. "Think Mezclantus, the Excelà."

"No way."

"Of course. That is the punishment for treason to the Áuqala and the Alliance. And for hurting you, my Eli."

I curled into Austin for a moment. He chuffed and kissed the top of my head.

We exited the ferry. Austin took my hand, and we made our way to Mong Kok, famous for the shopping on twisting streets, the architecture a blend of modern and old colonial styles.

"We have to get an egg waffle," Austin told me. After a while, we found a street vendor selling the delicacy.

We stood around, eating the waffles, enjoying the soft texture and delicious taste.

We polished off the waffles and went to another food stall, and Austin's eyes grew big. "Mm, fish balls! And after this we'll go to my favorite place for noodle soup."

We spent most of the day eating noodles, fish meatballs, siu mai, and octopus. Eventually, we made our way to the Tian Tan Buddha on Lantau Island.

I shaded my eyes, surveying the magnificent 112-foot bronze statue of the Buddha atop a small hill. The sun was setting. Austin held my hand.

"Someday, you'll make a big statue of Kangy, right, love?" Austin said. "Of gold, atop Homer's Peak, if you will. I know your family can afford it."

"You want me to build it atop the Verdugo Mountains so everyone in the valley can see it?

"Precisely," he said. "Everyone should feel the power of Austin Kang Jr."

"You might be slightly egotistical, Kangy."

"I'm a Leo; get over it, Eli." He reached over to tousle my hair.

We fell into comfortable silence. A breeze kicked up. Just enough to lessen the heat and humidity. That's when I heard a small voice. In my head. At first speaking to me in Cantonese.

"You must be careful, Elijah Delomary," the voice said. "Dig deep in you. Use your power to save the universe."

"Save the universe?" Dread came over me.

"Come again, love."

I shrugged. "Nothing."

"But watch out, dark forces are conspiring against you."

And then, the giant Buddha fell silent, looking so serene and peaceful above us. A while later, we were in Central Hong Kong at the HSBC building designed by acclaimed architect Norman Foster. I stared up at the glass and steel building while Austin did cartwheels on the sidewalk.

I concentrated, and the pot lights set in the ceiling above the escalators leading to the main lobby of the bank flickered on and off. A security guard, alarmed, hollered into his walkie-talkie. I giggled and turned his walkie-talkie into a cupcake. He shouted and ran toward a bank of escalators heading into the belly of the building.

"Having fun, love?"

"Yeah," I said. "It's fun to be mischievous."

"Remember the Oath, Eli."

I shrugged. "Yeah, I guess." My stomach rumbled. "Hey, wanna get a snack?"

Austin landed on his feet. "Of course! I'm always hungry."

"Always."

We laughed. Then Austin paused, looking around. "Something isn't right, love. I can feel monsters are here."

I threw my head back, staring up at the glass and steel superstructure of the building. Several windows shattered high above me.

Austin pushed me away from the street. Glass rained down on the sidewalk. I watched it pile up until it formed a large mound. Austin stood behind me, his arms wrapped around me.

"What the hell is going on, Kangy?"

The pieces of glass suddenly sprang to life, twirling around until they created the image of a man looking sort of like Kevin Costner from

The Bodyguard.

"Watch out, Elijah Delomary," a voice said. "The Master is mad at you. He is coming. He is getting stronger. He will destroy you."

Austin stepped past me. "Who are you?"

"One of the servants of the Master."

"We're not afraid of you." Austin and I pulled out our PlasmXs and assumed the fighting stance.

"You should be," a tiny voice said. "The end is coming. For you!"

And then, in a flash, the glass disappeared. We put away our PlasmXs.

Austin peered at me through his thick glasses.

"Don't worry, Kangy will protect you."

"Ah, thanks, Kangy."

"See, Eli. We're a great team. The A-Team, get it?"

I shook my head, "No."

"Team Austin."

"Oh God, you are too much, Kangy."

His chest swelled. "Kangy the Powerful!!!"

This guy is too much sometimes.

"You know you love me, Eli."

"That I do, weirdo"

Austin glanced at his watch. "Oh, bollocks! Well, we have to get back to the estate. Gran is having a dinner in our honor"

"Another one?" I laughed.

"I told you she's the best gran in the whole world."

Austin took my hand and flagged down a cab.

*

WE SPENT TWO weeks in Hong Kong, sightseeing, visiting Austin's extended family, spending time with his gran, and eating. We seemed to always be eating.

The day before we left, Victoria took me aside and said, "Elijah, I don't want you to worry about what I told you."

I looked at her. "I'm not worried. Confused really."

She smiled. "That's understandable. All I want you to know is that you are strong and powerful. Don't be afraid of the monsters inside you."

"Yeah, I'm learning to control them."

"You're going to be okay, you know that?"

"I hope so."

"I know it," Victoria said. "I am confident in you."

"Maybe I am too."

"Now, hurry along and get into your tuxedo. I'm hosting a ball for you."

"I didn't bring a tuxedo."

"I had one made for you." She winked.

I couldn't help but hug her. "You're wonderful, Mrs. Kang."

"Just call me Auntie!" She laughed. "I think you're wonderful too. And exactly what my grandson needs in his life."

"Me too."

"But let me ask you a question," she said. "Whatever possessed you to come out to your entire school?"

"Momentary insanity," I said. "I'm sure of it."

She laughed as we walked to the staircase leading upstairs.

*

A WEEK AFTER we returned home from Hong Kong, Austin and I wandered around the Huntington Museum and Gardens. We were inside the main building, the old Huntington mansion, to see an exhibit of old dolls.

"Not really my thing, love," Austin said, wrinkling his nose. "I used to torture my cousin Daphne's dolls along with Barn when I was a wee lad."

"These aren't just any dolls," I said. "These are the dolls of royalty."

Austin frowned, looking at a display of Raggedy Ann dolls. "What soddin' princess had these ugly dolls?"

"A poor princess."

"Certainly not the royal family," he said. "Maybe those Spanish royals."

I had no idea what he blabbered about, so I wandered around to look at the other side of the room. I noticed one of the dolls was frowning. I scanned the wall. The other dolls had blank looks on their faces. The exhibit was deserted except for Austin and me and a security guard snoring away, perched on a stool against a wall. I looked back at the doll. Now she had this angry expression on her face.

"Um, Kangy?"

"Right, yes, Eli?"

He sauntered over, his hands behind his back.

"Watch this doll."

"Why?" He wrinkled his nose in disgust. "She's ugly as hell!"

He peered in the display case.

"Is she flipping me off?"

I peered inside the case as well.

"Um, I think she is."

"What the sodding hell!"

Suddenly, she leapt for the glass.

"I will kill you, Elijah Delomary!"

We looked at each other. Austin and I pulled out our PlasmXs. The guard snoozed away in the corner, oblivious to what we were doing.

Glass shattered, and the doll sprang out of the case. She was on the floor in front of us, laughing maniacally.

"Wanna die today, boys?" Suddenly, she was holding a very large and scary-looking battle-ax in her cloth hands.

"How is she holding that when her arms are made of cloth?"

"SHUT UP!" the doll shrieked, flying through the air, slicing the battle-ax at Austin and me.

Austin's PlasmX connected with the battle-ax. Sparks flew, lighting up the room in purple light. The guard twitched, then continued snoring.

The doll summoned a bazooka and fired at us. We ducked as a missile incinerated the back wall. The security guard was still fast asleep. Flames smoldered against a shelf holding more creepy dolls.

Austin leapt through the air, kicking the doll against the wall. I followed behind him punching her head several times with my fists while she cursed me in the Dark Language.

"Do a bridge, mate."

I concentrated to find his magic to amplify my own to use against the doll. I muttered words to a spell in the Old Language, then shouted to her:

"I bind you, bitch!"

"FUCK YOU!" she hissed.

"*Eo-vovo-coentollo!* I bind you!"

A puff of gray smoke rose from the floor around her.

"Zid'dra, dammit, this sucks!" the doll complained. A moment later, she was seated back on the display case. Smiling with black button eyes.

"I told you dolls are creepy," Austin said, grabbing my hand and leading me out of the exhibit hall.

Later, we were staring at the world-famous painting of *Blue Boy*.

"I mean," Austin said, "he doesn't look exactly like a boy."

"More like a mini freak."

"Slimsu freak"

We both laughed really hard.

"Don't laugh, Master is coming for you," the boy in blue said, jumping down from the painting, then walking toward us, his silk pants making a swishing sound.

"Did the freak talk to us?"

Austin turned. "Oi, who is this bleedin' master? No one hurts my boyfriend."

"Master will," the boy said, staring up at us."He will kill you!"

"Is your master's name Master Bates?" I asked.

"You will pay, Elijah," Blue Boy said. "You have made your alliances known to Master."

"'Fraid we're out of cash," Austin said.

"Stop making fun!" Blue Boy complained, swishing back to the painting on the wall, then jumping back inside.

"Ah, I hurt the wee freak's feelings!" Austin laughed.

"Just because you are a Coaugelo doesn't mean you can talk to demons like that."

"Oh, so. Now you're a demon, yeah?"

"Shut up!" Blue Boy said before resuming his usual pose in the painting.

"Freak demon!"

We doubled over in hysterics. Eventually, we wandered outside to the extensive gardens surrounding the old mansion.

"Every day with you, Eli, is an adventure. Talking Buddhas. Talking dolls and paintings."

"Well, Little Ocho doesn't talk."

"You take that back." Austin peered at me through his thick glasses. "He is very much alive. He is our child."

"You're silly, Kangy."

"Am not," he said. "Little Ocho talks."

We sat down on a bench under a fragrant magnolia tree.

"I've gone and done it."

"Aye."

"Devlina is fighting the Gloom. The covens are warring with each other. I stood up for Devlina. In that alley, on Melrose."

"You did?" Austin asked. "But why?"

"Orville was there," I said. "And Àzmadus. Twenty against her," I said. "Oh, and an Orgma. Have you seen those monsters? They breathe out fire. It didn't feel right."

"Wow. Defending your mortal enemy."

"Yeah," I said. "I mean, I felt bad for her."

"Wow, next you'll tell me you forgave her."

I nodded. His eyes widened. "Eli! This is incredible."

"Arnulfo told me to let things go. To stop dwelling. My family likes to dwell. Not me. I let it go. And I tried to tell Devlina to let things go. She can't though."

"It's her nature."

"I suppose you're right," I said. "Anyway, I didn't want to get dragged into her drama like usual. But I had to help her."

"And now all the monsters of the coven hate you."

"Fuck them."

"That's the spirit, love."

Austin paused, scanning the sky. "Something isn't right. I feel it in my bones. Let's go inside."

"Are you hungry, again?"

"Upsy-daisy, love."

A shadow fell across us.

"Aah, look it's a giant heart, Kangy," I said, shading my eyes with my hand while staring up at the sky.

"That's not a heart, love, now RUN!"

Austin took off running, pulling me behind him, while I kept staring at the heart.

Black. Well that certainly wasn't romantic but fitting. Tory always joked that I had a black heart. Maybe before. Not anymore. Well, maybe still, but I could be—I was hit in the head with something wet. I looked up. Bird shit. Oh my God, those were birds! Suddenly, they began cawing and diving toward us.

"Master wants you dead, Elijah Delomary!"

Birds bit my arms.

"Ow, stop that, you bitch!"

"Die! Die! Die!"

"What the holy fuck!"

Austin suddenly reached down, lifted me up off the ground by my ankles, and pulled me over his shoulder, then ran as fast as possible toward the Huntington Library.

"Eli," he shouted. "I think you picked the wrong side to defend!"

I stared at his muscular, sexy, hairy legs.

"Thank God you play soccer."

"Football!"

A gardener leaned on his rake. "Damn, what did you do to piss off those pigeons?"

Austin carried me all the way into the library, depositing me on a bench near the front doors.

People stared at us.

"Why did you carry him in?" a woman asked indignantly.

"Can't he walk? He looks young," an old man in an electric scooter said.

"Oi, practicing for tryout." Austin panted.

"Are you British?"

"Oh, sod off all of you!"

A swarm of birds hit the glass doors, popping on impact.

"Oh my goodness!" a woman shrieked and collapsed onto a bench across from us."The poor birds!"

Austin glared at her, his hands on his hips, still catching his breath.

"Poor birds?"

The woman wept openly. Austin shot her an evil look, then spun around and said, "Oi, love, you are definitely in Zid'dra's crosshairs."

I looked up at him with my puppy-dog eyes.

"You'll protect me though, right, Kangy?"

Austin sank into the bench. "Those bleedin' puppy dog eyes. I hate them!"

He nuzzled my nose. "Oi, of course, I'll protect you, love."

Chapter Twenty-Eight

City of Darkness

THE WAR BETWEEN the covens, Devlina, and the Gloom continued.

"Devlina raised an army of the dead from all the cemeteries in the Valley to battle Princess Auhaqa, Prince Fido, and Prince Màdàmaxo," Mom read to me from a report from XAQ6 the next morning at breakfast. "Can you imagine, all those graves opening and the spirits of long dead Angelenos roaming the streets?"

"Sounds like a fright," Barn said, eating his congee.

"Stay alert, boys," Sean said. "You both have your PlasmXs on you?"

"Yes," I said. "Always."

"I won't be home for dinner," Mom said. "I'll be at the Temple of Magic in Hollywood in meetings of the regional Còngréhassa. Do you boys want to have dinner with Austin's parents?"

"Sure, Mom," I said.

"You'll be safe there."

The League and XAQ2 were trying to keep the peace. Aunt Christine was locked in her library with her familiars, Pinky and Agamemnon, making potions, practicing spells, and placing runes around the house and gardens to keep us safe just in case the battle between the coven and Devlina spilled over to the Alliance. Uncle George and Austin's parents were busy doing work for the League, coordinating tactical response teams.

XAQ2, the Macistráuto, busied itself setting up gramoras to protect Ordinaries, or, rather, protect them from the truth. If Ordinaries knew monsters were spilling ordinary blood, panic would ensue, violence would escalate, all-out war would erupt, like the Last Battle more than a century before. The Pácifimenta would fall apart; the Alliance break; and peace between monsters, Magicals, and Ordinaries end.

I shuddered, trying to imagine such a terrible scenario.

"The Macistráuto is doing a good job covering up the war between the covens," Austin said at dinner. "Coach Silvestri told me that Satanists were responsible for digging up the graves."

"Aye," Barn said, "I heard Chastity Arredondo talking about the brush fire in the San Gabriel Mountains. Little did she know it was really a battle between Malloupus and Àzmadus. Ten thousand dead on both sides."

"The fire was a gramora to distract the ordinaries."

"Áucúitus attacked the library at UCLA, hunting down Máunadas who were holding seances in the basement, trying to summon their own dead to battle Devlina."

"Yeah, the news said a lone wolf locked himself in the basement and threatened to kill himself unless the police brought him a thousand dollars."

"To Ordinaries, just another day in the life of LA. Mayhem, pandemonium, and chaos."

On the news, the war was nothing more than the daily mischief playing out in a metropolis of ten million people.

The next day, Austin and I decided to go surfing to distract ourselves from current events, the fear bubbling inside me of the series of monsters confronting me. Barn and Katie joined us for boogie boarding. Austin and I raced into the water with our boards. We sat waiting for the big waves. I looked around.

"Where are the Merpeople?"

"Aye, and where are the *Volqeńus*?"

"Merpeople love surfing, and wherever Merpeople are, you usually find fairies."

I squinted up into the sunlight, seagulls circling above us. Katie and Barn were laughing while boogie boarding. I was thinking about the glass shards in Hong Kong talking to me, the stupid Raggedy Ann doll, the damn birds.

Victoria said there was a conspiracy to strip me of my powers, to sideline me, maybe kill me. I gulped. That was scary.

My great-great-grandma Evangeline transformed into the Áuqala when she died, ascending to live in Cassiopeia. Mom cast a spell to summon Devlina to punish Dad and along the way connected me to Devlina. If I was connected to Devlina, and Zid'dra offed Devlina, would that off me? And if that happened, would that affect the Áuqala? What if Zid'dra's plan all along was to destroy the Áuqala so he could be the sole ruler of the universe? I shuddered at the possibilities. The universe would break in two, the balance between light and dark upended. Would Zid'dra remake the universe in his evil image?

No way. That sounded crazy. I was just one part in a huge puzzle making up the Shimmering, the Gloom, the Alliance, the universe.

"What are you thinking about, Eli?"

"My demise?"

"So dramatic, love."

"I am dramatic, we've decided that. And you have a temper, Kangy."

"Do not."

"You're funny to think you don't have a temper."

I laughed. He looked at me indignantly.

"You have the worst temper tantrums I have ever seen. The shower doors?"

He glared at me. Silent. His silent stare.

Austin continued staring at me. "It's not going to work, Kangy."
I removed my sunglasses and gazed into his eyes, smiling.
"BLEEDING PUPPY DOG EYES!"
We both laughed.

*

A FEW DAYS later, we sat beside the fire pit staring up at the stars.
"Senior year, mate," Barn said, squeezing my leg. "Can you believe it's our last year of high school?"
I stared up at the faint outline of Cassiopeia. "It's crazy. Then college."
We all grew quiet. I've never asked Austin where he was going.
"I'm thinking of going back to Hong Kong for university," Barn said.
Austin nodded. "Me as well, mate. Want to be roomers?"
"Sure, sounds delightful."
"What the fuck!" I exploded. Barn and Austin giggled.
"Oi, did you see the look on his face, mate?"
"Pure terror, mate."
"Stop making fun of me!"
"Face it, bro," Barn said, "you are so fucking lucky you met me when you were twelve. I mean, I put up with your idiosyncrasies and drama for four years until I ceded that duty to my cousin."
"You are very lucky to know both of us."
"This boy really needs us," Barn said. "We act as the voice of reason to his neurosis."
"Love, to fight his anger."
"His neurosis, bruv."
"Unbelievable, mate."
"French Creole boys. So much Catholic guilt and theater in their heads. He needs us Chinese boys to keep him safe and sound."
"Chinese *are* safe and sound."
Barn frowned. "Don't get ahead of yourself, mate."
They laughed. I rolled my eyes. They thought they were so funny.

Barn leaned over and began toasting marshmallows to make s'mores. Austin had never heard of s'mores.

"You are crazy," I told him. "How have you never heard of s'mores? Surely they have them in Hong Kong."

"You ever have Pi Dan?"

I shook my head.

"Then we're even, mate."

"You have *senlàpso*," Barn said. "Thousand-year-old eggs in Auntie Cecilia's congee!"

I stood up. The two of them were driving me mad. Maybe they were trying to keep my mind off the terror filling me. Or maybe they were tormenting me for fun. I never knew with those two.

"Anyone want a cola?"

Austin shot me a dirty look. "Rule number one!!!"

"I'm going to have one," I said, crossing the backyard, sliding the glass door open, and stepping into the dimly lit kitchen.

Austin's parents were in the media room watching Chinese soap operas, and the sound of the dialogue mixed with his parents' laughter drifted into the kitchen. I reached into the refrigerator, grabbing three sodas.

Outside, Austin and Barn stared at the pool, not moving. The bluish water gently lapped the side of the pool. Stepping outside onto the grass, I asked, "Are you guys okay?"

"Go inside, Eli," Austin said.

Barn agreed.

"Why?" I said, trying to balance the cold cans in my arms.

A shrieking sound filled the air.

Puxhàredo!

A monster from the Gloom. Not particularly fun to deal with on my *last* week of freedom before my senior year.

"Okay, what the fuck is that?" I said angrily.

The shadows from the dancing fire crawled across the grass toward me. I walked backward until I hit the sliding glass door. A figure rose through the flames, morphing into a very tall woman with pale skin tinged with green. Smoke poured out her nostrils. She growled at us.

"Oh my God, I smell shit!" I blurted out, covering my nose with my hand. I was in no mood to deal with another monster. "And look, it's the Wicked Witch!"

"Screw you!" she said, spewing her horrible stench into my face. "I am a princess of his majesty Zid'dra—Princess Ahacaca!"

"Caca?"

"Ahacaca! I am your worst nightmare, Elijah."

"Wow," I said in a bored way. "Look, shit breath, what do you want?"

"I want Devlina! And you know where she is."

"I have no idea where she is."

"You lie, filth."

"No, I'm not lying."

"You helped her! Master is not pleased."

"Look, this war is between Devlina and the coven. Leave me out of it."

"Give me DEVLINA!!"

"Fine. She's at 66669 Sandy Canyon Road, Beverly Hills. You need the phone number?"

She grabbed me by the throat, lifting me off the ground. "I want her dead. She killed my sisters."

I summoned a dagger from thin air and held it to her neck.

"I can kill you!"

She dropped me.

"You have magic!"

"Duh."

"We got rid of that."

"No, you didn't."

"That explains it all. As you grow stronger, she grows stronger. When you went looney tunes, she faded and almost died. Then you bounced back, asshole. And now she is growing stronger and killing us!"

"I know of your sick plot against me. It didn't work. And maybe I am getting stronger, but you aren't going to hurt me or Devlina. She can take care of herself. So I urge you to get the puxhàredo out of here before we destroy you!"

"Housà!" Austin and Barn chanted.

"And anyway, Devlina is Zid'dra's first wife. And if you knocked boots with him, that's bigamy, and illegal."

"Don't you dare judge me, boy!"

I turned my face. "Jesus, get a mint!"

"I need to kill you. To stop her."

"Look," I said, "you can't command or compel me, okay?" I tossed the dagger, in favor of using my PlasmX.

Ahacaca retreated. "Someone wants to fight!"

"Yeah, let's rumble!" I leapt into the air, lifting my PlasmX over my head, eyes focused on her head, my body charged with energy. I would slice her in two.

Ahacaca laughed and twitched her head to the left, sending me flying across the backyard, crashing into the cypress trees lining the wall. The air left my lungs. I slid to the ground, and my PlasmX flickered and dropped from my hand.

Austin gazed at me, shot me the peace sign, then launched himself at Ahacaca. She sidestepped him. He did a somersault and flip and landed on his feet facing her.

"Oh, look who thinks he's some Olympic gymnast!"

Austin growled, shouted "Housà!" and leaped at her, his fists out. She sidestepped him, falling onto Barn's legs, which connected with her torso, then sent her flying across the grass, rolling several times, and collecting grass and dirt as she spun. She landed on her back, muttering about disrespectful youth. Austin landed above her.

"Hiya, Cacaface!"

"Shut up!" Ahacaca lifted a hand and sent Austin spiraling skyward. I shook my head, stood, and summoned several knives. A twist of my hand and they shot at her at dizzying speed, impaling her against an old oak tree in the center of the yard.

Barn sauntered over to Ahacaca. "Looks like the disrespectful youth have you in a bind."

"I will end you!"

In a flash of smoke, she disappeared. Barn coughed and waved the smoke away with his hand. I joined him. "Where did she go?"

Austin floated back to join us.

"We scared her off!"

As we fist bumped each other, a cloud of smoke rose from beside Cecilia's prized petunia beds.

"Yoo-hoo!" Ahacaca called to us. "I'm still here, and now I will end you stupid jerks!" In a flash of red light, she morphed into a giant saw blade, spinning toward us, eating up the grass.

Austin leapt over her. I bridged Austin's energy and increased my magic. I waved my hands, sending the saw tumbling into the pool.

"Disrespectful youth!" Ahacaca shrieked as the water in the pool turned bloodred and boiled away.

I stood at the edge of the pool, watching the last of the water evaporate.

"Shit, that was totally legit."

"Bleedin' ace!" Barn said, bounding over to the side of the pool. "You offed that monster!"

"My powerful, Eli," Austin said, putting his arm around me and squeezing me. "So cute and cuddly and fierce!" He tucked me under his arm, chuffing.

"Ay yah!" Austin Sr. called from the sliding glass door. "What was all the noise?"

"Um, well, Dad, we had a devil woman here trying to kill my Eli," Austin called over his shoulder. I leaned up to kiss him on his cheek.

"You killed her right, son?" Cecilia said, holding a cup of tea. Austin shook his head. "Eli killed her."

"Oh, good for you," Cecilia said. "My three boys are Coaugelos, after all!"

"Only problem, Dad," Austin said, "the witch ended up in the pool and her evilness reacted with the water and now it's empty."

"Bollocks," Austin Sr. complained. "Water is expensive. You know how much it costs to fill a pool in La La Land?"

Chapter Twenty-Nine

Danger Grows

AUSTIN, BARN, CECILIA, and Austin Sr. went inside the house. Barn and Austin gave Cecilia play-by-plays of our attack, while Austin Sr. mumbled about having to refill the pool. I stood outside for a moment, staring up at Cassiopeia in the night sky.

A hand pulled me into the bushes.

"What's happening?" I squeaked.

"I need to talk to you," Devlina whispered.

"I killed Princess Ahacaca for you!" I said indignantly. "She was looking for you."

"You were saving your ass as well."

"Yeah, well, that's beside the point," I said. "She wants revenge. You know this whole battle of yours is a mess. The coven is in disarray; battles are happening all the time. Zid'dra has grown powerful again."

"Yeah, well Máunadas are making sacrifices day and night to make him stronger. Ten thousand monsters were killed only recently."

"I heard that was a battle between Àzmadus and Malloupus?"

"Think again."

"Okay, so look—" I pulled myself out of the bushes, pacing the grass, rubbing my face with my hands irritably. "—I've sorta become attached to you."

"Hoorah!" Devlina cried. "First you forgave me, and then you saved me, and now we're besties!"

"Yeah, well, don't plan the parade just yet, Devlina," I said. "As your friend, I am asking you to stop all this. Dial it back, for once and for all. I wanted this summer to be chill. It hasn't been. School starts soon. I'd like some peace and quiet, okay? Can you stop the madness?"

"We are on our way to destroying the coven!" Devlina said, doing a jig on the grass. "Isn't that what you always wanted?"

"The thought is enticing," I said, then lowered my voice. "But at what cost, Devlina? To you, to everything?"

"We are close to becoming gods, babe."

"You taking out God next?"

She chewed on a nail. "Not a bad idea."

"God is God," I pointed out.

"Says the boy who is richer than God."

"Fuck you," I said. "I am not rich."

"Oh right, beneficiary of the Delomary Trust VIII worth—" Glasses appeared on her face, and she peered at a ledger. "—six-point-eight billion dollars."

Puxhàredo. Was that true? How come I only received twenty dollars a week spending money? I was constantly "borrowing" from Austin, who, believe me, was keeping track of how much I owed him.

"You can pay me back, in-kind," Austin said last week, smiling mischievously.

"In-kind?"

"You know what I mean," he said, wrapping me in a bear hug. "Don't play coy with me, Eli."

"I'm tired of foot rubs and grabbing you colas."

"You can do something else, mate," Austin said. "Naked."

I tuned back into Devlina.

"Anyway, a little birdie told me that my hubs has been sending emissaries to scare you. Has it worked?"

"It has been unsettling."

"This is why we have to act and destroy him."

I rubbed my face with my hands. "Devlina, I understand what you are saying, but LA is a smoldering mess right now. Things are getting really scary. I worry about what happens next."

"World Builder!"

"Sure, fine," I said, "but what if the cost of your creating something new is too high?"

Devlina laughed. "Never."

"Isn't there a better way?"

Devlina gawked at me. "Like what? I am not apologizing to Zid'dra, and he won't apologize to me. We are too far into the game to retreat. I'm sorry, kid."

"Then this shit war is going to keep happening?"

"I'm afraid so," Devlina said. "Until one of us wins."

"What if it's not you?" I whispered.

Devlina fell silent. Crickets sounded around us.

"I guess that's the price I'll pay."

"And what about me? I'm stuck in the crossfire."

Devlina stared at me. She tapped her lips with her black riding crop, then waved a hand over me.

"Are you blessing me?"

"No, asshole, I am not a priest."

"You could be a priestess."

"Deity."

"Fine, deity. So what was that?"

"It's some evil to add to the spell your auntie cast on you."

"So, an add-on."

"It'll help, okay?"

"How do I believe you?"

"Go jump in that empty pool."

I stared at the pool and then back at her.

"Yeah right," I said. "I have grown to like you, but I still don't trust you."

"God, last year called and wants to talk to you." Devlina rolled her eyes.

"This is a perfect opportunity to finish me off."

"I'd die, you moron!" she said. "Did you forget our connection? And why Zid'dra is mad at you?"

"Well, he also hates me. And my family, and I get the impression offing me has enormous benefits to him."

"That's true."

"Great."

"Look, bestie, my spell helped you." She leaped at me, pushing me hard toward the pool.

"What the hell!" I cried out, stumbling toward the edge. I lost my balance and fell backward, arms flailing. "You jerk!"

I landed on the concrete, my heart racing, body aching. Devlina appeared over the edge. "See!"

"Wow, I'm not dead."

"Brain dead, maybe."

"You're a real comedian."

"*Comedienne.*"

"Sexist."

"Okay, comedian."

"You'll be fine. Stop worrying. Let go, let Devlina!" she said, and in a flash of black smoke, she disappeared into the night sky.

*

APRIL HOSTED HER annual end-of-the-summer barbecue and party. Next summer at this time, I and all my friends will be going off to college, all over the state, nation, and world. Austin's been accepted to Stanford. And me as well. They have a great architecture program and swimming team. Mom wholeheartedly supported the plan. Which was a big relief.

Austin and I sat on the sofa near April's grandma. She was snoring away.

We shot her a look. Then we both had an idea.

"Why not?"

"Yeah?"

"Kangy the Biggie is coming for a visit."

We made out like we were in heat for several minutes. Really getting into a groove when the grandfather clock in the hall chimed twelve times. We paused.

Someone was puking in the living room followed by another person giggling. "Did you have a purifying puke, London?"

"Yes, Cahuenga."

"Let's drink gallons more!"

"Slay, Cahuenga, slay."

Austin and I burst out laughing.

"Some things never change."

"Your hair is wild, Eli."

"So is yours!"

We tried to smooth each other's hair with our hands.

"These parties are always wild, love," Austin said, his arm draped around me. "Looks like all the heteros are doing *rumpy pumpy*."

"What does that mean?"

"Sexual intercourse," he intoned. We got up. I smoothed my hair. Austin jogged around for a moment. "I'm thinking of half-dressed cheerleaders to get my biggie to hide again, mate." We wandered into the kitchen to make ourselves Shirley Temples. The kitchen was deserted. The house was silent.

"Looks like we're the only two gay boys in the universe again."

Austin peered at me through his thick glasses and pulled me closer. "That's just how I like it. You and Me. No poncers."

"Just the two of us. Against the world."

Austin smiled. "You've grown a lot in the last year."

"Yeah, but I'm still not as tall as you."

"No one is, love."

"I mean, I have all this hair. Although it's well-groomed now."

"Manscaping is our friend."

He pulled me into a kiss.

"Get a room!" Barn said, holding Katie's hand. His hair was all mussed up. Her lipstick was smeared.

"Sod off!"

Austin glanced at the karaoke machine and mics setup at the far side of the room.

"Come on, love," he said, standing, "for old time's sake."

"I am not singing a depressing song." No way was I singing "Under the Bridge" or "Everybody Hurts."

"How about "Dear Prudence." I love the Beatles."

"Yeah!" Barn shouted. "Let's sing the Beatles! I'm Paul, and you're John Lennon, mate."

"Cool."

Austin grunted, "Who am I?"

"Ringo."

"Sod off!"

We sang for the next hour, then piled into Austin's car to grab late-night breakfast at Harry's Diner.

*

I WOKE UP at 6:00 AM, staring at the ceiling.

"This is the first day of the last year of high school!" the cherubs called down to me. "You're a senior now!"

"Yeah, I feel so weird," I said, "I can't believe this is happening. My very last year in high school."

"This year, you're going to change the universe, Elijah!" the cherubs said in unison, then began playing reveille with their harps. My cue to get ready and go downstairs to have breakfast with Mom and Sean, Tory and Barn. Mom was at the bottom of the back stairs in the kitchen, standing in the way of Mrs. Singh, who was trying to manage the chaos in the kitchen around her.

"My baby is all grown up!" Mom promptly shed several fat tears.

"Mom, I'm not really all grown up."

"You are."

"Mom, relax," I said, eyeing Mrs. Singh, "Mom, let's go in the breakfast room before Mrs. Singh begins talking to you in Hindi."

Mom turned. "Oh, am I in the way?"

Mrs. Singh grumbled in Hindi.

"Now you're on her list, Mom."

In the breakfast room, Mom said, "This is it, baby, senior year, prom, graduation. Then eighteen and you'll leave me."

"Not forever."

"Forever."

"Why do you say that?"

"Guilt."

"Relax, Mom."

"All right, Lin," Sean said, "why don't you sit down and have some food? Let's not get ahead of ourselves."

Tory and I exchanged glances that meant *thank God for Sean.* Later, as she was eating, Mom became inspirational. She was weird like that. I sometimes wondered if *she* needed medicine too.

"Savor every moment," Mom said. "Before you know it, you're fortysomething with kids."

"Lin? How about some more coffee?"

"Okay, okay," Mom said. "I'm losing it. I know. I can't help it."

*

AUSTIN WAITED FOR me outside in his black sports car. He leaned over to kiss me when I hopped in the passenger seat.

"Well, love this is it! Senior year!" he said. "And we get to experience it together as boyfriends!"

"That will make it more bearable. Having you with me."

We stopped to get breakfast at the drive-through. Yes, a second breakfast for both of us. Austin loved to eat, after all. And I was obsessed with the crunchy beef tacos from Tommy's. We drove forward to get our order from the window.

"Cash or charge?"

"Charge."

The girl threw a wireless POS device into the open window. "Swipe and then enter a tip." She glared at Austin. "Don't forget!"

"She's bossy," Austin said, then entered a tip.

"Sucker."

"She looks mean!" Austin said. A few minutes later, we were eating our food. Austin loved the fish filet.

"So bloody good," he exclaimed before attacking the fish sandwich like he had never eaten before. "American food is a wonder."

"You are too cute," I said. "I mean, a fish filet for breakfast, just like a cat."

He mummed contentedly. After he wolfed down three fish filets and drank his coffee, he turned over the engine and asked, "Do you have your emergency pill? Just in case. You know what Arnulfo said, big events like this can cause a panic attack."

"It's in my backpack with a bottle of water."

"Okay, good. And remember, if you feel one coming on, just let me know. We can work through it, okay, love?"

I nodded appreciatively, and I leaned in to kiss him.

A moment later, I said, "I sure hope this year is less dramatic than junior year."

He threw me an amused smile. "No chance, BHS seems to be filled with the most dramatic kids, and the weirdest things happen."

"I met you at BHS."

"Aside from that, of course, love."

"Best thing that happened to me."

Of course, once we arrived at Burbank High School, who was waiting for me at my locker but good old Blair, her blonde hair all puffy. She wore expensive pearls and oozed designer fragrance.

"Hello boys," she said, smiling at me. "Senior year. Can you believe it? Where did the time go?"

"You driving me nuts?"

Blair tittered. "You are too funny, mister."

"It's true."

"Anyway." She changed the subject. "War is raging between the covens. Are you safe from that?"

"As safe as I can be."

"Patricians are always here to help," she said. "Remember that, Elijah."

"Thanks, Blair."

"And to think, you thought we were enemies."

"Maybe frenemies?"

She laughed cryptically and walked away.

I turned to Austin as we walked into a classroom next to our lockers.

"Do we have homeroom together?"

"Yes." He pointed to a chair for me to sit in front of him. "Got to keep an eye on you. I mean, I am your boyfriend, love."

After homeroom, he clasped my hand and led me to my next class, English. I leaned against the wall while he towered over me.

"So, I guess I'll see you at lunch?" I said, looking up into his brown eyes.

He shook his head.

"Don't tell me you're in English too?"

"All your classes, love."

"Are you saying...?"

"Look, love, face it, you need Kangy with you at all times. God knows what those flailing hands will do without me to guide you, look out for you, provide you with an unending stream of unconditional love."

I rolled my eyes. "I happen to like my hands, thank you very much."

He grinned and leaned in to kiss me.

"Not going to thank me?"

"Thank you, Kangy," I said. "How did you...?"

"I have my ways, love," he said, peering at me through his thick glasses.

"You're sort of a stalker."

"Might be codependent. Didn't someone accuse me of that?"

I shrugged. "I'm codependent too. I mean, you have this pull on me…"

"It's my gravity…rule thirteen, love."

"Gravity keeps Eli and Kangy safe."

He grinned. "Come on, let's go inside, and then I can write you love letters."

"Kangy! You might be obsessed with me."

He shook his head. "No, afraid not. The hair. It's the red hair, love."

"You're only with me because of my red hair?"

He laughed. "Maybe your smile too."

"Is that all?"

"Nothing I can say out loud here, love, would be obscene." He chuckled. "America is so puritanical that way."

After English, we made our way to calculus. And thank God, Austin was in this class because I was terrible at anything related to math. My brain hated numbers. I think my eyes cross when I see equations and formulas.

Tyrone and Letitia were in class with us, which was awesome because Tyrone was a genius at calculus.

"Not me," Letitia said. "I'm more of a poet."

"A poet and lover, right?"

"Yes, Elijah."

"How's your girlfriend?"

Letitia rolled her eyes. "She went back to her boyfriend."

"Wait, we were all just at the movies two nights ago."

"He came and stole her from me," she said. "I'm heartbroken"

"You've been hanging with Stylo."

"Yeah, we went to Club Girls at Gingers. I already have a new girlfriend."

"What's her name?"

"Babe."

I looked at her. "Seriously?"

"Yes. You never call a girlfriend by her real name. In case you forget."

I narrowed my eyes. "How many girlfriends do you currently have, Letitia?"

"I don't kiss and tell, *vato*."

We went back and forth for a few minutes, while Austin and Tyrone talked about calculus until Mr. Jackson, our teacher, walked in. He cleared his throat and began talking about calculus. My mind just drifted off. I glanced up at the clock: 10:17. *God, this was so boring.*

My mind wandered from the clock in the classroom to the grandfather clock in Aunt Christine's library. Her familiars, Agamemnon and Pinkie, with their fur that changed colors. Mom's familiar, L'ocle, who spent most of her time outside surveilling the mansion grounds to keep my family safe from monsters and demons.

I closed my eyes as Mr. Jackson droned on. Austin mumbled to himself nearby.

"I love numbers and numbers love Kangy," he was saying. "Numbers keep gravity in place and that keeps Kangy and Eli together." The blackness behind my eyes was suddenly punctured by a tiny square of light. I walked toward it. Eventually, I spotted a doorway and stepped inside a brightly lit room. A blue pail sat dead center on the cracked and yellow floor. Floating nearby was the water from the pail, frozen and melting onto the floor.

Drip...plop...drip...plop.

What the hell was happening?

I leaned closer, examining the ice. Two black stains in the ice blinked. I gasped. Devlina screamed.

"Elijah, hide! He's found me, and he's not happy!"

"What happened?"

"The Máundas fully charged him. He has me, Elijah. Shit, you gotta be—"

Austin kicked my chair. My eyes flew open.

"You were snoring, love," he whispered.

I had just seen Devlina. What happened to her? I told Austin what

I dreamt on our way to tennis. In the locker room, he frowned. "That's really daft, love," he whispered, taking off his shirt in front of me. I stared at his chiseled chest and abs, momentarily distracted.

Puxhàredo. He was grinning at me as he slipped on his white-and-blue ringer shirt.

"Enjoy the show, love?"

"I'm hard, Kangy."

He leaned in to kiss me.

"Get a room, you two," Tyrell joked and pulled on his football jersey.

Austin and I walked to the courts holding hands.

"What do you think it means?"

"Maybe it's just a dream."

"It was really vivid."

"Look, maybe they made up. Maybe she came to her senses."

"Devlina is not the type to come to her senses."

"Maybe he's going to stop all this nonsense."

"What if he..." I hesitated. "Kills her?"

"Doubtful. He loves her."

"I doubt that," I said. "If Zid'dra kills her, what happens to me?"

Austin howled with laughter, throwing his racket in the air, punching the air with his fists, catching his racket, then kissing me on the cheek. "What Zid'dra doesn't know is how powerful Kangy is!!!" He pulled me in close. "I got you protected, love."

I smiled and kissed him back, but deep down, I feared he wouldn't be able to protect me. I mean, how do you fight Zid'dra, the King of the Gloom? Devlina was as evil and ruthless and powerful as they came, and if she couldn't protect herself from him, how could poor Austin?

I found Mom in the library with Aunt Christine later that night. After I asked about Devlina, they looked grim.

"Is it that bad?"

They exchanged glances.

"It's not good," Aunt Christine said.

"I mean, the enemy is Zid'dra himself," Mom said.

"He's part of the very core of the universe along with the Áuqala," Christine added.

"Destroying one destroys the universe," Mom concluded.

"So, I'm screwed is what you're saying." I pulled out a chair and sat down at the library table near the grandfather clock. I removed a piece of paper from a cubby filled with stationary engraved with the family crest. I began to write in earnest. Mom and Aunt Christine watched me.

"What are you doing?" Christine asked. "This isn't the time to be writing love letters to Austin."

"I'm writing my will. I'm leaving Little Ocho, Meow Meow, and Foxy to Austin. My supply of scented candles and my duvet with cats on it. He's obsessed with that duvet."

"Don't be so dramatic." Mom took the paper from me. "You're not dying."

"Then what?"

"Look. You're not going to die. You have powerful spells on you," Christine said.

"And the amulet around your neck," Mom said pointing to the necklace hanging off my neck.

"So, I'm fine, then?" I stood.

"Not really," Mom said. "You just have to stay away from anyone suspicious."

"Such as Zid'dra's minions," Christine added.

"You can protect yourself," Mom said. "You know Xem Sen Ou and have a PlasmX."

"And you have your powers," Christine chimed in. "You can bridge Austin or Barn's to make them more powerful."

"Powerful enough to fight Zid'dra?"

Mom and Christine exchanged looks. We all were aware that my power wasn't strong enough to save me from Zid'dra.

"The best we can do is hope he stays away from you," Mom said softly.

"Surely, he has bigger problems to deal with," Christine said.

"Right!" Mom said, "Everything will be okay, darling."

I walked over to Austin's house a half hour later. I was trying to be hopeful, but I was also worried.

A full moon floated in the sky above the Verdugo Mountains. We sat outside by the pool. The night air was still and balmy.

"I'm scared, Kangy."

"I know, Eli," Austin said, reaching for my hand. "All we can do is hope for the best."

I glanced over at the shadows from the far side of the lawn. A light breeze fluttered through the trees. For a moment, I was convinced I saw something. A presence.

"Austin, do you see that?"

"See what, love?"

I pointed toward the trees in the corner.

"Nothing. Just the croquet set we used a lot this summer."

"Looks like a monster to me."

"No monster here, love," Austin said. "Aunt Christine came by and placed powerful runes around the house. We're safe, love."

I changed the subject. "Who knew you were so into croquet?"

"I have many secret passions, Eli."

"Am I one?"

"Not a secret."

"My Kangy."

"My Eli."

I turned my head back toward the trees. Whatever was there earlier was gone.

"Oi, love," Austin said, swinging his legs out of the water. "Mum bought egg tarts from Chinatown; let's go in and demolish them."

He grinned and held his hand out to help me out of my chair. I looked over my shoulder as we walked across the damp grass to the house. For a split second, I swore two red circles blazed in the shadows of the garden. I blinked and they were gone.

Chapter Thirty

Vacuum of Space

I RAN INTO Orville Conry on the stairs. He was dressed in his usual uniform of black, only his face looked gaunt, like he hadn't been eating. Orville glared at me. "If it's not old Dimwitlomary."

"You're a jerk, Orville," I said. "You know I can punch you in the face if you want." I stepped back and whispered, "And I have my magic back. We can play, if you want."

He laughed. "Magic? Your magic don't scare me," he growled. "And I have protection now."

"Protection?"

"Yeah, from someone high up in the pecking order."

"Pecking order?" I stepped back. Orville's breath was pungent.

"Yeah," Orville said, "someone more powerful than you and your fucking family. You should be very afraid of me."

"I'm afraid of your breath."

He snarled at me, "What the fuck are you talking about?"

"Your breath stinks."

He grabbed me by my shirt and pulled me close to him. I turned my head, trying hard not to breathe.

"Finally, someone powerful is on my side, and he doesn't like you."

"Meh," I said. "Big deal. I think you're looney tunes."

Orville said, "Yeah, call me names if you want, but you have a problem, you know that?"

"How so?"

"You're going to find out real soon." He laughed. Then he did something crazy: he began to float a few feet above the stairs, a flickering red and orange light outlining his body. "You ain't the only one with magic, Douchelomary."

"What the hell!" I said backing away from him.

"Oi, everything okay, love?" Austin's head popped over the railing from the landing above us.

I looked up at Austin. "Yeah, it's fine, Kangy."

"Better watch out, *love*. You're in trouble," Orville said, sinking to the floor.

"How about we just ignore each other this year, huh?"

"Oh, you want me to ignore you?"

"We don't like each other."

"I hate you and your family." He grinned. "I don't forget, baby, and payback is a bitch."

I walked away from him to get two sodas from the blue-and-white vending machine nearby. I turned and then flipped him off. He watched me with a mischievous smile etched on his face.

Whatever he was planning, I wasn't afraid of him. He was just a goon with braces and acne. One with magical powers? I gulped. That was a new development.

Austin was waiting for me. I handed him an icy can of cola.

"What was that all about?"

I shrugged. "Who the fuck knows? Orville is nuts."

"It's the drugs."

"Heroin."

"Speed," he said, "definitely speed. Gives users bad breath."

"Dragon breath."

"I could smell his from up those stairs, love." He put his arm around me as we headed back to where Barn stood with Gina and Tina, the two of them laughing about some inside joke.

My last year of high school was unfolding to be mostly cool, but puxhàredo, Orville was a real troublemaker, and if he somehow had acquired new skills, well, that wasn't good for me. Not at all.

*

AFTER SCHOOL, I sat in the bleachers with Tina and Letitia watching Barn and Austin practicing soccer. They knew we were watching, so they were really showing off on the field, hitting the ball with their heads, running really fast, Austin casually lifting his soccer jersey to reveal his tight body in front of me.

"Damn, boy," Tina said, lifting her sunglasses, "your man is ripped."

"Yes, he is."

Letitia frowned. "I like my women curvy and luscious. I could never be with a man with pecs and a six-pack. Too firm."

"Eight-pack."

"Whatever, Elijah," Letitia laughed. A group of pretty Latina girls wearing knee-length black socks, plaid skirts, and cut-off black tank tops spotted Letitia and giggled.

One blew her a kiss. "Hola, guapa!"

Letitia caught the pretend kiss and sent one back. "Hola, Xochitl, chula!"

Tina laughed. "Ever since you came out, Eli, this school is getting a helluva lot gayer."

"Is that a bad thing?"

"Fuck, no!" Tina said playing with her braids. "More gays, fewer uptight, straight guys is a good thing."

"Amen, sister," Letitia said, high-fiving Tina.

"Do you still wish you didn't come out like you did?" Tina asked.

"Heck, no!" I said. "My dad told me to shake things up, and in retrospect, he was right. I needed to do it big."

"I wish you hadn't had such a hard time, babe," Tina said. "You went through a lot."

"You know what, Tina," I said. "Yeah, it was hard, it sucked, but I learned a lot about myself. And my friends who supported me."

Tina smiled. Letitia, not good with emotions, pinched me. "You made me come out to my familia," Letitia said. "And my parents were not happy."

"I know, but they're better now?"

"Yeah," Letitia said. "Tina and Gina coming over all the time and talking nonstop about how normal it was to be gay helped sway my very Catholic, very traditional padres."

"It is normal!" Tina said. "And, Elijah, you had it good, your family is so supportive."

"I did luck out."

"Your mom is pretty cool, you know?"

"Yeah, she is, huh?"

Gina, Tina's twin sister, appeared on the field coming toward us and looking angry. She stomped up the stairs two at a time. Gina sported red combat boots, tight black jeans, and a black tank top. She wore black lipstick and giant hoop earrings. Her hair was natural compared to Tina's braids.

"I am over all the gay boys in this school."

We all looked at each other.

"Armando is GAY!" Armando was her boyfriend.

"He dumped me for Ezekiel Barnes."

"The Jamaican kid?"

"Yes," Gina said, stepping over Letitia, who clucked irritably and forced herself between me and Tina. "Apparently, when we'd all been smoking weed and jamming to Bob Marley, they were secretly holding hands!"

"Austin did notice they walked very close together," Letitia said, slipping on her sunglasses and watching the cheerleaders kicking their legs up on a corner of the field.

"And what guy wants to sit on another's lap unless..." I added.

Everyone chuckled.

"What the fuck y'all laughing at? I am *heartbroken*."

I couldn't stop laughing.

"No, girl, it's not that," Tina said, putting an arm around Gina. "I was just telling Elijah that ever since he came out this school is hella gay now."

Gina scowled. "Fuck, yeah, it is. You and your fucking coming-out extravaganza!"

"Don't hate, Gina."

"Appreciate," Letitia added, high-fiving me.

Gina peered at the field. "Who's that hot guy who just came out on the field? He's fucking fine."

"That's Barn and Austin's cousin, Shang. He and his family just moved here from Singapore."

"How many fucking fine-ass cousins are *in* that family?" Gina asked.

"They're a huge family," I said. "Austin's grandma has ten siblings spread all over Southeast Asia."

We all looked at Shang. He was tall and muscular with jet-black hair that fell over his eyes. He strutted over to Barn and Austin. I could hear them speaking in Cantonese. He laughed, suddenly looking up into the bleachers.

"I should warn you, Gina."

"What? He's gay?"

"No. Not at all," I said. "He likes Black girls. Especially Black girls who dig comics, engineering, and science."

She turned to me. "You fucking kidding me? Hook a sister up!"

"I'll see what I can do when he comes over for a family dinner tonight."

"Invite me over!" Gina said. "Please?"

"Yeah, sure."

Katie appeared, holding a large iced coffee, and waved to us. "Are y'all cruising those fine-ass boys on the field?"

"He's gonna hook me up!" Gina beamed.

Katie turned, "Ooh, fucking Shang. Shit girl. I hear he's gotta big—"

"TMI!" Letitia screamed, covering her ears.

"Apparently, Shang's sister is single. And into Latin girls."

Letitia stared at me.

"*Increíble, vato,*" she said. "Am I coming to dinner too?"

"You better," I said.

"Okay, fuck y'all," Tina said. "If all of you end up with those fine-ass cousins, what the fuck about me?"

"I thought you were not dating," Gina said.

"I'm not, but how about a little fun?"

"Shang has a friend who's single and ready to mingle."

Tina just stared at me. "Does he like math?" Tina was obsessed with math.

"I mean, duh. He's one of Shang's math club buddies, after all." We all started laughing, while, out on the field, Austin, Barn and Shang pulled off their shirts to put on a real show for us.

"Dam those fine-ass Asian brothers."

"It's a blessing," Katie said.

"Why don't you all come to dinner tonight? It'll be a spontaneous party."

Gina and Letitia stood up to do a little dance.

"Heyyyyyyyy!" They paused to shout to the boys on the field, "What up boys!"

I looked down at Austin on the field. He was standing, peering at me, shirtless, through his thick glasses. He shot me the peace sign.

*

A FEW DAYS later, as I skated home with Stylo, we talked about dating and then about all the crazy shit happening in LA lately. The war between the covens, the palpable tension in the air, the sense that LA was a tinderbox ready to explode.

"You scared, Eli?"

"Yeah, sort of. Are you?"

"Usually I'd say, no, man, but yeah. Feels like something big is going to happen—something that could change everything."

I was quiet for a moment. "Yeah, I feel that too."

After dinner, we retired to the home theater to watch the latest *Fast and Furious* movie. Stylo and Austin were super into it. Barn reminded Katie he could drive like that.

"Oh, yeah, you can drift?"

"Sure thing, babe."

"Don't even try," Aunt Christine warned him, "especially not with any of my expensive cars."

I closed my eyes, tired after a long day. I was in a dark room. Everything was black except a square of yellow light in the distance. I walked toward the light, slowly, my sneakers squeaking on the cracked, black floor. Approaching the lighted square, I heard a raspy voice say, *"Tu desi mortarets!" You will die.*

I hesitated, goose bumps rising on my arms. The yellow square turned into a doorway. I stepped inside. The smell of sulfur tickled my nose. Flames crawled up a wall to my left. Screams and shouts of agony filled the air. A piece of ice floated in the air. Two black dots in the ice watched me.

"Things are out of control!" A voice filled the room. "We have to stop this!"

"What can we do to save everything?"

"You know what has to be done!"

"No, no, we can't...they...you will...kill...them?"

Flames erupted on the ceiling and floor and launched toward the ice, devouring it. I began screaming.

"Eli! Eli!" Austin shook me. My eyes flew open.

"Are you okay?"

Mom, Sean, and the rest of the family stared at me, looking worried.

"Yeah, sorry, just had a nightmare."

"LA is a tinderbox ready to explode," Stylo had said.

After the movie, Mom and Sean drove Stylo home. Austin and I went back to my room to work on homework and fool around a little. Eventually, we fell asleep. Devlina appeared in my dreams—she was running down a dark, creepy alley somewhere in skid row in Downtown LA. She was sprinting in her puxhàredo heels. She looked back behind her—a terrible monster at least twenty feet high composed of pulsing black light and eight legs followed.

"You can't run from me!" A raspy voice shouted at her. The voice echoed off the tall concrete buildings lining the alley. Devlina leapt over a fence, landing on her feet, and sprinted as fast as she could. A darkness followed her, devouring the asphalt, the concrete buildings, lights, bins overflowing with trash, puddles of water, rats, and cockroaches. Devlina stumbled. She fell and rolled onto her back.

"No, no, please, don't..." She crawled backward trying to flee from the darkness as it caught up to her.

"Elijah! Run! Save yourself!" she screamed before disappearing along with everything else on skid row, replaced with nothing. Space was a vacuum, cold and empty. A void, like the Excelà.

Chapter Thirty-One

The Sacrifice

I STOOD ON the front lawn of Burbank High School holding Austin's hand as Orville, wearing a black T-shirt with an image of a black hole made of tiny red dots set in the middle of a large Z, the symbol of Zid'dra, lead a group of Plebes marching in two lines behind him down Third Street. They stopped in front of the school.

"Plebeians!" Orville shouted. "Hail Zid'dra! We are *Destrùjantus*! Hail!"

The stone-faced plebs shouted back, *"Destrùjantus contraco Allégansa!"*

"March! March!" Orville shouted to the two dozen Plebs dressed all in black, looking like soldiers ready for war.

"Shit, Kangy," I whispered, "they called themselves destrùjantus! That means they are warriors for the coven."

"Aye," Austin replied, "but for who?"

"Zid'dra," I said softly, thinking back to the terrible dream of

Devlina the night before.

"This isn't good, Eli."

"I know."

LA was a tinderbox, ready to explode.

Orville stepped back to allow the Plebs to march up the steps into BHS single file.

Orville paused, turned to me, and said, "Your time is numbered, Fruitlomary!"

Austin growled, "Fuck you, Orville."

Orville launched for Austin, who came out swinging. A melee broke out, fists flying, legs kicking, until several teachers intervened and pulled us apart.

Soon, we were all in Principal Dustaffeson's office. She glared at Orville. He had shaved his head. He had tattoos on his neck—pentagrams, the large *Z* symbolizing the coven, and the numbers 666.

"Are you part of a gang, Orville?" She looked at him suspiciously.

He resembled a white supremacist.

"You could say," Orville said, sprawled out in the hard, plastic chair, a smirk on his face.

"Associating with gangs is forbidden here."

Orville sniggered. "You can't stop me or my Plebes. We answer to a more powerful authority than you."

"Who would that be?" Principal Dustaffeson asked wearily.

"None of your business, doll face."

"Excuse me?" Principal Dustaffeson said.

Orville settled into his chair, grinning mischievously.

"You better act right, son, you understand me?" Principal Dustaffeson snapped. I looked at her. I had never seen her mad like this before.

"What were you and those boys planning?"

"Showing solidarity with our new patron."

"And that is?"

"You don't need to know, hon."

"Orville, call me hon again, and you'll be suspended."

Orville made a pouty face. "Sawry."

"Why did you call Elijah names?"

"I don't remember." Orville snickered. "Maybe, because he's richer than God and *we* don't like God."

Austin's neck turned red. He was trying to control his temper.

"Orville, we don't use language like that here. And dress appropriately. No black shirts and jeans and boots. Got it?"

He stood up. "Fuck you."

"That's it, you're suspended!"

Orville stormed to her door, then turned.

"This ain't over, Delomary."

Austin launched out of his chair.

"What you going to do, lover boy?"

"Don't test me. I can destroy you!"

Orville laughed and skulked outside.

Principal Dustaffeson stared at Austin and me, worry etched across her face.

She stood from her chair. "Let me know if there's any more trouble, okay?" she said, showing us to the door, before returning to her desk and picking up the phone.

*

TWO TENSE WEEKS later, the sky was overcast, clouds shaded deep black, gray, and streaks of red covered the City of Angels. The first storm of the season headed to Southern California.

"The first Atmospheric River, folks," the jovial weatherperson on the news said from the TV in the breakfast room. "Bring an umbrella and batten down the hatches, Angelenos!"

The first rainstorm of the season was a big deal in the dry desert of Los Angeles. On TV, they had team coverage all over LA. Stationed near the LA River, at Santa Monica, up in the San Gabriel Mountains, out in Palm Springs, and on the Grapevine.

The city waited for nature to unleash her fury on the mountains and valleys.

"Slow down when you drive, as the first rain brings out the oil on the freeways," the TV anchored warned, "which makes it treacherous to drive, especially with rain."

"Be safe, boys," Mom whispered at breakfast, clutching her neck, fear and worry emanating off her.

"Sunny can give you all a ride home after school. That's when it's supposed to rain," Sean said. "He's an expert at driving in inclement weather. And this looks like it'll be a doozy of a storm."

A few hours later, I was on the tennis courts at school gathering loose balls after tennis class. We each took turns cleaning up after class. Everyone else was gone, even Austin, who left early for a dentist appointment.

I watched the clouds, ready to open up and drown Southern California at any moment. I had a sick feeling in my stomach that something was going to happen. Something terrible. My heart pounded. My face flushed. My emergency pill was in my backpack in my locker.

Just.

In.

Case.

Stay calm, Eli. Stay calm. Count backwards from twenty as Arnulfo taught you.

I wished we had session. I was like a pressure cooker with the safety valve blocked. I needed to fall apart in his office, so Arnulfo could put me together again, better than before. He was like that, with the patience and dexterity to put together the five thousand pieces comprising the puzzle of my life.

Someone whistled. I looked around, seeing only the oleander bushes lining the courts.

Was I hearing things?

"Stop taking medicine if you suddenly have fear or start seeing things," the label warned.

Puxhàredo. Was the medicine working against me? No, that was not possible. I was so much better now. No more dreams of dying. No more fear of every little thing.

A drop of rain hit my head.

Puxhàredo.

"Hey, asshole."

My eyes turned skyward. Orville stood on top of the chain-link fence behind the bushes around the courts.

The chain-link fence wasn't strong enough to hold the weight of a boy built like a refrigerator such as Orville.

He floated above the fence, his body glowing with a strange light.

I watched him. "What are you doing up there?"

"Havin' fun." The red and orange light flickered around him, casting shadows on his face making his features look more exaggerated and frightening.

"Little bitch!"

"That's not my name, Orville."

"Yeah, it is. You're an asshole and a fag."

"Don't call me a fag," I shouted. "You know I can leap up there and battle you. Wanna watch me?"

Orville snickered. "Relax, we don't care that you like boys."

"We?"

"Me and my homeboy."

"Jesus?" I squeaked. I hoped. The reality was too terrifying.

"NO!" Orville shouted.

Rain fell on both of us.

"Jesus can't do what my Lord can do."

"Like, um, make it rain in Southern California?"

Orville cackled, dancing several inches above the length of the top of the chain-link fence. "You're so sarcastic. And a bitch. Fucking De-lomary. Richer than God." He laughed mockingly.

"I've always hated you and your fucking family," he said.

"Why?"

"Because you're fucking rich, and I live in a fucking trailer down by the railroad tracks."

Was there a trailer park in Burbank?

"Yes, there is, asshole, right behind the power plant. Everyone gets cancer in the trailer park. My mom did last year. She died.”

Rain poured on me. I was getting soaked, but I couldn't seem to move.

“We petitioned City Hall to do something to help us. But your fucking family intervened. Apparently, your family owns a share of the municipal power plant.”

“That's not true.”

“You saying I lie, bitch?”

I cast my eyes down. My body quivered from the cold.

“Yeah, look down, you fucking pussy.”

“I didn't know about that. If I had, I would have helped.”

He snickered. “No, you wouldn't. You are too busy being this fucking victim.”

“I'm not.”

“You are. You rich kids. Like Blair and them Patricians,” Orville said, “have everything, live this perfect life, and you still whine and mope and act like the world is against you.”

“You know nothing about my life, Orville.”

“I know.” He snickered. “And I don't care. I hate you, bitch.”

I struggled to see, as the rain was drenching me. Orville was perfectly dry.

“Do you think it was an accident you lost that marathon? Tripped?”

“What?”

He laughed. “My homeboy did that.”

“I...uh...I know...”

“Yeah, he's so fucking powerful, Elijah, you don't even realize.”

“I understand.”

“Yeah, well, he was the one who made sure it rained so much last year to make you miserable. We were hoping you'd off yourself.”

“Shut up!” I cried.

“Yeah.” Orville did somersaults along the top of the fence. “He's been trying to destroy you. And you know why? Because you are pathetic. You make a big scene coming out. Force us to see you play the victim. Poor little rich boy. Fuck that."

"Why are you saying all these things?"

"Because...because I fucking hate you and I know we are getting even."

"Even?"

"My lord, you're fucking dense. That skank you've been scheming with is getting her just desserts as we speak, and soon, so will you, *tu desi mortarets*!"

"What are you talking about?"

He mimicked me and laughed.

"Devlina Du Vel," he said. "My Lord's First Wife. The arrogant bitch. She thinks she owns my Lord. But he is what he is. And he owes no one anything. Love? Fuck that. No one loves him because he loves no one."

Thunder rumbled. Orville smiled at the sky.

I gulped.

Puxhàredo.

I started to cry. I guess crying was progress. Arnulfo told me to feel my emotions. Damn medicine helped with that. Thunder rumbled in the distance.

A flash of light momentarily blinded me. A second later, a shadow fell toward me.

Orville.

And then I was knocked unconscious.

*

THUNDER RUMBLED OVERHEAD. Why did it seem to rain whenever bad shit happened to me? I opened my eyes. My head hurt. My eyes scanned the room. Lightning flashed in the cracked skylights overhead. Water trickled from the broken skylights and holes in the ceiling, splashing onto the uneven concrete floor next to me. I glanced up at the corroded metal ceiling and rusted steel beams supporting the ceiling. Blackness swirled around me, punctuated occasionally by bursts of lightning. My pulse quickened. Panic gripped my body. White light lit up the squares of glass in the ceiling. Thunder growled. Two red dots danced in the darkness. The odor of sulfur filled the air.

Puxhàredo.

Puxhàredo.

Puxhàredo.

Rain thumped high above me. Thunder grumbled. Sobbing sounded from nearby. My heart began to beat faster. My emergency pill was…in my backpack in my locker at BHS.

Crap.

Crap.

Crap.

The whimpering continued. My heart broke. I looked around. A figure slumped against the cold, damp concrete floor in a cage. I picked myself up and walked toward the cage. My head throbbed; my ankle burned.

I gulped. *No. Fucking no. This can't be happening. How the fuck did this happen…to him? Maybe I deserve this; maybe it's time that I paid the price for all the terrible things my family did, but surely not him. What did he do?*

Fuck. I need something to break open the lock? I have to help him. I feel him slipping away. I feel the gravity dissolving around him. I don't want to spin out into the cold, dark depths of open space. The Ex-celà. Fuck, I can't be the only gay boy in the universe again. I have to do something for him. For Austin.

"There's nothing you can do for him," a deep voice boomed in my head.

"He will be dead soon. What a fool. Love. It's the most terrible thing God ever created."

I looked around. There was no one with us. Just me and Austin.

I fell to the floor. "Austin, can you hear me?"

Austin's body squirmed. His eyes, partially obscured by his wet hair, met mine. He smiled faintly.

"I fought so hard, love," he moaned.

I tried to hold back the tears. "What happened?"

"He came looking for you. But I stopped him…"

"But why, Austin? I don't want you to get hurt for me." Fat tears streamed down my face.

"I love you, Eli."

"Kangy, no, you don't understand…"

"The most powerful Coaugelus are united with their Encantreinus. And no matter what those treasonous Estàntus did to you, you'll always be an Encantreino. *My Encantreino.* I *have* to protect you."

He screeched and moaned in agony. There was blood on the floor near him.

Red.

Hot.

Fury enveloped me. My amulet burned my skin. I rose to my feet, clenching my fists.

"Who the fuck did this? Show yourself!" I yelled.

Laughter, cruel and menacing, echoed through the vaulted space.

"*Sum Coa Imperiatoro deo Oscuriment, Iunio.*"

Zid'dra, of course.

"I am here to settle a score, boy."

Suddenly, my tears stopped. "Where the puxhàredo hell are you, demon king?"

"Here!"

Lightning flashed in the skylights above. For a split second, a bizarre-looking creature composed of a flowing, spewing tar-like substance, with two dots for eyes made of orange and red flames appeared in the darkness.

"What the fuck are you supposed to be?" *Why am I amused? This isn't the time to laugh.*

Lightning flashed and thunder reverberated nearby.

"You dare mock me, the Lord of—"

"Flies?" I said. "Why the fuck does it smell like dirty socks?"

"Shut up!" Lightning flickered in the skylights. Zid'dra lifted an appendage made of flowing tar. Austin shrieked. My stomach dropped.

"Stop acting the fool, Iunio, or do you want him dead?"

"No, stop, please..."

Cruel laughter echoed as lightning lit up the skylights.

"I thought so."

Thunder boomed in the distance. A fucking atmospheric river, rain rumbled on the galvanized-steel roof overhead.

"What do you want?" I murmured.

"You. Elijah. The great-great-grandson of the Queen of Queens. The Áuqala. You must die."

"I don't understand."

"I have to balance out nature."

"What do you mean?"

"You being here. Alive. Your mother—she did this."

"I don't understand."

"She joined your powers to my wife."

"So?"

"That's a no-no. We don't like that."

"We?"

"The Áuqala and me."

"What does my great-great-grandmother have to do with this?"

"She's one part of the universe. I am the other. The yin and yang. Light and Dark. We bring balance to the order of things."

"But what does that have to do with me?"

"My wife. She told you. She wants to destroy me," Zid'dra said.

He was speaking in English and the Dark Language simultaneously. An unseen chorus of voices filled the room with cruel glee. Austin screamed in pain. My heart broke in two.

"I do what has to be done. If no one kills the deer, then deer keep multiplying until they destroy their ecosystem. The Shimmering creates. I destroy. It's my job. Only, no one worships me."

"Devlina did."

"She's a fool. She fell in love with me, but I never promised her I would be hers only. I am not faithful like that. God is faith. I am fear."

"But Zid'dra—"

"Your Filthiness!" Zid'dra commanded.

"Yes, Your Filthiness," I repeated. "You don't have to do this. It was all a mistake. Mom was angry, upset with my dad. She made a mistake using Malac Malactańena and resurrecting Devlina from where she was entombed by the Alliance after the battle on Old Earth. Surely you can forgive?"

Zid'dra shuddered, bits of steaming tar flying off his head.

"I don't forgive."

"I implore you—"

"Enough!" Zid'dra's voice deepened, the floor trembled, and thunder roared overhead.

"Now, enough with these distractions. It is time for the ceremony."

"Ceremony?"

"Where I kill you," Zid'dra said. "So many times, I have come close to destroying you, and now I will fulfill my oath."

"Oath."

"To purify the universe. Of you. And once you are gone, then I will continue to rid the world of your family. And the Alliance. The Áuqala is too powerful; it is time for me to squash her. And return things to the natural order, with darkness and fear and monsters in charge."

Puxhàredo.

Puxhàredo. Panic gripped me. My heart was in my throat. Cold tendrils of fear wound their way like vines up my legs, slowly squeezing my body. Shit, I was going to have a panic attack. It was barreling toward me. After dodging death multiple times, this was it. I couldn't stop it. I was going to die. What will happen to Little Ocho and my skateboard? Damn. Shit. Puxhàredo.

An image of Dirk Delomary, lying in bed, eyes half-closed, whispering to Evangeline who huddled over him as he said his last words: *Nunma in Viacadeimo.* I am not a victim. I had come a long way since the day of that kiss on Lake Shasta. I didn't need any pill to stop the panic attack.

"No," I said, staring at the oozing tar man. "Let's rumble!"

"You think you can battle me?" Zid'dra hooted, gas rising from his head.

I centered myself as Máurso taught me, bowing to Zid'dra, then putting up my fists in front of my face.

"*Potentzea, imdentro, potentzea exancto.*"

"Power inside me, power outside me." A feeble, golden light flickered around me, brightening the vast, ruined foundry. Rain pounded the roof.

I was going to battle Zid'dra, if it was the last thing I did. Last summer, Mom and I watched a movie about a young family in their RV in the desert near Joshua Tree. A gang of motorcycle hoodlums attacked them. As the bikers beat her husband viciously, the woman collapsed to the floor inside the RV, crying, sobbing. Mom screamed, "Get up! Get a knife! Fight for your man, your family! Don't die a victim!"

Watching that movie summed up who Mom was raised to be—a fighter. She was determined to do what she thought was right. She had married a man she loved, and then when he walked out on her, on us, she picked up the pieces and carried on. Shit happened to her. Things went terribly wrong. She was taken prisoner and carried off to Old Earth by Devlina. I didn't cry. I was determined to bring her home. I did that. *Nunma in Viacadeimo.* Mom came back different. I was different. We changed, we had to. Life was about moving forward, no matter what. Mom had progressed. I did too. We were moving together now. "Elijah, do you understand that when the shit hits the fan, you have two choices: you give up and collapse on the floor and sob, or you stand up and you fight. And if you fail, well, you have to know you made a choice. This world loves victims. But let's embrace being heroes."

"Even if you die?"

"You have to take a chance; you have to stand up to fear, self-loathing, and doubt. You have to reach inside and be bigger than those monsters."

Those monsters rattled around inside my head. I was bigger than Zid'dra. I was bigger than him because a kiss on a lake had opened a key to my soul. And out of the door stepped a new boy—no, a man. He could do anything he put his mind to. I leaned down. "I love you, Kangy," I said, then summoned golden orbs of flames and played with them in my hands.

"Want to play with my balls?"

Zid'dra gagged. "Iunio, mal!"

I tossed the balls at him. Zid'dra ducked. The golden lights flickered out behind him.

I pulled out my PlasmX, the pink light glowing weakly in the dark space. Zid'dra extended a hand, snatching my PlasmX. He snapped his wrist. My PlasmX shattered, little pink stars filling the air and dissolving into the atmosphere. I strained to summon more magic; nothing worked. Was I out of magic? Puxhàredo!

The chorus began taunting me. Zid'dra was cackling. "You are nothing, Elijah Delomary. You don't even exist anymore!"

Unexpectedly, a door behind me was kicked open. I turned to face fucking Blair Winchester in a black leather motorcycle suit, her hair pulled back off her face.

"Hiya, Elijah," she said, chewing gum and looking entirely ferocious.

"Blair, what are you doing here?"

"Maybe Damien's rubbed off on me. Maybe the Alliance isn't so bad. Maybe our families can work things out. Maybe I can help save the universe."

I broke down. "Blair, I think I love you!"

"I know, honey. Of course, you do. Look at me. Look at you."

"Still gay."

"I have a boyfriend. Jesus, Elijah!"

"Who the fuck are you, iunia!"

"Blair Fucking Winchester. I am filthy rich and so much better than the likes of you. Huh. Do you have a titanium card? No, you don't because you're nothing more than a blob of crap, and I am a fierce woman!"

Zid'dra snarled. "Get out of here, you little gnat. I am going to do my job and destroy that red-haired freak."

"Not on my watch," Blair roared, then snapped her gum. "Get the fuck away from my man, beelzebub!"

Zid'dra and I both watched her. *This was fricking insane.*

Blair, in heels, clicked swiftly across the room carrying what looked like a giant water blaster.

I eyed Austin, who was still whimpering. Blair's eyes followed mine to the cage.

"Is that Austin? Fuck, is he okay?"

I shook my head.

"Fuck this." Blair walked over to the bubbling-tar man.

"You bitch!" she said before pumping her weapon and unleashing a clear liquid all over the bubbling tar creature.

Zid'dra hissed and shrieked. His gooey tar-like body convulsed. He was livid.

Lightning flashed; thunder crashed overhead.

"What the fuck is that?" I whispered as Blair kept pumping water on Zid'dra, snapping her gum, and tapping her left foot.

"Holy water, what else? Hurry. Help Austin."

"Okay."

A moment later, the water blaster was empty, so she released it and mustered pink balls of energy with her hands, then lobbed them at Zid'dra. He batted them with a tarry appendage. She conjured a thousand doves to swarm and beat him with their white wings. I scanned the room, lightning flashed—there was a hammer! While Blair used magic to battle Zid'dra, I banged the lock with all my might.

BOOM

BOOM

BOOM

Thud. The lock landed on the cold concrete floor. I rushed inside and kneeled beside Austin.

"Kangy."

He muttered, "Eli, love..."

I pulled off my amulet. It was warm to the touch. I wrapped it around Austin's neck. It shone with a pulsing pink light.

"Kangy?"

His eyes opened. "Eli, love, you came. I didn't want you to. This was a setup to get you. To kill you."

I began to weep. My tears fell onto Austin's hand. He grasped for me. "Eli, leave me. Save yourself."

"No, Kangy…"

"Elijah, if you die, the darkness wins, the Alliance could fail…"

"Kangy, please."

"Eli, save yourself."

"Elijah! I'm running out of juice. Do what you have to do," Blair yelled over to me.

Light flashed, followed by thunder, and then a sickening eruption. Blair shrieked. I was knocked down. I rolled onto my back. Fuck saving myself. I had to save Austin. He was all that mattered. He was pure love. He had sacrificed so much for me; at all costs, Austin must live. Maybe that was what Dirk meant, long ago, as the breath left his lungs. He was not a victim because he chose life and love after the struggles of his youth. And I chose to save Austin. He was worth it. He would make the world better. He would bring light to the darkness.

I scampered out of the crumbling building and rushed into the wind and rain. I looked around frantically. There was an old, beat-up pay phone hanging on the wall. I picked up the phone. *How do I use this? Where's the touch screen? Shit. Okay, well, shit. I'll just dial some numbers.*

Please work.

Please work.

"Nine-one-one. What's your emergency?"

"My boyfriend—he's hurt. We're at Forman Steel on Magnolia Boulevard. Please send an ambulance."

"They're on their way."

I hung up and rushed inside. Blair was nowhere to be seen. The tar blob had turned into a quivering mass of black points, hovering in the center of the room. Strange chanting filled the room. A sickly, green light danced on the rusted steel walls and beams above.

"It's time. Stop fighting this." Zid'dra's deep voice hummed, "Devlina has been dealt with. Balance will come. The Alliance will finally fall. Magicals will falter. Ordinaries will perish. The coven will grow stronger. The lion will devour the lamb. Order will be returned to the universe. Humanity is meant to fail, Elijah. Don't you comprehend?"

I was desperate. My mind raced to Mom and Barn and Tory and the Kangs and all my friends.

Blair. She helped me! Fuck. Austin. He was dying. He needed help.

The chanting grew louder. The walls quaked. Sickness crept up my esophagus. I bit my lower lip to stop it.

Shit. Shit.

Puxhàredo.

And, after a moment, peace enveloped me. I was right. For the first time in my life, I had clarity. Everything was going to be okay. I began walking toward Zid'dra.

"Eli! No!"

I walked toward the cone of black dots in the center of the room.

"Keep coming, Iunio! Death is your only choice. Death is wonderful. The Alliance must fail; humanity must fall. Balance and order must be restored to the universe."

I sluggishly trudged forward. I had to do this for Austin. He would live and rise up stronger than ever, and he would battle the darkness, and he would shimmer. I needed to purify myself. I had to let go so that balance was restored to the universe. Austin would do that. For me.

A blaze of lightning lit the skylights above. I saw a silhouette. I heard stilettos on the concrete. Thunder rumbled overhead.

"You have to live, Elijah."

"Devlina?"

Devlina, or rather a thousand tiny square-shaped tiles in a mosaic resembling her form, walked toward me, holding a ball of iridescent red light. I backed away.

"What are you doing?"

She observed the ball of light.

"It's the only way."

"I don't understand."

"For you to live."

"What do you mean?"

"Asshole over there wants to kill you. He already destroyed most of me, but I know a way so you can survive."

I watched Austin. He can—no, I can't bear the idea of leaving him. Alone. All alone.

Zid'dra beckoned. "Come to me and restore balance, Elijah," his voice instructed. "It's the only way, iunio."

No, I couldn't let that happen. I looked at Devlina.

"What are you going to do?"

"Save you; destroy myself."

"You are willing to do something to save me, even if you don't survive?" I said to Devlina

She shrugged. There were tears in her eyes.

"I've grown to love you, kid."

I stopped breathing for a second. I was baffled.

"Devlina, you only do things for yourself."

She snickered. "Not anymore, I guess."

This was colossal. *Unbelievable.*

"Devlina, could it be you've changed?"

She shrugged again. "I doubt it. I mean, I'm only doing this for you and lover boy. I can't stand the idea of you two being separated. True love. That's what I see. It's what I wanted..."

The thousand tiles composing her body reassembled and her hands wiped her eyes.

"Are you crying?"

"Fuck you, Elijah."

"You've gone soft, Devlina."

"I fucking know. It's you and your damn goody-two-shoes ways. Always helping people. Worrying about others. Fuck, you gave up your powers to save your familiar. That messed with me so much. I cried for days. I inverted myself and transformed to pure carbon and sank into the ground and leeched through the rocks and clay and mud and existed there in agony. I'll never understand why I felt that way after you did that. You gave up power to save someone you *love.*"

"I can't help it; it's who I am."

"I can help it, yet here we are. I'm going to do this... I love you, kid."

"I love you too, Devlina."

"You're like the son I've always wanted."

She was looking into my soul. We had a connection.

"I have to do this. To save you." She glared at Zid'dra. He had reverted to a gurgling creature made of tar, laughing manically, and spilling gasoline all over the floor.

"Elijah, you have to know something. You have great power. I lusted for power, but I was searching for something that doesn't exist. Hard power. No one follows a bully. You have soft power."

"Soft power."

"Your friends," she said. "They love you. Boxey—he followed your lead because he loved you. Your family loves you. People listen to you. You will rule the entire world with your soft power. You can be what I can never be. A true leader. One whom the whole universe will follow because you love. Love is all that matters."

She turned her attention to Austin. "And Austin—he loves you unconditionally. No matter what." She yelled at Zid'dra, "Fuck you, pookie! You suck!"

"Don't call me pookie!"

Devlina turned back to me, her eyes filled with hurt. "I just wanted to be loved. That's all." She groaned. "You can be the fulfillment of my dreams. Do you understand?"

I waggled and gazed at the floating red orb of light.

"You have to trust me."

"I'm scared."

"I know you are. I won't hurt you."

"How do I know that?"

"Faith. It's what God has. You trust in him or her or whatever it is. Trust me."

I nodded.

"I trust you."

"Close your eyes, son."

I shut my eyes.

Devlina said, "I love you, and I want Austin to live."

"But Devlina..."

I opened my eyes. Abruptly, she screeched and heaved the red orb at me. The red ball sped toward me connecting with my chest. The light absorbed into my shirt and then everything went black.

A terrible explosion surrounded me. I was flying through a great void of frigid space.

The *Excelà.* My body was pulled in every direction. I was ripping apart and spinning around and around and around in the great and vast blackness. All the pieces of me were tumbling down and falling deeper into a void.

And then, white light exploded into the black night. I opened my eyes. I was in Joshua Tree, seated on an outcropping of rocks. I shook my arms and kicked my legs. I was alive.

I spotted Áurmiddo sitting next to me. We were staring up at Cassiopeia.

"True Colors" played from a red speaker. Áurmiddo reached for my hand.

"You have to live. Don't you understand?"

I shook my head. I was muddled, my head filled with fog.

"It's about the universe and gravity and love."

"I don't understand, Áurmiddo."

"I was the key."

"To what?" I examined his brown eyes.

"To the universe."

"But why?"

"So, you could become who you are destined to be."

"What does that mean?" I looked at him. I was incensed. "You didn't love me?"

He smiled. "Of course, I did. But now, looking back, I know that when I kissed you, it opened you up to the universe."

"I loved you."

"You love Austin." He laughed. "I have a boyfriend now. Ours was puppy love, Elicêo."

"I hate puppy love. I was in love with *you.*"

"You're in love with Austin now and he adores you, and he keeps the light in you burning. Don't you see? They tried to douse it over and over again, but it can't be extinguished."

"I don't understand."

"You have to go back. Be with Austin. I'll be in Minerva. You can visit me. But you have to go back to Earth."

"Perhaps I don't want to."

"You have to. You think you're alive, but you're not."

"I'm not alive?"

"You're like a thousand tiles making up a mosaic."

"Yeah, well maybe then it's easier to be like this, a void, an Excelà. Nothing. No expectations. Nada. Rien."

"No, this is nothing. You have to be something. You've become a man, Elijah. You're no longer the scared boy living someone else's life."

"I'm not strong enough to pick myself up and go on."

He grinned. "You are. Don't you know that? You've always been strong, but you thought you were weak. How many things did you overcome? How many times did you live when you should have died? You are powerful. Remember that."

"I'm not."

I was crying.

"You are, Elijah. You are the great-great-grandson of our Glorious Queen of Queens. The bearer of light, the One Who Shimmers. You will always be powerful."

"I'm not powerful, Áurmiddo. I broke. I mean, I fell apart. I'm on medicine right now."

He held my hand. "Sometimes, you have to break to be reborn. Without destruction, there can be no creation.

"You need to go to that light. Be who you are meant to be."

A lighted red door appeared in the middle of the sand, next to a Joshua tree.

"Go to the door. Be with Austin. Be with your family. For me. But more importantly, for you."

"How do you know all this, Áurmiddo?"

He grinned. "I've been following you. On my scimitar. I've seen everything. Well, nothing too personal."

I looked up at Cassiopeia burning in the night sky.

"I'm frightened."

"Trust me." He smiled. "You can trust people who love you, Eli. Don't you know that by now? Your mom, Austin, your aunts, the Kangs, your friends. Even that silly Blair girl. She loves you."

I sighed.

"She helped me."

He laughed. "I know. I never anticipated that."

"And Devlina."

"She sacrificed herself for *you*," he said. "Don't you understand? People who love you will do anything for you. That's how you know you're loved. And a lot of people love you dearly. Even Devlina. And when you are loved, you can move mountains. That is real magic. Real power. They say that to be strong people have to fear you, but they are wrong. Love is power. Love is the law."

I broke down crying.

"Devlina sacrificed herself for me..."

He squeezed my shoulders.

"Go, Elijah, now, before it's too late."

I noticed the light fading as the door began to swing shut. I stood.

"Áurmiddo. Thank you. I mean..."

He laughed. "Go, now. Email me, Elicêo!"

I ran toward the door and squeezed through just in time as it closed behind me.

Chapter Thirty-Two

The Lightness of Being

AT FIRST, THERE was nothing. And then, slowly, I noticed the sound of buzzing in my ears, and something rough licking my face. I heard grunting and then barking in my ear. My eyes opened slowly. Dazzling sunlight poured over me. I rubbed my eyes. *Where am I? Puxàredo, is this it? Well, I guess at least I ended up here, not Down There with him. Zid'dra in his Gloom deep under the foundations of the Earth in all its seven dimensions.*

"Master!"

I sat up straight.

"Boxey?"

I looked over. Boxey circled me, his tail wagging merrily.

"I thought you were a goner, Master!"

"What happened?"

"You fell out of the sky!" he said. "I was shocked to see that!"

"Are we in heaven, Boxey?"

He barked.

"No, we're in the bumblebee garden."

The fountain in the center gurgled, and the wonderful aroma of the snap dragons, mint, dahlias, and lavender filled my nose. My eyes roamed the sycamore and poplar trees swaying in the wind as the marine layer pushed over the Santa Monica Mountains into the Valley.

"Welcome back, Elijah!" A bumblebee buzzed by me.

"We missed you," another said.

"Glad to see you again, young man!"

I closed my eyes. The buzzing was actually hundreds of tiny voices welcoming me back.

"Am I really alive?"

"Yes, Master!"

I opened my eyes. "Boxey, what are you doing here?"

"I was on my way to Old Earth for a new assignment, when suddenly I was pulled out of the *Messimenta*, the In-Between, and ended up here. Just now."

I shielded my eyes. It was so bright. I was not used to this golden light. Had it always been this brilliant in Southern California? I had been living in sepia tones, and now I was in vibrant colors.

"But what happened?"

Boxey circled several times and sat down next to me. "From what I heard from the bees, Zid'dra wanted to destroy you to finish off Devlina and your family, mortally wound the Alliance, and wipe out humanity. And most importantly you. You're important to the gravity of the universe, Master."

"I am?"

"Of course. You don't know that?"

"Yeah, well, I don't want to brag—"

Boxey barked. "You should brag, master!"

"Boxey." I stretched and pulled his warm, furry body close to me. He yelped but relented. I rubbed his fur. "Who's a good boy!"

Boxey yapped.

"Oh, Boxey." I started to cry. "I've missed you so much!"

"I've missed you too, Master." Boxey licked my face with his rough tongue. "I'm glad we're back together again."

I rubbed Boxey's fur for several moments, basking in the golden light falling on me from the sun above. After a while, I said, "Devlina had this red orb of light that she used to save me from Zid'dra."

Boxey nodded. "It was the last of her magic. Her entity."

My eyes grew big.

"When that orb containing all her magic touched you, it caused a chain reaction, sort of like a nuclear reaction."

"What do you mean?"

"Magic is science, Master. You are filled with positively charged atoms, Master. You are filled with light."

"I don't understand."

Boxey watched me, annoyed.

"Devlina is full of negatively charged atoms. She is filled with dark. When she transferred all her negative magic to you, all of her energy connected with your energy and caused a great explosion."

"I still don't understand."

Boxey rolled his eyes, which was weird to see a Golden Retriever do.

"You canceled each other out."

"So, I'm dead."

Boxey laughed.

"No, Master, you are very much alive. When Devlina's magic flowed into you, it released your true magic. It appears you are a far more powerful Encantreino than anyone told you."

"Really?"

"You can do anything. The Oath doesn't apply to you."

I squinted at the sky.

"I can muster sodas on command?" I snapped my finger. A blue-and-white can of cola appeared in my hand.

"A candy bar?" Snapped my fingers. One appeared in my other hand. "Wow! Maybe I want some dancing blocks of cheese!" I twitched my nose. Four six-foot-tall blocks of orange cheddar cheese with spindly legs began twerking nearby.

"Master, that's weird. Maybe, no?"

I shrugged. Twitched my nose. The cheddar blocks disappeared into the air. A moment passed. The wind blew through my hair. I snapped my fingers, and the grass changed from green to pink to purple and back.

"It's so bright. Has it always been this bright?"

Boxey laughed. "Of course, Master. You just couldn't see it."

I lay down on the grass, closing my eyes.

"Are you my Familiar again, Boxey?"

He barked and licked my cheek. "Of course, Master. When Devlina revealed your true identity, I was brought back to you. I'm your Familiar, until the time when I reach maturity and transition to being a human— Magical myself, of course."

I reached for his warm, golden fur.

"I love you, Boxey," I said. "I missed you so much. I am so sorry for everything."

"You gave the ultimate sacrifice for me, Master." Boxey looked at me with his big brown eyes. "I am eternally grateful that you did that for me."

I closed my eyes, listening to the bees singing around me. You know that the buzzing is actually bees singing, right?

A breeze rustled through the poplar trees nearby.

"What happened to Devlina?"

"She lives on."

I sat up. "Really? Where?"

"I'll show you tonight."

When the sun set, we hiked up Homer's Glenn, deep in the Verdugo Mountains and sat on the star-watching rock.

"She's there, right next to Cassiopeia."

"You mean, she's—"

I looked up at the stars.

Slightly to the left of Cassiopeia was a series of stars.

My eyes grew big.

Puxhàredo.

Wow.

Stilettos, the long legs, and miniskirt, the bodice, and her hair cut into a bob.

She even had her riding whip.

"She lives on, Master. Millions of stars," Boxey said. "She'll be called, 'The Paràsàfàna Constellation' and dwell there for eternity."

"I can't believe it."

"We're all made of stars, Master. Stardust, actually."

We sat there for a long time, staring up at Devlina glowing in the night sky.

"This is so perfect. And I know deep down she wanted to be free of the awful world she was trapped in. All that negativity."

"You released her. When your energy hit her, it changed her charge. She became positively charged and propelled into the heavens. To live for eternity as pure, white, and healing light."

We sat there watching her in the dark, listening to the rustle of night animals scurry in the dry scrub brush and chaparral for food. I looked back at the stars shaped like Devlina and swore I even think I saw her wink at me.

Fucking Devlina. She sacrificed herself for me. And in doing so, she freed herself. To shine light on untold planets all over the universe. Planets just like ours warmed by the life-giving light from the stars that burn with the energy that lived within her. She did what she wanted. She created whole new worlds. She was the goddess of entire galaxies. Worshipped for the life sustaining energy she benignly radiated onto them.

Fricking Devlina, she really was a world builder!

Finally, she accomplished what she'd always wanted, craved, to rule over the universe. And, in the process, the only one destroyed was her miserable old self.

"And Zid'dra?"

"Oh, the force of both your transformations turned him back into a black hole. And sent him spiraling out into the universe."

"So, he can't do any harm?"

"He's not gone. He can't be, the yin and yang, Master. But he's deeper in the universe now. His power is vastly weakened."

"Máurso weakened him before."

"No, this time is different; he's greatly diminished."

"And the Alliance?"

"It's stronger than ever. Monsters are in retreat. The coven is broken, disorganized. Ordinaries will not perish, Master."

"Thank God, Boxey."

Boxey barked and nudged my arm with his head.

"Puxhàredo, Boxey. I can't believe it." We fell silent, Boxey and me. He sat close to me, panting, his body glowing with golden light. An owl hooted from deep within the Glenn below.

Suddenly, I remembered. "Austin, Boxey!"

"Relax, Master. Your amulet saved him. He's in the hospital now. Recovering."

"Thank goodness," I said. "What happened to Orville? He was the one who kidnapped me and took me to Zid'dra."

Boxey looked away.

"What happened to him?"

Boxey looked at me.

"He's lost to the darkness," Boxey whispered gloomily.

I had more questions but didn't want to ask. Poor Orville. He was a lost soul. He thought he found someone to make him great, but, in the end, he was lost like so many others. I was heartbroken. Poor Orville never had a chance. Puxhàredo. It really sucked that Orville was gone. Maybe we could have worked things out like I had with Mom and Dad and Blair.

"Things happen for a reason, Master."

"Yeah, I guess."

"Are you crying, Master?"

"No," I lied. "I want to see Austin."

Boxey stood on all fours. "The sun is coming up...now!"

And, suddenly, golden light poured over the Verdugo Mountains.

Birds began singing. Volqeńus flitted overhead. A family of gnomes in green hats peered out at us from under the chaparral.

"And visiting hours are happening at the hospital."

I started jogging, then running toward the house. Boxey was running beside me, barking and racing ahead of me, then turning around, stopping, and urging me to hurry.

God, I was so happy to have Boxey back.

"I love the sun here on Earth. You are so lucky to live here, Master!" Boxey said, then paused to chase a squirrel into the chaparral. He tripped and flew into a clump of shrubs.

He whined, then laughed and floated up into the sky before me.

"I'm so glad to be back, Master!" He circled back to the Starry Trail, landing at my feet.

"Mom! Sean! Barn! Tory! Christine!!" I shouted as I stumbled along the path with Boxey to the pylons at the entrance to the park. A few joggers called out to ask if I was okay.

"This day is glorious!"

They nodded, looking slightly perplexed.

I couldn't wait to see my family.

To see my heart and soul, Austin Kang Jr.

*

I WAS SO nervous, standing in the hallway at St. Joseph's Hospital under the fluorescent lights. My eyes stung. I cried a lot last night. I was through with tears for a long time. I clasped and unclasped my hands. I didn't know what to expect. I gazed at the overhead lights; I heard the electricity powering them. My hearing was different now, more acute. I squinted in the strong light. *Why is everything so bright now?*

"Are you lost?" a nurse asked me.

"No, I'm just worried about going in."

She smiled.

"Don't worry, hon," she said. "You're still the two gay boys in the universe meant for each other."

I blinked.

"What?"

"I said I'm here if you need anything."

I grabbed the handle and pushed the door open and went inside.

Cecilia was asleep on a chair. Austin was hooked up to a bunch of tubes and things. He looked like I did months ago, almost like an octopus. Like Little Ocho, well, I called him Ocho but Austin changed his name to Little Ocho. One-night last week, Austin made up adoption papers, and we signed them. As did Austin Sr., since he was a notary. Little Ocho was ours now.

I didn't want to wake Cecilia. She was probably up all night worrying about Austin. His face was bruised and swollen. Puxhàredo, he put up some fight.

To.

Save.

Me.

I surveyed my hand. He groaned.

What if...?

Mom told me when I walked in the house this morning I was glowing. Golden light around me.

Mom looked at me. "Your hair—it's golden!"

I hated blonde hair.

Crap.

"Can I dye it?"

We both chuckled. Boxey said my powers were greater now... I closed my eyes. The universe and time slowed down... I opened my eyes. I touched Austin's hand. My energy flowed into his body.

Love! Pure love. The bruises disappeared off his face, and his cheeks returned to normal. The cuts on his arm disappeared too. His eyes flew open. He looked at his mom, and he sighed. He turned to me and grinned.

"Little Eli!!!!!!" He tried to sit up, but all the tubes made it impossible.

"Sit back, silly," I said, smiling at him.

He narrowed his eyes. "You did something, didn't you?"

I shrugged. "Used a little magic to heal you."

"Thank you, love," Austin said. "I was so worried that you were dead. There was this terrible explosion, and then you vanished. Devlina too…"

Cecilia stirred.

"Lie back and rest Kangy," I said. "You need to take it easy."

He nodded, then looked at my face. "Your hair… It's blond!"

I frowned. "I hate it"

"Little Eli, always worrying about ridiculous things," he said. "You're alive, and Kangy is so happy!"

"I'm the one who is happy. I thought you were a goner."

"The amulet saved me when the explosion filled the old, rotten steel mill."

He reached into his hospital gown and pulled out the necklace—only the necklace was made of black metal, and the charm was green jade.

The image was no longer the Virgin Mary but rather the Áuqala. "She's the protector of the Coaugelus," Austin said. "Did you know we're known as the Knights of the Áuqala?"

"Of course, Kangy," I said, sitting beside him.

"She told me. Well, in my dreams, I guess, love."

"Who told you?"

"The Áuqala," he said. "She's not even a person, really, but just a trillion lights circulating around a core of pure energy. It's so beautiful to see."

"Yeah," I said, "she's made of light."

"So are you," Austin said. "You're glowing."

"Are you on morphine?" I laughed.

He nodded. "Probably. But I see you, love."

I leaned over and kissed him softly on his lips. "I know."

He reached for my hand.

"I was so worried we'd be separated again, love."

"Devlina," I told him. "She intervened and saved me. So we could be together."

"Thank God for Devlina."

"Yeah, who would figure."

We both chuckled.

He smiled, closing his eyes. "I'm tired, love."

"I brought the *Cat Who Could Read Backwards.*"

"The first in the series."

"From 1966. Might as well start reading the series at the beginning."

"That's perfect, love." He opened his eyes. "Can you stay with me?"

"Of course. I have nothing else to do."

I opened the book to page one. I conjured up a soda and handed it to Austin. Then a bouquet of red roses, a bunch of sunflowers, some popcorn, and a heart-shaped box of chocolates.

I loved having all my powers back!

I began to read as Austin mumbled to himself and chuffed contentedly. Two gay boys, in love, connected to the gravity of the universe.

Chapter Thirty-Three

The Harvest Game

I TRUDGED UP the stairs to the third floor behind Mom.

"What are we doing, again?"

"Yoga," Mom said. "You'll love it"

"No, I won't. Last time I did it in the training facility, cousins Felicity and Inez kept farting. It was so gross."

"Farting means you're relaxing your whole body," Mom said lightly.

"That's gross, Mom."

Music played in the distance.

"Is that U2?"

Mom laughed. "Maybe."

"For yoga?"

"You kids like that kind of music."

"What do you like, Mom? Burt Bacharach?"

"Don't knock Burt. He's a genius."

We reached the ballroom, a huge room comprising the top floor of the entire north wing of our E-shaped mansion. Mom opened the door, then pushed me inside.

"SURPRISE!!!!"

My eyes grew huge, taking in the scene before me.

Aunt Christine and Uncle George, Aunt Lisa and Uncle Patrick, and Uncle Sweetie and his husband Uncle Tony. Barn, Tyrone, and Tyrell, their parents, Devereaux and Shamika, April and Kevin, their parent and siblings, Stylo, Aunt Dora and Uncle Ozzie, Letitia and several of her girlfriends, the Kangs, and even Gran from Hong Kong, were here.

In fact, my grandmother and grandfather were here as well as my great grandma, the matriarch of the family, whom everyone called Moms. She was small and had silver hair and birdlike eyes, and she was the mom to the whole family: various cousins, uncles and branches of our family from all over the globe, Mumbai, Bangkok, Cairo, Manila, Mexico City, Paris were here.

And standing front and center, wearing that ridiculous "I'm Special!" T-shirt and those awful high-water jeans pulled up to his belly button was Austin Kang Jr.

He held a sign reading, "How's it going, mate?"

The very first thing he ever said to me in Mrs. Biederman's class more than a year prior. The tall, dorky Asian kid. A sign strung across the room read, "Happy Belated One Year Anniversary." Austin, grinning ear to ear, held Little Ocho in his hand.

I mean, this was amazing. My phone vibrated.

Hashtags were trending on social media: #EliAndAustinAnniversary, #DelomaryHeirHappy, #BeautifulCouple, #AmericasSweethearts.

I stared at my feed. There was a link to *Fashion World* magazine with pictures of Austin and me eating lunch together on the field at school, holding hands, with the caption, "America's Boy Next Door and his Sexy Boyfriend Relaxing in the Sun."

Shit. This was crazy. All my fears about coming out, and my brand being tarnished, when in fact no one cared.

Well, I was the biggest dork ever. I started bawling like a little kid. And everyone gasped, then laughed because, well, they are my family and my friends and knew what a sentimental idiot I was.

Austin wrapped me in a huge hug. He towered over me, peering down through his thick glasses.

"I love you so much, my little Eli."

"My beloved Kangy."

"What's rule thirteen?"

"Gravity keeps Eli and Kangy together, forever."

He smiled.

"Exactly, love."

Suddenly a guitar started strumming the melody for "One."

I looked up, and I wanted to die because, I mean, puxhàredo Bono and U2 were on the stage playing "One" live.

"This is for Elijah and Austin Kang Jr. on their anniversary! Cheers for the boys!"

I was gobsmacked. Austin held my hand and squeezed. Bono saluted me.

Puxhàredo.

My family. I was lucky to be part of this wild, nutty family. I loved my family. And Austin. Damn, I must have done something awesome in a past life to have won the karmic lottery to be part of a great family *and* have an amazing boyfriend.

*

AUSTIN HELD MY hand to keep it warm—Southern California in the fall. Earlier, it was eighty degrees, and now, since the sunset, the temperature fell to the midfifties.

We sat in the bleachers ringing the field at BHS with Barn, Katie, Tyrone, Tyrell, Kevin, Tina, Gina, Letitia, and Stylo, waiting for the *Harvest Game*. Boxey was next to me, panting and taking in the scene. I was apprehensive. I mean this was where it all began. Me, the total senlàpso, announcing to the three hundred other fools that I was gay. Jesus. I was so dramatic last year.

"I like that about you, love," Austin told me recently. "I could never be with someone who was a pipsqueak and soft-spoken. You go all out when you do things."

I had laughed when he told me that. I do go all out.

"Here I am with my arch enemies," Stylo said, pulling her hoodie over her head.

"We're rivals," I said, "not archenemies. We go to different high schools, Stylo."

"Burroughs is better than BHS."

"No way."

"You people that live in the hills are snobs. We folk that live in the flats are down to earth."

"Your point?"

"Who knows?" Stylo said. "I think I'm hungry."

"Me too, love!" Austin said. "Treats for your cat!"

"Here here!" Barn added.

I summoned a funnel cake, smothered in strawberry sauce and whipped cream, handing it to Austin, who chuffed with delight as I invoked a chocolate and nougat bar for myself.

"I want a corn dog," Barn said.

"Cola, please?" Austin added.

Boxey barked. "Àzmadu arm to chew on, Master."

"No, Boxey, how about some kibble?"

Boxey growled and barked.

"Fine, enjoy the Àzmadu arm," I said, summoning a dripping appendage and pushing it toward Boxey. He yapped and took hold of it in his mouth, then settled onto his haunches contentedly.

"That's gross, Boxey."

"Woof!"

Barn glanced at the bloody arm in Boxey's mouth and rubbed his stomach. "I hate monsters! And as such, monster detritus makes me hungry." He reached over to pet Boxey on the head. "How about some cheese fries, yeah, mate?"

"And a smoked turkey leg for me," Stylo said.

"Anything else?" I quipped.

"A cherry slushie would be brilliant too." Barn smiled broadly. I wrinkled my nose, producing a steaming basket of cheese fries in one hand and a sweating plastic cup in the other and handed it to him. And a smoked turkey leg for Stylo.

"So glad you got your magic back," Barn said before digging in.

"Maybe summon some napkins, yeah?" Austin added.

"I want some water, Master. Sparkling!"

"Anything else?" I said, then snapped my fingers. In a flash, a stack of orange napkins appeared in the palm of my hand. "Here, I'm done conjuring snacks and such for you four."

I scanned the field. The football players lined up side by side. BHS and our archrival Burroughs. Cheerleaders waved their pompoms and kicked the air.

April walked to the middle of the field and waved to the crowd. Cheers erupted for April. Ever since her role in *Oklahoma!*, she was a celebrity on campus.

Austin squeezed my hand. He was mumbling, chuffing and humming something or another. And then I spotted a boy walking quickly toward April. Was this really happening? Now he was arguing with April, and then, a moment later, she rolled her eyes and handed the mic to the Asian kid with the pink mohawk.

"Hi, everyone, you probably know me as the Indonesian-American kid with the great hair. Ha ha. Well, anyway, the Harvest Game wouldn't be the same if I didn't do this."

Austin looked at me, eyes huge behind his thick glasses.

"My name is Brooks Wantanamnam, and well, I'm fucking gay, so suck it! Any single boys out there, meet me by the soda machine in five minutes!"

And he stuck his tongue out and shot the hang loose sign, then stomped off the field to applause. Clearly Austin and I stood up cheering him on. And all our friends. And even Blair, who shouted, "Atta boy!" Things settled down and April picked up the mic. And then we watched a line of boys and girls marching toward April.

"Oh, fuck," I whispered to Austin.

"Looks like half the school is coming out tonight, love."

"What did we do, Kangy?"

"Opened the universe to all the gay boys and girls, Little Eli."

And then he placed his hand behind my neck and pulled me in for a kiss.

And like that first kiss, stars exploded behind my eyes.

While our friends laughed and said, "Ooh" and "Aah, how cute."

Of course, someone shouted, "Get a room, boys."

I looked over, and, of course, Blair winked at me.

Jesus, fucking Blair Winchester.

Epilogue

SHEETS OF COLD, icy rain fell from the black clouds obscuring the skyline of London. Big Ben tolled nearby. A red double-decker bus zoomed by. Elijah Delomary, in his trademark blue parka, leaned in closely to Austin Kang Jr. A golden retriever outfitted in a yellow slicker stood between the boys.

They stared at the small, bronze plaque affixed to the brown stone facade of the *Edificea sie Dêtillus,* the Hall of Dragons, the home of the Còngréhassa sie Estàntus. The center of the Magicals Alliance.

"I can't believe Mom convinced the Còngréhassa to do this."

"Your mum is pretty powerful, yeah love?"

"Yeah," he said. "Your gran helped twist some arms too, I'm sure."

Both boys looked at each other happily.

"It's the right thing to do, Master!" the dog said.

Elijah peered at the bronze plaque, rivulets of rain running down the front. A tribute, written first in the Old Language then in English below, read:

Veo Gàrasimenta Ãe Paràsàfàna, Empra siec
Oscùrimenta porga eucraficeo aqel ensaàunoco
Allégansa Qu'elicantu.

"In Gratitude to Persephone, Queen of the Gloom, for her sacrifice that saved the Magicals Alliance."

"Zid'dra was very close to unravelling the Alliance," Austin said, pulling Elijah close to him, kissing the top of his head. "If he had killed you, he knew the Alliance would crumble and the monsters in the coven would crawl out of the Gloom and take over the Shimmering."

"A horrible thought," Elijah said.

"Terrifying, Masters!" the golden retriever agreed.

A gust of wind sent a torrent of water falling over the boys from the gilded dragons lining the top of the Edificea looming high over them.

"Come on, wankers," Barn, Austin's cousin, called over, "I want to get dim sum."

"It's cold," Katie, Barn's girlfriend, added.

"I was not meant to be in this type of weather," Stylo said, huddled in a voluminous black puffy jacket, a black beanie pulled over her head, with a bright-red scarf pulled across her mouth. Her bright black eyes sparkled at the boys. "I am from a tropical paradise. I don't like cold."

"Burbank is tropical?"

"Sod off!"

Barn shivered, thrusting his hands into the pockets of his gray ski jacket.

"Can't you take a picture of that soddin' plaque and be done with it?" Barn said, pulling Katie toward him, wrapping his arms around her.

Elijah turned around and snapped his fingers. In a flash, Barn disappeared. Katie frowned, staring down at a barking poodle at her feet.

"Not fair, Elijah." She frowned. "Turning my boyfriend, your brother, into a dog."

"He behaves like one."

"Turn him back!" Katie insisted. The dog yapped at Elijah's feet.

Boxey wagged his tail. "Master, be kind, turn Barn back into a human."

Elijah tuned out Boxey.

"We want dim sum!" several other kids nearby chimed in. Elijah's group of friends who had traveled to London to be with him as he saw the plaque that honored his friend who had sacrificed herself so he could live. They had, of course, traveled on his family's deluxe luxury jet.

"Fine, fine," Elijah said, "just because I get sentimental over *people who saved me*, I guess I wouldn't expect my friends to feel the same."

"I do," Austin said, winking at Elijah and pulling out a stuffed octopus from his red jacket.

"Ah, it's our son." Elijah laughed. "Little Ocho."

"Elijah."

"Yes, Katie."

"Turn Barn back into a boy, please."

"I like him more as a poodle. He's on a leash and quiet for once."

"Elijah." Katie glared at him.

"Fine, Katie," the boy with the strawberry blond hair said, "but I'm still going to punish him by making him talk like Mickey Mouse for a half hour."

Barn reappeared as a boy, very angry, shouting at Elijah in his small mouse voice.

The boys looked at each other. Barn's voice returned to normal. The boys howled, putting their arms around each other.

"You're a wanker."

"You love me, Barn."

"Oi," Austin said, "get away from my boyfriend."

"We're the Three Musketeers."

"My favorite candy."

"And we're your favorite Coaugelos in the whole world."

Stylo turned. "What am I, chopped liver?"

Elijah wrapped his arms around Stylo, who complained, "Yuck, hugs!"

Elijah, Barn, Stylo, and Austin caught up with their friends huddled under a yellow awning outside a brightly lit restaurant in the shadow of the Houses of Parliament.

"Dim sum!" Tina shouted. "Soup dumplings! Hurry up. It's freezing out!"

"Yeah, I am hangry!" Letitia added.

"She's mean when she's hangry," April lamented.

"Violent too," Kevin exclaimed, standing between April and Letitia.

"Coming!" Elijah called back to them. As they waited for the light, he whispered to his friends, "By the way, there's a headless horseman haunting St. Paul's Cathedral. You want to hunt some monsters after we eat?"

Barn and Austin exchanged glances. "Hell yes!" They high-fived.

"Food, friends, and kicking monster butt," Stylo said. "I love London."

The friends reached the doors of the restaurant, disappearing inside into the warm establishment where their close group waited for them as carts of steaming dim sum circulated around, the intoxicating and comforting aromas embracing them in the warm hug of food, friends and family.

"*I'm not normal*," Elijah realized, "a*nd thank God for that. I'm magical.*"

Tablica | Glossary

Lusa| Land

OSCÙRIMENTA (Oh-skoo-rah-men-tah)| The Gloom: home of the Monsters. The darkness, shadows; the underworld.

XHUXIMENTA (Shoo-shih-men-tah)| The Shimmering: home of Ordinaries and Magicals. Anywhere the sun shines is part of the Shimmering.

The Shimmering and the Gloom are the places, whereas the Alliance and Coven are organizations for Magicals and monsters respectively. Magicals tend to use both Coven and Gloom interchangeably to refer to monsters.

Langras (Lawn-grahs)| Languages

MINERVANA (Min-ur-vah-nah) "Old Language" language of the Magicals, Old Earth.

PASSIONANA (Pah-soh-nee-ah-nah) "Dark Language" language of the monsters and the Gloom.

ORGUMNAS (OR-GOOM-NAHS) | ORGANIZATIONS

ALLEGANSA QU'ELICANTU (Ah-luh-gahn-sah Cue-el-ih-cahl-en) | Magicals Alliance, an Alliance between all Magicals to protect Ordinaries from harm. They won the Last Battle and, as victors, are able to set the terms and enforce the "Pàcifimenta." The Alliance is divided into 9 specific groups:

COR ÀMBASSILONA (Core Ahm-boss-ih-loh-nah)—XAQ3 | The Embassy, the diplomatic organization of the Alliance meets with a shadow organization of world leaders, the few that know of the Alliance who coordinate protection of Ordinaries from monsters.

COR ÀPOJA (Core Ah-poh-jah)—XAQ9 | Magical Support, similar to 911 for Magicals. Summons emergency help and aid and attendance.

COR CÒNGRÉHASSA SIE ESTÀNTUS (Core Kahn-grah-hah-sah sigh Ehs-tahn-toos)—XAQ4 | The Council of Elders, the government of the Alliance located at the Edificea sie Calargos, (Ed-ih-fiss-ee-oh sigh Kah-lahr-goes) Hall of Dragons, near houses of Parliament in London. A parliament made up of the three hundred corpos sangrancto, the sacred families tasked with maintaining the Pàcifimenta, the Treaty of Malomo, which ended the "Last Battle" that spread across all dimensions, killing millions of Ordinaries, Magicals and monsters.

COR MACISTRÁUTO (Core Mah-siss-trow-toh)—XAQ2 | Magicals Alliance Service Two —The Magistrate—Investigate violations to the Pàcifimenta that jeopardizes the peace between the Alliance and the Coven. Similar to the CIA/FBI.

COR MÀDLINN (Core Mahd-lin)—XAQ5 | The court of the Alliance, final arbiter of disputes between Ordinaries, Magicals, and monsters.

COR MEZCLANTUS (Core Mez-klahn-toos)—XAQ7 | The Night Riders, an order of magical dragons that carry out the orders of XAQ5—usually to the Excelà (Ex-el-ah), the void where all magic and evil dissolve.

Cor Orancùladêro (Core Ore-ahn-koo-lah-dare-oh)—XAQ8 | The Regulators, responsible for regulating magical devices such as PlasmX, Pistolerro, PlasmET as well as Motáuvo and Avipro II along with the general use of magic among Magicals.

LLEGÃ CONTRA MÁUNAS (Lil-eh-gahn Cone-trah Mow-nahs)—XAQ1 | Anti-Coven League, warriors for the Alliance, who act as first line defense against the Coven. Similar to the police.

XUTACTIENDO SIEC ÁUQALA (Zoo-tack-tee-en-do sigh-ek Ow-kah-lah)—XAQ6 | Her Majesty's Secret Service. Top secret organization of "Numérantus" (New-mur-ahn-toos)—the triple numbered secret agents who secretly surveil the universe and all seven dimensions maintaining the balance of the universe. Simon Tong, Agent 888, is the most famous of all Numérantus.

GOÀNTUS (GOH-AHN-TOOS)| LEADERS OF THE SHIMMERING AND GLOOM:

COR ÁUQALA, EMPRA SIEC ESPRITISTUS (Core Ow-kah-lah, Emprah sigh-ek Ess-prih-tiss-toos) | Áuqala, Queen of Queens, Queen of the Sprites, dwells in the constellation Cassiopeia in the Astroluceas Càloreallen (Ah-stroh-loo-see-ahs Kah-lore-ee-all-en), the "Glorious Galactic Dimensions" (Fifth and Sixth Dimensions). She is visible to Magicals and Ordinaries in the night sky, a reminder of her never-ending protection and guidance.

COR ZID'DRA, EMPRO SIEC OSCÙRIMENTA (Core Zid-drah, Em-proh sigh-ek Oh-skoo-rih-men-tah) | Zid'dra, King of the Gloom.

MEMRANTUS | MEMBERS

HIERARCHY OF MAGICALS WITHIN THE ALLIANCE:

ÁUQALA| ÁUQALA- HEAD OF THE ALLIANCE.

ANTÉCALLANTUS (Ahn-tuh-kahl-ahn-toos) | The Immortals, famed Gods and Goddesses from Mount Olympus called Morra Êímpagońena (More-Ah Ay-ihm-pah-gohn-yen-ah), including Máurso (Mow-ur-so), Mars, God of War; Ammara (Ahm-mah-rah), Venus, Goddess of Love; Cupidêro (Koo-pih-dare-oh), Jupiter, lead god; Aveana (Ah-vee-ahn-ah), Diana, Goddess of the Forest.

ASTROÍSTUS (Ah-stroh-his-toos) | Wizards who draw their power from the four elements: earth, air, water, and fire. They have the most power of all Magicals after the Immortals. Limitations: cannot travel back and forth in time.

COAUGELUS (Koh-wah-jell-oos) | Glimmerers. Known as the "Qénocqus siec Áuqala," the Knights of the Áuqala. They are commonly armed with a simple weapon made of purple plasma that can either be soft or strong, a sword or a lasso or whatever tool the Coaugelo determines will be best to fight a monster. Known as a "PlasmX," it can be turned back into a small gold object akin to a lighter for easy transport.

Limitations: With little magic to draw from they are reliant on their training in Xem Sen Ou and their PlasmX when battling monsters.

ENCANTREINUS (En-kahn-tree-noos) | Magicians. Magicals who train to use their magic with spells, summonings, conjurings, along with potions and gestures such as snapping fingers or waving hands. Limitations: must adhere to an Oath, monsters can draw power from Encantreinus to make themselves stronger.

HIERARCHY OF MONSTERS WITHIN THE COVEN:

ÀZMADUS | Vampires, feed on life forces. Limitations: being excessively beautiful they tend to be slowed down while admiring themselves. Deathly allergic to cats, killed by catnip or wheat, except wheat grass, which makes them stronger. Obsession with pizza and spaghetti and meatballs.

MALLOUPUS | Werewolves, known as "Soul Reapers" feast on souls by cuddling Ordinaries to death. Limitations: prone to stop and have bouts of scratching, rolling around. Run in a pack. Allergic to chocolate and can be killed by catnip and wheat.

MÁU (Mow) | Mau, former Goddesses of the Shimmering, lured by Zid'dra to the Gloom. Known as Malevolents and embodying Lust, Gluttony, Pride, Sloth, Wrath, Jealousy, Envy, Famine, and Pestilence. The Wives of Zid'dra and leaders of the Gloom appear in all dimensions except Old Earth. Paràsàfàna, known as Mau Licuria or Devlina is the Queen of the Gloom, with all other Malevolents subordinate to her rule:

> MÁU ANVEDRA (Ahn-ved-rah) | Goddesss of Envy, nicknamed Medusanja (Meh-doo-sah-nahn-jah).

> MÁU AXEDIA (Ox-ed-ee-ah) | Goddess of Sloth, nicknamed Pàrasorendra (Par-ah-sore-en-drah).

MÁU CUPÁUDA (Koo-pow-dah) | Goddess of Jealousy, nicknamed Máu Máu (Mow Mow).

MÁU EUPRAVIA (You-prah-vee-ah) | Goddess of Pride, nicknamed Antigònansa (Ahn-tig-oh-nahn-sah).

MÁU FAMINA (Fah-mee-nah) | Goddess of Famine, nicknamed Mortalàmasà (More-tah-lah-mah-sah)

MÁU MÀLÙENA (Mah-loo-en-ah) | Goddess of Gluttony, nicknamed Tàntamaza (Tawn-tah-mah-zah).

MÁU PESTILENTIA (Pess-tih-len-see-ah) | Goddess of Pestilence, nicknamed Dragàmansa (Drah-gah-mahn-sah).

MÁU RABETICA (Rah-bet-ih-kah) | Goddess of Wrath, nicknamed Hêracansa (Hair-ah-kahn-sah).

MÁUNADUS | Witches, the most powerful and feared of all monsters; fond of cauldrons and baking deadly confections and pastries, riding around on broomsticks and dancing and telling terrible jokes. Limitations: Full moon, sponge cake, smoothies. Killed by catnip and wheat.

MORPHEIMUS | Shape Shifters, blobs of negative energy that can assume any shape. Limitations: Strong winds, metal detectors. Catnip interferes in the charges holding them together, destroying them.

ZID' DRA | Zid'dra- King of the Gloom, Master of the Dark.

GOÀNTUS SIEC MÁUNAS | LEADERS OF THE "LITTLE COVENS"

AUHAQA | Auhaqa, Princess of the Vampires.

FIDDO | Fido, Prince of the Werewolves

MADAMAXO | Madamaxo, Prince of the Shapeshifters.

MÁU RABETICA | Princess of the Witches.

DOMENSANABOS (DOUGH-MEN-SAH-NAH-BOH) | DIMENSIONS

The universe is divided into seven dimensions. Ordinaries, Magicals and monsters live in all dimensions. Time differs between each dimension as specified below:

FIRST DIMENSION: ARCENGA (Are-sen-gah) | Earth. Our dimension, our home. Present time

SECOND DIMENSION: ÁUTRARCENGA (Ow-trahr-sen-gah) | Other Earth, a realm of warring lands of Magicals and Monsters. Two thousand years behind Earth time.

THIRD DIMENSION: PARÀMORDEA (Par-ah-mohr-dee-ah) | Primordial Earth, a soupy swamp of magic and dark magic. Three thousand years behind present time.

FOURTH DIMENSION: CASSEOPLANA (Kah-see-oh-plah-nah) | Cassiopeia, the realm of the Sprite Queens and the Áuqala dwelling in the Milky Way. Four Thousand years behind present time.

FIFTH AND SIXTH DIMENSIONS: "GÀLÁUTIGOS CÀLORE-ALLEN" (Gah-lau-tih-goes Kah-lohr-ee-all-en) | The Glorious Galaxies, billions of planets and universes comprised of Magicals. Time tends to move back and forward in these dimensions.

SEVENTH DIMENSION: ARCENGA ÀNTIGO (Are-sen-gah Ahn-tih-goh) | Old Earth, the foundation of the universe, where the Immortals were born, home of the land of Minerva and where all Magicals come from. Ten thousand years behind present time.

About the Author

Timoteo K. Tong grew up in the San Fernando Valley of Los Angeles dreaming of living in a rambling Victorian mansion. He currently lives with his husband and way too many plants in San Francisco. He is obsessed with cheese pizza, drinking cola, and daydreaming about magic. He sold his first book when he was age eight, a story about his beloved stuffed animal named Crocker Spaniel. He is a member of the Society of Children's Book Writers and Illustrators International.

Email
Magicalsalliancebooks@gmail.com

Facebook
www.facebook.com/TimoteoTong

Instagram
www.instagram.com/Timoteotong

Website
www.magicalsalliance.com

OTHER NSP BOOKS BY AUTHOR

Magic, Monsters, and Me

www.ninestarpress.com

www.facebook.com/ninestarpress

www.facebook.com/groups/NineStarNiche

www.twitter.com/ninestarpress

www.instagram.com/ninestarpress